A TALL
DARK
TROUBLE

A TALL DARK TROUBLE

VANESSA MONTALBAN

zando
YOUNG
readers

NEW YORK

zando young readers

Copyright © 2023 by Vanessa Valdes

Zando supports the right to free expression and the value of copyright. The purpose of copyright is to encourage writers and artists to produce the creative works that enrich our culture. Thank you for buying an authorized edition of this book and for complying with copyright laws by not reproducing, scanning, uploading, or distributing this book or any part of it without permission. If you would like permission to use material from the book (other than for brief quotations embodied in reviews), please contact connect@zandoprojects.com.

Zando Young Readers is an imprint of Zando.
zandoprojects.com

First Edition: August 2023

Text design by Aubrey Khan, Neuwirth & Associates, Inc.
Chapter icons © NatalyaBurova / iStock
Needle and Thread by Caroline Mackay from Noun Project
Cover design by Aurora Parlagreco
Cover illustration by Liliana Rasmussen
Art direction by Lindsey Andrews

The publisher does not have control over and is not responsible for author or other third-party websites (or their content).

Library of Congress Control Number: 2022946739

978-1-63893-012-9 (Hardcover)
978-1-63893-013-6 (ebook)

10   9   8   7   6   5   4   3   2   1
Manufactured in the United States of America

*For all those who crossed seas and borders for
a better life, and to those who never made it.*

To all the halves that make me whole.

AUTHOR'S NOTE

With *A Tall Dark Trouble*, I wanted to write a story that explored the conflicting and harmonious parts of a multicultural upbringing, including the secrets, stories, trauma, and resilience that are passed down and fused to form a new identity that straddles generations and borders.

Although this is a work of fiction, I have woven together fantastical and historical elements to tell the story of the Sánchez women. While the experiences of the characters are invented, I reference the real oppression under Fidel Castro's regime, and real events such as the 1980 Mariel boatlift, an exodus that brought an estimated 125,000 Cuban asylum seekers to the United States—my father among them.

Similarly, while the references to magic in the novel are purely imaginative, they're undoubtedly interconnected with my superstitions, folklore, and religious inheritance. Alongside the invented magic practiced by the Sánchez family and by the fictitious Palomas, I've also included depictions of real Afro-Cuban religions and religious practices, including Regla de Ocha-Ifá, often also referred to as Santería or Lukumí, which are part of the rich cultural heritage of Cuba.

My hope is that, through a fictional lens, readers come away with a broader understanding of a syncretized, African diasporic religion that is often misrepresented and misunderstood, and which has often been the target of anti-Black sentiment and religious persecution. The references in my book are not intended to teach or disclose any specific practices, nor are they meant to be a definitive depiction of Regla de Ocha-Ifá. Santería, which was developed in Cuba following the slave trade and then brought to the United States by immigrants, is heavily syncretized, so religious rituals, practices, and even terminology can vary greatly from practitioner to practitioner, and from region to region. Some practices fuse elements of Yoruba, Catholicism, and European Spiritism. Other practices are more closely based on the religion's African roots.

Lastly, please note that in my novel, I have used the term "brujería" or "brujo/a" to denote someone who practices a magic unique to this fictional world. I do not use the term to reference practitioners nor practices of Regla de Ocha-Ifá, Santería, Palo Mayombe, or any other Afro-Cuban religion.

There is a disconnect that comes with the generational displacement of the diaspora—one that I can only begin to bridge through my creative exploration and imagination. Children of the diaspora, I hope you can relate, and find peace within these pages.

VANESSA MONTALBAN

AN INTRODUCTION TO THE WORLD
AND MAGIC OF *A TALL DARK TROUBLE*

Maldeados: A lost spirit unable to transition to the afterlife who has been captured and forced to obey the demands of a bruja. Derived from maldecido, the Spanish word for "cursed."

Orden de las Palomas: Secret order of powerful brujos that protect the Cuban president, known as el Comandante.

Elder: The most powerful brujos in la Orden de las Palomas, who have direct contact with el Comandante.

Guardia: Second-in-command to the Elders, they are apprentices training to take the Elders' places in la Orden.

Vasallos: Human followers of la Orden de las Palomas with no magical abilities.

El Ojo: Bruja or brujo who has the power to see visions from touching emotionally charged objects, like Ofelia Sánchez.

La Lengua: Bruja or brujo who can taste emotions, like Delfi Sánchez.

Magia del alma: The spiritual source of a brujo or bruja's power.

Trabajos: The Spanish word for "jobs" is used in some Santería communities to refer to spell work. In my novel, trabajos refers specifically to magical incantations and actions performed through witchcraft.

Obras: The Spanish word for "works," which is sometimes used interchangeably with trabajos in some Santería communities to refer to religious rituals. However, in my novel, I've chosen to only use "obras" when referring to rituals pertaining to Santería.

Tierra de Sombras: Spanish for "land of shadows." A realm within reality and death. A place where spirits roam and memories are kept.

PROLOGUE

Cuba, 1980

Anita had nothing left to cling to. Nothing to shield her from what was to come next.

She'd been forced to leave behind her beads, her cross, her *clothes* outside the door of the chamber. They'd stripped her of everything and yet they demanded more.

Her friends' cries rattled through her bones. Anita could hear their pain as the Elders branded their flesh with the symbol of la Paloma Eterna. The Eternal Dove. She would soon be next. She could practically feel the heat of the iron on her neck already, taste the bitter burn.

Today, Anita would be marked as one of las Palomas forever, her gifts bound to them in a way she could never hide or escape. Her life would be a mirror of her mother's, a path of blood and obedience.

The chant of the Elders amplified through the chamber, her mother leading the charge. Mamá Orti's eyes gleamed through the dark, urging Anita with her gaze to say the words that had been ingrained in her since birth.

Fidelidad, fuerza, y poder. It always came down to that—fidelity, strength, and power.

The maldeados, spirits of the condemned, circled her feet, slicking their cool bodies across her skin. The spirits were urging her to do something, anything, but she didn't know what. She couldn't think beyond her fear.

Ana met Gilberto's amber gaze from across the room, and saw her sorrow reflected back. They both knew they were in far too deep to leave las Palomas now. Her last bit of hope that she would be able to escape Cuba evaporated like mist.

Her mother had once told her, *Your destiny is already written in your blood, Ana. As it is in mine. Changing your future would mean leaving behind everything you are. It is a responsibility that ties this family.*

Ana closed her eyes, and mumbled the words of the binding chant, the promises heavy with burden, filled with the corrupted magic of her mother's lineage. Magic that would absorb the marrow of her own abilities until she was nothing. *Obey. Submit. Protect.*

Every bit of her power destined to serve one man. El Comandante.

A TALL DARK TROUBLE

ONE

Miami, November 6, 2016

LELA

My thoughts should be purely holy at this moment. What with "Tu Gloria" pouring out from the squeaky speakers and the old ladies singing off-key from the front pews. But I'm dying to get out of here. Church is just one of the many things I put up with solely for the sake of my mother.

The altar dude makes his way down the aisle with the collection basket, giving my twin the flirty eye.

"Think he'd pinch some of the cash for me?" Delfi—said twin—nudges my shoulder. She gives her admirer a little wave, then the finger.

I lock eyes with a bored cherub staring down from the ceiling. "You seriously have no chill."

Delfi laughs, and our mom tosses us a dark look from her honorary seat up front, right next to Padre Javier. He always tasks Mami with handling the golden goblet of wine and the silver tin of altar bread. Right now, she looks like a wrathful Lady Justice balancing divine gifts.

Delfi and I quickly rise, stifling laughter as we raise our hands for praise. Mami's grip tightens around the holy objects. In case her message still isn't clear, she does her scary wide-eyed, chin-jut thing that effectively shuts us up. I can practically see my full name spelled out in that look. *Ofelia Mila Sánchez, either you quiet down, or I will quiet you down.* In Spanish, of course, which sounds a million times more threatening.

My full name is reserved for special occasions only. *Lela* is the nickname I'm stuck with because when we were babies, Delfi was permanently affixed to her pacifier and couldn't properly pronounce "Ofelia," and Mami thought the nickname was the cutest thing ever. Though judging by the feral gleam in her eye, the fond memory is currently far from her mind.

The moment Mami does look away, Delfi's talking again, the main reason she spent the majority of senior year in detention.

"What the—" My sister's eyes flit to the gigantic portrait of Jesus. "What the *heck*, who's the DJ today? My arms are killing me."

She drops her arms with a groan. I shoot her a look, keeping mine up even though they're starting to shake. Usually, the church alternates between a song, a prayer, sit, kneel, stand, raise arms, rinse, and repeat. But Delfi's right; whoever's working the sound system has played three songs in a row, and even the pious Señora Benitez is sweating.

When the music finally ends, we plop down on the bench in relief. Delfi's loud sigh earns another glower from Mami. My sister takes out her tarot cards and begins to shuffle them until I kick her shoe. With a roll of her eyes, she puts them away, then laces her arm through mine, resting her head on my shoulder.

"Tastes like vinegar and olives in here." Delfi grimaces. I've gotten used to her announcing these random bursts of flavors. We only recently started keeping track of Delfi's emotional savoring, as we've been calling it, jotting down her tastes and emotions on my notes app. Delf's always been extra sensitive to emotions, especially once she gets to know someone, and gut feelings, uncanny guesses, that's always been our thing. But when we turned eighteen six months ago, things changed. Delfi's emotional perceptiveness went to another level and began manifesting through taste. For me, my ability manifested through sight. Visions that interrupt my life each time I touch an object attached to a strong memory. Every time it happens it feels like I'm pulled from my body and it's not something I can easily play off like Delfi can. Which is why my hands are usually jammed into my pockets.

But none of that helps when it comes to the disturbing dreams I've been having—to the plaguing images of someone being chased by death.

My whole body shivers and Delfi throws me a weird look as if tasting exactly what I'm thinking. We've tried to find out more about our gifts, hoping to find a way to control them, but it's not like there's a class we can take. So we're stuck googling, but the closest thing we've turned up was a generic wiki-superpower source on empaths and clairvoyants. We've found nothing on how or *why* she can suddenly sense emotions through taste and why I can pick up on visions from objects. And what we're supposed to do about the dreams we've been having.

All I know is we have to keep our weird abilities a secret because our mom would have a fit if she knew.

The closest thing to the supernatural she'll acknowledge are Jesus and saints, but that's her religion. That's different.

Another song starts, one of those intermediary piano solos that lets us know it's time to stand and take la hostia. My sister and I get in line to receive the communion wafer.

"I'm pretty sure it tastes like guilt," Delfi whispers, tossing back her long, highlighted hair. "Guilt or regret, one of those." My sister smacks her tongue. She knows I hate that sound.

"Not regret." I lower my voice, praying she'll do the same. "Last time you said regret tasted like Robitussin. I'll log it in once we get home, but *please* ya cállate." The last thing we need is for Mami to hear us.

"Well, then I'm sure of it. Tastes like guilt." Delfi looks around. "Guess someone needs to go to confession." She considers Señora Benitez's daughter, who plunks down in her seat to pick her nails, flicking cherry-red flakes onto the closed Bible in her lap. Her new Saint Laurent bag is strapped to her chest like a seat belt.

Delfi nudges me. "I bet she stole that. See if you can brush by her when we pass. Maybe you can see who she stole it from!"

"How about no." I take one giant step away from her.

We're almost to the front of the line. Mami comes into view, her gold cross necklace gleaming. She's about to don her scary face again but realizes there are people around, so she smiles instead—baring all her teeth.

"But—"

I shush my sister, and we bow our heads to Padre Javier as he grins wide, crinkling his owlish eyes under thick glasses, and getting us mixed up as usual even though we have completely different hair colors now.

As we shuffle back to our seats, I unstick the stale wafer from the roof of my mouth as Delfi nudges my arm. We watch as one of our single neighbors holds up the line trying to talk up our mom, but he's wasting his time. Mami doesn't date. None of us do. I once asked her if she'd ever loved anyone besides my dad. She'd said there'd been someone back in Cuba, but that, too, had only led to trouble. As all relationships do when it comes to us. Mainly because of what Delfi's dubbed the Sánchez Curse. Anyone who falls in love with a Sánchez

woman is doomed to slowly turn into a corrupted version of themselves, acting out their most dangerous impulses. A curse that's followed our family all the way from Cuba to Miami. So as much as
Mami refuses to acknowledge magic, the men in our lives have
always been the living proof that it's real.

For no particular reason at all, this makes me think of someone.

"So . . ." I whisper to Delfi. "Did Ethan say he was meeting us later?"

She raises a brow. "Yeah, *and* he's bringing the supplies we need."

"What supplies?" I lower my voice, but we're alone in the pews.
Everyone else is still waiting to give thanks to the priest and possibly
complain about the sound system and broken AC.

Delfi straightens in her seat. "For the trabajo I was telling you
about. Zuela says now that we've been getting those dreams so often,
we need the spell to strengthen our abilities. We need to figure this
out before—"

"Ya, stop." I flutter a hand. "I wasn't talking about that." And I
definitely don't want to talk about *Zuela*, Delfi's bruja mentor, or
whatever she calls herself.

"But we *need* to talk about what we've been seeing."

I deflate because I know we should. The woman's face springs to
mind, blue eyes glossed in fear, delicate features pressed in perpetual
worry—the woman from my nightmares. *Our* nightmares. Delfi and
I have been dreaming of her for weeks now. Unlike Delfi, I'm not
sure if the woman is real, or if we're dreaming about something
that's already happened or has yet to happen, but I haven't been able
to shake the feeling that we're dreaming about her for a reason. That
we're supposed to help her in some way.

I know Delfi's probably right. But I can't do it. Not yet. Not when
the visions are leading to someone's death and everything we've been
warned to stay away from. Not when a part of me still wishes we
could be normal, that we can ignore it away. I know Mami would
want the same.

It wasn't always like this. When we were growing up, our mom didn't exactly encourage our magic, but she also wasn't afraid of it. She defended us from the nosy neighbors who called us Las Brujitas for seeing shadows where they didn't exist, for guessing secrets or predicting outcomes too exact to be coincidences. But twelve years ago, after the fire at the Eighth Street house and after Papi's disappearance, Mami made it clear that any conversation that even hints of magic is off-limits. When Mami moved us to Cauley Square, far from anyone we knew, she meant for all of us to start over.

Before we moved, she'd taken us to see someone—an older woman dressed all in white and working out of her shed. I realized she was another santera, like Mami. We'd seen our mom do similar rituals throughout the years, and I recognized the woman's altars, like the one Mami kept by our front door. The old woman brushed our hair with a shell-encrusted comb that reminded me of something out of *The Little Mermaid*, pouring water onto our heads after each stroke. She was gentle and I liked her—until she took our dolls for a protection obra, wrapped them in twine, dipped them in viscous honey, and wouldn't give them back. Our mom told us this obra would help control whatever magic was corrupting our spirit. That the shadows would go away if we ignored them. They were merely restless souls hungry for attention. When we asked if the woman was doing a spell, Mami told us the obras were not magic, but faith. Divine power. She'd made it clear that whatever was inside us was something to be prayed away.

Keep that door closed, Ofelia, Mami would say. *Lock it away, or you'll invite in the unknown.*

But I want to tell her we never opened a door. For a while, the santera's ritual had helped restrain our magic, like a tourniquet cutting off circulation—not painful, but a low throb I could always sense beneath the surface of my skin. We've never been able to fully

8

keep the shadows from seeping past, from bleeding out. We only got better at hiding it . . .

"Are you even listening to me?" Delfi waves her hand in front of my face, and I snap back to the church again. "Ethan, full-moon party, the perfect night for a witchy duo debut?"

My nails dig into my palms. "I'll think about it, all right? And don't say *witch*."

"They've called us Las Brujitas our whole life; we might as well own it." Delfi already thinks she's going to win, like she always does. Her mouth curves devilishly. We're identical in every way, yet I can't imagine that expression on my face.

As we follow Mami out the church doors, an old beige van parked outside releases a loud pop. I press my hand to my chest, touch the wispy gold chain of my necklace. The woman's face from my nightmares blazes through my mind.

TWO

Miami, November 6, 2016

DELFI

My eyes snap open. I have no clue how the hell I got here. A second ago, I was sitting in the car with Lela, heading home from church, and now I'm standing here. Alone. The crisp, salty air of the sea whips against my back while the distinct reek of the city hits me. I look around to see the canopied strip of Miami Beach, crowds of people weaving from stores to restaurants to the bars that open only after dark.

This isn't right. We just left church. I *know* we did. It should be daylight still. I don't understand how an entire day has gone by, and I don't know where my sister's gone.

It clicks then. *Shit.* I'm having the vision again.

Idaly. A man's voice coalesces in my head, and I know that voice, recognize it from a memory that isn't mine. His voice is drenched in an overwhelming loss. I get a flash of other memories, brief images— of a small kitchen, an old town car driving down a dark mountainous road. My fingers running through a man's short-cropped hair, coming away bloody. No. Not my fingers—hers. This woman, Idaly's. These are her memories, her thoughts. Lela and I have been dreaming of her for weeks.

But this time, I realize something's different. Like the previous visions, it feels like I'm in this lady's skin, yet I've never had a vision this clear, this intense, where I can barely tell the difference between reality and dreams.

I'm looking out at Miami Beach through her eyes, the floral taste of violets overwhelming my senses. A car's horn blares, and I realize Idaly is standing in the middle of Ocean Drive and its infamous traffic. I try but I can't move my feet. It's cold and I go to rub my bare arms, but my hands won't listen. There's nothing I can do but watch the scene play out, no matter how creepy it feels to be lurking in someone's head.

Idaly starts walking with purpose. In past visions, her hands were usually fidgeting. She'd seemed nervous. But now her arms lie rigid by her sides, and she doesn't even flinch as a guy bumps her shoulder hard enough to jar teeth.

"Whoa, scary-ass contacts, lady."

She stares blankly at him, and I see her face reflected in his shades. Her eyes are bone white, empty as if she's completely checked out. The raised flesh of a burn or marking on her neck peeks out from under her hair. The guy quickly backs off.

The vision jumps ahead, leaving me disoriented. Now the night is pitch black. Idaly strides across a quay, her steps unwavering, as if no one—not even herself—can stop her momentum. She zeros in on a boat, the farthest one down the dock, and gets in. Goes right to the front and sits at the bow as if awaiting orders. The boat starts up.

That's when the smoky shadows emerge.

I flinch because I know those things too well, having glimpsed the shadows since I was a kid. Despite the obra the santera did to make

11

them go away, they never did. At least not for me. But I've never seen so many of them. They're everywhere, slinking across the handrails, drenched in an oily slickness, and overwhelming the boat deck. Idaly doesn't seem to notice as they wrap around her, winding up her arms and legs, as the boat carries her deeper into the bay.

Suddenly, the motor stops. I cry out as Idaly stands up at the boat's edge, but already, I know she can't hear me—doesn't know I'm here with her, experiencing this as if I *were* her. The night is quiet despite how loud I'm screaming for her to wake up. Idaly teeters over the side, and for a moment I feel her hesitate, snap out of whatever trance she's in, fear flooding her like a tidal wave.

No, she thinks, but it's too late.

The slithering, oily shadows coil around her neck, around her ankles, and *pull.* Idaly's body hits the icy water, and the ocean devours us whole.

◆ ◆ ◆

I jolt awake. My head knocks against Lela's as she shrieks.

Our mom swerves. "¡Por Dios, qué susto! Why are you scream-ing?" Mami whips around in her seat, nearly taking out a pedestrian.

I rub my aching head, grabbing hold of Lela's trembling hand as she tries to get her breathing in check. From the looks of it, she had the same vision.

We'll talk about this later, I convey with my eyes. *Don't say anything.*

Lela forces a nod, trying to swallow down her panic. "N—nada, Mami. We must've dozed off and smacked our heads together."

Mami grumbles but resumes driving. With a tremor working up my body, I grab my phone and shoot Zuela a text.

be at the botanica soon. something happened. you there?

Immediately, Zuela texts back. i'm here.

I smile in relief. Zuela's always got my back.

I look over at Lela as she wipes sweat from her brow. I hate that she's having these visions too. I know they're wearing on her. I pick up on her emotions stronger than anyone else's because, duh, she's my other half. I swallow back the metallic taste of Lela's fear and try not to linger on the cloying flavor I've come to associate with her self-loathing.

I still haven't gotten used to the way that others' emotions slip down my throat and wrap around my own, leaving an unnerving residue. It makes me question if what I'm feeling is my own emotion or just the lingering aftertaste of someone else's. But Zuela's helping with that too, helping me develop my intuition enough that I can tell the difference. Teaching me how to embrace the shadows I see, instead of shutting them out until my magic is banging on the doors of my brain, drowning out every other thought. Zuela has visions too and even though her gift is different than mine, she has this wealth of knowledge of what we are and what we can do. She makes me feel like I'm not alone.

Our mom sighs as she pulls into the plaza, parking in front of the bakery where she works. She stops the car and twists onto her knees so she can get a better look at us, gripping our chins so she can survey any damage.

"I thought we were past the stage of cocotasos," she chides, then smiles.

"It's only 'cause Lela's head is so damn big." I jump out of the car first, eager to get to Zuela's shop.

"Only we have the same-sized head," my sister grumbles as she climbs out after me, still looking pale as hell.

"Ya, enough." My mom gets out and stretches, adjusting the strap of her purse. Mami and Lela begin to make their way over to the crowded bakery. "Y tú? Where are you going?" she asks suspiciously as I back away to the other side of the plaza, toward the botanica.

"Getting an egg roll from across the street! Be right back!" I hurry away, hearing Mami mutter something about their skimpy portions. I look back over my shoulder to see Lela glaring. She may not know exactly what I'm doing with Zuela, but I'm definitely playing with fire.

Once I'm sure Lela and Mami are inside the bakery, I beeline toward the tiny storefront. The flashy neon sign proclaiming BOTANICA MAGICA winks down at me. I've been coming ever since the whole assault-of-emotional-flavors thing started and the shadows came back in earnest.

Mami would freak to learn I've been coming to *this* botanica without her. She frequents her own botanica across town for her obras and the altars to her saints, but it's a simple shop that caters to practitioners of religions like Santería, Palo, or Espiritismo who communicate with their ancestral spirits. Not like Zuela's shop, which serves a broader clientele beyond the realm of religion and faith-based work, people who delve into brujería and trabajos that manipulate otherworldly energies. People with special gifts like mine. To Mami, our intuition, our visions, the shadows we see are unnatural. Something to be stifled and ignored.

I've always assumed Mami's aversion comes from her experiences back in Cuba, from the bruja that cursed our family to live with a love that taints. It's part of why she sacrificed everything to come to the US. But what happened to our dad, and my ex, is proof that when it comes to magic, you can't really leave it all behind. Running might be her thing, but it's never been mine.

Zuela is the only one who's ever made me feel like maybe there's a place for me. Like maybe I'm not a complete freak. Even though exploring my gifts makes Lela uncomfortable, I'm going to keep turning to the only person who's been helping me figure all this out. I'm not ignoring who I am anymore, no matter who I piss off.

The bells peal as I throw open the door. Zuela stands at the back of her store, listening intently to a striking older woman wearing a long shawl with flowered embroidery. The older woman's hair is gray and stick-straight, a shimmery curtain against her russet-brown skin. They both turn in my direction, and I notice Zuela's strained expression.

Zuela holds up a finger for me to wait. I nod, but I'm nervous—my mom *will* come looking for my ass if I'm not back soon. I try to give them privacy, but I can't help but sneak glances at the other woman. Despite her tiny stature, the older woman emanates a too-powerful taste of tobacco that immediately coats my tongue. An earthy taste I've come to recognize as a bruja's magic—the kind you'd associate with the scent of a Cuban cigar.

I'm thrilled when I remember what Zuela told me during my last visit. *You will learn to sense others like you soon enough in your own way. Like attracts like. Power calls to power.* A faint taste of tobacco is what first led me to Zuela and her botanica, though I barely detect it on her now, and I've wondered why I never detect an earthy taste from Lela. Maybe we're too new or our powers are too weak, or maybe I'm too accustomed to Lela's magic. Like a perfume scent you've worn for so long that you no longer notice. I'm also not sure whether Lela can sense my magic, or how she becomes aware of another bruja's presence. I imagine it's something unique to her own visual gift. Not that she would talk to me about it.

Finally, Zuela and the older woman stop whispering, and the woman leaves with a package, the contents of which I can only guess at. Tobacco explodes on my tongue as she walks past me with a frown, seeming to assess me just as I'd assessed her earlier. Whoever this bruja is, she's definitely powerful. She had been in the back of the store where Zuela hosts her private psychic consultations and the religious services for the clientele looking for more than candles and prepackaged obras.

"Mi niña!" Zuela calls out as she walks toward me. "I've missed you." My mentor kisses both my cheeks with her bright orange lips, a lipstick shade my mother would say is way too flashy for someone their age.

"Zuze, I've *got* to talk to you."

"Wait!" Zuela peers out the storefront window, making sure the coast is clear. She shivers. "Good. She's gone."

"The lady who was just here? You don't like her or something?"

Zuze's mouth pinches. "It's not about *like*, corazón. It's about trust. I can't trust someone like her. Power is tied to intent. Hers is misguided." After seeing my confused face, she clarifies. "There are rumors that Doña Aura practices trabajos de desgracia—practices for the purpose of causing misfortune to others. She takes on the unsavory clients that no one else will. I don't approve of what she does, but if I tried to pick and choose my customers based off what I suspected they were doing, where would I be? No, it's not my place to judge what people do with my goods. Just be wary, mi niña. Come—" She grabs hold of my hand and leads me to her private space at the back of the store. "Tell me. Was it another vision?"

"Yes, but I think something's changed, Zuze." I follow her into a room cloyed with cigarette smoke that stings my eyes. Here is where Zuela offers her psychic gifts for a fee. On the other side of a partition that divides the room, she keeps her orishas in their wooden and porcelain tureens surrounded by shells, stones, and candles— among other things. When I asked why she keeps the two practices separate, she said, "Santería is my cultural inheritance, mi niña, my religious practice. My magia del alma, however, are the powerful gifts of my lineage—brujería, magic, psychic and spiritual power, whatever you want to call it. My magic is a different part of myself, so I must respect both practices by giving them their own space."

The cigarette smoke dissipates enough for me to make out three women around Zuela's age, early to late fifties, sitting around a table wearing varying shades of pink, teal, and animal prints. They smile warmly to greet me, their skin wrinkled from possibly centuries of smoking and a serious lack of SPF.

"Ah, está es la Delfi," one woman says, extinguishing her cigarette on an ashtray. "Zuela's told us all about you. Finally, something else to look at besides you all." Another one, weighed down under various amulets, cackles.

"Delfi, don't listen to these old crones," Zuela says. "Señoritas, we'll meet again next week."

The women crack jokes in Spanish as they pick up their bags, cleaning the scattered tarot cards and flecks of dried herbs laid out on the table. All of them emit that hint of tobacco, their magic weaving together in one subtle flavor on my tongue. They're like a family, I realize. The community of kindred brujas Zuela had mentioned.

I'm quick to squelch down the envy, but Zuela must sense it anyway. Once they're gone, she grabs my hand, petting it like a wayward puppy, and I try to ignore the subtle taste of sour, fermented pity. "Now, what did you see? Was it Idaly again?"

"Yeah, but this vision was different." My chest tightens as I remember being inside Idaly's head, the fear that she felt at that final moment before she sank below the waves. "I think she's going to die, Zuze. Or she's dead already, I don't know!"

"Cálmate, it's okay. Start from the beginning."

As she keeps petting my hand, I take a deep breath and describe my vision, watching Zuela's expression darken by the second.

"That is troubling," she says at last. "But it also seems your gifts are getting stronger. Your visions are getting clearer."

"Thanks to you and your teachings," I say, and mean it. Ever since I stumbled into this place, I've been picking up on more and more emotions, growing more comfortable with my abilities. "But what I still don't know is what we're supposed to do about these visions."

"It's a vision of the future, Delfi, it may not have happened yet. There could still be time," Zuela says. "Idaly's fate may not be your responsibility, but you must figure out why your gift chose *you* to see."

"That's exactly what I want to know! If that woman is still out there and we can help her . . ." I feel a burst of frustration toward my sister. "If only Lela would just come meet you."

"Be patient," Zuela says. "Has your sister shared any other details from her visions? Perhaps she's perceived more than you have."

I pause to think. "She doesn't talk about it. But probably. When we were little, she'd have these vivid dreams all the time—way more than I did." This time, it's my own bitterness that coats my throat.

"Yes, from what you've told me, her ability seems more visual."

"Yeah, but I still saw plenty on my own this time, trust me." I shut my eyes, though it doesn't block out the images. "Zuze, I gotta ask . . . the shadows I saw in the vision, they looked different, oily, like eels. They *drowned* Idaly. But you said the shadows I see aren't dangerous. That I shouldn't worry when they appear."

"The maldeados that follow *you*, corazón, are merely curious. They are restless spirits attracted to the energy of brujos." Zuela's soothing expression turns serious, but the buttery taste of sympathy remains. "The ones in your vision were likely under the command of a brujo. Carrying out their will. When the maldeados are being controlled, they take on that oily appearance."

"But why would a brujo want to attack Idaly?"

"That I don't know," Zuela says. She sighs heavily, then gets up and puts on a cafetera to heat. "Quieres?"

I shake my head. I'm already wired enough as it is. A Cuban espresso will send me over the edge. "You think I should go looking for her?"

Zuela considers this, her clever bottle-green eyes weighing me carefully. "I think you should learn all you can before jumping into something dangerous. Now, piensa. Is there anything from this vision that could tell us more about the woman?"

Closing my eyes, I think back to the vision and immediately the violet taste I've come to associate with Idaly fills my mouth. The memory of her desperation cinches my lungs. "When I've dreamed of her before, she's always seemed nervous. Looking over her shoulder like something was after her. I think she was hiding from someone."

Zuela's mouth tightens. A lot of women come to Zuela's botanica looking for magical or religious escapes from their abusive marriages or controlling boyfriends. She does her best to help, placing pamphlets for escaping domestic abuse meaningfully in their hands, but there's only so much she can do.

"Can't we do like an Obí or Diloggún or something to get answers?"

Zuela shakes her head. "No, corazón. The coconut shells are for when we consult the orishas, not for magia del alma. Some of our rituals may appear the same, but what have I said?"

My shoulders deflate. "We keep our practices separate."

She taps my nose. "Exactly. Alma Magic and Santería are two different things, but they share a common prejudice riddled with misconceptions, and as with anything in life, the integrity of a practice is left to the individual. Intention matters." She smiles. "And we *learn*. Open your spiritual center first and your craft will follow. Do you still have the cards I gave you?"

I nod and pat my pocket.

"Good."

The bell at the front door goes off, and Zuela calls out that she'll be right there. She wipes away her lipstick from my cheek. "It's unfair, mi niña. Your visions are both a gift and a curse. But you're not alone in carrying this burden." She raises a finger. "Now, let us channel our alma magic and do a quick trabajo for mental clarity."

With her ever-loving patience, Zuela guides me through a spell she says will help make the visions clearer. She's out of the bitter bush known as abre camino in Cuba, so instead she burns rosemary to open passages, rubs an egg against my skull, then cracks it, to clear away uncertainty, and then I chew something disgustingly salty and quickly spit it out when Zuze informs me it's freeze-dried lizard brain to sharpen the mind.

As Zuela and I work together, the knot in my stomach loosens. There's a meditative quality to the rituals, a comfort and a *rightness* that I wish I could share with my family.

As if she can sense my thoughts, Zuela says, "The trabajo might help, mi niña, pero remember, there is power in blood. In strong bonds. With your sister at your side, you can achieve anything. Talk to her, Delfi. She may need you more than you know. You've said yourself, you sister's visions are more vivid. Her gift is in touch and sight. She's el ojo." Zuela points to her eye.

"She doesn't want anything to do with magic."

"Sometimes we don't know what's best for us and we could use a little nudge. When she is ready, hold something you both have a connection to as an anchor and use your magia del alma to revisit your vision of Idaly. Working together, you can fill in the gaps."

"My alma as in my power, right?"

"The power within us all, our *souls*. We brujas just know how to tap into our metaphysical potential."

My eyebrows lift. "Okay, Walter Mercado, thanks for the lesson."

Zuela gives me a light smack on the arm and laughs, and I give her a big hug, falling into her familiar flavors of sage and lemongrass and the faintest whiff of tobacco that conveys her strength.

"I couldn't do this without you, Zuze." I sink into her embrace, reminding myself I'm not alone. All I need to do now is convince my sister to embrace her own alma magic before our visions come true.

THREE

Cuba, February 21, 1980

ANITA

In the quiet hollowness of the town church, Anita stood alone.

She missed the guidance of her grandmother with a terrible ache. Abuelita had not only been her grandmother but her spiritual teacher as well. Before her death, she'd taught Anita how to practice Regla de Ocha-Ifá, Santería, with integrity, with a deep ancestral respect. But with the passage of time and under the scrutiny of her mother and las Palomas, Anita's worst fear was that she'd stray from the path her grandmother had laid out for her.

Anita lit a candle for her statue of Our Lady of Candelaria, honoring her Yoruba patroness, Oyá. Fittingly, a deity warrior who rules the winds and the dead. It'd become her weekly ritual to visit the makeshift church that operated under the guise of an old school before she cleansed her room in the hacienda, a necessary step to keep the spirits that roamed the grounds from entering her space and demanding her attention.

As she hurried back home, Anita ignored the stares of the other campesinos filtering out from church. A group of iyawós—Santería initiates—running a great risk by dressing all in white in public looked at her as if she were something evil to ward off.

She'd heard plenty of the whispers before. The townspeople knew what she was—a bruja, or what the santeros called an ajé. They were aware her mother was a Paloma, and Anita was part of the lineage and therefore corrupted by association. The local communities of Afro-Cuban religious practitioners and Espiritistas disapproved of las Palomas because they believed the way that las Palomas channeled and controlled spirits as maldeados was a corrupted and twisted form of power, and that their practices painted all spiritualists in a bad light. And while under Castro's regime religious practitioners were forced to hide their faith, host their gatherings secretly in the confines of their homes or old abandoned buildings because of the government's religious prohibitions, las Palomas were given an exemption because they were secretly and hypocritically sought out by el Comandante and his cabinet for magical protection. The *only* aquelarre of brujos dedicated to el Comandante's welfare. Castro may have declared Cuba to be an atheist country, but the man had his superstitions, and he was not one to leave any part of himself vulnerable, whether he fully believed in las Palomas' magic or not.

Anita tried to ignore the way the santeros muttered prayers or the way they crossed themselves around her. Even though she hadn't been officially initiated yet, her association with las Palomas made her a target and it was for that reason her mother kept Anita under such strict watch—church and school had been her only forms of diversion for as long as she could remember.

Anita quickened her steps. As soon as the hacienda came into view, so did the militant jeep. She was late.

The intimidating figures of the militants leaned against their vehicle, waiting to escort her mother to her secretive monthly meetings with el Comandante and with her aquelarre, the infamous Orden de las Palomas. In the back seat of the jeep sat two gaunt-faced vasallos, loyal yet powerless followers of las Palomas. They kept sharp eyes on Anita as she ran to the open courtyard located in the hacienda's center.

The courtyard was Anita's favorite space in the hacienda. There were wrought-iron benches and handrails, emerald stones on turquoise mosaic tiles. Dozens of birds flitted from one branch to the next on the massive tree that grew like an arrow straight through the hacienda's heart. The hacienda was always full of birds—doves, crows, and those little yellow-necked finches in the summer. Anita often wondered if they were her mother's little spies, but despite that, she loved to sit at the tree's roots, where her late father had carved their names into the trunk.

She spotted her mother. Mamá Orti walked briskly down the steps, her white headscarf billowing behind her. "You're late."

"I'm sorry."

"Either you go to early Mass or you don't go at all. The church is too crowded at this hour for you to be there, and I cannot prevent another raid."

Anita bit her lip. Talking back would only make things worse, and soon Mamá Orti would be gone for two whole days. Two blissfully quiet days when Anita could forget that she too would soon be forced to attend these gatherings.

Her mother continued briskly toward the front door, expecting Anita to follow.

Her mother was required to attend las Palomas' gathering as one of the five Elders, the highest ranking of brujos within the aquelarre. Mamá Orti's hereditary strength made her a target within her own circle. Their bloodline was the strongest, the most potent, had been ever since Anita's grandmother formed las Palomas, turning local, extraordinarily gifted mediums and curanderos into a team of occult bodyguards that were meant to protect their community. Mamá Orti had twisted las Palomas' original goal, and they now devoted their unique abilities to serving one powerful man. And instead of helping lost spirits find peace, las Palomas condemned them to do their bidding as maldeados.

These days, the Elders acted more like jealous, bickering politicians vying for el Comandante's favor rather than a circle of dignified brujos.

And Anita was to be the successor of Mamá Orti's magical lineage. She'd been the one to inherit her mother's formidable magia del alma. Her brother had gotten lucky. He'd always had another choice while she'd been left with none.

Having just turned eighteen and come into her full abilities, Anita knew her mother was now grooming her to become a Guardia, second to her mother's command. Upon her mother's death, Anita would ascend to the role of Elder and tie her life force, her alma, directly to the next comandante—Castro's successor.

The idea terrified her.

"Protect the house." Mamá Orti raised an imperious chin. "And do not leave." She stood by the front door and its impressive brass knocker shaped in las Palomas' symbol—la Paloma Eterna, the immortal dove, pecking a snake coiled around its foot in an endless struggle.

Her mother paused. "Remember, it's not safe out there for you."

"Sí, mamá." *Please go.* Anita kept her hand tucked inside her pocket so her mother wouldn't see the twine she had wrapped around it for a trabajo.

With a satisfied nod, Mamá Orti walked outside to the jeep, where the two militants waited, rifles gleaming in the sun. Their berets drooped, as if the stitched military insignia weighed too much.

Mamá Orti greeted them stonily, her colorful bracelets and rings clattering as she climbed into the jeep, tucking in her dress, white as milk, before shutting the car door. The last thing Anita caught was her mother's scarf fluttering in the wind like a goodbye.

Anita flexed her twine-wrapped hand and let a full breath fill her lungs. Finally.

She skipped back into the house, thin sandals slapping against heels, then broke into a run. The sun was high overhead, dazzling through the courtyard as she tore toward the kitchen, which was thankfully clear of any maids. There was only one oblivious spirit rocking in the corner, but Anita was already used to the presence of Señora Martha, who spent her afterlife roaming the kitchens. Whereas other brujos sensed the dead nearby, Anita saw them as clearly as if they were still alive. But she'd perfected the ability to ignore them rather than risk her mother noticing and transforming the poor lost souls to maldeados.

Anita grabbed an empty rice sack and filled it with as much food as she could sneak out without notice. She snapped bananas from the hanging bunch and took cans of the Russian beef that was shipped in droves from the Soviet Union—Cuba's largest trade partner.

She knew that what her mother had done to secure el Comandante's successful revolution and continued to do for him was the reason they lived so well amid so much misery. Most of her classmates at school went hungry because the government-issued food ledgers claimed one pound of rice was enough to feed a family of six. But the food that filled Mamá Orti's pantry was never recorded in the ledgers.

Hedging around the ghostly Señora Martha, Anita hefted the sack and stole through the back door. She shooed away the cats teasing the chickens in their pen and continued down a well-worn path through the trees.

Anita pretended her father was waiting for her at the edge of Mamá Orti's campo, where the hillside dipped and the red-trunked trees grew like hair. She could picture him tapping out a thin cigarette from his front pocket, his guayabera shirt glowing like a boat at sea.

Her skin prickled, as it often did when she thought of the dead.

She imagined how her father would greet her with a story, perhaps ask, "Do you know the tale of Doña Magdalena? The woman who enchanted a sun god?"

And she'd reply, "You mean, the woman who lost everything for love? Yes, I know it well." In return, he'd give her a toothless grin, his warm smile decayed from years of smoke and drink.

But of course, her father wasn't there. Of all the spirits Anita could see, he wasn't one of them. Instead, she was too often visited by the betrayed, the victims of her mother's curses, those disappeared by the Palomas. As much as she longed to see her father again, Anita took comfort in the knowledge that his soul was free.

She heard a rustling behind her, a whip of cool air, and nearly dropped the heavy sack of food. She jerked around to see a black crow coasting overhead, feathers shining. Its jet glass eyes seemed to stare right through her.

She couldn't afford to be watched. Not now. Although she hated doing it, she shut her eyes and concentrated on calling forth her spirits. The maldeados weaving out from the trees now were wanderers, always curious and never slithering too far behind Anita. They appeared as detached shadows, their shapes inhuman at this point, but still surprisingly sentient.

"I need you to hide me." She gestured at the bird above. "Please."

The shadows suddenly shifted as one—like a dash of movement at her periphery. A wave of darkness wrapped around her like a cloak, and she felt the airy chill before the shadows disappeared into her skin, as if absorbed. It was the part she hated most, but it was necessary with Mamá Orti's spies always near.

After a moment, the bird finally stopped circling and took off, unable to detect her through the shield of maldeados. Anita was so busy watching the crow retreat, she missed the signs of someone else approaching.

"Espantápajaro!"

Anita screamed as her brother burst out from the trees, calling her a scarecrow. He doubled over in laughter.

"Rafa, you idiot! You scared me half to death."

"I know! You should've seen the look on your face." He mimicked her ghoulish expression. "What's in the sack? A body?"

"None of your business." Anita huffed, charging ahead and ignoring her brother's calls to wait for him. The fool was always so amused with himself.

Even though Rafa had to keep stopping to laugh, his long legs caught up to her in seconds. "You still believe her little birds are spying on you?"

She scowled. "Would you risk it?"

He planted himself in her way with a secretive smile. "I have my own ways of keeping hidden."

"Good for you. Now move or make yourself useful." She pushed the rice sack into his gut, and he let out a whoosh of air.

"Is this why you called me? To run your errands?" Rafa dropped the sack and scratched at his palm in frustration. He grabbed Anita's hand, wound with the blessed thread of the trabajo.

Anita smiled. The trabajo never failed to get her brother's attention. It was a little spell using her magia del alma that involved consecrated linen thread and a white-flowered weed ground to a dust the locals called yerba mala. Rafa sighed with relief as he disentangled the string from her hand and discarded it.

"You're lucky I was already on my way to see you," Rafa said. "Could you perhaps find a less annoying way of contacting me? Like, say, a telephone call?"

"Oh yes, and which infuriated lover should I call this time to see where you are?"

He picked up the sack again with a smirk. "Where are you going, anyway?"

Anita's smile faded. They'd arrived at a dirt field where brown grass grew like mold around a small house. Rafa's expression tightened when he spotted it. He knew exactly who lived there. Even from here, they could smell the rank of rotten and abandoned things.

"Come on." She walked ahead before he could protest, waving him on impatiently. They crept close to the shabby home with its yellow, cloudy windows, ringed with dying shrubs and weeds.

"There he is," Rafa whispered, and Anita peered over his shoulder, standing on the tips of her toes. She spotted their former groundskeeper, Silvio. The old man was asleep by the open front door, hunched in a chair, his mouth open. A string of drool fell across the bulging purple tumor on his neck.

"Christ," Rafa muttered, following Anita as she made her way up the front steps. She prompted Rafa to go in quietly, but he couldn't stop staring at the tumor on the old man's neck. She felt a prickling of shame at her mother's handiwork.

"How long have you been coming here?" Rafa asked.

"For as long as he's needed me." Anita grabbed the rice sack from him and stepped inside. But although she took care to keep quiet her foot kicked an empty glass bottle, sending it clattering. The old man stirred.

"Mi ángel de la guarda?" Silvio asked sleepily, sitting up. "It is you. Have you found the thread, ángel? Have you come to end it?"

Her brother raised a brow in question. Anita said nothing. She knew exactly what the old man meant. It was the thread that held his fate. The black thread their mother had used to stitch Silvio's name onto a cloth and curse him. And she also knew his request was pointless. The only way to reverse a curse was to kill the one who'd cast it. It didn't matter if someone found the thread. It would not change his destiny.

"Come lie down," Anita soothed, dropping the food by the door and bringing the old man inside. She led him onto the couch, tucking a pillow under his head, and his saggy face smoothed. "Better, no?"

The old man smiled, then winced. "Promise you'll look for the thread, mi ángel. And that you'll feed my goats. They'll starve if I die."

"Shh, I will, no need to get worked up." She patted Silvio's paper-thin hands until the old man's eyes closed. His head drooped to the side. He could barely breathe with the tumor. Every attempt was strained, wet.

"*Anita*," Rafa hissed. "Does she know you've been coming here?"

Anita checked to make sure Silvio had fallen asleep, then dashed for the door, toward the open, fresh air. "Don't be stupid. Of course, she doesn't know."

Rafa followed her out, and they both nearly leapt off the porch in their haste to be free of the house. "You're leaving? What about his goats?"

Anita laughed without an ounce of mirth. "*What goats?* They're dead. What do you think a curse of ill will does? Makes someone lose their shoes? Lose a bet?" Anita's voice tightened with anger. "Our mother made sure Silvio lost *everything*. All because he stole a few chickens."

Rafa's fists clenched. "This happened because I wasn't here. I would've never allowed—"

"Allowed! How mighty of you, Rafa. Just because you're never here to see what she does doesn't mean you don't know what's going on."

"And why do you think I'm never here? Huh? You think I can condone this?" He flung a hand in the direction of the house, toward the old, dying man. "I'm not just running away, Anita. I'm trying to help people like Silvio. There are others out there like us, fleeing and forming their own communities! Who believe magic shouldn't be used to make the powerful more powerful. People are getting fed up with las Palomas, Anita. Mamá Orti may be mighty, but I know what my gifts can do too, and I know how to use what I've been given. For good. With good intentions."

Anita rolled her eyes. "Those parlor tricks you do? Getting scraps from the desperate for pretty predictions?"

Rafa grabbed a fistful of his hair. "It's better than cowering under her shadow. Forced to join her aquelarre of zealots! I'm learning other ways, from santeros who respect the gifts given to us, who honor the saints and spirits and channel their abilities for good. At least I'm trying."

"I'm trying, too." Anita spread out her arms. "I'm here, aren't I?" Here was a dried empty field. Here was defiance at her feet, squashed beneath quaking shoes. She stopped her chin from trembling. She could be as stoic as her mother when she wanted to.

Rafa's shoulders dropped as if sensing the shift in her. "Yes, you're here, and I want to be here for you too." He leveled his gaze with hers. "What's truly holding you back?"

"Nothing," she said. Anita knew Rafa was watching her intently, trying to tap into his ability to see the colors of her emotions. He did it out of habit—it always drove Anita crazy growing up. But she was no longer a novice. She knew how to block herself from being read so easily. At most, he would just pick up on a murky halo around her head. She didn't want him to read anything, especially not the hopelessness that'd permeated her heart ever since Mamá Orti declared she'd soon be ready for her initiation.

After making a frustrated sound, he said, "Leave with me, Ana. We'll stay in Havana until I can figure a way to get us off this island, start fresh. If you could stop being so afraid—"

"Stop." Anita stepped back. "I'm not like you, Rafa." As if to prove this, a sliver of black mist coiled at her feet. It slithered across her ankles like an old, venomous friend before disappearing into the grass.

Her brother didn't notice the maldeado. He rarely did. They'd always craved *her* presence. She was the one who'd inherited the gift of death and manipulation. Like her mother, she had the ability to destroy someone with a few words and a sacrifice. By exploiting the spirits of the lost and lonely to carry out her will, she could tear someone's world down like Mamá Orti had done to this poor old man and countless others. Her magic wasn't used to heal, or to bless.

No, she wasn't like her brother at all. The venomous gift was her lineage, and Mamá Orti knew it.

"This is my home," Anita continued. "And she's our mother. I can't abandon her."

Rafa looked at her in disbelief. Anita couldn't hold his gaze. She had often wondered herself why she couldn't leave. Was she that much of a coward? Or was it that deep down, she feared that if she turned away from her mother, there wouldn't be anything to keep others from turning their back on her?

Rafa's face fell. Anita knew that even after all this time, he expected more from her.

"If you want to stay, fine," Rafa said. "But do something more. Use your magia del alma for good. Use what you've learned from her to become someone better."

Anita bristled. Her brother's words were foolish. Naïve.

The mango-bruised sky above them grew dark as the wind pushed against Anita's back, ever persistent.

"You've always asked too much of me, Rafa."

He made it sound so easy, but he didn't understand what their mother would do to keep Anita at her side. It'd be impossible to turn her back on a lineage where magic ran as thick as blood. But perhaps he was right. She could still do more for Silvio's suffering.

Maybe her gift could fix what was broken. Even if the magic came at a cost.

FOUR

Miami, November 6, 2016

LELA

Blood or not, I will seriously kill Delfi if she doesn't hurry up. It's unfair I have to cover for her each time she goes running off to that botanica. The clock above the bakery pickup window ticks with a relentless reminder of what I'm supposed to do today. What my sister wants me to do. What my mom always expects of me.

As a nervous habit, I almost absentmindedly touch the decorative antique cat by the cash register before I catch myself. These kitschy things tend to hold sentimental value and the last thing I need is to be thrown into a vision of some cat lover's childhood memory in front of Mami. The images usually pop into my head in quick bursts but sometimes last long enough that it doesn't simply look like I'm staring off into space, daydreaming. Delfi says my eyes take on the creepy vacant stare of a sleepwalker. Not cute.

I drum my fingers on my thigh instead, staring into the white cardboard box on the bakery counter, full of gleaming honey-glazed pastelitos oozing guava goodness. Mami closes the lid.

"For your lunch!" She whisks away the Cuban ambrosia before turning around to add two Materva sodas. "Two croquetas for each. Two empanadas de carne and two guavas with cheese. But pick something up for dinner." Mami packs extra napkins and utensils though it's only for me and Delfi. She always acts like she's feeding an army.

"Thank you, Mami." I go behind the counter, which is covered with dozens of delicious mini cakes our mom spent all night preparing. I grab the bag with our lunches and kiss her cheek, breathing in the vanilla and bread scent that always clings to her. "We'll order something from work after our shift."

"Tell your sister to eat," she instructs. Both of us glance out the window to see Delfi pacing back and forth on her phone, finally back from "getting an egg roll." She waves her arm around as if she's conducting an orchestra.

"I will," I say, but I'm distracted by the parked van across the street, an old beige van with a brown stripe along the side that prompts a case of déjà vu. The windows are tinted, but I can make out some kind of badge hanging from the rearview and the shadowy silhouette of a man directly facing the bakery.

I get a prickle over my skin even though I know this is a public parking lot and there could be any number of reasons he's parked here. Why does that van look so familiar? I lean forward and manage to get a quick glimpse of the man's face, intense eyes and thick, caveman-like features before he suddenly drives off. Probably because the guy caught me staring at him like some paranoid weirdo.

I seriously need more sleep, free of any more nightmares. The thought of visions, of *her*, starts a low thrum of panic under my ribs and I turn away from the window.

"Lela, escucha . . ." Mami trails off with a sigh, worrying her lip. It's the beginning of the Watch Over Your Sister speech. The one that starts with "You know she's kind of loca."

She always uses the same tone for her lectures. Reminding me to stay focused on work and school. To keep our guard up with friends and be wary of strangers. And, of course, her favorite lecture anytime she senses either Delfi or me are about to catch feelings.

She'll gravely remind me of the curse wrought upon the Sánchez women from an old bruja in Cuba—*stay away from love, Ofelia. The curse will sour it.* As if I needed any more reminders. As if having to run from our addict father all our lives hasn't been incentive enough. Or seeing the aftermath of Delfi's first and only boyfriend. I still remember his cries outside our window after she broke up with him for his own good . . . Delfi's phone sliding out of her hand after we got the call from his mother saying he'd hurt himself. To anyone else it'd seem like we just have the crummiest luck with romantic partners. But the reality is they've never seen the curse cling to those we fall in love with like a rabid dog, bringing out the worst sides of them. We change those who love us, and it's never for the better.

But today, Mami doesn't say any of those things. She doesn't need to. One look is all it takes, and I understand what she's asking of me because I've heard it all my life.

Sometimes I think they all ask too much of me.

"Yes, Mami," I say. The smile she gives me in return is genuine, knowing her obedient Ofelia would never break the rules. And I never have—until the visions of that woman Idaly started happening. Delfi made me swear to keep them a secret, and I didn't want Mami to freak out, either.

I take the lunches and let Mami believe we're on our way to work. Just one more lie, one more thing we need to hide from her.

◆ ◆ ◆

I sit cross-legged in the back seat of my friend Soraya's car, keeping my feet away from the floor. She's giving us a ride to the beach, where we're meeting Ethan before the full-moon party. The wind whips Soraya's poof of curly hair around the tiny hatchback, lashing Delfi, who sits beside her. Still, we'd never dare ask Soraya to close the windows—not unless we want to suffocate from her car fumes and die a slow, painful death. The Dominican Republic air freshener dangling from her rearview mirror can only do so much to mask the car's smell with coconut lime.

"You talking shit?" Soraya lowers the radio volume and looks back, flashing me an arched brow.

I laugh. "Oh, now *you're* the psychic?" I glance down at the car floor—it's a garbage abyss of dollar-sandwich wrappers, mismatched pairs of heels with worn soles, and . . .

"Soraya!" I say. "Why's your government textbook propping up the passenger seat?"

"What?" Delfi cries, holding on to the *oh-shit* handle on the roof. "My seat's not connected to the *car?*"

Soraya ignores us and beeps at a scarlet-red Maserati that cuts us off. "Baboso!" she yells out the window, beeping again for good measure.

Soraya taps her temple with a sharp nail. "It's all here, boo. Besides, college is an entirely different ball game. I'm in for the real shit. Tired of all those low-effort mock trials. I need a worthy opponent. A cause I can stand behind. You know what? I'm going to be the first Afro-Latina congressional representative, bitches!"

I slap her arm. "Okay! That's my girl."

Soraya sticks out her tongue, but in the rearview, I catch her dorky smile.

It's strange now that the nauseating whirlwind of essays, acceptance letters, finals, here-sign-my-yearbook-person-I've-never-spoken-to is over. Now, everyone's started college, heading off in different directions. Everyone has a plan, a destination—everyone except me. I feel stuck. As if a giant hand slammed into my chest and stopped me in place. Even Delfi knows what she wants. My sister's decided to go to the local community college, earn a degree in the arts, and take credits for whatever the hell she wants at the moment.

When Mami or teachers ask me what I want to do next, I say I don't know. But that's not true. I do know what I want.

I've always known I wanted to be an archaeologist. When my mom would take Delfi and me to the old ruins of Coral Castle as kids, something in my heart felt right. Even before I had the ability to pick up visions through objects, I'd run my hands over the rough coral stone of the castle, built in the 1920s by a man as an act of unrequited love, and feel as if each piece were infused with magic. A good magic. Stones that had absorbed decades of whispered promises, declarations of love, secrets. I still want to know every secret. Hold something real and ancient in my hands and have it transport me to another place, another time through knowledge-based trials, *not* magic. I want foreign dirt under my nails, the tedious lonely hours of working under the sun to unmask something spectacular—life-changing.

But I want too much for someone so broke.

Delfi looks over her shoulder, but I glance down. There's no telling which of my emotions she tastes to look so concerned. I avoid her gaze for the rest of the ride.

Eventually, the air goes thick with the scent of the ocean, and it takes only three more songs and ten more dollars for the parking garage before we arrive at South Beach. I grab our Hula-Hoops from the trunk of the car, slinging Delfi's gold one around my neck and my silver one over my shoulder. Soraya gives us each a quick kiss and skips off to work.

"Ethan says he's already here," Delfi says. I scan the people lying on the sand, coolers, and oversized umbrellas beside them. I register the bright pink flamingo swim shorts first—the ones I gave him last

Christmas as a joke. Our best friend, Ethan, jogs toward us with his diaper bag full of photography crap strapped against his chest. He's glow-in-the-dark pale, almost as blindingly bright as the sparkling ocean behind him.

I try to rein it in, but a smile breaks across my face. The kind that makes everything melt, turns everything syrupy and warm.

Delfi straightens like a cat picking up an interesting scent. "Oh. What's that I taste?" She pinches my side.

I smack her hand away. "Shut up."

My sister sucks her teeth. "Mm, so sweet. Like butterscotch."

"Seriously, Delf. Stop."

"Or what?" Her arms cross.

"Or I'm leaving."

A shadow falls across Delfi's expression, no longer teasing. "You can't leave yet. I told you. The nightmares are only going to get worse. If we just do the trabajo, our combined gifts—"

I hush her. "Ya. Not now. I told you that's not why I came."

"My villains!" Ethan stops in front of us, fists stacked on hips like a superhero greeting an obliging crowd. His smile loses its sunny stretch as he catches my expression. "Wha—what happened? What'd I do?"

"Nothing." Delfi huffs and passes him. She grabs her Hula-Hoop and bumps her shoulder with his. "Did Lela tell you she got offered that internship in Antarctica?"

"Argentina." I shrug as if it's not a big deal. As if it's not the biggest opportunity of my life dangling out of reach.

Ethan pushes up his glasses to rest in his moussed hair. It used to be mostly blond, but over the years, it's gotten darker.

"You're kidding?" he says.

I shake my head, and Ethan whoops and wraps his arms around my waist, lifting me into the air before my feet touch sand again.

"Ofi . . ." He's the only person that calls me that and it warms my heart. There's a wildly happy expression on his face. "Holy crap. You got the thing! You did it. That's amazing!"

"Yeah, amazing," Delfi parrots. "But it's *unpaid*, and our mom can't afford it." Delfi's face softens. "Which is why we'll be busting our ass extra hard this year. If I can just concentrate on work rather than . . ." She gestures between us impatiently. "Everything else going on."

"You don't have to save money for me, Delf. I can do this on my own."

She glares. "I *want* to, but do you honestly think we can focus on anything else right now besides Idaly? Something's happening, Lel. Whatever this is—it's getting stronger. You can't tell me you don't feel it too." Her eyes catch mine—a little feverish, a little worried.

I do feel our powers getting stronger. But doing this trabajo meant to enhance my already volatile "gifts" and open up a metaphorical can of magic juju is not something I'm ready for. I'm supposed to just step aside and let everything come crashing in? No matter what kind of grim and unknown things waited?

"¡Ay! *Please*," Delfi says. "Enough. I can feel you worrying." More like she can taste it. "Look, I even brought you something—" Delfi digs through her beach bag.

Ethan sidles closer, wrapping an arm around my shoulders so I can rest my weary head on his chest. I breathe in the smoky flint scent of his favorite soap as he draws comforting circles onto my back, and all my awareness is on the pressure of his fingers over my skin.

I'm not sure when Ethan's touch stopped feeling so casual. We've always been touchy. Hugs, kisses on the cheek, holding hands during a scary movie, lying on the same bed to study, sitting on his lap in Soraya's packed car have always been normal things. Best friend things. It had never been a big deal before.

So why was I ruining it?

I flinch as Delfi comes up from behind and pulls us apart.

"It's your azabache," she says. "I got mine on, too." There's a small jet stone charm on the palm of her hand, an identical one already hanging from her thin gold chain along with the letter *D*. My necklace has a small gold *O*, a gift from Mami when we turned sixteen.

Delfi gestures for me to take off my necklace so she can add the azabache charm. It's the same one we used to wear as babies pinned to our clothes, meant to keep the evil eye at bay. The stone is lumpy and oh-so-tiny.

"I didn't know we had these anymore," I say as she clasps the necklace around my neck again.

"You know Mami doesn't throw anything away. I thought we could use it"—her eyes grow pleading—"for the trabajo. I mean look where we are—the same beach we saw in our vision. If we channel our powers together, make the vision clearer, maybe we can find her before it's too late. I already made Ethan bring, and *buy*, everything else we'd need, and it's not even that hard to do."

"It's not a big deal," Ethan adds, making it clear he's not adding onto the guilt trip. The transition lenses on his glasses hide his green eyes from view, and right now, I want nothing more than to see the reassurance in them. The azabache stone feels suddenly too warm, too heavy on my chest.

When you open that door to the spiritual world, it pulls you. Traps you. Leave your door closed, Ofelia. What would happen if I unbolted the locks and flung that door open? If I let everything come crashing in?

I can't.

Delfi studies my expression, her mouth puckering with my thoughts. Whatever she tastes must tell her my answer. Her sigh is heavy with disappointment. "Fine. You're not ready. We'll just go to the party tonight and have fun." She points a finger at me. "But I want you to know that these visions, *our gifts*, aren't just going to go away. I'm giving you the space to come to this on your own, but I hope it's not too late when you do. A woman's life depends on it."

My mouth is too dry to say anything. Guilt stabs at me like a needle, but it's not fair to put this pressure on me. Of course, I want to help Idaly, but where would we even begin?

"It's settled then," my sister says, and the sun glints against Delfi's Hula-Hoop as she spins away, twirling around and around, dusting sand in her wake. She's a shadow against the glare—a curving silhouette against a white sea. It's truly a wonder how anyone so graceful could be so pushy. And how anyone with a twin like her could always be so scared.

◆ ◆ ◆

Not for the first time, I wonder if it's already too late. Delfi's so sure the vision is yet to happen but I'm not convinced. The one thing I haven't wanted to admit, not to her and not to myself, is that the last vision of Idaly felt too real to have been a prediction. It felt more like a memory, something fated that's already come to pass.

From the shore, I can make out the distant boats bobbing ominously in the waves. The woman from our nightmares could have been on any one of them. Along with her killer.

I shift my gaze away from the horizon, wrapping my arms around myself.

Once the sky darkens and the beach fills up with people gathered for the full-moon party, it's easy to get lost in the crowd. The drum circles are always a surprise, always a different vibe each time we've come. Sometimes it's hyped electronic music with pookie heads waving around glow sticks near their faces, or shroomies sitting cross-legged on the sand swearing they can hear the trees cry.

But I like it best when it's like this—fire poi and Hula-Hoop dancers, people huddled around a crackling bonfire, and the light of a full moon. I prefer this crowd with their firmer grip on reality, with their gentler escapes in music and smoke. All of us dancing beneath a plush black sky like a swathe of velvet.

Delfi hasn't said another word to me, but I don't need magic to sense the radiating disappointment. I'm not like her, though. I'm not willing to trust some stranger with our secrets like she is. I don't want to make my already unstable abilities stronger, and I'm not sure I want to see more of this vision-nightmare.

Now she's off dancing with her friends and Ethan's getting us a drink. From my solitary perch in the sand, I let my head fall back, bathing in the moonlight as if it could cool the fiery burn of my skin.

There's something about the full moon that reaches deep into the center of my chest and tugs, pulls at me as if I could float away. I dig my fingers deep into the sand, leaning back onto my arms.

I sense him hovering nearby, the gentle weight of his lingering gaze. For a few heart-rendering moments, he doesn't move and neither do I.

"Praying to the moon goddess?" Ethan finally speaks, walking over. He sits down beside me, cross-legged.

"Yes." I peek at him. "And she sends a divine message."

"Wait. Are you being serious?" His glasses glitter.

I nod solemnly. "She says the tide will rise within the hour and drown all the dorks from the beach." I sit up. "You will be missed."

He hands me a cup. "Hilarious."

Delfi's distinct laugh rings out and we both look up. She's with a group of dancers at the edge of the shore—lithe figures in bohemian wear swaying as much as the waves behind them. My sister trades her sparkly Hula-Hoop to some chick with the biggest ear gauges I've ever seen for a poi stick with fire blazing on each end.

The sight of flames encasing her makes me shudder.

"She's going to get herself killed." My throat is tight.

"Nah, she'll be all right." Ethan rummages through his diaper bag, stuffed with earmarked books, and withdraws Pearl, a giant camera with a lens the width of my arm. He removes the cover, the flash popping out, before snapping pictures of the fire dancers.

Click. Delfi twirls the fire stick out in front of her, creating a circle of orange-white light.

Click. She waves it over her head, mouth tight in concentration.

Click. A crowd gathers as she gains speed with the fire stick, forming figure eights, circles, blurry spirals. The drums pick up tempo.

Click. My heart is in my throat. My twin is buried in a cocoon of shimmering heat. Even across the distance, Delfi's eyes meet mine. She smiles, and for a moment, the sight of her blurs with the memory of her small, panicked face as she shook me awake when our house was on fire. I was so tired. I'd cried myself to sleep that night because I'd overheard my parents arguing. The last words I ever heard my dad speak were the ones he screamed at my mom. *There's something wrong with them! You're all maldecidas!* And then everything went up in flames because he was right. We are cursed.

Click. The camera's on me now, and when I face Ethan, he lowers it, flushed.

My phone lights up with a text from Mami.

ya, you finish? did you eat?

She'd flip if she found out where we are. At least there's one thing I can be honest about. I sigh.

si mami, we ate. don't forget to eat too! we're finishing up here, and don't forget we're staying over soraya's house because we have an early shift tomorrow.

"Everything okay?" Ethan asks as I gnaw my lip to bits, trying to shake the memory of fire lingering in my mind like a mold.

"Yeah, it's my mom." We fall into a comfortable silence, and the more I watch my sister dancing, ecstatic and unharmed, the more I feel at ease. My finger swirls against the sand, drawing a circle.

Scooching closer, Ethan adds a happy face with a big nose. His straight hair, in need of a trim, falls over his eyes.

"Oh, is that supposed to be me?" I tease.

"What? No." He adds a weird helmet-hair shape to the happy face, adds giant lips. I snort. He scrutinizes it for a moment longer, scrunching his nose and contemplating his masterpiece. He holds up a finger. "Ah." He adds two tiny hearts on the happy face's cheeks. "*Now* it's you."

I consider it. "Hm, not bad. But why the hearts?" My gaze brushes upward, his face inches away. He's taken off his glasses, and in the dark, his eyes look black, fathomless and unreadable. I can smell the fruitiness of his drink, the tiniest bit of spice from the rum as if its flavors washed over my own tongue. As if his mouth were already over mine.

This is dangerous. I can't let myself go there. Not with Ethan.

"Ofi—"

The phone pings with a message, and I scramble for it. My skin too warm, my mind too muddled. Ethan sits back as I glance down at the screen.

ok. don't be on the road late. it's dangerous. tell your boss. and tell your hermana que if she doesn't answer her phone, i will return it to el best buy.

I roll my eyes and laugh, showing Ethan the text.

"Is it weird I can hear her voice perfectly in my head?" he says.

"Nope, I hear it too."

Delfi runs up to us, skin glossy with sweat and seawater.

"Will you guys stop being so boring?" Delfi whines. "Get up and come dance with me. Help me convince the DJ to play something more upbeat." Apparently, she's over giving me the silent treatment.

I groan as she reaches for my hand, but when her fingers touch mine, she freezes. Stands absolutely still. Color drains from my sister's face, and I immediately sense why. It comes over me like another wave of déjà vu. The phantom pain starts in my throat, curling down into my lungs, and I lean forward, trying to contain it. Delfi doubles over, too, her own hand fisted against her chest.

"Hey, you two all right?" Ethan asks, sitting up in concern.

I can't answer him. My stomach twists into knots, and I feel an unbearable pain around my neck, in my lungs. *Idaly.*

I shoot to my feet, hands shaking. Delfi and I stare at each other in horror.

"Delf—?" I can't finish. The beach, the moon, the music. The visions we've been having for weeks . . .

"Lela, something's happening," Delfi gasps.

"What do we do?" I choke out. Delfi's hand still clutches her chest. As if her lungs burn as much as mine do. As if we were drowning.

"What's wrong?" Ethan demands, standing too. The guy with the drums picks up speed again, the banging in tune with my heart. I can barely breathe, the pain has grown so intense. It's impossible that no one else feels this.

A shrill scream stabs through the air.

My skin turns to ice.

Another scream rings out and Delfi takes off running. I chase after her, following the cries to the edge of the ocean.

We run up to a gathering of people. The girl with gauges scrambles back from the surf, a hand smothering her shrieks. Delfi and I shoulder our way forward. Ethan calls after us, but he's quickly lost among the crowd.

My body is heavy with dread, already knowing what awaits. No. No, no, no.

My sister clutches my arm. "Shit."

We're too late.

We look down at Idaly's body, tangled on the shore.

FIVE

Miami, November 7, 2016

DELFI

Idaly's face, now so familiar to me, is bloated. Her eyes are open and filmy, lips blue. The seaweed is caught around her creamy-white limbs, and for a moment, I can almost pretend we're not looking at a human. It must be a sick joke, a prop.

Someone beside me throws up, but I can't tear my gaze away even though I'm about to be sick too. People are crying, screaming, shouting into their phones, but it's all muffled, distant except for the roar of my blood and the ocean lapping at Idaly's corpse.

Wake up. Wake up.

Lela's arm presses against mine. Warm, alive. We stand side by side, shaking, both of us searching the body for the marks we already know are there. Idaly's hair is wound around her neck, obscuring my ability to see any strangulation marks, but her legs . . . the dark bruises are stark against her dead flesh.

Lela gags, pressing the back of her hand to her mouth.

I crouch to push aside Idaly's hair and Lela yanks me back, but I'm done just watching. We're too late. We're too late, and it's all my fault. If I would've just tried harder.

I give my sister a pleading look, a desperate one, and she knows what I'm asking her to do. It's the least we can do for her now.

Already I hear the sound of police sirens coming, can hear Ethan shouting our names.

Lela leans forward and presses her fingers to the frigid, stiff skin of Idaly's neck, making contact with a heart-shaped charm still dangling around the base of her throat.

My sister closes her eyes and mumbles the words that come to her in Spanish. "No. I have to warn them." The last words Idaly must've thought.

The memory of our last vision of her strikes me like an arrow through the chest. She was so full of terror. Awake when she died, pulled down into the ocean by maldeados.

Then the other realization hits—Idaly's last thought wasn't about her own life, but to warn *them*. Someone else is in danger.

My sister turns hastily away from the body and I take the moment to gently yank the thin chain off Idaly's neck. The woman from our dreams doesn't even flinch, because why would she? She's gone, because we couldn't save her. We let her die, and now other people might die, too. Pocketing the necklace, I grab hold of my sister's hand and we back into the crowd as a swarm of officers runs toward us like frenzied fireflies, flashlights bobbing in the dark.

The cops won't find a weapon. They won't uncover who did this. We might be the only ones who know how she died except for the brujo who did it, but we can never breathe a word to the police. How could we ever explain that we've been dreaming about Idaly for weeks? That we know this woman like the inside of our own eyelids, know that her eyes were a pensive blue and not the filmy, unseeing gray currently peering at the sky?

I can't stand idly by anymore, not when the consequences are staring me in the face.

An accusing reminder that we failed her.

◆ ◆ ◆

Three hours later, we're still waiting for the police to finish taking our statements, and I'm staring at the picture on my license like it's the first time I've seen my face. I read over my full name and hear it in my mother's voice, middle name and all. Her pissed-off voice, reminding me of the deep shit we're in.

I toy nervously with the thin chain hidden in my pocket.

Police cars and yellow tape cordon off a section of the boardwalk. Only a few witnesses are still sticking around, which is a relief after the emotional tidal wave from before. You'd think a crowd at a crime scene would bring on the taste of worry, concern, shock, even sadness. But nope, the most overwhelming flavor I got was the nauseating citrus taste of excitement. Apparently, some people will welcome any break from their dull lives because humans suck.

"Didn't I already get your statement?" A cop walks over with a teasing smile, as if we're at a damn barbecue and someone forgot to introduce us.

I jut my chin out toward Lela, shivering against the back of another cop car across the lot. "You were talking to my sister."

Lela shoots me a worried glance, and I give her what I hope is a reassuring look.

The douchey detective who interviewed me earlier in the night approaches my sister. His greased-black hair shines under the lamppost, hands tucked into a pressed suit as if he has all the time in the world. Some forensic expert with quick-firing questions and, despite his smile, a taste of sharp, acrid spice—like suspicion.

Come on, Lela. I propel the thought at her. *Don't say anything you'll regret.*

This other cop, with his yellow notepad follows my line of sight. "Twins, eh?"

I regard him with a flat look, proceeding to explain everything I've already told douchey forensic expert, which is to say not much. It's not like I can share everything I know without being charged with murder. While the cop jots down the information, a rusty gurney grinds up from the sand onto the pavement. There's a lump strapped to the top—a black body bag.

This sight, more than Idaly's gray skin, her blank eyes, is what hits me. She's gone. Really and truly dead. Guilt rakes against my insides, but so does a bitter anger. We could've done more. I have to convince Lela.

The cop finishes up and I look for my sister, but she's no longer talking to the cops, she's calling after some guy in a windbreaker hoodie. He's standing with all the other straggling rubberneckers behind the yellow caution tape but as she gets closer, he hurries off.

"Hey!" she yells. My sister books it after him, like a quarterback, astonishing the hell out of me. She gets close enough to brush his jacket and I can see the moment her gaze spaces to another plane of existence. The zombie stare. It's quick but lasts long enough for the guy to run across the street and get into some old beat-up van.

I run toward her and we watch as the man drives off in the van, Lela staring like she's seen a ghost.

"What's going on?" I ask. "Who was that?"

Lela is shaking, out of breath. "That's the third time I've seen that beige van today. Brown stripe on the side. I know that guy. I've seen his face. He was by the bakery earlier."

We're getting curious looks from the police officers nearby, and I gesture for her to lower her voice.

"Are we being *stalked*?" Lela asks.

I shush her again, pulling her away from prying ears. Ethan follows, confused and concerned.

"This is because of you!" she says, her anger catching me off guard. "You've been visiting that witch at the botanica and you—you blew open our door!"

Our door? My gut twists as my sister's features rearrange themselves to mimic our father's—angry, disgusted. But then it's gone like a trick of the light. A stubborn trace of the man who abandoned us. Who'd done more than abandon us. I want to defend myself. I want to tell her this has nothing to do with me finally accepting who I am and seeking Zuela's help, but . . . I don't know. Did I bring this on?

Lela's face falls, the minty green taste of regret coating my tongue, but more potent is the barbed flavor of dread that makes me want to pull her into a crushing hug. Before either of us can move, her phone rings.

"Mami . . ." she starts in exhaustion. I can hear our mother's screeching. "Sí, I told you we're fine."

Ethan pushes his glasses to the top of his head and rubs his eyes. Still, I can't unsee my sister's face from a moment ago. Her accusation. She has no idea that everything I do at Zuela's botanica, all the things I keep from her and Mami, are to keep us safe, to understand ourselves and our gifts so that we can control our magic and not the other way around. So that no one can turn around and tell us what we don't already know—we're different but I no longer think that's a bad thing.

Protecting her from the full truth of the curse is why I've never told her about what really happened with our dad. Mami said that our childhood house burnt down because of an electrical failure. But she and I both know that's another lie. I was six, but I know what I saw, even if I never told anyone.

Our dad stole into our room that night, lit the blessed candle that Mami would keep on our nightstand to chase away our nightmares. My eyes had blinked open, hazy with sleep, and met his—darkened by that fanatic glaze that'd replaced any bit of kindness. The Sánchez Curse.

He'd told me to go back to sleep, and I pretended to. Pretended like I didn't see him nudge the candle until it brushed against the gauzy, billowing drape. Pretended like he didn't leave us to burn while he ran.

So whatever magic thrums through us, whatever power we carry, the very thing he shunned us for, I prefer to his meek legacy. And I know that even though my sister favors him, Lela's nothing like our father. She is everything he wasn't—gentle eyes for a gentle heart. The soft center to my spiky flower. I'll protect her, no matter the cost, even if she doesn't like it.

Lela leans her bare arm beside mine as if sensing my turmoil, and I relax into my sister's offered touch and breathe.

"It's too late to head home—" she continues while our mother's pitch rises in response. "No, we can't call out. Okay. Okay, I said! We'll call for a ride. See you in a bit and try to relax, you're going to have un patatún." She ends the call and shoves the phone deep into her pocket.

"You don't need to call for a ride. I got my car." Ethan pats the jingling pocket containing his keys. His gaze flickers to Lela, his concern a sweet spongy flavor like angel food cake left out too long, stale with long-repressed desire. I've picked up on Ethan's little crush before, but lately, it's different. Stronger. And for a while now, I've been noticing the way Lela returns his looks.

My stomach twists and I nudge myself between them, flicking Ethan's forehead. "Duh, she only said that so our mom wouldn't think we were hanging out with the likes of *you*."

I've let it go on longer than I should've. If Ethan were to finally grow the balls to ask my sister out, I'm not sure Lela would refuse. My sister has never seen the family curse take hold like I have, never felt its clawed grip on her heart, shredding it to pieces.

Losing Christian like that broke my heart. Losing Ethan like that would kill her. Like Zuela said, sometimes people just need a nudge for their own good.

"Delf, listen—" my sister starts, but I hold up a hand.

"No need. I get it. We're all freaked out. But we have some talking to do, starting with where you've been seeing that van. So let's get out of here." I whirl around, catching sight of a familiar face. "Oh my god. What's *he* doing here?"

"Who?" Lela says with a tinge of fear, as if afraid to find another aspect of our nightmares brought to life. But she quickly spots who I meant. "Oh."

Out of all the spite-fueled flings I had after I lost Christian, Andres is the one I regret most.

Dressed in his security uniform, Andres ducks under the yellow police tape like he owns the place or the crime scene or whatever. I duck behind my sister and then realize how futile that is since we look exactly alike. Luckily, he doesn't look our way.

Andres fell into my path at the wrong time when I wasn't in the right state of mind to be gentle or kind. Not that I've ever had much capacity for either. Still, I'd been feeling extra vengeful those days, and the threat of his feelings had only stirred rage in me. I resented him for wanting something I could never give, demanding something that would only destroy him. For his own good, I hooked up with his friend. Better for him to hate me than love me.

Still, my regret, that annoying guilt, is sometimes overshadowed by other feelings. Other memories. Maybe it has something to do with my gift, but I still remember exactly how the taste of Andres felt on my tongue, the smell of his skin, the feel of his chest—

It's then I notice who he's walked over to greet. The douchey forensic expert claps him on the shoulder—same wide jaw, same brown skin and tilted mouth.

"Detective Jerk's his dad," Lela says, coming to the same realization.

I huff a laugh. "I named him Douchey Forensic Expert."

Ethan shrugs. "I just called him an ass."

"That works too." As if sensing our smack talk, Andres looks up and locks eyes with me. He looks startled, but his surprise is soon overtaken by disgust. It's a look that stings.

"Come on," I say. "Let's get out of here. It's depressing."

We walk in silence into the city until the crashing of waves fades and the police lights and never-ending nightlife of the beach are far behind us.

Lela glances back. "God, Delfi, do you think we should've said something to the police?"

"Are you *high*? Hell no. They'd lock us up." I glance around, making sure no one's around, as we finally walk up to Ethan's car.

As I get into the car, I sense Ethan's bursting with questions. I taste everything from peppery confusion to licorice impatience. The boy tosses off emotions like a dog shaking off water. But there's a subtle, almost rosy, taste that makes me think of trust. Like he knows we won't leave him in the dark, but understands we need to get all this out in our own way.

I turn on his AC. "Okay, explain. Where else have you seen that guy with the van before? And what do you mean he's stalking us? Do you think he has something to do with Idaly?"

I look back at Lela, ready to dig into everything she knows, but it's as if the whole night just caught up with her. She's got her hands over her face, trying to cover up the fact that she's crying.

Ethan's face drains of color. "Oh . . . please, don't cry." He seems ready to launch himself into the back seat with her, but I stop him and stretch my hand across the console to capture my sister's.

"Drive," I say quietly, giving her a moment to collect herself.

Ethan spears the key into the ignition and we take off. It's not until we hit the expressway that Lela finally speaks up, roughly wiping the tears from her face. Like me, she's never been big on crying.

"I thought it was weird this morning when I saw that same van outside the church, then again, outside the bakery. I only caught a glimpse of his face this morning, but I knew it was him tonight in that hoodie, standing there behind the police tape."

"What'd you see when you touched him?"

At this she gives me a look like, *you saw that, huh?* "It was so fast but . . . he was searching for someone in the strip, close by where we saw Idaly in our last vision of her. This other guy—a Black man with a silver-streaked beard and a fedora—grabbed his jacket and spoke to him in Spanish. 'We have to find her. She's been here, I know it.'"

My mouth drops. "You think they were looking for Idaly?"

"I don't know."

"Wait. You were having more visions?" Ethan's glasses capture the glare of headlights.

I breathe in crisp, stinging air, even though the windows are closed. It tastes like the thick humidity before a thunderstorm. It's the taste of what our mom calls el sereno—moist night air that supposedly causes sickness—but this time it evokes the pang of betrayal. And it's coming from Ethan.

Lela hesitates, possibly having sensed something similar in his tone. "You already put up with so much of our weird stuff. I didn't want to add dreaming up murder victims to the list."

"Ofi." He turns to face her so suddenly that the car jerks to the left.

"Whoa, whoa!" I say as he quickly flips back around. "Eyes on the road."

"Sorry," he grumbles, glancing at her in the rearview mirror instead. "Look, I don't know how else to make you understand that nothing you tell me will scare me away. Nothing."

A tender smile curves along Lela's mouth like a shaft of moonlight. My tongue is met with a burst of minty vanilla ice cream on a sunny day, and I can't tell which one of them it's coming from. I forget what it's been like to be alone with these two. The havoc of emotions I'm forced to taste because they're both a wreck of repressed feelings.

I impatiently dig through my bag for a cherry Jolly Rancher and pop it into my mouth. It doesn't dull my ability completely, but it helps.

"Focus," I snap, garbled words around the candy. "Why was he searching for Idaly in the first place? What if he knows who killed her or if he had something to do with it?"

"And why has he been following you guys?" Ethan's grip tightens on the steering wheel, knuckles white. Ethan shifts in his seat. "You didn't see him or anyone else in your dream—when she died?"

The maldeados we saw had no will of their own, they were only carrying out the commands of someone with power—now who that brujo is, I have no clue. "No." I say, just as Lela says, "Kind of?"

My blood boils. "*Kind of?*"

"I—I thought you saw it too," she says, her voice small. "You didn't see the hazy silhouette waiting for Idaly on the boat?"

I point a finger at her. "See, *this* is why we should've discussed this sooner. No, I didn't see anyone else."

She bites at her thumbnail, something she's done since we were kids whenever there was a whiff of confrontation. I get a hint of the vinegary taste of her guilt.

"Did you get a good look at them? Is it a man, a woman?"

Lela shakes her head. "It was just a shadow. Not . . . one of those maldeados, but a human shadow."

I fall back on my seat. Zuela was right. Because of the nature of Lela's gift, she's seen more than I have.

My phone lights up and I glance down at the flood of unread texts from my mom.

"So what do we do now?" Lela asks softly, but there's steel in her voice. "Because I'm ready now. I'm sorry it took me so long. We can go over our dreams, our abilities, whatever you want. I just don't want this to happen again."

I look back at her in relief and grab hold of her hand. I recall what Zuela said about power in strong bonds. About working together with Lela to fill the gaps from our visions. Using our gifts, our combined almas.

"Are you sure, Lel?" I ask. "I have the materials for the trabajo right here."

Lela nods and I know then it's time.

I pull the azabache necklace from under my shirt, gripping it in a tight fist.

"Now, we do a bit of magic," I say.

SIX

Cuba, February 23, 1980

———

ANITA

Use what you've learned from her to become someone better. Her brother's words had been eating away at her since the other day. Rafa was right. She wasn't doing enough.

"Damn him," Anita whispered. The words curled around her and she regretted them immediately. Words carried weight. Curses determined fates. And even a simple one could follow someone to their grave.

Anita stepped into her mother's divining shed. She weaved through the smothering cigar smoke, clutching the bowl of river water tightly in her hands. She was careful not to knock over the porcelain saints dressed in money or the candles with flames flickering blue and bloodred.

The candlelight spilled onto a man in the center of the dark room. He was curled in the fetal position, forehead pressed to the cold, cement floor. Mamá Orti did not usually cast trabajos for las Palomas in her sacred space. Anita's grandmother had taught them that in

Santería, a practitioner was meant to honor the spirits of her ancestors, her eggun, with devotion and offerings. As a santera, doing these rituals for las Palomas felt like a contradiction to Anita's very being, to the teachings she first learned from her abuela in order to channel and tame the disruptive power bestowed on her.

But a lot had changed since Mamá Orti became the head of the family. The man huddled on the floor today, invading their sacred space, was a member of el Comandante's cabinet. A dying member of his cabinet. El Comandante had ordered Mamá Orti to save him, and her mother would do anything to keep her regarded position as his most sought-after Paloma.

The man let out a groan and her mother's warning rang in Anita's head: *Never look straight into the eyes of someone possessed by a spirit, Anita. Unless you want that spirit to find a home in you.*

She shivered, and with a lowered gaze, placed her offering for the trabajo down near the man, next to the large conch filled with black clay and an inlaid face of cowrie shells. The Orisha Eleguá. She turned the conch away from the scene. It was this merging of her mother's practice with their Santería worship that made Anita uneasy. Two practices that had no business being in the same sacred space, not when they so often contradicted each other's purpose.

The river water she'd carried was speckled with animal blood and the torn leaves of the rompe saragüey herb, meant to entice, then expel the wayward spirit. Soon, her mother would complete the ritual with her magia del alma, pouring the bloody water over the visitor's head. Cleansing. Purifying.

The deep vibrating hum of Mamá Orti's chant reached inside Anita's bones, chilling her. Anita shuddered as she felt the spirit pull free from the man's body. She sensed its presence, a caress of cool air, awaiting her mother's next command.

The man threw his head back in a garbled, broken scream.

Don't look, don't look.

And she wouldn't. Because Anita was never supposed to disobey her mother. Instead, she clenched her fists, waiting for it all to be over, for the wayward spirit to be sent free, but Mamá Orti's chant continued. She was speaking so fast, Anita could hardly make sense of the words, but caught enough. Buscal al insurgente. Transfiere la maldeción. Amárrate cede a mi voluntad.

Anita gasped, and her mother cut her a sharp glance. Mamá Orti was ordering the spirit to seek another. Burden someone else with the man's sickness. Punish an enemy. Mamá Orti was transforming the spirit into a maldeado—forever destined to be under a bruja's summons, lost between the living and the dead.

Anita's eyes watered as she watched Mamá Orti complete the ritual, stitching a name onto a cloth—just like with Silvio.

Anita felt useless. Powerless.

That is, until she noticed where her mother stored the cloth with black thread, along with all the others.

◆　◆　◆

This time, as Anita made her way to Silvio's decaying home, Rafa was waiting for her on the path. Her brother followed close behind, silent as if reading the colors of Anita's dangerous mood.

As she marched up to the man's front door, a wind began whipping her dress, slashing her hair against her face.

"Anita . . ."

She ignored him. She was there for only one reason.

The pockets of shadows within the trees detached, slithering like a pit of snakes toward her. She began to sing a prayer. The maldeados swirled around her feet and up her body, cradling her face like an old friend. Shielding her from prying eyes.

"What are you doing? At least let me help," Rafa said.

Her words barreled on as she stared at Silvio's door, knowing the old man suffered on the other side. She felt a crack of power inside her, saw the sky darken in response. She knew she was summoning a twisted magic. A magic that threw off the balances of the world and tipped them in her favor. An obra de maldición.

She held up the cloth that she'd stolen from her mother's shed and the blade she'd brought with her.

"Anita," her brother pleaded again with a hitch in his voice.

But it was too late. It was all she could do. With one quick motion, she ripped through the cloth stitched with Silvio's name, severing his life, freeing him at last from her mother's curse. The maldeados rushed like a flood into the house and disappeared. The old man didn't even have time to cry out.

"Do you see what I am?" Anita whispered, slumping to the ground. "Is this a kindness, Rafa?" She begged an answer from him, her voice and body once again her own. "Hastening his death because I can't save him? Do you see that all I can be is *cruel*?"

Rafa came to his knees and held her small hands in his. "I see what you are, Hermana. I see your power, and it is far from cruel. It is miraculous."

She raised her chin. "What if I'm just as corrupted as her? What if it's too late for me?"

Her brother shook his head. "It is never too late for you. I won't allow it." He helped her stand.

"And if she finds out what I've done? If she captures Silvio's soul and he's never free?"

Her brother thought this over. "Then I know an olorisha who can show me how to prevent it. I'll make sure Silvio moves on. I promise you."

The adrenaline and power of what she'd just done was beginning to fade, and with it the weight of an incredible burden.

Rafa squeezed her hand. "Anita, this is proof that you are nothing like our mother."

She looked up at him. "You really believe that, don't you?"

He smiled. Proud, compassionate, and always loving. "I do. And I'll show you how your magic can heal."

SEVEN

Miami, November 7, 2016

DELFI

I s it bad that a part of me feels relieved? Not about Idaly's death, of course not. Not even about the proof that our visions are real and not just some parasite slowly eating away at our brains, showing us random images for giggles. I'm relieved because I'm not alone in this anymore. Lela believes, and most importantly she's ready to learn.

Ethan pulls onto the forested road of Cauley Square. Despite everything that's happened tonight, I feel a small sense of peace settle as I take in our home, the small, historic community filled with restaurants, art galleries, and antique shops. At night, hundreds of lights strung from the massive oaks are turned on, illuminating the pathways to the gardens. It's an abrupt contradiction to the rest of South Miami, where everything is concrete roads and buildings pushed right up to the edges of sidewalks. This little village is our world.

Ethan turns off the headlights and parks a block away from our apartment. Light spills from the windows like two watchful, waiting eyes.

Ethan has the stuff for the trabajo out before I can ask. He's been keeping it at his house in case my mom snoops through my room. I light the twin candles, smear the oil Zuela gave me on my hands, and wind my azabache necklace around my fingers. I tell Lela to do the same.

"You sure this will work?" she asks.

We both hunch over in Ethan's car, clasping hands over the center console.

"For sure," I say. "Just—close your eyes and shut up. I need to focus."

She frowns but does as I ask. I follow suit and wait for the magic to come. The power of my alma magic that Zuela told me I'd know instinctually how to channel, but all I feel is cramped and anxious.

I'm straining to sense anything, but I keep getting distracted by the whoosh of wind outside, the hum of the car's engine, and the loud, nervous tapping of Ethan's foot as he waits in the front seat because it's impossible for that boy to stay still. I concentrate harder, squeezing my eyes shut until I hear a yelp.

"You're hurting me!" Lela says, and I realize I've been clenching her hand in a death grip.

"Sorry," I grumble.

She peeks an eye open. "Maybe I can help. Tell me what I'm supposed to be looking for."

"I'm not exactly sure. Let's work together to see if we missed anything. Zuze thinks you have a stronger gift for visions." My sister stiffens even as I try keeping the envy from my voice. "Which, given the revelations this past hour, I'm assuming she's right."

"Don't worry." Ethan places his hand on Lela's. "I'll be here. I'll pull you out of it if you need me. We just got to think of a code word."

I roll my eyes. "We don't need a code word and *you* don't have magic."

"Haven't you ever seen a witch movie? There's the power of three." He holds up three fingers.

Whatever. At least Lela seems comforted. She and I both take one of Ethan's hands, and all three of us close our eyes like we're auditioning for *The Craft*.

"Now let's concentrate on Idaly," I say, bringing back the last vision of her as much as I don't want to. I remember the sea wind biting her cheek as she stood on the boat. I taste the floral violets that always accompany visions of her. Like the baby cologne my mom used to put on us.

Something stirs in me then as my sister's hand tightens on mine. There's a heat coming from the azabache necklaces, from inside my stomach, and at last, I feel it. My magia del alma. I almost cry with relief knowing my magic is there, waiting, despite having been locked away for most of my life. Maybe there is something to the power of three.

I can feel the discomfort of the car melt away. Can barely feel the grip of Ethan's or Lela's hand, just a sense of growing cold. Almost like drifting off to sleep except I'm less sure of what waits on the other side of these dreams.

I plunge into darkness.

◆　◆　◆

My bare feet pad into a cavernous room. No, not my feet. Not mine. There are others in here holding up flickering candles to light the room.

I hear a chant that rattles my bones. *Obey. Serve. Submit.*

Someone grabs hold of my neck in the dark. A robed figure. The glint of a fiery branding iron. The pained cries of others echo around the space. The figure lowers the metal to the soft skin of my neck. I want to scream, but I'm wrenched away to another dark space. Another vision.

I recognize this part of Miami Beach, near South Pointe and the abandoned lifeguard tower where Idaly washed ashore. A large man with a teardrop-shaped birthmark under his eye walks with his hands tucked into a tattered windbreaker. It's the same man Lela chased after. Teardrop walks near the area where police tape still lingers on the palm trees. There's a maldeado following close behind, slithering at his heels, but he can't see it, and I can't warn him.

The fading sun casts the sand in a haze of peach. He walks along the shore, but not leisurely. More like he knows exactly where he's going.

Like Lela said, there's a person following close behind—a brujo, lurking in the darkness.

Teardrop doesn't notice. Or maybe he does because his pace quickens. He goes behind one of the alleys behind the clubs and shops. He doesn't look behind him. His long, dark hair is falling over his face but he doesn't stop to brush it away. The footsteps are loud now. Using a key card, the man dashes into one of the back doors of some sort of nightclub with the logo of a radioactive-green mango.

A gloved hand slams over the closed door, and I jolt as the vision cuts to black.

My sister and I let go of each other's hands and the azabache necklaces drop to the floor. Something must've cut me because there's a small bloody gash across my palm. A matching one on Lela.

"You're bleeding," Ethan says, opening his center console and handing us napkins from Dunkin' Donuts. "That's what you guys go through each time?" Ethan runs a shaky hand down his face. "I don't know how you deal. That man we saw with the birthmark . . . is that the same guy from the crime scene today?"

"It is," Lela says, making a fist and keeping pressure on her cut. "If only I could've held on longer to him, maybe I could've seen what he wants with us. What he wanted with Idaly."

"So," I say slowly. "I might have something that'll give us more answers. And before you freak out, remember this would've rotted away at a police station."

I pull out Idaly's charm necklace.

My sister covers her mouth. "Oh my god, Delfi. You didn't? Please tell me you didn't."

As I hold it up in the light, I realize it's a locket.

"Wait," I say, suddenly excited. I open the locket and stare at the tiny picture inside. It's another guy, not Teardrop but someone else entirely. A man with light hair and light eyes.

Lela's expression fills with alarm.

"Lela, it's going to be fine, just—"

"Look behind you," Lela hisses, pointing frantically toward the road.

I turn to see a nightmare heading straight toward us. Ethan frantically blows out the candles, throwing them in his bag and spilling wax all over the place. We sit, frozen, as a ghostly figure skulks up to my side of the car, wearing a faux-silk nightgown and a gaze promising death in Spanish.

"Shit." I sink into my seat. Ethan rolls down my window to face the apparition.

"H—hey, Ms. Sánchez. I—uh, made sure to bring them home safe and sound."

But not even Ethan's good-boy smile can melt the fury from Mami's face.

EIGHT

Miami, November 12, 2016

LELA

I'm pacing my room as if it's a jail cell. Mami hasn't let us out of her sight this entire week except for work. It's not like I've had any extravagant plans, but the clock is ticking on tracking down Idaly's killer.

I have to warn them!

I flinch at the clarity of her final words in my mind. I still don't know who Idaly wanted to warn. If the man Delfi calls Teardrop is the one in danger or if *he's* the brujo who killed her. Who was Idaly hiding from, and why, why, why are me and Delfi the ones left to deal with this? What connection could we possibly have?

I look over the text we sent last night in our group chat. It's a screenshot of a website for Elektric with the logo of a radioactive mango. The same logo we saw on the door that Teardrop escaped into, and one I knew I'd seen before. A kid we knew from school named Sam is always there because his dad owns the club. That's a connection, I guess. Though it's not that big of a coincidence, considering our magnet school was only a few blocks south of the beach. Not all of our friends had to take the morning train and a bus to get to school every morning. When Ethan got his car senior year, it literally saved our lives. So the plan is to go to the club tonight and see if Sam knows anything about the big hulking man with the teardrop birthmark and a keycard to his dad's club. Because even if we did have Sam's number, this calls for more than a text or phone call, and it wouldn't hurt to scope out the place ourselves, see if we can pick up any other visions.

Aside from constantly checking Florida's databases for unidentified and unclaimed deceased to see if there's been an update on Idaly's case, we've been waiting for a sign or another vision, anything that'll tell us what to do next, and this is as close as we've gotten.

I stop doom-scrolling and toss my phone onto the bed and head to the kitchen, beckoned by the smell of mouthwatering food. As well as the trace of magic. Even from the other side of the counter, I can feel that prickle of power over my skin. Delfi's still wearing Idaly's locket with some mysterious man's face in it. Someone else we don't know added to the mix.

Ever since we did the trabajo in Ethan's car, I've been dealing with this new heightened sense of awareness, as if every object nearby is sending out a tiny ripple that only I can pick up. Even *more fun*, the shadow things have also started showing up more. Delfi said the maldeados were normal. As if any of this were normal. She said she'd noticed them lurking around once she'd started practicing with Zuela.

Delfi yelps as the pan pops and a spittle of oil lands on her exposed stomach. Wincing, she turns over the caramelized plantains, exquisitely brown on both sides.

"Quick. Pass me the good stuff," Delfi says.

I keep clear of the sizzling oil and reach on tiptoes to the highest shelf, where we keep the good stuff. "Do you want the all-purpose seasoning or Badia packets?"

"MSG packets." She flourishes a hand over the slabs of red meat on the cutting board like one of those models revealing prizes on game shows. I wrinkle my nose and toss the seasoning to her before sitting down on the wobbly bar stool. I remember when I first came out to our mom as a vegetarian. I honestly thought she would murder me.

"So, who's asking Mami if lockdown is over?" My thumbs swipe across my phone. "Soraya wants to know if we need a ride to Elektric tonight." We miss Soraya and even if tonight's purpose is to investigate, it doesn't mean we can't take our friend to a party. Two birds, one stone.

"Tell her *hell yes*. She can pick us up at the beach and we'll change at her house." Delfi lowers her voice. "Now we just have to get out of this damn house. You ask her. It's your turn."

"How the heck is it my turn?" I stop texting to look up. "Besides, you always know how to convince her. She's been acting extra paranoid lately, so make it good."

A few mornings ago, Mami barged into our bedroom and splattered coconut juice on all four corners of the room. She brought fish from the market and placed it in her entryway cabinet, where she keeps her altar, stinking up the whole house. And now she's outside in the woods doing who knows what. It makes me wonder why, what's changed that she suddenly feels the need to produce so many ebós for protection.

Delfi motions for me to get up. "Turn on the sink for me."

"But I'm so comfy . . ." I groan. Still, I get up and do as I'm asked. Delfi grabs the heavy pressure cooker, squealing with steam, and places it under the cold water.

"Keep complaining," she warns. "I won't cook for you all week, and you'll have to burn yourself some eggs with toast."

I pout, but then Delfi cracks open the lid and out swells the mouthwatering scent of perfectly cooked beans swollen with the taste of peppers, cilantro, onions, garlic . . . I moan.

"Don't be cruel, *Delfina*." My tongue grows thick with a heavy telenovela accent as I throw the back of my hand over my brow dramatically—only halfway kidding at the thought of having to cook for myself. "I promise to be your humble servant in return for your"—I search for the right words—"godly food."

"Godly food, eh?" Mami comes into the house, her shoes all muddy, and takes a deep whiff. "You forgot the vinegar." She's already dressed for a day shift at the bakery. Her hair is neatly coiled away from her face, and her skin shines dewy wet from the outside heat.

"No," Delfi huffs. "I did not. I eyeballed the perfect amount."

"Move." My mother pats her on the hip to scooch and produces the jug of vinegar from under the sink. Mami knows the beans are perfect, and she's only blocking our view so we can't see the tiniest drop of vinegar she pours in. She hates that she hardly has time to cook for us. Hates relinquishing her kitchen. So, any bit of control Mami wants, we give.

We all jump as a bird taps its beak against the kitchen window. Mami dives for the blinds and pulls them closed.

"Mami?" I ask, completely weirded out. "Is everything okay?"

"Fine," she says, her face pale as milk. "I can't stand those birds. Ahora, what is it you want to ask me?"

We snap a surprised look at each other, which, of course, gives us away. Mami has a superior jut to her lip. "You both have esa cara." She gestures to her own unamused face. "So, qué quieren?"

What do we want? Freedom. When do we want it? Now.

"Mami, you know we love you," Delfi starts, already softening her eyes, shoulders humbled. The picture of innocence if it weren't for the bloody knife graphic on her crop top. "But we need to get out of this house. You know it's not healthy to be cooped up."

"Out? For what?"

Delfi skips over and wraps an arm around our mother. Mami's expression sours even more.

"Just for a bit. It's our friend Sam's birthday today, and he's having a party near Soraya's house."

Technically true. Maybe not the party our mom imagines, but still.

Lying to Mami has always been tricky. She has this nose that can sniff out BS in a hot second. We would think it was magic if she weren't so vehemently against it. Though lately, our mom's been so tired with work, it's like her detector has gone cold, and she's been waving aside the half-truths with exhausted resignation. Guilt gnaws at my insides.

"Which one is Sam?" Mami asks. "El bonito who looks like Jesus?" She nods at the tapestry of *The Last Supper* on our kitchen wall.

I cough. "Yeah, Mom. That one."

Really, to her, anyone with long hair and a goatee looks like Jesus. Mami glances at the time on the oven display and rubs her face. I feel another needle of guilt, but it's also laced with triumph. Thanks to Delfi, she's going to say yes. And Delfi says *I'm* Mami's favorite.

"Okay. Pero—pick up your phone when I call and ask Soraya if you can stay at her house after. I don't want you driving home so late. Only borrachos drive at that time. And don't drink!"

I release my thumbnail from my mouth, a smile swooped across my face. We descend on Mami and pull her into our safe-place hug. Nothing bad can happen when you're in the safe-place hug.

It's always been Delfi and me on either side of our mom, clinging to our foundation whenever we're crumbling. But now we're so tall, towering over her. Now it's like we're the markers holding Mami steady in a wild sea.

It hurts lying to her, especially since I feel like I finally understand her. All those warnings of magic and shadows, the consequences of opening that door, and here I am, letting everything in because I no longer have a choice. There's too much at stake. There's a brujo out there who may know where we live, who for some reason may have us in their sight, who already proved they're willing to kill. It's all as dangerous as Mami said it would be.

"On your way out, don't step on the ashes I left outside," Mami whispers, and Delfi catches my eye—identical to hers, same color, same shape, and the same worry threatening to break free.

In a way, it's like we're the ones taking care of Mami now, keeping her sheltered and safe from a world that's always frightened her, but it doesn't mean I'm not terrified. It doesn't mean we know what we're getting ourselves into.

NINE

Cuba, March 1, 1980

ANITA

Anita felt like an unmoored ship threatening to sink, as if the tides of her life had shifted.

She'd ended Silvio's life. Everything felt tilted on its side, every orderly rule and fact tumbling to chaos. She wondered if the old man would haunt her now, or if Rafa and his santero friend had been successful in setting him free. If she'd finally done one good thing with her power.

Naturally, there wasn't a viewing for the old man. No family to dress the body, no wreaths or sashes. Silvio's death came and went without the world knowing any better, without anyone breaking routine.

Mamá Orti certainly hadn't noticed. She'd just returned home and el Comandante had already called her back to Casa Santa. Anita thought perhaps Rafael was right, something big was coming. The people were restless. The political upheaval must be troublesome enough that it'd require Mamá Orti's continuous presence—her protection. After her initiation, Anita was expected to join Mamá Orti. Whether she believed in el Comandante's revolution or not. It was a cause that had lost its intended purpose: freedom for the Cuban people, equality for all, the promise of a self-governed country. Instead, the people were left with a one-party dictatorship and the streets were painted with the blood of those silenced.

Her thoughts were mutinous. And mutiny was swiftly dealt with in her country.

Anita nearly jumped out of her skin as she felt a tap on her shoulder.

"It's just me!" Rafa said, barely dodging the swing of her broom. He threw his hands up to ward off another swipe.

"Por Dios, Rafa. Why do you *do* that?"

A husky laugh came from the hacienda's door. Her brother hadn't come alone.

Gilberto stood at the threshold, wearing the same ironic smile he'd had since they were children. But he was now practically a man, Rafa's age, his dark skin made darker from years spent in the sun, his body strong from years of hard work. He was as handsome as Anita remembered.

"Ana, it's good to see you."

She swallowed, grasping for words. "Hello."

God. Was that all she had to say? It'd been years since she'd last seen him. Mamá Orti used to drag her and Rafa, barely in their teens, to gatherings for las Palomas. The adults would filter in and out of rooms where smoke and a steady thrum of voices escaped in bursts, while the younger brujos would be kept in another room, juntos pero no revueltos, meaning *together but not quite*. They were instructed to wait in silence until the adults were finished, but

Gilberto was never one for rules and he would always try to get her to talk. To make her laugh.

He was often successful. As he stood there smiling at her, Anita was surprised to realize her childhood crush on him had lingered.

"I took care of Silvio like I promised," her brother said, clearing her fog. "With Gilberto's help, he showed me how to cleanse the body. How to release the negative energy. He consulted the Diloggún and all that's left is to leave this at the cemetery gates as an ebó."

So Gilberto was the olorisha her brother had consulted. She supposed she owed him a great debt, and she knew he was taking a risk by helping her. To be an olorisha, he'd had to have practiced under the guidance of a padrino or madrina—one not associated with las Palomas. A mentorship Anita was sure las Palomas wouldn't approve of, and that he must have taken great pains to keep secret. Gilberto risked exposure just by being near them.

"May I come in?" Gilberto asked her.

Anita worried what her mother would say but Rafa beckoned him forward.

Gilberto stood before her, his eyes still that amber like hardened honey. "Rafa told me that you might want to learn. You received your elekes? Your warriors?"

Anita nodded. "Yes. My grandmother said I'm of Oyá."

"Perfect," he said, his smile gentle and mature. Different yet still the boy she knew.

"Thank you for your help," Anita said. "I don't know how much Rafa told you, but I didn't—I wouldn't have—"

Gilberto held up a hand. "No explanation needed." He looked around the hacienda. "Anything to keep another soul from their grip."

Before she could respond to this, her brother placed a heavy arm across her shoulders. "The cemetery is on the way to Havana. We'll go and complete the ebó so Silvio's spirit can move on, and you can come out to the Malecón with us tonight and celebrate."

"Celebrate?" she balked. "A man died, Rafa."

"What better way to honor Silvio than to celebrate his life?" Rafa said. "Gilberto and I will show you all the wondrous things you can do with your gifts besides sulk, cower, and manipulate, but for tonight, we dance in Silvio's honor. And in yours."

◆　◆　◆

Anita was still indignant over her brother's words as she prepared to leave for the Malecón. She knew how to do other things besides sulk, cower, and *manipulate*.

She blew out the candles in her room, knowing she'd have to invite in the maldeados to keep them hidden tonight, hoping her brother wouldn't notice the shadows spilling into the hacienda. Would he consider *that* cowering?

Her brother and Gilberto waited as she got ready. She chose a red dress with flecos that she'd bought on a whim, on the unlikely chance she'd go out to dance. Now it was actually happening, and with Gilberto of all people. Not that she expected to actually dance with him.

The three of them first headed to the cemetery, leaving the wrapped bundle for Oyá. Gilberto instructed Anita to gather nine small aubergines for Oyá in her altar the next day.

After they said a final prayer for Silvio's spirit, they left the cemetery and made their way to the Malecón's promenade. The three of them walked along the seawall, falling into easy conversation. They stopped to listen to a man playing the trumpet, and Anita smiled, swaying to the music.

All along the seafront promenade, couples held each other while Havana glittered like a gem. This contrast was what she loved best about the Malecón. It was here that people from all walks of life fused to a single beat, where a dark sky met a lit one, and where civilization met the vast ocean in a thread of concrete. Still, they couldn't ignore the occasional person walking past with the red CDR armband—the eyes and ears of the revolution, searching for any anti-government sentiments among the whispered words and groups of elderly Cubanos playing dominoes. But there was no escaping that surveillance anywhere in Cuba, so she tried not to let it bother her.

A man strolled by, giving Anita an appreciative look. He mouthed the word *bella*, pressing a hand to his heart, pretending to stagger back. Of course, she waved him off, and the man's friends laughed as they pulled him away.

"He's right, you know?" Gilberto whispered near her ear as her brother yammered on about something up ahead. She felt every part of her body flush.

She did feel beautiful in her red dress and curled hair, but most of all, she felt grown up.

Free. Even if just for a night.

They made their way to El Paraiso, one of Havana's classiest clubs. Anita froze when she saw the military police at the door, checking identification, but Rafa whispered, "Don't worry, for tonight, you're Yeneisy Valdés." He pinched her cheek. "A baby-faced twenty-year-old student."

"It'll be fine," Gilberto assured her.

Anita tried not to wring her hands as her brother handed over their identification and a few pesos to the soldier wearing an ominous rifle on his back. The man pocketed the money quickly and barely glanced at their IDs before letting them through. Once they'd walked inside, Rafa beckoned them toward the music, and finally, Anita was able to relax. A bubble of excitement swirled up from her chest as they entered the courtyard. There was a stage planted in the center, a live band playing soulfully. Like the rest of the city, the walls were a mosaic of colors ranging from turquoise to grapefruit orange to sunflower yellow.

The dancers slinked from one side of the courtyard to the other, carried off in expert arms and dipped precariously low to the checkerboard floor. The music slipped itself into every stiff muscle of Anita's body until she found herself swaying, moving her hips.

"Ayi, al fin," her brother needled, poking her side. "Let's get a table first, then you can show these tiesos how a real dancer moves."

Anita pinched his arm but felt immensely pleased. She was afraid of a lot of things, too many to count—her mother ranked among the top—but if there was one thing Anita was not afraid of, it was dancing. She felt the rhythm in her bones.

Once they sat at their table, Rafa cursed. "What are *they* doing here?"

Anita followed his glower to a couple sitting across the courtyard, around their ages.

She recognized them with a spike of apprehension. They were brujos from her generation, the other children of las Palomas. Not related by blood but connected by the gifts of their magia del alma and the manipulations of power taught by their parents. Anita was surprised she hadn't sensed them right away. The maldeados usually whispered to her if any brujos were nearby.

The girl was Idaly, the only person besides Gilberto that Anita had ever spoken to in stolen whispers at those gatherings. Beside Idaly was Emiliano, now a young man but with the same blond hair and elegantly long nose. Anita recalled the two had been sweethearts, and judging by the way they leaned into each other now, they still were. Between all of them, the only two missing from her peer group were Elder Madroño's children. They'd been older than the rest and acted far too superior for Anita to say more than a few words to either of them. The Madroño boy had always had a cruel, hungry look to him that made Anita uneasy, and his sister was just as cutthroat.

Anita was thankful they weren't there now. She raised a hand to wave at Idaly, which Rafa quickly yanked down, but not before Idaly's mouth quirked in response.

"¿Estás loca? Don't look over there," Rafa said. "I shouldn't have brought you. We can't all be seen together."

Gilberto did wave but even he didn't beckon them over. Anita remembered Idaly was his cousin, and still he hesitated.

Rafa lit his cigarillo, the brand her father used to smoke, a sparkle of an idea in his eyes. A bad idea, probably. Her heart tightened as the familiar scent of clove wafted over, but she was growing impatient with her brother's inquisitive stare. "*What?*"

"Maybe you and your shadows can keep us hidden." He ignored her startled sound of protest and called Idaly over by whistling and signaling to their table. "Let's test how effective your method of cloaking is."

Idaly gave him a wary look but she and her novio Emiliano made their way across the dance floor to their table. Anita swallowed hard. She'd called to the maldeados before they'd left, asking for their protection but there was no telling how well her cloaking would work here, especially not with such a large group in such a public place.

"Rafa, I see your manners haven't improved," Idaly said. Anita watched with astonishment as Idaly leaned down to give Rafa a kiss on the cheek and Emiliano gave him a familiar handshake. It was clear that Rafa knew all of them much better than he'd led on. She wondered if this was the group her brother had gotten himself into all kinds of mischief with last year. Mamá Orti had flown into a fury when she'd learned that Rafa had been visiting a church of Santería in secret with an unsanctioned community, against the law and forbidden by the aquelarre. Mamá Orti decided to cover for him as long as Rafa agreed to never speak to those friends again. El Comandante didn't tolerate any religious practices . . . unless they were in direct aid to the revolution.

Idaly put a warm, friendly hand on her shoulder. "Hello, I remember you." She kissed Anita on the cheek and sat beside her. Her eyes were the blue of a deep ocean, with a secretive depth that pulled Anita in.

Emiliano, the light-haired boy with the thick set of brows, pecked her cheek as well, smiling pleasantly when he said, "This feels like a reunion."

"Or an ambush," Rafa added, breaking the stiff tension, and they all laughed. Soon, they were all exchanging stories from their many misadventures until Anita was sure this was the group Mamá Orti had forced Rafa to dissociate from. She realized how little she knew of his life outside of the hacienda.

"And what exactly happened between all of you?" Anita asked, a trace of hurt lacing her words. How much had her brother kept from her?

The four of them fell silent until finally Gilberto spoke, his voice so low she could barely hear him. "Last year, the Elders discovered we were meeting on our own and accused us of forming our own aquelarre." A criminal offense. An unsanctioned community practicing without the permission of the government would've landed them all in jail as traitors. It's what Mamá Orti had helped Rafa avoid. Not out of motherly concern but to preserve her esteemed position with el Comandante. "But all we were doing was learning. I was teaching them what my godfather had taught me. The beliefs my ancestors bled for. The path of the orishas, of Aché—the true animating source of where our power comes from. Of the practice we're meant to study, in order to respect and honor our roots," Gilberto continued passionately, his eyes lit with fire. "But the Elders forced us to disband and we were forbidden to meet until we could be officially initiated with las Palomas or face the consequences. At first, we didn't believe them, and we kept meeting in secret."

Again, the momentary silence.

"But there are no secrets from las Palomas." Idaly's words were haunted. A wave of gooseflesh swept over Anita's skin.

Her brother banged a fist on the table. "They didn't understand or care that we were doing important work, too—for our community. For the sick and the hungry. Not for the political figureheads that charged in with a revolution and promises of a bright future where the Cuban people would hold the power, and yet here we are."

Anita met her brother's fevered gaze from across the table. "Rafa, what did las Palomas do to you when they found out? Is that why you left home?"

"It's in the past, Ana," Rafa said gruffly. "If I had wanted you involved, I would've told you when it happened."

"Do not treat me like a little girl." White-hot anger shot through her. "You've kept enough from me. What did they do?"

"Fine." Rafa's expression hardened. He pushed his empty glass away. "You want to know so badly—I was beaten by a group of militants. Las Palomas threw me in a windowless room for a month, and they unleashed their maldeados on me every night. Made sure my dreams were horrific." A catch tightened his voice. "I dreamt of you in my place. I dreamt I put you there. And our mother didn't do a thing to stop it."

Anita felt her blood run cold, a fist of pain in her chest. All this, all this Rafa went through alone because he wanted to protect her. He'd been so sure she couldn't handle it.

Could she?

"I'm sorry," Anita choked out, but her words felt small. Rafa looked down, appearing lost in his hellish memories.

"We all knew what we were risking," Idaly said, lacing her arm through Emiliano's, resting her head against his shoulder. "Our parents made sure we wouldn't disobey them again."

Rafa folded his hands over the table, the drink already making his face flush. "But we've learned a lot since then. I never stopped what I needed to do to fight back, and I would be willing to risk it all over again, especially now that Anita can hide us." As Rafa boasted to the others about her cloaking abilities, unease wound its way up her throat. His faith that she could keep them safe was placing too much pressure on her.

Emiliano and Idaly leaned in, invested, ready to risk it all again.

"Mi gente." Gilberto sat back, noticing how loud they'd become even over the din of the club, but he was also looking at Anita with concern as if aware of her growing fear. "I think we should leave this discussion for another time and do what we came here to do and celebrate." Before she knew what was happening, Gilberto got up from his chair and stood in front of her.

"Ana." His smile was devilish, amused at her surprise. His voice was like morning coffee, rich and warm. As he extended his hand, she recognized the act for what it was—a lifeline. "Would you do me the honor?"

Anita knew with every ounce of her being that she should not accept. What if this got back to her mother? As Anita hesitated, heart pounding, she caught sight of something over Gilberto's shoulder.

A small, translucent, paunchy-hipped Black woman stood behind Gilberto with a loving expression. Her dark curly hair met at a distinct point at the center of her forehead, much like his did. She ran nearly transparent fingers down the back of his shirt as if smoothing it, but Gilberto didn't flinch, because he couldn't see or feel her.

Anita's eyes widened. She'd grown accustomed to the spirits around the hacienda, but was shocked to see one here, in this place and in this moment, wearing such a tender expression. The woman nodded encouragingly at Anita, patting Gilberto on the back, before fading away.

Gilberto's grin slipped a little. "Is everything alright? Did I cross a line?"

Anita wasn't sure what message the old woman wanted to convey, but she was struck by the love with which she'd gazed at Gilberto. Maybe that's what made Anita shake her head and say, "All right. One dance."

A trumpet blared as they took to El Paraiso's dance floor, and Gilberto's hand slid down Anita's spine. He swept her back as if opening a silk fan before pulling her flush against him. He lifted a teasingly arrogant brow and Anita laughed as if her insides were made of feathers.

He knew when to move his hips along with hers, when to twirl her away and curl her back. She couldn't remember the last time she'd danced this way—with someone who seemed to speak the language of her body. Perhaps she never had.

Eventually, the music wound down. A singer crooned on stage, voice easing into the night, a soft ballad that had them swaying cheek to cheek.

Gilberto's voice caressed her skin. "Do you think you're ready?"

Anita's eyes, which had begun to close, blinked open. "For what?"

She expected his expression to appear playful, as it had all night, but the set of his jaw was serious. Perhaps even tense. "For what we have to do. The initiation ceremony is soon."

Anita's body tightened. Gilberto quickly picked up on it and they paused, letting the other dancers break around them.

"I'm sorry to mention it. It's only that with the ceremony coming up, I know it's weighing on all our minds. I want you to know, we don't have to be like our parents. The backstabbing, the secrecy . . ."

"The eternal devotion to the regime?" she asked, perhaps too loudly, but the drinks and the relief of being away from Mamá Orti's influence made her bold.

His clean-shaven cheek dimpled in a smile, and she hid her face in his shirt, breathing in his smell of spiced cologne and, charmingly enough, anise seed. His voice rumbled past her cheek.

"That too," he whispered. "We can simply be whatever we like. *With* whoever we want."

His words rang like a promise, and for the first time hope flared in Anita's heart like the first strike of a match. Maybe she could keep them safe, and then she wouldn't have to be so alone.

Maybe Rafa was right, and her magic would be enough.

TEN

LELA

I have to remind myself that I don't get to do what I want. Even
if the distant music is already worming its way into my skin,
tonight, I can't simply be a girl going out with her friends to a
club. We're here on a mission to corner Sam, ask him if he knows
anything about Teardrop, and hope for a miracle, another vision or
clue to point us toward Idaly.

Still, even if tonight's outing is for a crucial purpose, it doesn't
mean we can't look good while we're at it. I check my deep burgundy
lipstick in the reflective windows of Soraya's car. The color matches
the blossoms on my satin dress, and I have to say I look pretty sultry.
It's a shade Ethan might've once mentioned looked really good on
me. Maybe.

Delfi gives me a suspicious look, probably having savored something incriminating, but I ignore her.

"What the hell? How does this lot not have the U-Park app?"
Soraya shouts, irritated. "You have change?" She sticks her fingers

into the cup holder, peeling away syrupy dimes and nickels. "I don't think the meter will take these."

"Sure, let me check." Delfi makes a show of looking down at her skintight dress. "Sorry, got nothing."

Soraya flashes her two front teeth like a bunny, her weirdly disturbing way of insulting someone.

"Here," I say, laughing, pulling some quarters from my small purse. "That'll give us two hours before the parking's free."

As we near the boardwalk, I keep my eyes peeled for any sign of a large man in a windbreaker, for a teardrop birthmark, or even of that blond guy from Idaly's locket, both of whom would stand out among the scantily clothed partiers. But it's impossible to pick out anyone as we weave through the hundreds of sweaty people walking from one stretch of restaurants and clubs to another. Soraya and Delfi keep me snuggled between them. They know how overwhelmed I get in large crowds, never sure what accidental touch might set off my gift. And ever since the trabajo, it's been on another level.

When we reach the venue, I realize we're right across the beach and the abandoned lifeguard tower from the full-moon party. In front of the nightclub, I spot the giant, neon-lit logo of the radioactive mango. It's all like it appeared in my vision, which means there's a real chance Teardrop could be nearby. He used a key card. It's probably where he works and he could be working here tonight.

"Yo, look who it is!"

I turn to see our old friend Marco, a loud, Honduran musclehead, whom we happen to adore. He peels away from the graffitied entrance to walk over to us.

"Don't say it." I hold up a hand in warning.

"Double Trouble!" he says anyway, giving me a fist bump because he remembers how I feel about hugs. Then he wraps Delfi up in his massive arms and gives her a peck on the cheek, reserving an especially tender one for Soraya. "Aw man, and they brought my queen in all her fine-ass glory."

Soraya slaps him lightly on the chest, but she's pleased.

Delfi looks like she's about to make fun of Soraya, but her words get lost in the heart-thumping bass as we enter the club. Strobe lights pierce the hazy mist of smoke and fog, giving flashes of raised arms, bare skin, and a couple's stolen kiss caught in the swell of music. My gaze automatically looks for Ethan in every glimpse of messy hair but there's no sign of him yet.

Focus, Ofelia. You're here to find someone else.

Our group gravitates toward the bar, and there's some guy already hitting on Delfi. She arches a brow, mouth slightly smiling, slightly puckered as she looks up at him doe-eyed. I call it the come-hither look. Soraya has a more colorful name for it.

But behind them, I spot Sam. I tap Delfi's shoulder to get her attention. She gives me a nod, ignoring the flirty guy's protest, and we hurry over to him.

Sam smiles once he sees us, and I guess he does kind of look like Jesus.

"Sam!" Delfi says. "We have questions for you."

Sam pouts, gesturing at the bartender. "Hi to you, too, Delfi. It's not like I haven't seen you in forever."

"Whatever, you know I missed you," my sister says. "I wouldn't have come if I didn't."

"Right, sure," Sam says, handing us each a drink. "Rum and coke, just don't ask for it at the bar."

I take a sip, and it's like drinking liquid fire. "Are you sure there's soda in this?" I sputter as they laugh.

"So what's your question?" Sam asks. Marco is leaning in intently, nosy as always, so we pull Sam away to a corner farther from the music where we can actually hear him.

I decide to start. "We need some info on a guy who works here. He's hard to miss. Really tall and bulky. Longish dark hair a little past his ears, super dark eyes, and a teardrop-shaped birthmark under the left eye."

Sam blinks at us, and Delfi interjects, "Think Javier Bardem with a Cindy Crawford mole, but higher up."

He taps a finger to his chin. *"No Country for Old Men* Bardem or *Vicky Cristina Barcelona* Bardem?"

"Vicky Cristina Bardem, for sure."

"Ah," Sam says in understanding, and a jolt of excitement shoots through my chest. "Sounds hot, but I'm afraid we're all out of Bardems here."

"But we saw—" I glance at Delfi. "We're pretty sure he works here."

"Look, I know every single person on staff. No one like that works here."

Delfi grimaces at whatever taste she's getting from him. "Okay, but what are you not saying?"

"Y'all are being weirdly persistent."

We stand firm in unyielding silence until Sam sighs in surrender. "Okay so, don't go around saying this stuff; my dad could get into some serious trouble." We lean in. "But once in a while, he'll take in undocumented workers for a job or two to help them out. That's how he started out, too, you know? We just had a crew clean out our refrigeration units. The guy you're looking for might've been part of their team, but that crew isn't here anymore."

"And you don't keep any of their information filed away?" I ask, already knowing the answer.

"Hell no. Are we done?"

I sink in defeat. Delfi pulls something out from her pocket though and I immediately feel the hairs on my neck stand up. She hands him the locket, showing him the picture.

"What about this guy? Have you seen him?"

He looks at us like we're crazy. "What the hell are you guys up to? This is an old-ass photo. Do I look like an antiques dealer or something?"

"Forget it." I snatch the locket back. As soon as the metal hits my hand, I gasp and nearly fall back as an image flashes in my mind.

Idaly holding someone to her chest, cradling a man's blond head, an anguished scream. Her hands bloody.

I snap back to the club with a gasp. Delfi's arms are around me, holding me steady. Her eyes are wide and panicked.

"Blood sugar drop, right?" she asks, and I nod.

After I reassure them both I'm okay, Sam excuses himself to another group of friends that probably won't hound him over his dad's hiring practices.

"What'd you see?" Delfi asks, and I tell her with a shaky voice.

"Was the guy she was holding dead?"

I swallow hard. "I'm not sure, but I think it was the guy in the locket."

As the music melts into a gritty electronic song, Soraya comes over with Marco at her heels and I try my hardest to wipe the images away, the sensation of suffocating in grief, but I can't help the tremble still vibrating down my skin.

"Are you two done being all mysterious and witchy, 'cause I'm ready to party, and someone just got here looking all over for you, girl."

My heart rattles in my chest, a yearning for his steady comfort. Because in this moment, I know who Soraya's talking about even before I spot Ethan's sweet, lopsided smile heading my way.

ELEVEN

Miami, November 12, 2016

DELFI

On the dance floor, a ray of pink light strikes Lela's face as Ethan whispers in her ear. By the looks of it, she's moved past her horrifying vision from earlier, or at least doing her best to ignore it. His pale hand slips around her waist, resting on her lower back as if she were precious glass. Lela and Ethan disappear from sight as the lights go wild, as the fog surges into the air. I see a flash of black hair flipping, of glasses, and that sweet smile that's too delicate for so much heartbreak.

Her look of pure happiness shreds me, peels away at my heart until it reveals the black poison at its center. It's not like they haven't danced before. We've known Ethan for years. Hell, I've danced with him. But what they're doing now is something else. It's slower, softer.

What they're doing is falling.

I see this for what it is, a familiar collision. The point of no return.

A name comes to me, unbidden, one I desperately want to forget. And now I'm drowning in the memory of him. Of his smell, of his touch. Of two kids falling in love.

Christian.

A stab of ice-tipped pain, and I give my back to my sister, to Soraya and Marco flirting at the bar, and take long swigs of my drink until my body feels heavier, my thoughts cloudy.

Before I can even formulate a plan, the solution quite literally walks through the door.

I sprint away from my friends, waving to Jay, an old friend from high school who'd been Lela's obsession until he'd graduated and left for the Marines. Jay makes his way over.

"Hey!" I say, and wrap him in a hug. "I didn't know you'd be here. You should come say hi to my sister."

"Ofelia's here?" Jay asks. And I don't have to be a psychic to sense his wanting.

"Yup!" Looping my arm through his I lead the way. "Look who's here," I say brightly as we walk up to Lela. She pauses in surprise, mid-sentence with Ethan, but shoots me a look that doesn't seem entirely annoyed. Which I consider a win.

"Ofelia. Man, you look great," Jay says. He engulfs my sister in a hug. Okay, so he forgot to ask first, *but* . . . luckily, she doesn't space out with a vision.

"I know, right," I chirp since my sister still seems stunned. "So who wants shots? Sam saved us a booth in the back."

"Me!" Soraya squeaks like a kid raising her hand for an answer. Jay steps aside, making space for Lela to walk beside him like a true gentleman. She hesitates, so I toss an arm around poor Ethan, shooing the others forward. With one last glance over her shoulder, my sister follows after Jay.

The moment they're out of sight, Ethan shakes me off. "I know what you're doing."

"Good. Then we're clear."

"Delf, come on. This is ridiculous. You, of all people, know how I feel about Ofi. You know I would never do anything to hurt her."

"You think I'm worried that you'll hurt *her*? After everything you've seen, everything we've told you, you still don't believe there's a curse? Death clings to us. God, I thought Idaly would be proof enough." I throw my arms up. "What's it going to take, Ethan?"

He rubs at his face. "It's not that I don't believe you." His expression is pained. "But what if it's different with us? We've been friends forever. There are feelings there already, from long ago."

"It doesn't work like that. It'll *destroy* you," I tell him.

"Delfi," he snaps. "I'm not your dad. I'm not Christian. At least let me try."

Now I'm shaking, and I grab his arm to haul him away from the crowd.

He groans, wiping a hand down his face. "I'm sorry. I shouldn't have said that."

"You're right," I say, taking a steadying breath. "You're not them. You'll be worse. Because she'll do anything to keep you from hurting yourself. She's not me, Ethan. She won't give up and walk away, and it will *kill* her to lose you like that."

"There has to be a way around the curse."

"Ethan, stop," I spit out. "Do you know the last thing Christian ever said to me? He said he wished he'd never met me. Said it was all my fault." My laughter is sharp, jagged. "And he was right."

"Hey—" Ethan moves forward as if to comfort me, but I back away.

"Do yourself a favor. Don't regret meeting us. Don't regret knowing her. Be her friend, and just . . . save yourself the grief."

The never-ending, suffocating grief.

I shoulder past him and find the bathroom, skipping the line of girls and their drunken complaints, heading straight into the first empty stall. I lock myself in and push my palms against my face, trying to breathe past the ache expanding in my chest.

I'm doing the right thing. I'm saving them both.

As the grief inside of me deepens and grows, I feel the slithering shadows circling my feet. Like cobwebs you can never shake loose. The maldeados thicken and the lights flicker, the hum of electricity thrumming through the stalls.

Stop. Stop. Not here. Not right now.

A breath in, a breath out, and the shadows slowly recede. Zuela's right—I can control them. At least for now.

One last look in the mirror, and I leave to meet the others. I find them sitting in a booth. Ethan's nowhere to be seen. Jay and Marco are griping about how much they hated the last Dolphins game, and Lela seethes quietly, fiddling with a cocktail napkin shaped into a rose—the kind Ethan always makes for her.

"Finally! We've been waiting for you." Soraya pats the empty space beside her and slides a tiny cup my way.

I sit and Soraya begins chattering away, but my attention's on my sister. She looks at me as if she knows exactly what happened. What I said. What I did. Her hand tightens on the rose. I wonder if my sister is absorbing every bit of emotion Ethan poured into that thing. I notice the rose is a little torn around the edges, as if made with angry, jerky movements.

Marco arrives with another round of shots, and my sister and I toss them back in one motion, locking eyes once we're finished.

I'm sorry, I try to convey silently.

I know you are, is what she seems to say in return. *You always are.*

◆ ◆ ◆

On one of the lounge loveseats, Lela smiles at something Jay whispers into her ear—a quieter, sleepier smile that doesn't quite reach her eyes. She still has Ethan's rose crumpled in her hand, and I know she's still mad at me.

"I'm going for a walk," I inform Soraya, who's busy getting a shoulder rub from Marco.

"By yourself?" Soraya hesitates, then shivers as Marco's thumbs knead her spine.

"Yeah, just to the corner. Tell my sister, will you?" I say, and she agrees, uncertainly.

I leave the club and dart across the street toward the beach, weaving through cars stuck in traffic along the strip. Despite the hour, there are still groups of people clustered on the sidewalk and on the grass, eating greasy, face-sized pizzas or sipping alcoholic slushies.

Once I get to the first dusting of sand, I whip off my heels. Already, I see the shadows swirling around my ankles. Almost as if the maldeados were leading me there.

The lifeguard tower comes into view first. With a pang, I realize I'm out of my depth here.

How could I help anyone when I couldn't track down the one person who was haunting my dreams? When I can't even keep the people I love from suffering?

Ambling to the shore, I stretch out close to where the water is gently lapping, keeping my eyes out for anyone who might approach.

The night's cold and quiet. It would be peaceful if it weren't for the memories of dead eyes, of dreams, and things I could never redo, never get back. Christian.

"Let me help you."

"You can't help, don't you get it? It doesn't want you. It wants me. It talks to me."

"Who talks to you? Chris, please, let me be with you through this."

"No, you can't. You'll only make it worse."

Everything inside me recoils. At least Christian's doing better now. His parents got him help, and from what my friends have told me, the more time he spent apart from me, the more he started acting like his old self. I realize why I've been so fixated on controlling my magic, on helping Idaly. I think I believed that if I could prove that I can do more than destroy, that my magic isn't just toxic, then maybe I can move on, too.

The light from my phone beams, startling me back to reality. A text from Lela.

you okay?

I stare at the words until the light fades and the message is lost. I bring my knees close to my chest, the maldeados around me thickening. I curl inward, wrapped into the smallest form possible, and the anger surfaces.

The curse isn't just mine, but sometimes it feels like it is. I know my sister's not to blame. I'm the one who chose to keep what our dad did secret from her. I'm the one who pretends like I barely remember Christian. I don't want her to know what that pain feels like. I want to keep her safe from it. But I also don't want to shoulder that burden all by myself.

I look down at my hands, nearly hidden in a mass of roiling, slithering shadows, like wisps of night sky. It's beyond darkness, a void weaving through my fingertips.

Zuze would tell me to let them in, to understand. To accept.

"Delfi?"

I jump, the maldeados receding, sinking into my skin like a child hiding behind its mother.

"What are you doing back here?"

I can barely make out his shape, but I recognize the voice. My ex, Andres, holds up his phone as a flashlight. I cringe, shielding my eyes against the glare.

His voice loses some of its sting. "Are you—you all right?"

"Can you stop pointing that thing at me?" I stand to face him, awkwardly maneuvering so I won't flash him my goods. I quickly wipe the tears from my face. "And I could ask you the same thing. I mean—about why you're here."

Andres puts the phone away, and a mess of blue-green spots blooms behind my lids as I rub my eyes.

"You look like you were crying." Andres comes closer. His voice is casual, but a sweet, toasted taste wraps around my tongue, like warmed waffle cones, before burning to bitter. "Break another heart?"

I dust the sand off my thighs and the back of my dress, but it's still everywhere. "Are you saying I broke yours?"

He lets out a short laugh. "Seriously, why'd you come back? Some morbid fixation?"

"What, I'm supposed to avoid this place forever? It's Miami. Murders happen all the time."

"How do you know it was a murder?" His expression turns shrewd, that faked indifference vaporizing like smoke.

I wave a hand. "Lucky guess."

He looks annoyed, which only makes him look hotter. I can't help but let my gaze linger over him. His tan skin, his dark hair cut close in a fade, the light shadow of a beard trimmed to perfection, and a body that has a close relationship with a gym. He's certainly filled out this past year.

Andres digs his hands into his pockets. He'd pull off the disinterested look if not for the sweet taste of definite *interest* on my tongue. I casually stroll closer, near enough that I can feel his heat, smell the heady spice of cologne. The sweetness intensifies.

"Did they find out who she was?" I ask.

For a moment, I think he won't answer, but then he sighs, so quietly the waves nearly drown it out. "She's a Jane Doe—no one's claimed her. She was traced back to some stolen boat found abandoned not too far from here."

"And you know this because you've been snooping through your dad's case files?"

Andres ignores me, but I taste the tartness of guilt. It's then I realize, Andres could be my ticket to uncovering more about Idaly's death. He has access to way more information than I could ever get on my own.

He sucks his teeth. "Forget it, I don't even know why I bothered talking to you about this." Honestly, I'm surprised myself. "Everything is a joke to you. I'm out."

I groan as he turns to go. "Andres, wait. I'm sorry. Tell me why her death doesn't feel right to you."

"Why? What's your interest in this?"

I cross my arms. "Maybe it doesn't feel right to me either."

"Sounds like a you problem." He keeps walking away. I hurry to catch up, but his steps are longer than mine. He can't leave now. There has to be a reason I came here today. That I ran into him of all people.

"I said I was sorry," I call after him.

"Yeah, I've heard that before," he tosses over his shoulder.

With my growing agitation, the maldeados begin to creep around us, pulled from the shadows of the nearby boardwalk like a gathering fog that only I can see. Zuze says any bruja can control the maldeados, that they can help you get want you want. Maybe now it's time to find out if that's true.

This time when the maldeados circle around me, I don't resist. For the first time, I'm practically calling them to me, feeling the seductive magic swirl in my stomach.

"Wait." I finally catch up, grabbing his arm, and he stops, going rigid, but my tongue is heavy with the flavor of honeyed wine and I think part of him still wants, still remembers, what we were like together. I brush against him, looking up sweetly at his broad face. The air seems to grow hazy with heat and salt. My fingers skim across the buttons of his shirt, right across his chest. He stills my fingers with his hand but doesn't let go.

"Andres, come on. What else do you know?" Not a question, but a sweet, soft command. The maldeados wrap around my words, etch my will to the wind. It's not only compulsion, but an anger I can't stop from bubbling to the surface. An anger for everything I can't have. "Promise I won't tell anyone." The maldeados swirl around us, vibrating with anticipation, taking on that same iridescent sheen that means they're under the command of a bruja. *My* command.

"I can't," Andres insists, but his voice is strained, husky.

The maldeado shadows curl around his neck, oily-slick, and although his face is calm, there's a thick frothy taste of his apprehension. Deep down, he's starting to realize something's wrong. I've let my fury, my resentment, fuel the magic and now the maldeados are ready to make him obey, no matter the cost.

For a second, I'm tempted.

But I can't do that. I can't force someone against their will. I stumble back, hugging my arms around myself as if I were cold.

Go, I command the maldeados. The shadows withdraw. That was too close. I took it too far.

Andres's blank gaze soaks in life again. The noise of Miami Beach comes rushing back—of the distant clubs, the ocean, the crowds—as if we'd been held underwater until now.

"What—" He backs away. Face white as bone as if I were a monster, and maybe I am. To nearly force someone to do what I want. "I got to go."

"Please," I try again. No compulsion, no magic this time. "I think we can help each other."

He almost decides to leave, but then curiosity sparks in the seductive, smoky taste of a lit match overpowering everything else. "How?"

"I'm psychic," I say, chin raised. "I've . . . seen things."

Surprisingly he doesn't look at me like I'm baked, but rather seems intrigued. "So what? My grandmother is, too. She's a santera and a medium. What can you offer that's so different?"

Interesting. I decide I need to let him in if I want some of his trust in return. "I've seen *Idaly*—that's her name, by the way. I'm not just harboring a sudden interest in dead people. I have a connection to this woman for some reason. I knew she was going to die before it happened, but before you ask, I didn't see who did it. That's what I'm trying to find out."

He's still eyeing me warily.

"Let me guess," I say. "She had some kind of brand seared on her neck?"

His eyes widen. "You could've seen that when you found the body."

"But I didn't, Andres. You know I'm telling the truth."

He looks at me for a long while and something in my eyes must convince him because he says, "The cops called my dad down because the woman—Idaly—is the second body they've found in the last two months with similar patterns: similar wounds, no family, and no local affiliations. It's like they're already ghosts before they die. They both had the same markings on their necks, almost like a cattle brand or maybe some sort of gang mark, but the marking was practically seared off before they died. Someone purposefully wanted to keep the brand mark hidden."

Two bodies. I think of the man from Idaly's locket, from Lela's vision earlier in the night.

"Was the other body a man with blond hair? Light eyes?"

His brow knits. "Yeah."

Her lover. He must've been Idaly's lover, her partner, someone special to her. And now they were both dead.

"I shouldn't be telling you this," Andres says. "I came out to meet some friends and bailed on them because something was pulling me here tonight, to this spot again. And here you are, like a damn twist of fate."

I arch a brow but only because I'd been thinking the same thing. He chuckles darkly. "Not the good kind of fate. I was just brooding over the case. Everyone else seems to think it was just an accidental drowning, but I know something's off, and now you've *seen* her—" He notices my expression and pauses. "What?"

I hide my thrill of excitement. "I could be your psychic sidekick, and you can be my inside source."

"I don't need a sidekick."

I know I pushed the limits with him earlier, and I refuse to turn into an asshole that takes what they want because they can. There are other ways to get what I need. Though I'll keep my plans to myself for now since I already know what Lela would say to the idea of me working with an ex. Speaking of which, I need to get back to her.

"You want my help," I say. "And you're hell-bent on proving something to your pops." His face twists and I smile, dropping my voice. "So why work apart when you know we work so well together? Who knows, I might have some more information to share next time we meet." He's taken aback as I saunter past him.

"My cell number's still the same, by the way," I call out. I know he still has it stored, or he'll find a way to get it. "See you around, partner."

I glance back to see Andres shake his head, eyes a little wary, a little warm against the cold dark. "God help me," he mutters.

Something in my gut tells me that we'll be needing all the help we can get.

TWELVE

Miami, November 16, 2016

LELA

I can feel you lurking." I keep my eyes shut, my head resting over the tub's rim. It's the first time I've spoken to Delfi since Elektric Mango four days ago. We've each been trying to make sense of what little information Sam gave us while dealing with the weird friction that's settled between us after Ethan left.

A drop of frigid water falls from the showerhead and plops onto my exposed knee, raising the stubborn leg hairs I missed while shaving.

The door squeals open. "I wasn't lurking." Delfi scoffs. "I gotta use the bathroom."

I hear the ceramic lid clack back.

"Really?" I can't get a minute of privacy in this house. I forgot Delfi was off today. "You couldn't have waited for me to get out?"

"Whatever, it's just pee." The toilet flushes and I hear the rustle of my sister pulling up her jeans. But Delfi doesn't leave, quiet except for the small hesitant sound of an unasked question.

I crack open an eye and peer sideways at her, Delfi isn't looking at me. Well, she is, but at my shoulder. At the smattering of dark freckles and the patchy scar from our long-ago house fire. Her eyes flicker between my scar and the purple candle from the third spiritual bath that Mami's made me take this week.

"Don't say you're fine." Delfi reaches forward, smoothing back my wet hair.

"Then don't ask me what's wrong." I sink deeper into the fragranced spiritual bath, now gone cool. The woodsy lemon scent of Kolonia 1800 overpowers the tiny bathroom.

"What is this stuff?" Delfi asks, swirling the milky water.

"Eggshell, milk, some herbal concoction Mami said is meant to *cleanse* me of negative energies."

"She hasn't made us take any of these since we were little."

"I know, but you're next. She said to tell you it's your turn." I pause. "And don't answer that."

Delfi cocks her head. "Answer what?"

My phone vibrates above the sink, a tune that's supposed to evoke a magical forest but now sounds grating. Delfi peers at the display and presses the silencer on the side.

"So. I'm not the only one you've been avoiding," she says. The hurt in her voice only worsens the ache in my heart. These past days, it's been a constant war to keep from crying when I think about the look on Ethan's face, what I saw when I held his rose. The regret comes up like vomit, no matter how hard I keep it back, expanding in my throat like a balloon.

There's no point in denying that I had, in fact, been avoiding Delfi. I've been avoiding everyone.

"At least tell me what happened with Jay."

"Nothing happened."

"Um, yeah, figured that much. But why, exactly? Are you saving yourself for marriage or something?"

I glare at her. "Because he's nice. Because he's respectful and actually wants to get to know me. Plus, he's moving away in a week."

"And that's bad because?"

The edges of my vision fill with the shadows I always pretend are never there. I sit up, the fluorescent bulb of the bathroom flickering above with a crackle of static.

"I don't just want sex, Delf," I say. "I want something more."

Someone who looks at me like I'm the only thing that matters. Someone who knows me. Understands when I'm anxious. Knows when I need to be alone. Has seen my faults laid bare and still likes me despite them. Because of them.

I expect my sister to snap back, tell me to stop being so dramatic. To stop wishing for impossible things and suck it up. And I will. I'll suck it up, but I need the reminder. I'm practically begging for it. I know the only reason I can get away with these whiny episodes of wanting and needing and wishing is because I have Delfi, who will always bring me back, grab me by the ankle, and yank me down to reality.

But this time, she doesn't.

My sister's face remains soft, almost sad, as if for once she's given into the wanting and needing and wishing, too.

Delfi nudges the lit purple candle farther away from us. "You must hate me."

"No." I don't hesitate, not for a moment. "Never. I know why you told him what you did. I know that you're only trying to keep us safe. I saw what it did to Christian, how it made our dad so obsessive." Delfi makes a face at this. She's always been much harsher on our dad, but I remember some of the good times. How he'd cook us dinner, our early morning drives to school, the way he looked at Mami.

"I live with this curse over my head too, Delf. I know you're right, but sometimes a girl just catches feelings." I splash the water, my voice cracking, and when Delfi lifts her chin, her eyes are shiny. I can't remember the last time I saw Delfi cry.

"Scoot over." She stands, unzips her jeans, and wiggles out of them. "I'm taking my spiritual cleanse now."

My sister strips down to her sports bra and underwear and climbs into the tub, sending murky water spilling over the sides and onto the floor. I should get out and mop it up before Mami comes home and whips off her rubber sandals. But I don't move. Our knees press together, hands clasped as if we're keeping each other afloat.

"I don't want to be right, Lela. I want you to have that stupid, all-consuming love that makes you feel weak and strong all at once. I want you to have that person who looks at you like you're everything. Especially you, hermanita, because you *are* everything. But I worry."

"I know." A lump builds in the back of my throat. A tiny brown moth floats down from the window and lands on our clasped fingers, as if attracted to a shimmer of light shining within us.

Eventually, one of us breathes, and the moth flutters away.

I squeeze her hand. "We do have that stupid love, though. We've got each other."

My sister rolls her eyes. "Yeah. There's that."

◆ ◆ ◆

Right after I showered off the residue of Mami's spiritual bath and got dressed, I got a text from Ethan saying he had an update on Idaly's case. So while Delfi skulked off to the botanica, I headed to his place, mainly because Delfi's right, and I need to make it clear that we can't be anything more than friends. Like ever.

My heart is in knots when I get to Ethan's house and his stepmom tells me I can wait inside his room. The room, in reality, is a detached pool house that always reminds me of those Tennessee cabins in the brochures, with wood-infused everything and fluffy, burgundy blankets.

I debate for a few seconds whether to wait on his bed. It'd be the first time I've climbed into his bed for something other than *Mario Kart* marathons. I imagine the touch of his sheets would bring on the flurry of Ethan dreams, the surge of restless nights and jumbled thoughts—the overwhelming sensation of him would no doubt rush over me. If I'm an emotional leech, then Ethan's an emotional bleeder. As if his supply of whatever makes Ethan himself is endless.

Chewing on my bottom lip, I grab a throw blanket and plop down on his leather couch instead, surrounded by shelves stuffed with books and sketchpads.

Through the tall, open windows, I spot someone crossing the yard, heading toward the front door. My heart gives a traitorous leap. *Play it cool, like nothing's happened. Like nothing's changed.*

The knob twists freely since he never bothers locking up. And in he strides.

Cheeks pink from the outside sun, hair un-styled and tossed back in brown waves. He looks tired. Unaware, unguarded, and as always, beautiful. It's when he grabs the edges of his shirt, readying to undress that I let out a squawk.

"Holy—" Ethan quickly tugs his shirt back down. "You're here."

Not a *What are you doing here?* Or *How'd you get in?* Just *You're here.*

"You texted," I say. "You said you had a lead on Idaly? I hope it's okay I just came over."

"Of course it's okay. I'd have picked you up, but—"

"I know." But I didn't answer. We both stay quiet for a beat longer. I watch the dust motes swirl against the falling light.

"Ofi, could I start by apologizing—for leaving so quickly the other night?"

"And . . ." I hedge. "For not saying goodbye?"

Ethan's warm laugh fills the room. "Yeah, for that too."

He'd left me with a black napkin rose, knowing I'd figure out exactly why he was in such a hurry to leave the Elektric Mango. He wanted me to know.

"Forgiven," I say, patting the space beside me. He plops down.

"Did you have a good time?" He fiddles with the edge of the blanket.

My stomach knots. I want to tell him nothing happened between me and Jay, but I'm not sure if I should. Maybe he should believe something happened. But the thought of hurting him, even for his own good, is unbearable.

"It was all right. A little boring."

"Oh. That sucks," he says, but seems to perk up. "So let me tell you about the update on the case!"

Ethan grabs his laptop and shows me the screen, unfurling an email thread between him and a Miami-Dade medical examiner custodian, according to her email signature. "Have you checked NamUs today?" he asks, and I shake my head. Anytime I check the National Missing and Unidentified Persons System, I'm always left shocked by how many people go missing daily. How many crimes are never solved.

"Well, they updated it this morning," he continues. "Thanks to my annoyingly persistent personality as implied by Stephanie in her last email. My years of journalistic sleuthing have struck again!"

"What's it say?" I press.

"Right, right. So, it's not an autopsy report—an ordered copy would've taken too long—but the NamUs database now has public record of how Idaly died *and* forensic evidence that she was indeed from Cuba." He clicks on the link, and there's an entire profile on Idaly, including photos of what she was wearing, a detailed list of every bruise and strangulation mark that I'd rather not keep reading, and an added note stating evidence of fluid found in the lungs and stomach, suggesting the victim drowned.

"How'd they find out her name?" I ask, stomach tight.

"I asked the same thing, but the police have it as her alias. They don't have a last name or any matching fingerprints to missing persons. If they did, she wouldn't be considered unidentified. But look closely at the descriptions list."

My eyes skim the list, then widen. "They were able to make out the mark on her neck."

"A dove and a snake," he says. "But I did a Google search on the mark, and I couldn't find anything other than generic tattoos. No matching emblems or symbols."

An idea strikes me. I take the laptop from him, and on the same database for unidentified bodies, there's a description search. I type in "dove and snake burn," like it said in Idaly's description. The search generates only two results, one of which is Idaly.

Ethan peers at the screen. "I should've thought of that."

"You've done plenty," I say, and click on the name *Emiliano*, my heart beating furiously. This guy's body was found only a month before Idaly's. DNA traced ethnicity to Cuba, and he was blond, pale blue eyes. The last name is unknown, listed as "Doe."

The image of Idaly cradling someone to her chest blazes in my mind, of her hands coming away bloody.

"It's the guy from the locket, isn't it?" Ethan asks.

I close the laptop. "Yeah. They both had the same mark—the same brand as if they were in a gang."

"Or a cult," he adds.

I let my head fall back against the wall. "We're dealing with something a lot bigger than we can handle. I just want like . . . one day of normal. Focusing on scholarship applications. Hell, I'd even settle for a boring workday if I could get more shifts."

Ethan pauses, debating something. Leaning really close to my face. His breath skims my lips. "Can I show you something? I think it might help." He stands up and holds out his hand. "It's by the old barn."

"The old barn? Okay, Farmer Joe." I keep my tone light. I thought he'd been about to kiss me, and my insides are warring between relief and something heavier, something colder.

But when I grab his hand and he draws me up, a glimmer of light falls across his cheek, and I forget that cold exists, that sadness ever dared touch me.

◆　◆　◆

I blink at the *thing* Ethan wanted to show me.

"Well, what do you think?" Ethan wags his brows.

I try and make sense of what it is but fail. It's like a school bus had a baby with a wagon and turned into some sort of camper, painted with so many colors it burns my retinas.

"Where'd you find this?" I ask.

Ethan inspects something under the hood, then reaches deep into the engine, eliciting a clicking noise.

"My dad's friend found this bad boy on his lot just dumped there! Can you believe it?"

"*Who* would dump this treasure?"

He squints and points at me. "I can't tell if you're being sarcastic. *Anyway*, she's coming along nicely."

"You said a second ago *she* was a bad boy."

He gives me a lopsided grin, wiping his hands on a rag. "I know it doesn't look like much on the outside," he says, closing the hood with a slam that makes the long, rusted side mirror fall onto the grass. "Yeah, I can fix that. But check it—" He grabs my hand, eagerly pulling me toward the door.

Ethan has to use both hands and exceptional strength to pry open the rusted door. "I can fix that, too," he says.

He looks at me, then shifts nervously. "Holly helped decorate. She added lace and stuff, thought it was a nice touch. I think it is too, but I'll take it down if it's too much."

"Eth," I tease. "Don't keep a girl waiting."

"Right." He smiles, biting at the edge of his lip in what could only be an attempt to kill me. "Would it be dumb if I asked you to close your eyes?"

"Yup." I close my eyes and hold out my hand. "But I'll do it anyway."

He grabs it, his hand a little shaky, and guides me up the steps and into the caravan. He situates me in a spot that feels fluffy beneath my shoes, as if I were standing on a rug. "Can you wait here? Just don't open your eyes yet."

"Got it." I cover my eyes to avoid temptation, but I don't need to have them open to see Ethan. My mind can draw his face like a photograph. Highlighting the bright parts of his cheeks that round when he smiles. The creases at the corners of his eyes. Those freckles that trail along his jaw, leading to his mouth.

I hear a lighter clicking as he moves around me and suddenly the caravan grows warmer, with the heat of the candles he's lit, his body so close to mine. I can feel him there, studying me. "You can look now."

And I do. My hands drop from over my eyes and fly to my chest.

Inside, it's an entirely different world. The caravan is bathed in a yellow velvet glow.

The candlelight and twinkle lights dance along the edges of the window, hung with a lace curtain. It belongs in a fairy tale. I can find Holly's touch in a lot of things—the frilly pillows, the crystals dangling from the ceiling. But it's Ethan's presence everywhere.

"You did all this?" My fingers brush the window frame, engraved with roses by skillful hands, the gold paint still not quite dry.

"Well, it's not entirely finished, but I've been working on it little by little. Do you like it?"

When I look at him, I expect to feel that feathery sensation in my stomach, as if I were falling and falling with no end. What I get instead is this surety in my feet, like I've landed on something sturdy, as if it's been waiting for me to reach it for the longest time.

"It's incredible," I say, walking around the space. I feel his eyes on the bare skin of my neck, tracing the curve of my back. "What are you going to use it for?"

"Whatever you want it for."

I turn. "Whatever I want it for?"

He nods. "Yeah, you can take it to college. Drive it to your internships. I hear those excavation sites get pretty hot—you can cool off in here. And if you ever decide to try the whole tarot thing out with Delfi, this could be a pretty cool place to practice your magic."

I feel lightheaded. "Ethan, I can't accept this."

He rubs his face. "I promise this doesn't come with any strings attached."

"Eth—" I start. "I know, I would never think that."

I place my hand against the cool surface of the table, weave my fingers through the black crochet tablecloth. The vision comes on like a light wind. I see Ethan here, holding the crochet in his hands like I am right now, eyes closed. So proud of himself. It's a brief image, gone too soon, but it warms me to my bones.

Ethan leans closer and wraps his hand around mine, unaware I just had a vision. "I want to do this for you. I want you to travel the world, be the one to discover—I don't know, Cleopatra's tomb. Find the lost civilization of Atlantis." He pauses, and I smile. "I want you to believe in this power you have. The visions, the intuition, all the magic. I think that not only can it help you, but you could help so many others. And I think you'd like that."

I'm surprised to realize he's right. I've been so focused on all the bad things that could happen when I use my magic, but a part of me is curious. I mean, could I use my abilities for more? To help others, and maybe, to fix the harm magic's done to my family? If magic is what cursed us, then what if magic is what can undo it?

Slowly, my shoulders unwind. It's impossible not to feel hopeful when Ethan is looking at me like that. For once, I find myself curious about what could happen if I open that door.

"Fine," I say. "But I want it to be ours. You can use it for photography gigs or for whatever."

"Deal," he says, his smile making me feel like I'm lost in a sea of stars.

"And in case it's not clear, I think the caravan's beautiful."

"You're beautiful." My mouth parts, but he looks back unflinchingly. "Eth—"

His steps consume the small distance between us. "Tell me this isn't what you want. Tell me, and I'll never bring it up again."

I try to stop the tremble of my lip. "I can't tell you that."

Then his hands are cupping my face. Ethan tilts my chin up, searching. Every inch of my feverish skin is alive with the nearness of him.

"Can I kiss you?"

God, I want to. But I've buried this feeling deep, and it's bad enough I've already involved him in a dangerous situation. My mind flashes to Idaly. Her blank eyes accusing me of not doing more, of being too late. Her final plea echoing in my head.

I have to warn them.

Ethan must see my expression change because he lets go. "I'm sorry," he says, stepping back. "I—I crossed a line." He hurries around the room, blowing out the candles. "I'm here offering you a van, and then I just—god, I'm sorry."

"Wait," I say. He stops, his expression tense as I walk toward him. "Will you look at me? *Please.*"

He does, and I reach a tentative hand up to his face. My fingers trace along his jaw, and he winces as if it pains him. It's practically cruel of me to lean up toward his mouth. But I can't help it. I want him too badly. When our lips finally meet, there's a sharp intake of breath against my mouth. His hands slide across my neck, tangle into my hair until we can't breathe but we don't care and can't stop and just give in.

A release. A sweet escape into each other when all this time we've been lost, searching, and it's been *right here.* When his tongue slides across mine, an electric jolt zips through me.

He mumbles into my mouth, and I hesitate, thinking we're moving too fast, but then I realize he's whispering my name. My *real* name.

"*Ofelia.*" The candles around the room flicker like wild, as if a wind had swept through. When had they been lit again? Light dances across Ethan's face, all over my arms.

"I shouldn't—" I start. I want to tell him that I've liked him for a while now, maybe more than like, and that it might kill him. Or at least twist him into a person he was never meant to be—the opposite of everything that makes him Ethan. I need him to understand the curse is real, as much a part of me as my beating heart.

His forehead touches mine. "Be with me, Ofelia. Be with me for as long as you can."

And because I'm an awful, selfish person, and because I'm determined to change my fate, even if it means blowing open the door I've kept under lock and key, I whisper, "Okay."

THIRTEEN

Cuba, March 4, 1980

ANITA

Ever since she met the other children of las Palomas last week, Anita felt like she had electricity running through her veins. She wasn't sure if it was her excitement over the new possibilities in her life, or her fear of being caught.

The spirits were more restless than ever, and they'd gotten into the habit of whispering to her—*soon, soon, soon.*

Anita was certain it was a warning, but for what, she wasn't sure. What would happen soon? The initiation? The lessons that Rafa and Gilberto had been promising to teach her, like channeling her magic?

With a clothespin held between her lips, Anita hung the freshly washed sheets along the clothesline. The sun was a hazy eye against the horizon, casting a timid heat on her skin, and the billowing white sheets reminded her of sails, of clouds.

She tensed when a shadowy figure moved on the other side of the linen. She nearly screamed when the sheet was thrust aside, revealing a smirking Gilberto.

"What are you doing *here*? Have you lost your mind?"

The very next day after their dance in El Paraiso, Gilberto had shown up at her school, where she'd started pre-university courses, insisting on carrying her books. And the day after that, and so on. But this was the first time he'd dared to appear at her house so brazenly. Her mother could find them at any moment and would murder them both.

"In a manner of speaking, yes." Gilberto grinned as he reached for her hands. "I wanted to see you. When you didn't meet me after your classes this morning, I was worried."

Anita's nervousness was only partly due to the threat of Mamá Orti. No matter how many times they'd seen each other this week, Gilberto still made her heart race. Every time she'd spoken with him, she'd learned something new about Santería, a connection to her grandmother's old teachings and an introduction to new practices she'd only ever glimpsed through twisted versions by las Palomas that had never felt right.

Gilberto was making everything unwind within her, like a long thread coming loose, and Anita felt a bit undone, like her future wasn't as certain as she'd thought, in a way that was both exhilarating and frightening.

Beyond that, Anita found that she enjoyed spending time with him, Idaly, and the quiet Emiliano, and being close to Rafa again. It had been a long time since she'd had friends and she liked hearing the group make plans, talk about escaping from el Comandante and las Palomas as if it were a tangible, possible thing. Even if deep down she knew they were being unrealistic, it made her feel as if she was a part of something bigger, no longer so alone.

"I told you yesterday I couldn't meet you after class anymore," Anita chastised, then glanced around anxiously. "My mother expected me back *early*. She's noticed I've been getting home later and later each day."

"Really?" Gilberto plucked one of the clothespins from her basket and clipped it to her hair. "Sounds like you've been dedicated to your studies. Your mother should approve. In fact, I should go tell her how *attentive* a student you are."

He made as if to march to her house, but she yanked him back, her heart jammed in her throat. She pulled too hard, and he was left too close, his face inches from hers. His honeyed eyes swimming with an emotion she couldn't decipher.

But something darted past them, and Gilberto stumbled back as a ball of white feathers came bounding into view. It was only Preedi, their most adventurous chicken, but still, it was a reminder. Anita backed away, smoothing her skirt. The blood must have stopped flowing to her head, robbing her of common sense.

"You need to go." She picked up the wet sheets again.

Gilberto bit his lip, for once rendered quiet. He helped her tack a few more sheets to the line. "Did your mother tell you we'll need to be at the next gathering?"

Anita sighed. "This time, she says I must go." She was of age now, and the Elders must have been wondering why she'd been absent. "She said it was time I took a more active role in Las Palomas."

"It's only temporary, Ana. Until we can go."

"I want to believe that."

Gilberto crossed his arms, studying her. "Our destinies are not written in stone. There's always another choice."

She groaned. "Now you sound like my brother."

"Ah, I'd like to say he's a wise man, but the admission would eat away at me."

She smacked him lightly on the chest and he held her hand there. Close to his heart.

Brujita, run home. The whisper slicked across her ear as a gust of wind blew by. Anita stiffened. At the edge of her vision, she could see the maldeado. Gilberto's head perked up as if he could sense it too, and she realized with horror that she'd forgotten to cloak herself.

"I have to go," she whispered. "I'll see you soon."

His expression wavered. They both knew they were on borrowed time. In a few weeks, everything would be different between them. After the gathering, they would begin the initiation into las Palomas, and once they accepted their oaths, their lives would revolve around what was best for the aquelarre—and for el Comandante. Mamá Orti would never allow Anita to become involved with Gilberto, who has always been more of a radical thinker like Rafa, and who could jeopardize her path to becoming the head Elder. No, there would be no more of this unless they could figure out a way to leave Cuba and Las Palomas for good.

"Promise me you won't give up hope, Ana. They can't control every aspect of our lives."

She wanted to be swept up in the promise, but it'd be a lie. The shadow's cool embrace, wet at her heels, reminded her of that.

Run, run, run.

She didn't say anything. She didn't need to. Gilberto knew better than she did that those promises would be wisps of smoke. Her heart ached as he kissed her cheek, bittersweet like a goodbye. As she ran back home, he became a speck in the distance.

Anita found her mother perched by the framboyan tree in the center of the hacienda's center. Her skirts were layered in blue, her scarf a bloodred atop her head. She was surprised to see her mother sitting so close to the tree, so close to her father's carved initials. There was something in her mother's hands, too, a cloth. And a black-threaded needle. Anita's heart hammered as she wondered which poor soul her mother would be punishing next.

Her mother did not glance up as Anita walked in. She tried to make her way up the stairs, quiet as a cat, so as not to draw her mother's attention.

"You know," her mother began, voice echoing through the large courtyard. "We de Armas women, we are great at many things." She set down the cloth, but Anita could not make out the name stitched there. "But never at love."

Her mother fixed on a spot in Anita's hair, and Anita realized the clothespin Gilberto put was still there. She removed it quickly. "I don't know what you mean, Mamá."

Mamá Orti continued as if Anita hadn't spoken. "We turn our men into monsters. Our love rots inside them. Spoils them from the inside out." Her mother looked up at her, and it was not anger Anita found there. "Just look at what happened to your father."

Anita's blood ran cold. *Could she know? Had she seen Gilberto? Had they grown too bold?* Her mother's next words were answer enough.

"After initiation, Ana, it ends. Are we clear?"

"Sí, Mamá."

FOURTEEN

Miami, November 16, 2016

DELFI

I swear, sneaking to the botanica has been getting harder and harder. It doesn't help that the main entrance to the plaza is easily visible from the bakery. While Lela headed over to Ethan's, I came here. I basically had to pull a James Bond to get to the botanica's back door. But once inside, I'm golden.

Zuela listens as I tell her everything, then I wait as she mulls, trying not to cough. She goes a little overboard with the incense, and it dulls my ability, making it hard to taste anything through the thick scent.

A text comes through, and I think it's Lela again with another update from the NamUs site, but it's from an unknown number. Once I read the message, I know exactly who it's from.

not a sidekick. and this truce is only temporary.

My smile is catlike and entirely too self-satisfied. I save Andres's number.

whatever you say, robin

"So I must not have heard you right."

I look up to see Zuela staring at me over her reading glasses. A tiny gold locket lies curled in her palm. "Where did you say you got this again?"

I bite my lip. "Off the body of a dead woman?"

Zuela shakes her head. "Ay, Delfi."

I get that a lot. She opens the little gold heart and finds the same water-logged picture of the blond man I've kept studying for just over a week since we found Idaly's body. Emiliano, according to the database and my sister's text a few minutes ago. The other dead body marked by the same dove and snake symbol.

I feel a pressure on my chest. We've come nowhere closer to finding out who's behind their deaths or what's up with Teardrop in the van stalking us, so I knew I had to call in the big guns. I'd wanted to come sooner but Zuela had been on a trip across the Gulf making a special delivery for a client—apparently, animal skulls aren't carry-on approved.

Zuela takes off her glasses and sighs. "This is dangerous, mi niña. I worry about you, Delfi. Maybe it's best that you don't get involved."

"I think it's too late for us not to get involved," I say, and I tell her about Teardrop. His appearances near our home, Mami's bakery, and Idaly's crime scene. Plus, the vision we had of him in Ethan's car, running from a shadowy figure we assume belongs to a brujo, maldeados at his heels.

Zuela looks grim. "Delfi, do you think he might be trying to get close to your family?"

"That's what I'm afraid of." A sharp sting pierces my eyes. "I wouldn't know what to do if something happened to my sister, or my mom. I'd rather die than—" My throat seizes, trapping my words, and perhaps it's for the best. Thoughts like those should never be voiced aloud. "I can't wait for another vision."

Zuela reaches across the table and squeezes my hand tightly. "I understand, corazón. Let's get to work then."

. . .

Zuela closes the curtain between her psychic space and where she houses her orishas. Ideally, we'd do this in a completely different room or house out of respect for the religion, but we're in a hurry and money's tight and resources are limited. Though she's careful to reiterate we're using our alma magic. Calling to her psychic intuition, her connection with the spirits, through organic materials.

I'm distracted by another text.

this is a two-way street. what do i get out of this?

I should've known Andres wouldn't offer up information for nothing.

are you propositioning me? I ask, too tempted not to mess with him.

you know i wasn't. this is strictly business, delfi.

I narrow my eyes at the screen. What can I offer him?

"Whenever you're ready," Zuela says with a raised brow.

I put my phone away. "Sorry, let's continue."

"Okay. Cow tongue, for the last words spoken and the last words heard." Using tweezers, Zuela places the tiny bit of bloody meat into the melted black wax. The macabre chunk slowly sinks down and disappears. She drops in a small magnet next, to draw in our desires.

"Trabajos like these can be tricky. Magic is never straightforward. It's best to ask in a roundabout way what you seek. A way to trick it into an answer. In this case"—she swirls the tip of a smoldering incense around the wax—"we want to know who Idaly last spoke to, who she last saw. Chances are, that is who's responsible for the deaths."

"You can do that?" My mouth drops. "How will I know if it works?"

She holds up a finger with a weighty emerald ring, and then grabs a pen. She writes down Idaly's name in blue ink on a strip of paper and places that into the wax as well. "Now the necklace."

I give it to her, watching as she lifts the chain, and it uncoils like a rattlesnake ready to strike. The locket spins, swirling through the smoke, and only once it's settled does she slowly dip the charm into the wax, sealing it shut. She places Idaly's locket, still hot, back onto my palm and I flinch.

"Make a fist," she commands, and I do, wincing. "Now, reach deep into that restless part of yourself, Delfi. Into the unquiet you've fought so hard to tamp down."

I close my eyes and reach. I know exactly what she means. It's a pit in the center of me that's filled with uncertainty. And hunger. It's constantly fighting, ready for me to just . . . let it free.

"Let it go," Zuela says. "Trust that it will fill you before it spills. Do not shy away from your power, mi niña."

I take a deep breath and hold the locket tighter. I know this power is what my father must've seen in me and tried to destroy. What he found and named *monster*. But today, with Zuela by my side and my family's safety at risk, I push past my fears. I may be a monster, but at least I fight for those I love.

"That's it," Zuela encourages, ever patient. She clasps my fist with both her hands. "Revela, revela," she repeats. *Reveal.* The wax hardens in my clenched fist until it feels like stone.

There is so much more to me than what others see, and the same has to be true for my magic. There has to be a goodness, a light, even if all I've known are shadows.

I open my eyes and Zuela is beaming. "It's done. Now, the trabajo is complete and the wax will only melt if you're near the person who last uttered Idaly's name. Her killer.

"That taste you get—with the visions of Idaly's death—should be lingering on the one who caused it. You said it was violeta?" I nod.

"Well, it could serve as a clue. Judging by what you've seen, this is a powerful brujo to control so many maldeados, so you should be able to sense their presence. Magic like that is not easy to conceal. And remember your sister saw another man in her visions searching for Idaly. It may be more than one brujo behind this. You must be careful, mi niña."

She's right. Uncovering one killer is hard enough, two's a dangerous crowd. But now I know what to tell Andres.

fine, i have something for you. two men were searching for Idaly on the day leading up to her death. they were around her age

His response is pretty quick.

that's a pretty broad clue, delfi

I sigh.

one was tan with a teardrop-shaped birthmark under his left eye, and the other was black with a salt and pepper beard wearing a fedora. might be dealing with more than one killer. or more than one potential victim? and so far you haven't given me anything

Despite the risks, I feel excited—at last, there's an actual lead if only I could get close to whichever brujo did this. If we could find out who it is, what they have to do with *us*, then we can figure out a way to stop them.

Now if only a certain detective's son with access to confidential files would help me fill in the blanks.

As if I'd manifested it, his text comes through.

idaly was renting an efficiency under the books, and the landlord called the hotline. says idaly was living there with her husband who also went missing. the efficiency was mostly cleared out but police found evidence of ritualistic paraphernalia. no identification.

I must have read over his text a dozen times. So Idaly and Emiliano *were* a couple, and apparently, they were practitioners of some kind. Why would the killer be targeting others with magic? Is this some sort of dominance thing? Is that why my sister and I are seeing these visions, because we might be next on the list simply for having abilities?

Ice goes down my spine. I can't let that happen. I can't put Lela at risk.

"Is everything all right, amor?" Zuela asks, and I try explaining as quickly as possible when another text comes through.

can i call you?

Instead of waiting for an answer, Andres calls and I put him on speaker, putting a finger to my lips.

"Figured you'd have more questions. You alone?"

I meet Zuela's eyes.

"Yeah," I say. "I'm alone."

"Okay, good. So they brought in a religions expert to investigate some of the stuff Idaly and her husband left behind and the expert doesn't recognize the items or their placement pertaining to Santería or any other known religion, at least not in the way they're commonly practiced."

"Are there any pictures?" I ask.

"Check your messages."

I open the image of what looks like an altar. Chalices of dark liquids and bundles wrapped in twine. Herbs and different seeds and rocks in a ceramic bowl. He's right, there are no effigies to gods, saints, or otherwise. It's not like any religious practice I recognize. And it all looks broken, as if someone messed with it. Most likely the police.

"If you zoom in, you can see a last name stitched on one of the strips of cloth."

I show it to Zuela, but she makes a face like she's not sure what some of the trabajos were intended to be. I zoom in on a specific cloth laid out with others on a table. The name is hard to read at first, but once I do, I feel my stomach hollow out.

It says: de Armas.

The ground seems to open beneath my feet. "I'm going to have to call you back."

◆ ◆ ◆

Stepping out of Zuela's botanica, I try to get a handle on my breathing. De Armas was my mother's last name before she changed it to Sánchez.

It's got to be a coincidence though, right? I mean, why would Idaly have something with my mom's last name on it?

Zuela says the trabajo could've been for anything—control, damage, or protection. Since it was ruined, trampled, it's impossible to know.

Could this be why Mami's been acting so strange? Maybe she senses it. Maybe the brujos who cursed our family in Cuba have come back to look for her. Or maybe . . . maybe we're dealing with another de Armas. Mami never talks about her family. Could Idaly or any of the other people from our visions be related to us?

I can't ask Mami because she'll freak, demand I tell her how I've come across this information, and she'd probably move us out of the country before she'd tell us the truth.

I take a deep breath and try not to panic, forcing myself to calmly go through what I know, or what I think I know, about the killer.

They have powerful abilities, so I should be aware of the taste of tobacco denoting a brujo. They're most likely Cuban since that's where Idaly and Emiliano fled from. And it's possible the killers could be one or both of the men Lela saw in her visions—Teardrop and Silver Fox. That's way too wide of a net for my liking, considering there are Cuban men on every corner—two of them hollering right now across the street.

I'm so busy worrying that I take the corner too sharply and run straight into my mom.

I quickly rein in whatever magic I felt at Zuela's botanica until it feels like nothing more than a tender bruise.

My mom takes me in, glancing toward the botanica before her expression hardens. "¿Qué haces?"

Discreetly tucking the wax-caked locket under my shirt, I walk past her, steering us back to the parking lot. "Coming over so you can feed me. The bus was running late."

Her shoulders slump in relief. "Running around in circles for nothing," she chastises. "There's food at home, vamos."

I get a surge of frustration. There's so much I need to ask her. So much I feel she's been keeping from me. What have you been running from, Mami?

But I bite my tongue and follow her to the car. Only once we're inside does she hand me the grease-soaked bag with half a pan con lechon inside. "Hurry and eat. I have a lot to do for Friday."

I'm too nervous to eat, but I grab the bag from her. "What's happening Friday?"

"Celebration of the Saints Festival," Mami says.

Wait. Celebration of the Saints Festival is a yearly event hosted in Cauley Square for the local Catholic schools. My mom tries to get me to volunteer for it every year, which I usually do my best to avoid. The festival usually hosts a variety of practitioners including santeros, or psychics and mediums offering their services. It also draws in those who delve into the occult, which is why Mami always turns in early, preferring to avoid the late-night crowd.

I realize this will be my best chance of scoping out the local practitioners in a relatively safe public setting. If I spot Teardrop or Silver Fox, or if the wax locket melts, I'll call Zuela. There's no way in hell I can do it on my own. There are binding spells or other trabajos for containing a brujo, but it'll take all of Zuela's community to handle this.

"Count me in," I say.

"Really?" Mami looks surprised. "Está bien. You can help your sister with the scavenger hunt for the children."

Oh, right. Of course, Lela's already volunteered. I'll have to find a way to get her to leave the festival early, too. I consider telling her about the trabajo on the locket, but I can handle this on my own and there's no point in putting both of us at risk. But I will have to tell her about the stitched name found in Idaly's apartment and what that means for us.

Mami clears her throat awkwardly. "And have you decided por fin if you're going to start the next semester con Lela?"

Talk about a gear change. "Yeah, for sure." My hand goes to the wax-coated locket under my shirt. *But first, I plan on tracking down murderous brujos and finding out what you're hiding from us about our family.* "I'll start a class or two once financial aid kicks in. As planned."

"You said you were going full-time, what happened?"

"I still need to work," I say. "I know funds are tight."

This seems to soften her. "Delfi . . ."

"Mom, listen!" I quickly cut her off, not wanting to get into my future right now. "It's your song."

And thank god for Luis Fonsi because she is legit obsessed. I turn the volume up and can't help smiling at her little squeal of excitement. She looks so young and happy that I can't help but feel a pang. When was the last time I saw her laugh? I don't even remember.

FIFTEEN

Miami, November 18, 2016

LELA

I knew it. Delfi *wanted* to volunteer at the festival today, but now she's bailing on me. I'm going to be stuck hauling out all the papier-mâché saints onto the garden paths by myself. I'll have to watch over the Catholic school kids from St. Mary's on the scavenger hunt and deal with the aftermath when only one team wins the stuffed lamb. Those kids are ferociously competitive. Plus, I was hoping I'd get backup when the eighth graders ask me what it was like to go to a school with boys. And if I have a boyfriend. And if I've had sex yet. That's Delfi's department, and definitely not something I'm willing to dive into right now.

want me to come help? i'd much rather be with you than at work

I fail to hold back a smile, a warmth spreading across my chest when I read Ethan's text. He follows it up with a selfie of him in his dad's office. He's got a sticker label on his forehead that says SENSITIVE MATERIALS.

I rifle through the basket of scavenger props I've been hiding around the gardens and send one of me wearing St. Bosco's clown nose while pretending to guzzle down whatever's in St. Benedict's goblet. My hair is up and sweaty because it's humid as heck and I've been running around Cauley Square since seven in the morning. But he's seen me at my worst, so, oh well.

okay, this is the best photo ever. you win. saving as my home screen now.

I'm about to follow it up with an even better one. I cover my eyes with St. Lucy's two giant googly eyes and am concentrating on aiming my phone at my face when my mom's voice rings out.

"Ofelia! The kids are about to start the scavenger hunt and you're here playing."

I jump, sending the two eyes clattering to the floor. Seeing Mami makes my stomach clench. Delfi told me last night about seeing the de Armas name stitched on a cloth among Idaly's possessions. I can't look at Mami without wanting to ask her if she knows Idaly or other brujos. But Delfi's right, she'll clam up for sure and we'll never get answers. "Sorry, Mami. I only have a few more items to hide."

A quick glance at my phone and the last message reads: i can't stop thinking about you, ofi. no regrets, right?

I hesitate, but I can't lie to Ethan. I leave him on read until I can figure out what to say.

Mami takes the basket from me and pats me on the arm. "Go get something to eat. I'll finish here. I want to have everything picked up before nighttime."

"No, it's okay. I'll help you."

Mami looks like she's going to protest, then nods with relief. She seems exhausted, and a bit pale too. I wonder again if Mami's been so busy protecting the house because she senses something coming for us. Because she has all these secrets from her past, including another possible de Armas relative. Or maybe *de Armas* is just a common name and we're making too much of it. Mami's tightlipped but she's always done what's best for us. I need to believe that.

Mami and I weave through the scattered decorated shrines throughout the gardens in silence. Despite the Celebration of the Saints Festival being a Catholic event, this is a predominately Cuban area, so it's not uncommon to see iconography that melds both the saints and orishas. People will dress in yellow to honor both Our Lady of Charity and Oshun or leave a tray of fruit for Yemayá under the guise of Our Lady of Regla. There are so many ways to honor the saints and orishas through different religions, and today is a day when people come to Cauley Square to practice openly.

Like Mami, though, I've never stayed after dark, and this year, I'm especially nervous. If what Delfi's source told her is true, then the brujos could be tracking down others with magical abilities, making tonight especially dangerous for us.

I wipe the sweat from my brow, taking back the empty basket from Mami and pulling her toward the crowd in the main square to kick off the morning's activities. She's never been touchy-feely, so instead of holding my hand normally, Mami claps our hands together a few times like a paddle ball, always in motion.

I know Delfi said not to bring up the de Armas thing to Mami because she'll freak out, but we've all spent way too long not communicating and it's only made things worse.

Maybe I can give it a shot. "Mami?"

"Hm," she hums.

"You know . . . I've always wondered. You said you had no one left in Cuba, but what about distant relatives?" She wraps her arms around her stomach. "A cousin maybe? Another de Armas?"

Her mouth is a thin line. "No. There's no one else. We are Sánchez now. We left all that behind."

"I know, but—" Before I can continue, we hear flip-flops slapping against the concrete pavement.

Delfi runs up wearing ripped shorts and a T-shirt that says SATAN'S SUGAR BABY. Mami's eyes look as if they're going to fall onto the floor like St. Lucy's googly ones.

"Delfi, por Dios. Go change." Mom pinches the bridge of her nose.

Delfi glances down at her shirt as if only now realizing what she's wearing. "Oh, sh—I mean, excuse me. I'll change, Mami." She kisses her on the cheek.

After reminding Delfi to hurry up and change, Mami leaves.

"Where were you all morning?" I say. "I could've used the help."

"Chill, I'm here now. Lead me to the deprived pubescents and I'll take over." She sidles closer. "Once the sun goes down, Lela, I want you out of here."

My face screws up. She needs to stop pulling this protective act. If anything, she needs me to keep her in check. "No way," I say. "If you're staying, then I'm staying."

She hesitates. "Fine. But don't wander."

◆　◆　◆

Right before dark, everyone gathers to listen to the padre's sermons, and I'm on full alert, waiting for the prickle over my skin that tells me power is nearby. But I don't sense a thing. Though, it doesn't mean they can't be hiding in plain sight.

I haven't answered Ethan's text yet, and I know my silence is cruel. But I still don't know what to say.

I watch my mom and the others light the row of candles, dress the saints, spend hours on their knees in repetitive prayer. It reminds me that everyone's looking to make sense of the unknown, and there's a power in that too. A prayer is like a spell cast onto the universe, hoping to attract the things you desire. I think Mami's aversion to magic is because it's unpredictable, uncontrollable. Rituals, religion, well, there are rules to those. And I wonder if maybe I just haven't found the right rules for my gift. If maybe I could learn the rules, so I'd have more control. So there would be an order to the chaos, and I could decide what visions I see, what I could touch, and maybe, if I grew strong enough, who I could love.

Maybe our curse is only proof of a lack of control, a leeching of toxins, because we don't know how to properly contain whatever magic is inside us. But what if we could master it, like we master our magic? I could kiss someone without regret and tell them honestly how I feel.

The thought is incredibly enticing.

As the sun goes down, we help Mami clear up the main square, then walk her home, offering an excuse that we're meeting friends on the other side of town. Far from the things that terrify her the most. And what would ever make her believe otherwise?

◆ ◆ ◆

The Celebration of the Saints Festival is transformed at night. In the main courtyard, vendors sell everything from love potions to talismans that supposedly prevent ever losing a gamble. Large tents with sheer fabric nettings are set up in the surrounding forest and along the garden paths leading away from the courtyard. There's a distinct chittering of animals from the crates, along with the scent of burning incense and aromatic oils. Cauley's art studios are transformed to centers for meditation and ceremonial dancing for cleansings. Which is where I expect to find Delfi, but she's nowhere to be seen.

She'd told me not to wander, but she went off to do just that, and I'm starting to worry. Tonight is not the night to disappear. The energy here is different. I keep catching the tail ends of maldeados tucking into the dark. Here, many of the visitors wear all white or bright dresses layered with beaded jewelry that clatters when they walk. I force myself to brush close to people, welcoming the intrusive visions, but there's no prickle of awareness. No brujos yet.

What I don't expect to see is Delfi's ex, Andres, coming from the direction of the tents. He's carrying a large box to the back of a pickup truck and taps the bumper before the driver pulls away. I watch as he gets onto a motorcycle, texts someone, then roars off.

Odd. I wonder what he's doing here. Either way, it's a good thing he left before he could bump into Delfi again. The last thing we need is more drama. I continue searching for Delfi, keeping mostly to the lit paths, following the bend of one until I come to a tent illuminated with a red light settled under the deep cover of a banyan tree.

As I get closer, I see a propped-up sign outside with a list of services, including MANIFEST LOVE, PROTECTION SPELLS, CLEANSINGS. Curiosity springs in my chest as I wonder what else this practitioner can offer. Curse removal, control of abilities? I know it's not that simple, but maybe with the right tools . . .

I'm about to glance inside when the hairs on my arms stand on end, as if I were touching a live wire.

"What are you doing here by yourself?"

Delfi materializes behind me, coming up the path.

She stops right outside the tent, too, grabbing my arm and savoring something in her mouth. "Lela, do you sense that?"

We hear a clattering sound and look inside the tent. There's an older woman pacing, her long gray hair and white shawl shimmering under the red light. She's electric, ripples of energy pouring off of her. I know the power we sense is from her.

"I recognize her," Delfi whispers, swallowing hard. "That's the bruja who was at the botanica. We got to get out of here." Delfi tries to haul me away but it's too late. The woman looks dead at us, watching as we back away from her tent.

Delfi makes a pained sound, clutching at her neck.

"Delfi! Oh my god, are you hurt?" I try pulling her hand away so I can see, but she grabs hold of me again and we run down the path toward the main square.

"You're bleeding!" I say once we're sure the bruja isn't following us. Delfi's grabbing her neck again and something red oozes out between her fingers.

"I'm fine," she pants. "It just burned a little."

Delfi pulls out a thin chain from beneath her shirt, the dangling charm smeared with something red and drippy.

"It's wax," she says. "Melted wax." She stares back toward the direction of the tent, though we're too far away now to see it.

I get a good look at the charm. Idaly's locket. Delfi explains the trabajo she did with Zuela.

"If it worked like it was meant to, then we just saw who last spoke to Idaly, making it very possible that she's the bruja who killed her. She's a well-known practitioner who deals in obras de desgracia."

Malicious practices? I touch the wax as if it's something alive.

"I got to call, Zuze," Delfi says. "If we wait for her, we can—I don't know, trap the bruja."

I rub my hands over my face. "You want to trap a bruja who's got years of experience over us and a *serious* killer instinct?"

"Come on, answer." Delfi paces, clutching her phone to her ear before hanging up. "Crap. She may not even be working alone. Maybe Teardrop and Silver Fox are her followers and they're circling us now. Then again, I didn't get that strong of a tobacco taste, or a violet taste."

"You're not making sense," I say, trying not to panic.

Our voices echo in the dark. The woods are eerily quiet, filled with the snap of twigs and distant cry of trapped birds from the local sanctuary. Most of the guests are on the other side of the grounds, closer to the main square.

"She's not answering," Delfi says. "Should we go back? Maybe I should go look for Zuela. She was here earlier."

I gape. "No! That's it. Night's over. Zuela didn't come through and we are not about to go running around in the dark to try and trap this person alone."

But my sister doesn't answer. Instead, she's frozen as something detaches from the night and slithers across the cobbled pavement, leaving a sheen of grease behind like a slug. A maldeado.

Delfi's arm tightens on mine. "You see that, right?"

I nod.

"It wants us to follow it," Delfi whispers. That much is clear, but is it trying to lead us to safety or danger? We cautiously begin to follow the maldeado as it snakes ahead of us, and we realize it's following someone. The path forks to the right, toward a small chapel that should be closed at this time. I gasp when the moon's light illuminates the person.

It's Mami.

Delfi grips my arm. "Don't say anything yet," she whispers, as if it's perfectly normal there's a maldeado chasing after our mother.

A gathering of white doves perches on the peaked roof as Mami goes inside the chapel. I haven't seen that many white doves here before, let alone at night. Their beady eyes track our movements with an unnerving ruby glimmer.

"Something's wrong," I say, but Delfi follows Mami and the trailing maldeado inside, so I have to follow.

Terror lodges in my throat. As we walk inside, every candle surrounding the lectern is lit. The chapel is empty save for Mami on her knees and the maldeados gathering behind her like a bridal train. My mom's voice trickles along the small space—a mumbling prayer I can hardly make out. It seems like she's talking to someone in front of her we can't see.

"No," Mami mumbles. "Leave us alone."

Delfi and I look at each other, clasping hands, then step cautiously down the aisle. "Mami?"

She doesn't respond. We creep closer. "Mami?"

Our voices cut through her prayer and she stills. She slowly twists in our direction, but her eyes are blank. Milky white and empty.

I cover my mouth, holding back a scream, and Mami breaks her unbearable quiet with the words: "No se metan donde salir no puedan. No se metan donde salir no puedan."

Do not enter where you can no longer exit.

"La Orden, La Orden," she says, and I want to sob. This isn't her. Mami isn't here.

A warning, they're delivering a warning. And they're using our mother as the messenger. Fear gnaws at my stomach, so large it's consuming me from the inside.

She rises to her feet, but just as I'm about to scream for help, Mami blinks.

The cloudiness in her eyes clears. Her irises are back to normal.

"Ofelia? Delfi?" She stands on wobbly legs, swaying.

Delfi and I rush over to help. We offer to call an ambulance, but she can't imagine why on earth we'd suggest it. Mami assures us repeatedly that she's perfectly fine, despite the tremble of her knees, and the fact that she can't remember how she ended up in the chapel. Despite the obvious fear in her expression. She knows something's wrong. She knows something's happened, but she won't admit it to us.

The hollow pit in my stomach grows.

We take Mami home and lay her in bed. As soon as Delfi and I creep out of her room and collapse into our own beds, my sister voices exactly what I'm thinking.

"Mami's like us," Delfi says. "She's like us, and somehow, she's been hiding it all these years."

A tear escapes my eye. I felt it, too. I felt the ripple of power off her when her guard was down. I still feel it even as she sleeps in the next room.

"We're connected to this, Lela. This has something to do with Mami's past."

I swallow hard. "I know."

The warning words are still ringing in my ears. No se metan donde salir no puedan. But maybe we've already entered a place we cannot escape.

Whether the bruja in the red-lit tent had something to do with Idaly's murder, I recognize we're out of our depth. We need help, even if it means going against everything Mami taught us. For her safety and ours, I need to do it.

"We'll go tomorrow," I say, and I don't need to specify where, because Delfi already knows. We have to find out more, or the next deadly vision we see might be about one of us.

SIXTEEN

Cuba, March 18, 1980

ANITA

Anita knew she'd been getting involved in things she shouldn't, with people she should stay far away from. But lately she'd been more preoccupied with what she wanted, rather than with what should be done.

She quickly stocked the items in her mother's shed. She'd been working hard to finish her chores before Mamá Orti had to ask. The less she was needed, the less she'd be missed.

Fortunately, over the last few days, her mother had been preoccupied with el Comandante anyway. Foreign governments were trying everything to remove him from power, from planting explosives in his cigars to sending female spies to seduce him, and he was in urgent need of his Palomas. Anita knew he would survive, and god help whomever they caught. Her mother would make sure it was taken care of.

After her mother's warning, Anita had to be even more careful. Until the initiation ceremony in two days, she'd been given a bit of a longer leash while her mother was engaged in other pressing concerns, but Anita was afraid the tiny bit of freedom from these past weeks wouldn't be enough. Would never be enough.

None of her friends ever spoke of the dangers of leaving. No one wanted to break the illusion of freedom just yet. They were living as normally as any of them ever had, and Anita relished it. She woke with the echo of Gilberto's laugh in the mornings. She looked forward to Idaly's warm greeting as they would pick her up after school. She thought of Emiliano and his steady presence. The way he looked at Idaly made Anita think that perhaps love did exist after all.

She supposed having her brother around was also nice, despite how determined he was to tease her at every turn. As he was doing now when the group picked her up a mile down the road from her house. Anita handed Rafa the sack of sugar he'd asked her to sneak out, worth more than gold now for its scarcity. He meant to use the sugar as a bartering tool for whatever he planned to show her today.

As she got in the car, he gave her a funny look and asked, "Why are you wearing lipstick? You never wear that."

Anita flushed furiously. Gilberto sat in the seat beside her, watching her mouth with rapt attention.

"¡Ay, qué pesado!" Idaly reached back and smacked Rafa on the leg. "Because she can, that's why." She winked at Anita. "And I love that color. You must let me try it some time. I'll trade you for some of my agua de violetas that you said you liked so much." This made her perk up. The violeta scent Idaly always wore was divine.

"I'd love that," Anita whispered as Gilberto threaded their fingers together, taking her by surprise. She looked out the window, hiding her smile, but the moment's lightness quickly died.

They all ducked down as the car passed a campesino on horseback, his ribs as prominent as the animal's. Anyone could be keeping watch, forced to spy on neighbors in exchange for being left alone by the military police. Anita couldn't risk staying out past sundown or being seen. There was always the possibility her mother could return and not find her in her room. The leash only went so far. As quickly as things had changed for the better in their lives, Anita knew they all felt the disquieting certainty that it would change again just as swiftly at the ceremony.

"Where to?" Emiliano asked, turning off the dirt road onto the highway.

After a careful glance at her, Rafael leaned forward. "The infirmary."

"Why?" she asked in surprise.

Rafa shrugged. "It's where I perform my parlor tricks and pretty predictions for the desperate."

Anita looked down, hearing her own harsh words repeated back. She had said that, hadn't she? She gave her brother a small smile. "Well then, we must go."

◆　◆　◆

The infirmary was an old, abandoned hospital with rat-eaten cots and mold-coated sinks swarming with flies. It was made more unbearable by the relentless heat pouring in from the broken windows. Anita forced herself not to flinch as she walked among the sick.

The hospitals in Havana were often overfilled, and medical equipment and medicine in short supply. Before her time, perhaps before the revolution, las Palomas served the community as powerful healers who offered their support to the sick and comforted the ones they couldn't save in their final hours. But their priorities shifted long ago and with the ongoing US embargo cutting off Cuba from exports, the healthcare infrastructure was struggling with a lack of medical supplies and inadequately maintained hospitals. These illicit clinics with their black-market medicine and unorthodox healing methods were the only way many could be treated.

After helping her brother distribute the sugar to the nearby homes in exchange for silence, Anita watched as Rafa and the others got to work right away, going to different patients. Anita was left standing there with no clue what to do. She saw Rafa grind up herbs and bring them to a young boy who'd taken a fever. Idaly rubbed the boy's feet with some thick mixture, and the boy's father hovered over them with a candle, as if already at his son's vigil.

Gilberto read others the Obí, tossing the coconut divination rinds again and again to better understand what the will of the orishas required or which spirit of their eggun—ancestral spirits—needed special attention. She watched, mesmerized, as Gilberto prayed in the Yoruba language, acknowledged the other santeros in the room, and calmly delegated the right rituals and sacrifices for each person seeking help. There was no book or Bible to refer to, he'd told her days ago when teaching her the words to a prayer. *"The traditions, prayers, and ebós of Regla de Ocha-Ifá were passed down orally from one generation to the next, syncretized and dependent on the practitioner's morality. It was a cared-for and protected practice by my ancestors, rooted in African slavery and oppression."*

Looking around at all the Afro-Cuban santeros and paleros, Anita was amazed at the resilience to continue a practice and maintain its truth despite the opposing powers of governments and colonial exploitation. It ignited a fire in her, a sense of responsibility to be as true to her orishas as she could.

Her gaze lingered on Gilberto. He was a skilled diviner, Anita noticed. Tender and compassionate. Knowledgeable and truthful. It made something in her chest ache like a bruise.

What others couldn't see however were the restless spirits of the dead. The ones who were beyond help but couldn't move on, trapped in their final moments of pain and despair. They hovered near the edges of the room, hungry for someone to notice.

"Here." Idaly came forward, handing Anita a large bowl of cereal to share with the patients. "We start small," she said with a kind smile. "That's all we can do."

Anita spent the next hour feeding the sick. For the ones who could eat, there was only dried bread and cereal to be washed down with warm milk. She watched as a fatherly spirit laid ghostly hands on a young woman as if wanting to offer healing. He couldn't help, but perhaps she could.

"Show me what to do," she told Rafa. He nodded and handed her gauze that had been soaked in honey and herbs. Anita wrapped it around a young woman's middle, her elderly mother helping her sit forward because the woman had no strength of her own.

Rafael instructed Anita to lay hands on the woman and Idaly and Emiliano joined her.

They waited for Gilberto to approach with another elderly Afro-Cubano, an Obá Oriaté, who was cradling a chicken, soothing the animal.

"Call to your alma, Anita," Rafa said quietly. "Use the strength of our lineage and redirect it to heal."

His words from their long-ago argument came back to her. *Do something more. Use what you've learned from her to become someone better.*

She wasn't sure she was ready yet, but with the smell of the sick around her, and Gilberto's steady praying, she knew it was about time she tried. Anita called to the sacred part of her.

The Obá Oriaté calmly rubbed the chicken against the body of the sick woman, and over Anita's hands. As humanely as possible, the elderly santero killed the bird and instructed Gilberto to take it away where it would be discarded according to the orisha's will. Most ebós were sacrifices of food, drink, or even prayer. Her abuela had taught her the meaning of animal sacrifice, the care a good practitioner took to honor each life. And though in many cases the animal would be consumed and shared for nourishment, the animals used for cleansings are meant to remove osogbo, or malignant energies.

Anita sent a small prayer of her own to thank the animal for its sacrifice and once again redirected the thrumming power of her alma into healing. Gilberto looked at her with pride, and for the first time in her life, she felt as if her magic were a gift instead of a curse.

The moment between them was cut short when a harsh voice rang through the room.

"¡Oye! Por ahí viene un comité! Un comité!"

Immediately the people who were well enough to walk began rushing out the back door. A comité was a member of the Committees for the Defense of the Revolution, the CDR, tasked to alert the government of any suspicious behavior. They could be as young as fourteen, sometimes younger, obligated to "volunteer" to spy on their neighborhood. Whatever they saw, they had to report or risk their own family being targeted. And no one knew when the government would test their loyalty.

Gilberto peeked behind the window's tacked sheet and cursed under his breath. Anita went and peeked outside too. There were several comités, and they were circling Emiliano's car. Rafa quietly whistled from the back door, indicating that their group should abandon the car and leave on foot.

They silently crept after Rafa, following him out to an alley, up a stairway that led to a series of connected rooftops. It was clear to Anita that Rafa and the others had done this many times before. Some of the roofs were in such bad condition that Anita could glance down and see families cooking or people lying in bed with a fan pointed at their sweaty faces.

Just when Anita thought they had escaped, they heard a yell. Anita turned and saw a young comité in a tattered red tank and a pair of new shoes that looked as if they'd just been shipped from la Yuma. He shouted again for them to stop, running at full speed now.

The group ran faster until they came suddenly to a ledge overlooking a stretch of road too wide for them to jump over. Anita whirled around to see the comité catch up to them. Gilberto shifted to stand in front of her, but Rafa stepped toward the comité.

"Don't worry, I know him," her brother assured them.

The comité was panting hard. The boy looked at their group, then glanced back to make sure they were alone. "I'm going to say you disappeared, okay? But don't go down that way—" He pointed to the fire escape they'd been eyeing. "They'll be waiting for you there. There's a hatch farther down, leads to a condemned building. Hide out there for a while, and you'll know when it's time to go."

Rafa nodded. "Thanks for the help, Hermano. Has there been any word yet?"

Anita wasn't sure what her brother was talking about, but the comité handed Rafa a folded note.

Rafa grabbed the note and placed a soft fist on the boy's shoulder. "Gracias, compadre."

Once they'd made their way to the building and were safely hidden, Gilberto spoke up. "What's it say?"

Rafa skimmed the words, his face drawn tight. His eyes flickered from curiosity to pure fire as he read. Anita felt every warning thrum through her.

"Well?" They all asked in unison.

He drew a hand down his mouth. "It's a call to action for counterrevolutionaries to be ready in the next thirty days. A plan's been put into motion."

He read the note aloud.

The counterrevolutionaries were planning to reenact the bus crash from last year. A few Cuban citizens had driven a bus into the Venezuelan embassy in an attempt to claim asylum. Once on the grounds, the Cuban government couldn't remove them without the Venezuelan embassy's permission. They'd been allowed to leave Cuba after strained negotiations with the Venezuelan government, but their departure had inspired a flood of other desperate asylum seekers to force their way into the embassy. The Cuban regime's suppression of the dissidents was swift and violent, leading to many deaths, some publicized and others not.

"It's not possible," Anita whispered. "After what happened last time, el Comandante won't allow anyone to escape again."

"If there are enough of us, can he stop us?" Gilberto insisted, his eyes glinting. "The underground radio has been saying that Peru is willing to accept any asylum seekers who attempt to escape. And perhaps Chile and the United States will, too."

"Plus, you don't think el Comandante's patience is wearing thin with counterrevolutionaries?" Idaly asked, placing a hand gently over Anita's. "If he thinks of us as traitors undermining his power, he should be more than willing to cut us loose."

Her brother's expression brightened by the second.

Anita glanced back down at the note, now crumpled in her brother's hand. According to the coded note, the rumors were true, and some of the guards posted at the Peruvian embassy had been made aware of the plan, and were willing to give people a chance to go through. Could this really be happening?

Her brother ripped the note to pieces. "We're leaving, starting over." Rafa held Anita's gaze with a look of challenge. "This is your chance to lead a different life than what Mamá Orti has planned."

"To live for yourself and no one else," Gilberto added.

"To be free," said Idaly, an arm around Emiliano, beaming at her.

What Rafa and her friends were talking about was risky and dangerous, likely to get them all killed—or worse, if Mamá Orti and the aquelarre found out.

She hated to be the one to say it, but she had to. "What about the initiation? It's in two days."

The group looked at each other, Gilberto keeping his steady gaze on hers. "We pretend, lie, whatever we have to do for now to get through the initiation, but the moment we get our chance to escape, *to choose*, we take it."

SEVENTEEN

Miami, November 19, 2016

LELA

Even with Ethan's warmth at my side, I feel unbearably cold. I get a good look at the botanica, situated in the back of the plaza. Its windows are blacked out. The neon red sign above has the first A in Magica blinking out.

My mom is so close, just around the plaza's corner and it feels like I'm betraying her by coming here. But after what happened last night—the terrifying moment something took over her body and delivered a message that was clearly meant for our family, I have no choice but to do this. After feeling the waves of power coming off of Mami, knowing that she has magic of her own, I almost feel like *she* betrayed me long ago.

"You don't have to be scared," Delfi says, misreading whatever tastes she's getting from me. "Zuela can help. She always comes through for me."

Hurt pinches my insides. Don't I always come through for her? Through Chris, our dad's reappearances, all the visions. For every single event of our lives?

My sister runs her tongue across her teeth as if ridding herself of the taste of my thoughts. Her face softens, but before she can say anything, the door of the botanica opens, releasing a cloud of incense vapor and cold air.

"Come in," a voice calls out, and we walk in.

Zuela's eyes are an intense amber green, like a boggy lake, but she looks less scary than I expected. More like someone's flamboyant tía.

"Hello," she says, in a careful tone. "You finally made your way here. I'm glad."

I give a tight-lipped smile.

I stand stiffly as Zuela leans over to give me the reflexive Hispanic kiss on the cheek, but at the last second, she pulls back as if remembering something. Delfi gives her an appreciative look and my prickling anger returns. Apparently, my sister's blabbed all of my secrets to her without even asking me.

Zuela greets Ethan quickly, then beckons us in.

"I received your messages from last night, corazón. Come, let's discuss."

We follow Zuela deeper into the store, and I gulp down the rising panic. Ethan's fingers brush my arm as we walk into a back room so cloyed with smoke I can barely see.

Once my eyes adjust, I take in the room. The walls are painted a deep iron red. A table is wedged into a corner and shelves are lined with books and glass chalices filled with different substances. There are fewer saints displayed than in the main store, but they're still present and nearly half my height.

I pause when I see the objects piled in only one half of the room. The staffs of bamboo and clay plates holding coconut husks decorated to have faces. The covered tureens piled with food and charms. The stains of gooey honey and crusted rust. But what stops me in my tracks are the ripples of power emanating from all directions.

"There's no need to be intimidated, amor," Zuela says, drawing the curtain that divides the room. "Those are my altars, and this side is where I utilize my magia del alma. My one true belief is that we receive the forces we expel onto the universe, and I don't wish to spend my gifts on causing harm." She lowers her voice. "Unless necessary."

"Ven—" She leads me and Ethan to sit at a small table, where Delfi's already perched. Zuela plucks a satin blue pouch from the shelf, then picks up a water glass and a candle, placing them in the center of the table along with the satin pouch's contents—stones and what looks like a tiny bone. She takes off her eleke necklaces and stores them away in a drawer.

Delfi dives into what happened. "We were delivered a message last night. Through our mom."

Zuela's eyes widen. "That is serious magic. What did it say?"

"Do not enter where you can no longer exit," I answer. "It was a warning."

"Someone like—possessed her," Delfi rattles. "And she's been super cagey lately." Delfi looks at me. I'd come here under one condition—we keep our mother's bruja nature out of this. It's been her secret this long, and even though I'm angry she kept it from us, it doesn't mean we need to tell everyone else. Delfi gives me a little nod. "We saw that cloth with the de Armas name, and then the stalker guy with the teardrop birthmark showed up where our mom works and where we live. We think he wasn't looking for us, but for her. We think maybe . . . this has something to do with the people she knew in Cuba."

"That guy also showed up at the crime scene," Ethan adds.

Delfi crosses her arms. "Further proof he has some kind of connection to Mami *and* Idaly. I think Mami knows them. All of them."

"We're not one hundred percent sure, though," I say defensively, not liking how this makes our mom look to this stranger.

Zuela puts a hand up. "What about the wax trabajo? Your message wasn't clear. Did it work or not?"

"Oh yeah, sorry. I was a bit hysterical." Delfi hands her the locket, explaining last night's events in detail from running into the bruja in the red tent leading up to the moment we found our mom. Zuela shakes her head as Delfi speaks.

"Do you think the bruja sent us that message? Doña Aura?" Delfi asks. "You said she's a shady character and the wax melted as soon I got within a few feet of her."

Zuela's eyes sharpen. "Aurelia could have something to do with it. Though perhaps inadvertently. Doña Aura has a habit of sticking her nose into things she shouldn't. Could've drawn the wrong kind of attention to herself, but she's a minor bruja, like I am. Nowhere near powerful enough to control other people in that manner. To deliver that kind of message—" Zuela releases a long, shaky breath. "The truth is, I believe I know who's behind this. Which is exactly as I feared."

A crash comes from the shelf, and we all whip around.

Ethan falls to his knees, scrambling to pick up wood chunks that spilled out of a small basket labeled sacred ceiba bark. "I am so sorry," he says, looking up at Zuela apologetically. "I'll buy whatever's broken."

"Damn it, Ethan," Delfi says. "I can't take you anywhere."

"Leave it," Zuela says. "I'll get it later."

Ethan sits, keeping his hands tucked close to his body.

"So you knew who was behind these murders and you didn't say anything?" I ask. Delfi shoots me a look.

"I didn't at first," Zuela says with a patient smile, "but when Delfi mentioned the warning was issued by la Orden, it confirmed my suspicions. La Orden de las Palomas. You don't usually hear them mentioned outside of Cuba. They tend to keep a low profile in the

US, unless they're dealing with one of their own or with someone who crossed them."

What category would Mom fall into? Going by the curse that's followed her to Miami, I'm going with the latter.

Zuela closes her eyes as if deep in thought, her fingers worrying over the beads of her necklace. *La Orden de las Palomas* resonates in my mind like the gong of a bell, leaving me unsteady.

Delfi rubs at her bare arms. "Who are they?"

Finally, Zuela opens her eyes again. "They are a society of powerful brujos that protect the Cuban president at all costs, but their focus is on him, and surely Idaly and Emiliano posed no threats to him. No, if Idaly and her husband were targeted, they must've terribly transgressed against las Palomas. Las Palomas are known to be merciless unless shown complete devotion."

I gape, and for once, Delfi looks as shocked as I am.

"And you think this secret society came here to Miami just to hunt them down?" Delfi asks.

"Certainly not; they would not leave the comandante's side. I think they sent someone on their behalf. I'll get what we need," Zuela says, pivoting with surprising grace toward a metal cabinet against the wall. "This is going to require all of our combined strengths."

I pull Delfi to me. "We're trying to go against an entire cult backed by the Cuban government?"

"A society," Delfi corrects as if that makes it any better. "Which is why we should be armed with as much knowledge as possible."

"Delfi?" Zuela prods, handing her a lighter and sitting across from us. "Let's go into this with clear intentions. Choose: Do you want to focus on who's in danger or who's responsible? Which one do you think needs you most?"

The question is obviously meant to be some sort of a test, but I'm not sure why we can't focus on both. Delfi leans forward and lights one black candle and one white.

"My intent," Delfi intones, "is to find the ones in danger." Her gaze strays to Zuela, seeking approval. "I want—I need to know how we're connected to the victims, how we can stop the killers from claiming anyone else. Before any of us can get hurt."

Smoke swirls up from an incense. Ethan tries to look reassuring, but he's white as sugar. A drop of sweat rolls down my neck, and I swear everyone in the room can hear the pounding of my heart.

Zuela peers at me closely. "Give me your hands. Since you are the ojo, this will work even better on you."

"Since I'm a *what?*"

Her expression is pitying. "Delfi is la lengua, and you are the ojo. *The eye*—you see moments from objects, no? Don't you receive more insight into the past, present, and sometimes future?"

I digest this. *An ojo.* So there's a word for what I can do. Does this mean I'm not the only one? So far, I believe I've only seen glimpses into the past. Can I do more?

Delfi dips her chin in encouragement. "It's okay, Lela. She knows what she's doing. I would do it myself, but my visions aren't as strong as yours."

Zuela bows her head at this. "I'm going to transport your spirit. It'll take you where you need to be, to the Tierra de Sombras where memories and reality intersect. You'll be safe, but this is powerful magic. It'll take our combined almas so we must hold hands. Except for you, sweet boy." She pats Ethan on the cheek.

Um, excuse me? Transport my spirit?

"Cover her eyes, Delfi," Zuela says. "We don't want her to bring anything back with her."

Delfi nods, plucking a satin scarf from the shelf.

"Hold on," I start, grabbing hold of Delfi's wrist before she can blindfold me. "This is not what I had in mind when you said we were going to get answers today."

"I wouldn't put you through anything dangerous," Delfi reassures us. "I've seen Zuze do this before—I mean, not to this level, but I'll be right beside you. You gotta trust me."

I do trust her, but she's not the one sending me god knows where *spiritually*—whatever that means. But what choice do we have? The brujos know where we live, where Mami works. We have to find a way to stop them.

I nod at Delfi and she beams, brandishing the scarf.

Right before my eyes are covered, I see Ethan's glasses catching the candlelight and his eyes behind them, just as fiery. I place my shaky hands over Zuela's. After a moment, Delfi's hand covers ours.

The moment we touch, I plummet.

◆   ◆   ◆

I fall back into a room, whipping around like an errant breeze. Distantly, I hear a gasp, and the hands around mine tighten like a rope. The pressure slows me down enough that I can look around the room without wanting to throw up.

Everything's gone—my sister, Ethan, the botanica, and all the saints.

"What do you see?" Zuela commands. Her voice sounds far away, as if I'm underwater.

My breath shudders, jaw trembling. I can't speak.

"Hurry." Delfi's voice now, urgent. I try to focus on what's in front of me.

"I—it's a room. But I don't know whose."

"Look harder."

I want to rub my eyes, but there's nothing to touch. No body to control. Fear wells up. What if I get stuck here? What if I can't get back to my body?

Then I feel the familiar pressure of someone's hand on mine, like a tether to the real world. The image of the room sharpens until I can see it clearly.

I scan the room. "Um, there's nothing on the walls. One TV." I panic, trying to take in everything. How do I know what's worth mentioning? "A newspaper on the bed. Dog hair everywhere. Scattered men's clothes. Looks like maybe a hotel?"

"What else?"

I move around. "A window. There's construction outside—a half-demolished building, a red crane," I say, stepping into another room. "There's a bathroom with . . . blood on the sink. A needle. Like from a shirt pin."

"Look in the mirror," Zuela says.

I brace myself to see my reflection, wondering what I'll find, but I'm not there.

Instead, I see a familiar face, an older handsome Black man with a salt and pepper beard. It's Silver Fox, the same guy I'd seen in my vision searching for Idaly when I brushed against Teardrop's jacket. As I continue looking at Silver Fox's reflection, the light outside the hotel window flickers and shifts, as if the days are filtering by. Silver Fox's reflection begins to change. Sometimes he's shaving, other times he's talking to someone I can't see, growing agitated. Maldeados gather around him until he disappears, and someone else is reflected back.

It's him. It's Teardrop. Our stalker.

He's staring into his reflection, almost as if he could see me on the other side. I see his birthmark, but it's his eyes that draw me in—hooded and brown with a rim of black, his widow's peak similar to our mom's, his square jaw, and serious mouth. Features that are entirely too familiar. Features that could easily belong to a de Armas.

I scream.

I feel a painful tug, and then I'm on the floor, looking up into Ethan's frantic face. Back in the botanica.

He pushes back my hair. "What happened? Are you okay?"

I gulp for air.

"Lela—" My sister shoves Ethan out of the way, her own face pale as she helps me sit up. Somehow, I'd ended up laid out on the floor.

"I saw him," I manage as they help me back onto my chair. "I saw him so clearly, Delf. I think . . . I think he's related to us."

The blood drains from Delfi's face. "Teardrop?"

I nod.

"And I'm afraid we've been seen as well." Zuela stands abruptly and blows out the candles on the table.

"How do you know?" Delfi asks.

Zuela murmurs a prayer under her breath and slips her beaded necklaces back over her neck. "I felt them. Those maldeados in the vision—they belonged to las Palomas. I saw into la Tierra de Sombras—the moment the shadows appeared in your vision, I saw who sent them. Those two men are being watched."

"So you don't think they're the murderers?" I ask. "Or Aura's accomplices or anything?"

Zuela shakes her head. "I don't know, but the way I interpreted the vision, the shadows are hovering close behind, waiting to strike. If you think this Teardrop man is related to you, perhaps he was watching your mother for a different reason. We must find this hotel they're staying in. Mark them under our protection with un trabajo. Las Palomas will believe they've been taken under the wing of another community. It'll delay them, but I'm afraid it won't stop them."

"And what about us?" I ask. "Are las Palomas coming for us, too?"

"I don't know," Zuela says again. "You must protect yourselves. I'm sorry—I misjudged the extent of their connection with las Palomas. I should never have opened that channel."

"But he's—*why* is he related to us?" This is breaking my brain. "We got to talk to Mom."

"No," Delfi says. "You think she's lied to us this long only to tell us the truth now? There's a reason she doesn't want us knowing about her past. Something she's ashamed of."

"Or scared of," I say.

But Delfi ignores me. "Zuze, you think our mom has something to do with las Palomas?"

Zuela shrugs. "I wish I had all the answers, mi niña, but if you really are related to this . . . Teardrop, and both of you are gifted with magia del alma, it stands to reason your mother is too."

Delfi and I stare at each other. That we already know.

"The point is," Zuela continues, "it's imperative we find them as soon as possible." Her sharp expression turns affectionate. "We will figure out what your mother is hiding. I would tell you to leave it be, but I know you won't, so I will do everything I can to protect you. Hand me your necklace." She gestures to my neck and the azabache. "I'll place a protection over it, a mal de ojo trabajo that'll keep you safe for now until we can figure out a better way to keep you hidden from las Palomas."

"What about Delfi's?" I ask.

"She already did mine," Delfi says, and Zuela pats her arm. "The day I walked into her botanica."

I hesitate but eventually hand over my necklace. While the two of them work through some complicated process of blessing the stone and a separate protection trabajo for Silver Fox and Teardrop, my phone vibrates in my pocket. I know the message is from Mami.

I feel as if I'm being torn apart. Maybe Mami is keeping all this a secret for a reason. Not from shame, but to keep us safe. Whether we share DNA with Teardrop or not, it doesn't mean he can be trusted. Family doesn't always have your back. But I also know

Delfi is set on tracking these men down, and I can't let her do this alone.

"How are we even supposed to find them?" I ask, exhausted.

"Um, I might be able to help with that." We all turn to look at Ethan, who's remained quiet up until now.

"Oh my god, he's actually raising his hand," Delfi mutters.

"You were talking in your vision. Something about a red crane—" He places his phone on the table so we can all see the screen. He's pulled up his dad's website on the browser, which features a photo of a construction site with dozens of different types of machinery, all in red. "My family's the only one who rents out red equipment for the American Heart Association here in Florida. Excavators, forklifts, rollers—cranes. He's got me doing bookkeeping on some days, which sucks because his office reeks, and the water filter's crap so the coffee's—"

Delfi clears her throat.

"Right, right. So I have access to everything that's out of the warehouse, and its current location. It wouldn't be hard to figure out where they're staying if we find the red crane."

"But how many red cranes are out there?" I ask. "We don't have time to track them all down."

"Actually, there's only two."

Delfi's mouth splits into a grin. "I knew there was a reason we kept you around."

Ethan shrugs, looking more pleased than offended. After a quick look through his phone he sits back. "Little Havana and Key Largo. But the only place with residential or commercial buildings nearby is in Little Havana."

"You have the full address?" Zuela asks.

"Yup." He shows us the screen. We have a location. I know there's no backing out now.

Delfi's phone chirps with a message. She stares at the message a beat before she gets her scheming face.

"Okay, here's what's up. You two scope out the address and see if you can find Teardrop, but don't do anything without me. Something came up."

"So now you're going to dump this on us?" I say. "We should stay together."

"I'm not dumping anything on you. I'll be doing the hard stuff. As usual." She goes up to Zuela and kisses her on the cheek. "Zuze, I love you. I'll pick up the protection trabajo tomorrow morning."

Zuela says goodbye, the anxious expression on her face doing nothing to soothe my nerves. As we head out, Delfi takes a few other things off the shelves without asking. "Cover for me? I'm sleeping over at Soraya's after my shift."

"Like hell you are. Where are you really going?"

She gives me a hard look, halfway out the door. "If you must know, I'm meeting with Andres." Before I can protest, she adds, "It's solely for the investigation, nothing more. And he doesn't want me bringing anyone else. He's paranoid like that."

I grit my teeth as she takes off. *That's* why he was at the Celebration of the Saints Festival yesterday. To meet with her. Purely for the investigation, my butt. I can only hope Andres will help keep her safe.

I look to Ethan who's waiting patiently. I know whether I choose to track the men down, fully embrace this mission that'll wedge us deeper into trouble or leave it be, he'll be with me every step of the way. He'll support whatever I decide even if it means facing the dangers of a love curse or worse. But I really wish I didn't have to keep putting him in jeopardy.

His mouth pulls into a smile, another thing I can always count on. Like the rising of the sun. "Where do you want to go?"

EIGHTEEN

Cuba, March 20, 1980

ANITA

Athick air of tension ran through the dark like a riptide at sea. Anita, along with the other children of las Palomas, stood at the ocean's edge as the Elders prepared for the tracking ritual.

This gathering was different from the congregations of prayers and offerings she'd glimpsed as a child. Anita, like the other soon-to-be Guardias, was not usually invited to these rituals and it was only proof that they'd soon complete their initiation. As imminent as the bus crash.

She reminded herself that all of this was only temporary. This ritual was intended to help introduce her into a society that she could no longer see herself being a part of. She would pretend, lie, harden her heart to what was in store until it was time to go.

A row of vasallos, the powerless followers of las Palomas, stood like emaciated soldiers in front of the Elders until it was their turn to confront their fate. Waiting behind the Elders, Anita's hands trembled, the needle and thread rattling on the clay plate she held. Gilberto looked straight ahead but she could feel his attention focused on her. Feel the radiating warmth of his body beside her. He carried his own plate with a thread and needle, as did Idaly and Emiliano at Anita's other side. The fifth and final soon-to-be-Guardia was nowhere to be found. The Madroño children had lost their place when Elder Madroño betrayed las Palomas by fleeing the country.

It was because of that betrayal they were all gathered.

Despite the cool breeze and vastness of the bay, she was sweltering. Maldeados detached from the dark to bear witness.

Elder Amoros stepped forward. He pushed back the veil of a vasallo, smeared something dark across their forehead, and intoned, "Your sacrifice is acknowledged, Hermano, and las Palomas are forever in your debt."

"My service is to las Palomas now and always. Fidelidad, fuerza, y poder." *Fidelity, strength, and power.*

Everyone gathered repeated it, including Anita, who did it without thinking. She'd practically been born with those words on her lips.

Her mother glanced back at her, dipped her chin. An owl shrieked against the dark as the Elders parted and Anita stepped forward, bringing her instruments for the ritual. Her hands shook even harder. She knew the vasallos had chosen this fate, but it did not lessen her terror or her guilt in taking part in the ritual.

Pretend, lie. It's almost over.

Elder Amoros withdrew the needle from Anita's plate and held it aloft. The vasallo leaned forward, so that their face was illuminated by the moonlight, their glazed eyes empty. Anita shuddered as the Elder threaded the needle, then sank the pointed tip into the vasallo's lips.

She nearly cried out, but Mamá Orti turned, her stare pinning Anita in place like a dog held by the scruff.

"Elder Madroño, the traitor, the deserter," Elder Amoros said as he stitched the lips of the vasallo who'd begun to make soft noises in the back of their throat.

"Where he goes, his words will not be spoken," the Elder continued.

Acrid horror built in Anita as she watched Elder Amoros finish stitching. Another vasallo came forward to repeat the process. Another willing sacrifice.

The next Elder took the needle and thread from a stricken Gilberto, and this time, the Elder sank her needle into the vasallo's ears, speaking quietly as she stitched them closed, one by one. "For the traitor Elias Madroño, where he goes, his words will not be heard."

When Gilberto was back at Anita's side, he was shaking. He spoke low, too low for the others to hear. "This isn't supposed to be like this. In our faith, there are protections against an enemy. Humane ways. Ways that don't twist your soul." His grip tightened on the plate. "They've taken old practices and corrupted them."

Anita wanted to comfort him but knew she couldn't. The most she could do was whisper, "We will be different."

He gave her a slight nod. A warmth in his gaze that was in stark contrast to everything around them.

Anita repeated the mantra, *we will be different. Pretend, lie. It's almost over.* Until it was her mother's turn. The final act.

Mamá Orti stepped forward and took the thread from Idaly's trembling hands. As Idaly stepped back, Anita saw Emiliano brush her arm comfortingly. The needle's glinting point pierced into the last vasallo's eyelid. "For the hermano who betrayed us, where he goes, he will not be seen again," her mother said.

The entire aquelarre began to chant, the layered voices of magia del alma drifted into the night.

Blood dripped down the vasallos' faces, soaking the sand. One by one, the vasallos stepped into the sea, where their blood could be washed away and the trabajo would be swept out to all the distant shores. No matter where he ran, Elder Madroño would never be safe, would live only long enough to regret his betrayal of las Palomas.

Gilberto met Anita's gaze. He wasn't chanting, and neither was she. They'd contributed enough to the man's fate.

All this for an Elder who defected to the United States, who'd believed he could go against the order. Who wanted another choice. But all he would get now would be a slow, painful death, with no one to hear his silent cries, or a life of running. Although Anita had never particularly liked Elder Madroño's children, her heart twisted to think of what their lives would be like now.

Anita and her friends looked at one another. They were confronting the reality of what they would face, the horrors if they stayed, the consequences if they left. It made their dream feel further out of reach, but Anita wanted to try everything in her power to leave this world of vicious magic behind. In defiance, and in fear, they all held hands, forming what they hoped was an unbreakable chain of resilience.

NINETEEN

Miami, November 19, 2016

LELA

I didn't wait around Zuela's botanica any longer than I had to,
that's for sure. I decided to scope out the address of the red
crane with Ethan, and if I die because I run into a society of evil
brujos with a bone to pick with the de Armas clan, I hope Delfi
knows it's her fault.

Just in case, once Zuela returned my azabache necklace, I asked
her to give me that protection brujería concoction meant for Silver
Fox and Teardrop, which apparently was an offensive way of putting
it. Zuela's eyes had bored into mine, and when I apologized, she gave
a nonchalant shrug with enough flair to make any drama teacher
jealous.

Now the tiny vial of oily substance rests in my hands. I roll the
smooth glass between my fingers and repeat the protection words
she told me to say.

All we need now is to find the hotel where the men are staying.
Ethan surprises me by grabbing my hand, rubbing his thumb across

my knuckles, and my heart is fired up for an entirely different reason.

I'm watching the side of his face. The sunlight outlining his profile and the alluring smile forming at the corner of his mouth. When his phone starts trilling, connected to his car's stereo, it makes us both jump. He's maneuvering the car around a tricky blocked intersection, trying to find his phone, when I see it's his dad calling on the car's display.

"Oh, here," I say, pressing the button and his dad's big voice fills the car speakers.

"You feeling better, kid?"

"Hey, Dad." Ethan shifts in his seat.

This snatches my attention. Had he been sick?

Ethan's trying to wrangle driving and disconnecting his phone from Bluetooth. "I'm fine. I'm out right now. Getting some stuff done."

"That's good. I don't like seeing you cooped up in that room, eating all your meals alone—"

"I said I'm fine, Dad. Drop it," Ethan snaps. "I'll call you later." He ends the call.

I've never, *ever* heard him talk to his parents like that.

"What was that about?"

He avoids looking at me. "I didn't want him worrying you for nothing."

I cross my arms. "Well, if I wasn't worried before, I am now."

"I'm sorry. I'll call him back and apologize, I promise." He glances over quickly. "Nothing's wrong. I'm not sick or depressed or anything. I've been spending time alone in my room because . . . I just prefer to be alone. I mean, sometimes. Not when I'm with you. I love being with you." He reaches over and grabs my hand again but it's not as soothing. "Would you mind putting the address in the GPS? I don't want to get lost."

And I don't want to lose him. I feel his heart pounding beneath my fingers.

"Promise, I'm okay." He squeezes my hand for a bit longer, trying to be reassuring, but it doesn't ease the worry settling like an anchor in my chest. I've been his best friend for a long time, and I know when something's wrong.

◆ ◆ ◆

About twenty minutes later, we're pulling up to the construction site in Little Havana.

The street's closed off, so Ethan takes a back way through a narrow road of clustered homes.

The red crane catches the fading sunlight, shining like a bloody heart. I recognize the bare bones of a building right beside it. We park and make our way over.

"Hey, can we check on the other side?" I say. In the vision, the hotel's bathroom window faced the construction building where graffiti letters were painted on its side.

"No problem," he says. "But can you jump a fence?"

"You mean you don't have a key?"

He snorts. "My dad *rents* out the machines. This isn't his contract, and even if it was, I wouldn't have a key." He walks over to me, threading his fingers with mine with an ease as if we've been doing this forever.

He smiles. "Come on, I'll give you a boost."

I grimace as we walk up to the gate. "This is illegal."

"So is stalking." Bending on one knee, he laces and cups his hands so I can step into them.

"It's not stalking if I'm trying to save their lives," I mutter. "What if I can't tell which room they're staying in?"

His brow furrows. "Then we come back tomorrow with Delfi and knock on every door."

Because only Delfi would be brave enough to do that. I shoo away his hands. "I know how to climb a fence."

I take a deep breath, then scale the chain-link fence, hopping over to the other side like a pro. I give Ethan a smug smile while dusting off my hands.

"You're a hardcore criminal now, huh?" he says, laughing.

I kind of hope he'll struggle to climb the fence so I can tease him, but he moves over with ease. When he drops down beside me, he touches his lips to my cheek and walks off. Whatever smart remark I had fizzes out as I chase after him.

"Ofi—look."

I look at where he's pointing. The building's naked cement façade is marred with letters spray-painted in neon orange. Which looks similar to the angle of the building in the vision.

I whip around, and the only thing directly across from it is a two-story hotel shaped like a horseshoe. The kind of hotel that rents out by the week. We walk a few yards, and I find a break in the fence that we can easily slip through.

That's when I see him. Anxiety spears down my spine. We duck behind a cluster of palms.

Even at this distance and with the waning sun, I recognize Silver Fox as he comes out from one of the units carrying a box. He loads it into the back of a pickup truck already filled with stuff. He wipes a rag down his face and goes back inside.

He's leaving. By this time tomorrow, or whenever Delfi deems this important enough to break away from flirting with Andres, it'll be too late. We might never find them again.

I can't take that chance.

TWENTY

Miami, November 19, 2016

DELFI

The alley behind the now-closed botanica smells like old bacon grease and sewage, but it's the first bit of quiet I've had for hours, and I melt into it.

After I got Andres's text about finding a new lead, I ran home to change and came back here to meet him, right as the sun was beginning to set and the flickering lampposts powered on. A neutral spot for a meet-up. On the opposite wall, someone graffitied a girl biting into a candy bracelet with the words *The World is Ours* on her forehead. It's disturbing but also beautifully drawn and strangely enthralling, and I need something to focus on besides the fact we're on the radar of an extremely powerful society of brujos *and* that my mom has apparently been lying to us our entire lives. We are not the last de Armas. My sister and I aren't the only ones with abilities, and she's kept us in the dark because she got involved with the wrong crowd of people.

I take a deep drag from the cigarette I swiped from Zuela earlier, along with a fancy Zippo lighter, and the smoke burns my throat. It's as disgusting as I remember. Still, it stops me from gnashing my teeth, so I take another drag.

"I didn't know you smoked."

I whip my head toward the voice, heart in my throat. Andres is standing at the end of the passage, nearly filling the narrow alley. I cough, the smoke going down the wrong pipe.

"That's what that stuff does to you," he says.

I flick the cigarette at his feet. "Shut. Up. I don't—" *wheeze.* I almost go into another fit as my lungs burn from the acrid smoke. "This doesn't count." I shoot a sharp look at him. "Didn't anyone ever tell you not to sneak up on innocent girls in alleyways?"

He leans against the wall. "Didn't anyone ever tell you there's nothing innocent about you?"

Hmph. Fair enough. I look him over. He's dressed head to toe in dark clothing. Black sneakers, dark jeans, and a black, tight-fitted shirt under a jacket. He told me to wear sneakers, which I am, but he didn't say I had to come in a Morphsuit.

"Where are we going exactly?" I ask.

"A boatyard, close to Black Point Marina. The boat Idaly went missing from was linked to this warehouse, but the owners said it's impossible because the place has been shut down for ages. Maybe we can find something there that tells us what she was getting herself into before she died."

Like something that definitively links my mom or Teardrop to Idaly's death.

My brow lifts. "And is this source of yours the dad detective? Has the place already been ransacked by the police?"

"Like I said, the police have done the bare minimum with this case. I did my own digging."

"Anything else you'd like to share with your crime-solving partner?" I ask in a super-sweet tone, the kind that could rot teeth. I can't
get a read on his emotions since the cigarette smoke momentarily
killed my taste buds.

"Not really. Do you?"

I bite the inside of my cheek. I still don't know how much I can
trust him. He could run to his dad and have me arrested for—
whatever you arrest people for when they know too many things
they shouldn't. I'm also not ready to share what I know about Silver
Fox and my potential relative.

"Thought so," he says, checking his watch. "We have a short window. Park security stops patrolling at eight and the overnight shift
doesn't arrive until midnight."

I check my phone. "Well, shit. Let's go."

The gap between plazas is narrow, and he goes rigid as I squeeze
past him. I smile up at him, chest to chest, as I wiggle to the other side
and toward the street. The subtle scent of his aftershave lingers.

"You know, you could've said *excuse me*." He walks up behind me.

"If that's what you're into." I glance back, shaking my hair loose
from its clip. "Next time, I'll make sure to whisper it in your ear."

"Keep dreaming."

"So, where'd you park?" I ask.

Andres gestures with his chin toward a sleek cobalt motorcycle.
My mouth drops open. When he swings his long legs over and hands
me the extra helmet, I give him what I think is the first genuine
smile he's ever seen from me. He smiles back, and I tell myself it's
not the reason my stomach flutters.

"Hold on to me," he yells.

"No way!" I spread my arms, air rushing past, head tilted back.

We speed down the back roads toward the marina. There are no
streetlights or traffic, not another human soul out at this time of

night in the middle of nowhere. Only starlight reminds me the world still exists beyond the strip of headlights from his bike.

"Seriously, hold on. You're going to fall."

I pout, though he can't see it, and lean forward to curl against his back. He tenses as my hand slides across his stomach. Sweetness pours over my tongue, tasting like fizzy soda. I lick my lips, not sure what feeling I'm tasting, but knowing that I like it.

For a second, I nearly forget we're not on a joyride.

I need to stop myself from getting distracted. We're here for a reason. He would never have let me get this close again if it weren't for a purpose, for Idaly and Emiliano. At this point, I need to figure out who las Palomas sent to kill off their old members so I know who I'm facing when they show up for my family. If the killer used a boat registered to this place, maybe they left other clues to their identity there too. I grip my necklace and the azabache in a tight fist, absorbing as much as I can of the protection Zuze infused into it.

"We're almost there," Andres says.

I look around, but there's nothing but swampland. It's not one of the more well-known harbors with fancy boat rentals or luxury yachts. Black Point Marina never gets super busy unless it's Labor Day or something, and hardly anyone goes fishing around here unless they enjoy getting eaten alive by mosquitoes and breathing in the garbage mound that lines the coast like Florida's version of a mountain range.

Everything looks familiar, but not from my visions. It's because I used to come here with my father. Back when he was a decent human being, before the curse broke him, he used to take Lela and me on his boat. I learned to fish in these waters, how to snell-knot a hook and cast a line.

But that was a long time ago, and it's not what we're here to do.

Andres slows down to take the next turn. It's easy to miss because it's not the main entrance for visitors, and it's congested with trees.

There's a cacophony of mating frogs and buzzing insects. A musty salt smell twists my stomach with memories. My dad shucking oysters behind a red pickup truck. Lela and me jumping from rock to rock along the stone jetty. My dad watching us from behind a film of cigarette smoke, head cocked, eyes narrowed. Maybe even then he could see the shadows that clung to us.

We approach a secluded rusted building, deep in the groves near the water's edge.

"This is it." He stops the bike and lifts his visor, examining the building. "Can you wait here? I'm going to hide the bike."

I glance over my shoulder to the thick congregation of trees. "Sure." It's not like I'm scared of the creepy woods or the dark or anything. It's who may be lurking in them. I've never felt more like prey.

Andres cuts the engine and walks the bike toward a thick underbrush. There aren't any signs to indicate what kind of business uses this warehouse, but I pick up an unsettling taste of desperation that stings the inside of my mouth. Then, the faintest taste of floral violet lingers on my tongue.

My eyes widen. It's the taste of Idaly's visions—the traces of magic that Zuela said would cling to the killer.

"There's no cameras around." I jump as Andres walks up, hoisting the strap of his bag. "Come on, let's check if there's a door."

There's not a regular door, but an industrial-sized roll-up steel door shut with a padlock. He crouches and examines the padlock before taking out a small pouch from his book bag, rummaging through all kinds of tools.

"You don't know how to pick a lock," I say.

He doesn't look up. "Watch me. I can also get out of zip ties if I need to."

"Well, in that case, Houdini, let's throw you in the bay and see how long you can hold your breath."

He ignores me, his face pinched with effort. It takes a few minutes longer than they show in movies, and I'm nervously glancing around in the dark for any movement. Finally, there's a click, and the padlock unhooks. His dark eyes slide to mine, pleased, and although I would never admit it, he looks pretty damn good.

"What are you waiting for? A cookie? Go in."

He smiles. One of those rare full ones and I remember why we stopped talking in the first place. He's too beautiful to resist.

"After you." He yanks up the metal roll-up door partway, the sides screeching. I duck under.

We look around, up to the three stories of stacked boats with rusted bottoms. None of them look like they've been in the ocean in years, let alone the outside of this warehouse. Some of the boats have faded names like *La Sirenita* and *The Pearl*, and I even spot a small dinghy called the *Motorboater*.

The walls are peeling gray. Exposed pipes and circuits dangling from the roof. Even a busted-out window that we could've easily crawled through instead.

"It's abandoned," I say.

"Or it's a cover."

"A cover for what?"

He shrugs. "Meet-up spot. I mean, this is supposedly some sort of, abandoned business. But how many derelict buildings have new locks, fresh tire tracks outside?"

I hadn't noticed those, but I do notice a swirl of darkness in the corners. I realize we're being watched by a swarm of maldeados.

"Something's not right here," Andres says.

Understatement of the century.

I imagine this is the perfect spot for a haunted house. The ideal scene out of a scary movie where the bimbo dies first. If me and Andres start making out, I'll know for sure I'm going to die here.

"This shit is creepy." He points the beam of light at my face and I squint.

"Agreed. Let's look around and get the hell out." I find myself walking close, arms crossed to keep myself from touching anything.

"Wait." Andres shines a light on a row of vials lined up on an exposed beam.

"These look new. No dust on them. Santería?" he asks, and I shake my head, recognizing the objects.

"A type of brujería," I correct. "There's no saints or effigies here either." It could be alma magic. Or a combination of things, a syncretic mashup of beliefs and abilities that's common for brujos.

"This place isn't abandoned at all." I pick up one of the containers, which feels like it's not made out of plastic or glass, but something more organic like bone. The shelf below has a row of metallic tins filled with feathers.

"You think Idaly's been here? Do you . . . sense anything?" Andres asks.

I nod. The residue of violet is still on my tongue.

"Either she came here, or her killer did. The boat she was pushed from was registered here, and I think it's safe to assume this wasn't Idaly's hangout spot or anything."

"You said she was pushed?"

I see the maldeados gathering at the center of the room. Although Andres can't see them, his shoulders tense, and the light he carries trembles across the floor, illuminating a crystal gleam of water.

"An assumption," I say, crouching down to examine the bowl of liquid on the ground surrounded by tied wooden stakes. Without thinking, I plunge my fingers into the basin, feeling the scratch of sand at the bottom and the sleekness of a plastic bag.

"Killers or not, whoever left this knows what they're doing as far as their practice." I pull out a plastic bag from the basin. A clear sandwich bag with something inside—a picture.

"That's her," Andres says near my shoulder, pointing at Idaly, his interest scrubbing out any apprehension.

I study the faces, finding a teenaged Idaly holding tight to Emiliano, and two others—a young Silver Fox before the salt and pepper beard and a young Teardrop, his eyes a penetrating brown in a shape that's all too familiar. Lela was right, he has to be a de Armas. Practically a male version of our mother. Like a twin.

This isn't some distant relative. This has to be her brother or something. Our . . . uncle?

But before I can look closer, we hear a muffled bang. The sound of a car door closing outside.

TWENTY-ONE

Miami, November 19, 2016

LELA

What should I even say?" I whisper as I watch Silver Fox disappear inside his hotel room.

Should I apologize for not having saved Idaly? Should I ask how they know my mom? Everything I come up with makes me sound completely baked. Silver Fox, and maybe even my relative, are right here, right on the other side of this door. Room 10B. But if Mami didn't want us involved with whatever family she has left, I'm sure it was for a good reason. I don't know if I can trust them yet.

All I can do is deliver the warning. I'm just a messenger. I don't even have to mention that I'm a de Armas. I take a deep breath.

"Tell them you're a psychic," Ethan suggests. "And that you think they're in danger. If he doesn't find that completely ridiculous, then he'll know what you're talking about and maybe be open to help. If he gets defensive or weird, then we call the cops and we run like hell."

"Okay. Solid plan."

I knock on the door, way too softly, but the lock unlatches, and the door cracks open. A man's dark eye peers out, a thick brow like a boomerang. It's Silver Fox. He looks shocked to see me too, but I can't tell if he recognizes me, or if he's just wondering who the hell I am.

"Sí . . . eh." He pauses. "¿En qué te puedo ayudar?"

I respond to him in Spanish. "Hello, we just want to talk to you for a moment." *Excuse me, sir. Do you have a moment to discuss the murderous cult that you may or may not know about?* "It's something . . . you might know about."

"Yo no sé nada, ni quiero comprar nada."

"We're not here to sell you anything."

"No debes estar aquí."

I shouldn't be here? So does he know who I am? As he moves to close the door, I surprise myself and grab his hand to keep the door from shutting.

Silver Fox lets out a sound and freezes as my fingers brush against his, against the gleaming ring on his index finger, like a crackle of electricity. An image bursts into my mind.

I see blood, a circle of robed figures in shadows. I see an old, bearded man, lying on a huge white bed. A face too iconic to confuse for anyone else's—the Cuban dictator.

The vision sputters out abruptly like a faulty wire come loose. Not because the vision was over, not because I let go, but because something went wrong. Did he shut me out? Is that possible? What did I even see? He shakes off my hand as if I'd burned him.

"You're in danger," I say, this time in English. "Something's after you. But I think you know that already."

Silver Fox doesn't say anything, so I repeat it in Spanish.

The man shakes his head. "What are you?" he asks in English.

The question cuts deep. It's one I've asked myself my whole life.

I step forward. "My name's Ofelia. I know this sounds weird, but I've had visions about you, and judging by what I saw, I know you're in trouble."

I have to warn them!

His red-rimmed eyes don't blink, but after a beat, Silver Fox extends his arm out, making room for us to enter the hotel room.

"Entren."

I waver at the threshold, debating if this is a smart thing to do, but instinct pushes me forward and we follow the man into the dark room, which smells of cigars and Chinese takeout. The living room overflows with crumpled newspapers and paper plates as if he hasn't left his couch in days. As if he's been hiding out here. The straw fedora I'd seen him wear in my vision is on the coffee table.

The guy watches me warily as I come in. Now I get a clear glimpse of his face. Not as imposing as I'd imagined him to be, but handsome, like one of the actors on my mom's telenovelas.

I give him a watery smile. My palms start to sweat. We're in this guy's *room*. We have no idea who he is. He could be an ax murderer for all we know. Or a brujo murderer. Basically, any kind of murderer. But I came here for a purpose.

"¿Quieren café o agua?"

I shake my head quickly. I don't think I could drink anything right now.

"Americano?" the guy asks, gesturing to Ethan. He makes a face like *go figure* as if he hasn't run across many white Americans in Little Havana. Yeah, go figure.

"Yup, Americano," Ethan says. "Nice to meet you. I'm Ethan." He offers his hand. The guy hesitates before shaking it.

"Gilberto," the man introduces himself, then motions for us to sit on the couch.

"Entonces," he continues, "what are you?"

I squirm. "Cuban?"

"No," he says forcefully. "You said you had visions about something hunting me. So tell me."

I press my knees to keep my legs from bouncing. "I—I'm a psychic. An . . . ojo." His eyes light with understanding. "I've had these visions—well, my sister and I have these visions and we've seen you and another man with a birthmark here—" I point to my cheek, and Gilberto's face goes grim. "It's hard to explain, but I did this spirit transport thing—anyway, I know something's after you."

"Do you know who?"

"I do," I say, my gaze flickering to his neck. To the scarred mark I have a feeling is hidden under his collar—a dove with a snake.

"I see." Gilberto leans back in his own chair, steepling his fingers. There's something sharp about him and refined, despite the surrounding mess and his rough appearance.

"So, you came to warn me?"

I nod. He gives a dark laugh, and the hairs on my arm stand on end.

"I brought something that can protect you," I say, pulling out the tiny vial of enchanted oil and feeling more ridiculous by the second. Especially as Gilberto looks closely at the vial and scoffs.

I sit up straighter. "I'm only trying to keep you from getting killed. If you could call your friend or whoever he is, I can help him too. I know people who can protect both of you."

Gilberto puts his hand out for me to settle down. "Though I appreciate it, I won't be calling anyone. My question for you is, do you understand what you're doing? This—" he snatches the vial from my hands, holding it up by his face, "is useless. Or do you mean to tell me you have a community to take us in?"

My expression must show my response because he shakes his head. "Who sent you?"

"No one," I say. "I mean, I had help finding you but—"

"Didn't they tell you that *you* could be the one in danger by coming here?"

I feel Ethan tense beside me. "They did, but—"

"But nada. I don't know what kind of person you're working with, who's whispering this nonsense in your ear, but it was foolish of you to come."

My chest rises and falls. "Yes," I tell Gilberto angrily. "It was reckless to come here, and they did warn me, but I couldn't let someone else's death haunt me for the rest of my life, even if that person is a stubborn jerk!" My mouth snaps shut.

"We should leave," Ethan says, grasping my arm.

Gilberto's eyes flash. He sits forward. "What do you mean by someone else's death?"

I want to stuff the words back in but it's too late. "A woman named Idaly, and her partner."

Surprise . . . and pain registers in his face. "And what happened to them?" he asks.

"They died. And I'd seen her—Idaly. I knew it was going to happen, and I didn't even try to stop it. I can't let that happen again."

Gilberto clamps a hand over his mouth, gripping hard. It's clear he knew Idaly and Emiliano, and that he cared for them. With his movement, his collar shifts to reveal the mark on his neck. A strange puffy scar that looks like a bird pecking a snake. A paloma. Just like I expected. It's the same pale mark we'd seen on Idaly and Emiliano's necks. As if they'd been branded like cattle. So they were all former members of las Palomas, including Teardrop. Maybe including my mom.

He pulls up his collar, hiding it, and I force my gaze away and look up at Gilberto. This is my only chance to ask.

"Do you . . . have you ever met anyone by the name of Ana de Armas? In Cuba maybe?"

His hand clenches on his knee. No matter how impassive he tries to appear, it's obvious he knows the name. He knows Mami.

"I think you should go. This is dangerous."

"Have you thought about going to the police?" I ask.

He jumps up abruptly. The vial of oil clatters onto the table. Ethan quickly stands between us, using his full height.

"Have you spoken to the police?" Gilberto demands. "Do they know where I am?"

I stand, too. "N-no, I swear. The police wouldn't believe me anyway."

Gilberto scrutinizes me with an intensity I can feel inside my skull. "La policía en Miami can't be trusted," he says finally, softly but still not backing down. His steps are slow and deliberate as he leads us to the door like an angered animal who's done being cornered. "Remember that. And, ojo, I suggest you keep any future visions to yourself. For you and your family's sake. *Please*, stay out of this."

As Ethan and I reluctantly walk out, I'm reminded of the warning delivered through my mother. No se metan donde salir no puedan. *Do not enter where you can no longer exit.*

Gilberto shuts the door in our face.

TWENTY-TWO

Miami, November 19, 2016

DELFI

There's a man outside the boatyard.

So we hadn't imagined the sound of a car door slamming. Andres clicks off the flashlight and grabs my hand, moving toward the hallway of the abandoned offices. "Stay close," he says. I hear the rumble of the man's voice as he gets closer, entering the warehouse through the metal door we left open.

The adrenaline kicks in, and I almost tug my hand away from Andres, try to run, but I pull back. *Think, think.* There's an empty office room with a window facing the front of the warehouse, a storage room, and—

"There's a bathroom." My throat is dry, eroded with fear. The bitter taste of metal gets stronger, mingled with the earthy taste of tobacco—a brujo. "The room before this one, i-it was a bathroom with a window facing the forest." We inch our way closer to the door, trying not to trip on the debris.

Andres holds tight to my hand, presses his face close to mine, nearly forehead to forehead. "Delfi, listen. Whatever you do, don't turn back. I'm going to create a distraction and when you hear my signal, run. Jump out of the window and run."

"Like hell," I say. "I'm not leaving here without you."

We freeze as we hear the man's steps getting closer to where we're hiding. It sounds like he's on the phone. He's talking in Spanish as he walks around, peering under the boats and saying that he thinks he's in the right place.

My blood runs cold as I catch "hay alguien aquí," and "sí es ella, la mató."

He knows someone's in here. He said he'll kill her if she's here. But who's her? *Me?*

"He'll hear us trying to escape," Andres whispers harshly. "These windows are rusted shut and haven't been opened in years."

"Forget it. I'm not leaving by myself." I yank at his arm, making sure he stays close. We slip out of the room and into the gutted bathroom we'd passed earlier. We make it just in time. From the main storage room, a shaft of light slices through the dark.

The man's steps echo through the hall.

My nails dig into Andres's arm, and I force myself to grab hold of his jacket instead as we move toward the bathroom window. Our shoes stick to the floors, and I know he's going to hear us because it's impossible to get around without stepping on something broken or slippery or disgusting.

There's a crash outside in the main storage area. The man's speaking into his phone. *I don't sense her. Maybe she hasn't been here in a while.* It sounds like he's about to go, but then he tells the person on the other line to shut up, he hears something.

He hears us. He has to hear us. All I hear is us.

Andres slowly wedges the window open, and it lets out a small pop. We tense. It's an agonizingly slow process, but eventually, he manages to get the window half open. We're squeezed together right under the window, in the shower stall that smells of piss doused with something more overwhelming . . . something putrid and cloying sweet like rot. Like rancid, maggoty meat. There are flies everywhere, landing on my arm, crawling over my face and neck. They're in my hair. I might scream any second.

The window creaks, and Andres gives up. It's too risky.

His face completely drains of color. It's impossible to tell if it's his fear I taste or mine. "I'm going to have to ram open the window. It's going to be loud and you're going to have to jump. I'll be right behind you."

My gut is twisting and riling and threatening to spill everything I have in my stomach.

"You've got this, Delfi. You're the toughest person I know. Are you ready?"

I nod shakily. "Open it."

Andres wrenches the window open with a loud splintering crack and there's no way in hell the guy didn't hear. He's a brujo, so for all I know he can envision our next steps. He could be the one las Palomas sent and there's a whole squad of them on the way.

We don't wait around to find out. I fling myself out the window, falling like five feet and landing hard on my side. I spring to my feet again, Andres tumbling out after me. There's a shout, the sound of running feet. The brujo's spotted us. We won't make it back to Andres's bike.

A gunshot rings out.

Andres throws himself over me, but it didn't hit either of us. We look around. The sound of a door banging open splinters the night, ripping what remains of my nerves to shreds.

The brujo is outside with us now. He must've gone out another door. For a moment, his face is in full view and shock ripples through his features when he spots me. It's Teardrop. The man with de Armas blood.

"Go!" Andres startles me out of my frozen state, and I book it with everything I've got into the woods, Andres right behind me. Hands at my back, urging me to run faster.

Teardrop shot at me. My own blood shot at me.

We cut through the trees. The branches claw my cheeks, my shoulders. As hard as we're running, I can hear Teardrop's feet crashing over dead leaves, getting closer and closer.

I plunge through the forest. Through the dark. Maldeados whip past, tugging me forward, and I'm worried they might give away where I am. Can Teardrop see them too?

We finally reach the public boat ramps—completely empty. A few feet away, the windows to the bay's waterfront restaurant are dark. No one around who could help.

I don't know where to go. Beneath the docks, in the sloshing black water? Inside one of the boats moored at the pier's end?

"I have an idea," I say to Andres. "But you're not going to like it." I run toward the slippery edge of a boat ramp closest to the dockside restaurant, Andres at my heels.

"What are you doing? We have to hide!" He tries tugging me away, but I gather the largest rock I can find and aim it at the restaurant window. The rock soars through the air and crashes through the glass.

After a second, the sweet sound of an alarm peals.

"Let's go!" I pull Andres with me, the maldeados pushing me toward the water. I whisper for them to go, leave. And they do.

We slip down the filmy boat ramp, dive toward the murky unknown. We swim as far as the end of a dock, where an old, tied-up boat offers cover. It's tethered to a mooring pole attached to the pier, covered in prickly barnacles. We swim under the wooden pier and cling onto the pole, where the shadow of the boat can keep us out of the harbor lights.

For a while we don't hear anything but the wail of the alarm and the sound of police sirens. Then we hear the footsteps above us, quiet, searching. As we tread, my mouth fills with salt water and that overwhelming taste of tobacco.

We barely make a ripple, gripping onto the barnacled pillar supporting the dock, so we don't kick our feet. Seaweed and garbage drifts near my face, tangles around my arms like eels.

Andres shields my body with his, arms wrapped around me, clinging to the pillar while I cling to him. It leaves him more vulnerable if the brujo does find us, but I'm also pressed hard against the post. There's a sharp sting on my shoulder as a barnacle pierces my skin.

Teardrop still hasn't seen us. He calls out in Spanish, "Come out! I know you're here!"

I don't understand why he was at a boatyard associated with the boat Idaly was on the night of her death. Why he's chasing us, and why he shot at me. I came expecting to find out more about the killer—and I run into him. I think we got it wrong. He might work for las Palomas, but I'm no longer sure if Teardrop is the hunted or the hunter.

One long shadow wavers above us. The tremble of boots. Through the dock slats, I can make out Teardrop's outline. His chin-length hair. The brujo hesitates right above us.

He whispers something into the night. The alarm is so loud I strain to hear a string of Spanish words that resonate in my chest. A trabajo.

I gasp quietly as something latches on to me, as surely as if I'd been hooked with a reel, as if he branded me with magic. Then it's gone. Teardrop's footsteps slowly recede, fading away into the blazing night.

We wait until we see blue and red lights overwhelm the dark, after the police have gone inside the restaurant to investigate, giving us the chance to wade out of the water.

We can't risk going back to the boatyard for Andres's bike, so instead we begin walking back, using his still-functioning iPhone to order a car.

On the ride back, neither of us says a word. Instead of feeling like we've escaped, I feel as if I've led Teardrop right to me.

TWENTY-THREE

Cuba, March 25, 1980

ANITA

The day of the initiation had finally arrived. Anita had foolishly allowed herself to hope that she and her friends would be long gone before then. But there was no escaping this.

Mamá Ortí had kept her isolated from everyone since the tracking ritual, and now she had been traveling for hours, driven up a long, winding mountain road overlooking nothing but emerald jungle. She wasn't even sure what city they were in anymore. The militants who picked her and her mother up had yet to say a word. Perhaps angry they were forced to chauffeur el Comandante's aquelarre around when the cities were full of protesters boldly proclaiming their dissatisfaction with the government despite the deadly consequences of doing so. But the militants had their orders.

Anita's stomach was twisted in knots, the nausea made worse by the steep drops and sudden curves of the mountain road. She'd heard stories of people who stood against the revolución taking an "accidental" dive off mountains like these. Rumors about men and women who'd disappeared off the face of the earth for going against el Comandante's regime. Anita eyed the rifles mounted on the side of the van doors warily.

Mamá Orti placed a hand on her leg. Anita glanced down at the touch, surprised. Either it was an unusual show of affection from her mother, or a reminder to remain still. Anita willed herself to breathe deeply until the jeep pulled up to an enormous building waiting at the very end of the path.

There were other unmarked jeeps parked outside. More militants than usual, an increase in security because of all the political turmoil. The building was at least five stories tall, ringed with concrete ribs that strangely reminded her of the exterior of a cathedral. It looked abandoned, but the doors featured la Paloma Eterna. Looking at the symbol, Anita felt just as trapped as the bird and snake. Ready to be devoured. Dread gnawed at her insides. Everything inside her screaming to run. *Pretend, lie, whatever it takes to get through this before we can leave for good.*

One of the militants opened Anita's door and escorted her and Mamá Orti up the steps to the building's entrance. The other militants looked uncomfortable, as they often did when made to work under las Palomas' direction. But, like her, they had little choice. All in service to el Comandante.

Anita searched for the familiar crop of tightly curled hair and amber eyes, the soothing sight of Gilberto. Or Idaly and Emiliano. Anyone to make her feel as if she weren't so alone. But they must've already been inside.

The doors opened and Anita felt her stomach turn to stone.

"This is your future, Ana," her mother said. "Remember what I've taught you. Today, you show them you are a de Armas and they are *nothing*. Today is not the day to be distracted. Ojos al la tierra, niña."

As they continued walking, Anita kept her eyes to the earth as promised, wondering what it would be like to have had a loving mother, one who felt concern and care for her in this moment of initiation into a society she didn't want to join, to protect a dictator she didn't support.

Her mother held her head high as they entered the ceremony site, as striking as the Virgin María carved from marble but without her tenderness. Anita had expected the ceremony site would be dark, filled with candles, animal skulls, and the metallic scent of her mother's divining shed. Instead, the space was cavernous, concrete, perhaps an abandoned hospital or a gutted factory. Anita did not find the presence of spirits here.

Mamá Orti brought Anita down a long, dark hallway where two vasallos waited, their slight frames swimming in their robes. Anita realized they were girls, long-lashed and younger than she was. They held out a bloodred robe in their hands.

Anita shivered. The girls approached her with blank looks, as if they were hollowed out of anything human. Their hands went to her clothes and Anita yelped, backing away.

"Está bien," her mother reassured her. "Here, you leave everything behind." She walked back into the main, cavernous room, leaving Anita alone with the stone-faced girls.

The vasallos grasped her clothes again, their vacant eyes stamped with dark circles. This time, she allowed them to undress her. She couldn't stop the tears as she stood there, bare and shivering, touched by indifferent, icy hands. The robe they placed over her shoulders nearly sank her. Its weight was overbearing. It was the physical weight of inevitability. They made her remove her elekes of the orishas and even her gold cross. After securing the hood over Anita's head, the girls ushered Anita back into the main room that was now filled with the rest of las Palomas. She caught her mother, standing back in the shadows along with the other three Elders. There was a gap where Elder Madroño and his initiate would've stood had he not defected.

A single light shone on an empty chair in the center, where she saw the three other red-robed initiates waiting—Gilberto, Idaly, and Emiliano. She stepped toward the center, facing Gilberto, while Idaly and Emiliano faced each other, the four of them arranged in a cross.

Gilberto shifted to peer at Anita from beneath his hood. She could see the urge to run written across his face. She knew he wanted to push through the circle of Elders, take her by the hand and disappear.

She looked away. It was too late for any of that. Their only hope was to make it through the ceremony.

The Elders began to pray, and she felt their chants run through her, rising in pitch. There was an oil drum lit with fire in one corner where some vasallos stood. She tensed when she heard the scrape of metal, then the sound of something dripping, soft, like water or candle wax. Or blood. She didn't turn her head to look.

As the wave of smoke from the fire thickened the room, the maldeados materialized.

She felt them everywhere, the room filled with the dominated spirits.

Was this truly her fate? Anita had hoped that maybe her brother was right, maybe there was another way to use her magia del alma. Another path. But what if there was only this?

In the corner of the room, Anita saw a vasallo hold an iron branding rod up to the fire. La Paloma Eterna glowed a fiery red. The Elders' words finally caught up with her. It was un amaro—a trabajo that would tie them to las Palomas with a mark on their flesh. She felt herself go faint.

If she was marked, there was nowhere she could go where they couldn't find her. She would be shackled to las Palomas and to Cuba. Like Elder Madroño, there would be no corner of the earth where she could hide. *No.*

The maldeados moved around her, swirling near her wrists, her ankles. The chorus of the Elders' voices grew even louder, agitating the spirits, quickening her heart.

From the dark, the Elders appeared, stepping up to their charge. One Elder per initiate. She felt her mother's presence over her shoulder, the cloying smoke of her cigar constricting her throat like a collar. Mamá Orti was bathing her in the smoke, not preparing Anita for a cleansing but for a ceremony that would take over her life.

Anita could hear them all. Not only the Elders' chanting, but the maldeados—the faded, corrupted spirits of the dead. Some shrieked, others chittered, but they all asked for something in one pleading wave.

"Have you found—"

"Help me, I'm—"

"Where am I—"

She didn't know how to make it stop. How to help. Her hands pressed over her ears as the room spun.

Anita felt a hand on her shoulder and staggered back. Her mother grasped Anita's hand, and her touch burned as she ran a black-tinted palm down Anita's face.

She spoke, her voice enhanced by her magia del alma, *"Acepta—"*

Anita didn't have time to react. Another Elder, his eyes the same hazel color as Emiliano's, appeared, grim-faced and looming. A knife gleamed in his hand. *"Obedece."*

The Elder turned Anita's hand, dragging the blade across the flesh of her palm. She cried out as a stinging pain vibrated up her body. She could hear the others now too, their shouts echoing in the dark.

Shuttering like a deck of cards, the face of all four Elders appeared before her, one after the other.

"Acepta, obedece," their voices merged. "Por todo tu vida hasta la muerte."

Finally, a striking older man with coal-black eyes stepped forth. Gilberto's father. "Speak," he commanded. "What must you do?"

She didn't want to say it. Not as the screams of the spirits amplified around her.

"Free me—"

"I'm lost—"

She didn't want to, but she had no choice. She was her mother's daughter. Her heart turned to stone.

"Acepta, obedece . . ." She clenched her fists. "Por todo mi vida hasta mi muerte."

For all her life until her death.

Her mother squeezed Anita's cut hand over a wooden bowl, her blood to be mingled with the others, to be thrown in the fire that would heat the branding iron.

At the last second, Anita tried to rear back, silently pleading with her mother but Mamá Orti's grip only tightened.

It was then she heard the muffled scream, not from her own throat but from Elder Madroño as he was dragged into the room, bleeding from his eyes, mouth, and ears.

TWENTY-FOUR

Miami, November 20, 2016

DELFI

Three rings. Four rings. Come on, Lela. *Please.* Answer. I know it's late and that she usually silences her phone for bed but god I wish she'd just answer—even if it's to tell me to fuck off. Or in her case, fudge off. Anything to let me know she's okay, and that Teardrop hadn't suddenly shown up at our house looking for me because I'd uncovered his boatyard hideaway.

I thought Teardrop would be the good guy, but I'm not so sure. What could he have been doing there? Could he be off on a rampage, tracking all his old friends including our mom because they left las Palomas? Or maybe they all left together and Teardrop's only trying to protect himself since he's next on las Palomas hit list? Maybe he thinks reconnecting with Mami would help, but why hasn't he approached us then? Instead, he tried to shoot at me. He didn't know I was also a de Armas, but still.

The phone finally stops ringing and my sister's groggy little voice mumbles, "Hello?"

"Lela, it's me!"

I hear a rustle as she sits up. "Are you okay?"

"I'm fine," I say. "I'm fine. Are *you*?"

"Yeah, everything's . . . good. Why are you calling so late? Are you coming home?"

I can't risk going home tonight. I still feel Teardrop's whispered words in my chest—tugging me back the farther we drove away. Whether it's a trabajo to track me or not, I can't risk bringing the threat back to my family right now. Not until I'm sure Teardrop or las Palomas won't suddenly appear. I'll call Zuela in the morning and see what she thinks.

"No, I'll explain everything tomorrow. Meet me in the gardens in the morning. I'm—I'm so glad you picked up."

"You're scaring me."

Good. I don't want to scare her, but she needs to be on alert. "It'll be okay," I say instead. "Make sure the doors are locked and get some sleep. I'll see you in the morning."

Lela gives a big yawn. "Okay. Don't do anything reckless, Delf."

Too late. We say good night and I give Andres his phone back.

"Don't worry, we'll keep an eye out," he says. He hesitates at the door of his apartment, hand poised to turn the key. "And, I'm sorry about the mess."

He glances back. Finally, he's able to meet my eyes. On the ride back, my mouth had filled with the taste of everything from acidy fear to saccharine concern and the sharp, smoky taste of interest, that curiosity that always clings to him.

Tonight unraveled something between us. He'd offered for me to spend the night at his place instead of having me risk going home. He'd braced himself, waited for the bite of my refusal, or worse, the smugness he'd come to expect from me. But I was too scared, anything caustic carved out of me. I'd thanked him, grateful to have somewhere to go. A place where I wouldn't need to explain myself.

Especially since the night had brought up more questions than answers. Like why was that picture in the boatyard? The basin of water suggested some kind of containment trabajo, which could have been done to protect the people in the photo—or to track them all down.

Andres opens the door to his apartment with a wan smile. I take off my sodden shoes by the door and pad over to the quaint living room. A stack of pillows serves as a couch on the floor, next to a scratched-up dining table piled with papers, textbooks, and a coffee mug with a stale croissant. The black screen of a television bears witness to the scene.

It's bare and lonely. It's reserved and comfortable.

And it's entirely him.

Now I'm the one who feels unsteady, feeling the heady pressure of his gaze as I move around the room. I pause near the table, catching the title of one of the books—a study on occult practices and beliefs. I snatch my hand back. Was this for research?

I think back to our conversation at the beach when he mentioned his grandmother was a medium and a santera. He's definitely gone into this with more information than he's led on.

Then again, so have I.

"Is there a bathroom?" I gesture down to my body. The salt water has dried my clothes to a stiff mess. "Maybe clothes I can borrow?"

He drops his keys and phone onto the kitchen counter, a muscle at his jaw working. Peeling off his jacket, he reveals his equally clingy and soggy shirt beneath. "Yeah, I'll get you something." He points down the hall. "Bathroom's to the left."

"Great." I suck on my teeth. "Thanks."

The awkward tension between us has to be because of what we went through tonight. It's like the disorientation after a bomb drops when everything's gone to shit, you're wading through a haze of smoke and ash, and you're still not sure you made it out in one piece.

That's what this is.

It's why he can't look at me. It's why my heart tries to punch its way out of my chest when I look at him now. Why I don't have a single rational thought to work with. Except the loudest ones pounding in my head—*he'd been willing to sacrifice himself for you. He said you're the toughest person he knows.*

No. Nope, not going there. This is simply sexual tension heightened by adrenaline. The Sánchez Curse doesn't apply to being "in lust," I've proven that much. And after the night I had, I deserve to catch a break.

I walk toward the bathroom and call back, "You know, you're welcome to join me."

He glances up. His face lights up as if those simple words washed away the cloudy uncertainty between us.

This is comfortable. This is familiar, and he wanted it too.

But he shakes his head, struggling to suppress his grin. "Take a cold shower. I'll leave the clothes by the sink."

I shrug. "Your loss."

It's only when I shut the door behind me that the smirk slides off my face. I lean against the doorframe, press a hand to the nape of my throat, and let the entirety of the night bring me to my knees.

◆　◆　◆

I'm not sure how long I've been in here, but I'm starting to prune. I've finally managed to stop shaking even though my heart will probably never settle back to a normal cadence. When I release my hair from the towel, the smell of Andres surfaces. He had only a bottle of generic all-in-one shampoo and conditioner but it got the scent of salt water and warehouse off me.

Wincing, I press an oversized Band-Aid to the cut on my arm from when my shoulder struck the barnacled dock. Luckily, the guy keeps a fully stocked first aid kit under the sink like an ex-Marine. I pull his plain white T-shirt over my head. I'll need to let my bra dry, so it would've been nice if the shirt he lent me wasn't so thin, but again, I shouldn't complain.

Checking my reflection, I doubt he'll complain either.

I tighten the cords on the cotton sweatpants, roll up the bottoms until they rest over my ankles. It's the loosest thing I've ever worn, and it's like I'm enveloped in a cloud.

I emerge from the bathroom in a puff of vapor to find Andres in the kitchen. He's changed into dry clothes, and I smile when I see a bowl of dry rice, my phone buried halfway deep in an effort to revive it. He's facing away from me when I approach, peering down at something on the counter, but I know he senses me by the way the hard planes of his back tense.

"What you got there?" I lean on the kitchen counter, craning my neck to see what's captured his attention so fully. My jaw drops as I study the picture. "No way! I thought I dropped it."

It's the picture of Idaly and the group. The one I dug out of that basin of sand and water.

"You did. I picked it up. It's evidence." When he looks at me, his gaze travels down to my white shirt before snapping back up. The tops of his ears redden. Clearing his throat, he uses his pinkie to gently point at Idaly's pretty face, alive and teeming with a determination I never witnessed in my visions.

"This is the woman you saw," he says, and I nod. Then his finger slides to the man with an arm around Idaly's shoulder. His features fit the edges of my memory like a puzzle. The same man from her locket—Emiliano. He's tall and slim, with a head of light-colored hair and a long, straight nose. "And this man was the first victim. Same marks as her, and the same landlord confirmed he was married to Idaly."

I already know that, but I never found out how exactly he died. "What happened to him?" I ask softly.

"He jumped off a roof in Wynwood, or he was pushed. Another untraceable ghost with that brand on his neck. Same elements, different scenario." He presses his knuckles to his mouth, thinking.

A wave of sadness crests over me. Another one I couldn't save.

"Back at the boatyard, you said you'd seen them in your visions. Did you see their murders, too?" Andres asks.

I push off the counter. "I saw Idaly die, but not who did it. I wasn't even sure it was real until Idaly turned up on the beach." My jaw hardens. I can tell he wants to ask more, dig as much as possible until he uncovers a motive or a suspect. Unfortunately, I don't have much to offer. He must read the exhaustion in me, like I can taste it from him, because he doesn't push.

My gaze seeks the picture again, focusing on another person in the group. Teardrop, the guy that could be my family. The one that possibly tried to kill us tonight and placed some kind of trabajo on me. He wears a pair of flared slacks and a striped button-up, straight from the eighties. His presence demands attention. The others shift toward him as if he were magnetic. But it's his eyes that draw me in the most—the slightly drooped corners, the rich brown color evident even in the picture. The birth mark right under his eye is like the first splash of milk in coffee.

"That's the guy that was chasing us," I say, and tap the photo. I keep the fact we're possible blood relatives to myself and pray that Andres doesn't pick up on the resemblance.

"So they all knew each other," Andres says, eyes widening as he peers down at the man's face. "Maybe he's hunting his old friends because of some vendetta?"

"I was thinking the same thing," I say. "He wasn't exactly friendly. Or he could just be trying to protect himself from whoever killed Idaly and her husband."

Andres's gaze cuts to mine and he points out Silver Fox. "These are the guys you texted me about."

I rub at my face. "Yeah. We thought he or Teardrop could be the next ones in trouble but I'm honestly not sure anymore."

Idaly's last words were that she had to warn *them*. But whether she was trying to keep her old friends safe is anyone's guess.

Andres shifts his weight on the counter so he's facing me, flipping the photograph so we no longer have to look at them.

"Do you have anything to eat?" I ask.

He looks surprised, then smiles as he slips the picture under a book. I note exactly where he places the book—I need to find a way to get the photo into Lela's hands.

He pads over to the kitchen barefoot. My mom would freak if she saw bare feet over tile, but I'm not my mom, and I'm not about to scold him for it—it's actually kind of sexy.

Ugh, I sound like I have a foot fetish.

I hear a loud crash, and I scream, ducking down to the floor. *They're here, oh my god they found us.* Andres comes running over to me, panicked until we both see the mess of DVDs on the floor.

He rubs a hand over his face. "Shit, that scared me, too. Sorry about that. That stand is always falling over." He moves to help me up, but I wave him off, mortified.

I clear the panicky copper taste from my mouth. "Those things are obsolete anyway."

He watches me carefully. "You're right. I'll donate them tomorrow."

I nod at this. As if that takes care of everything. As if that's all I need to stop feeling terrified.

"Are you hungry?" He heads back to the kitchen and opens the empty fridge, "I don't have much here, but maybe there's something open for delivery."

I sigh and start opening up his cabinets. Pathetic. Plastic silver-ware, billions of soy sauce packets, and cups collecting dust, and—oh, this can work.

"Please tell me you have a pan. Maybe some oil?" I brace myself.

A little-boy grin graces his face. "Those I have."

His expression thaws something in my chest. The pureness of it, the way he loses some of that intensity that's so captivating but intimidating.

"Great, pancakes it is," I say, holding up the box I'd found. My fingers brush against his as I take the pan and oil from him. His eyes narrow into a look that takes me back to the days when we had just started dating. Before he knew what kind of person I was. Back when I was something rare and desirable.

"You don't have to look so worried," I say, turning away quickly. "I can handle pancakes. Besides, I like a little dessert before bed."

He blushes, and I smile. This is safer.

"Fine," he says. "Make whatever you want. I'll go set up my bed for you. I'll sleep out here."

I point a scavenged plastic spoon at him. "I am not taking your bed."

"I'm not going to let you sleep on the floor," he says with finality, going into his room.

Fine. The least I can do is accept his gentlemanly act. I peruse his pantry and score a can of leche condensada with the graphic of a woman with a breadbasket over her head.

This is going to be fire.

Stabbing through the can with a knife, I pour a swirl of the condensed milk into the batter and make perfect circles with it on the pan. Each pancake comes out with just the right amount of brown edges and spongy middles.

I make space on his kitchen table, moving around books and files. It's obvious he's in school—I angle my head to the side—and, by the looks of it, he's taking some criminology and law courses. I flip one of the books open and snap it shut when I see a graphic crime scene photo.

Okay. That's enough snooping.

He emerges from his room, summoned by the scent of the steaming pancakes. I push the other plate toward him with a fork.

His mouth quirks. "Thanks."

"You're welcome." I watch as he takes his first bite. His eyes shut, and he releases a resounding noise of satisfaction deep in his throat that tightens my stomach.

He pauses before taking another bite. "This is amazing. What'd you add to this?"

"Secret ingredient."

He grunts but we keep eating, devouring our plates in minutes. We lean back in our chairs, drugged by the sugary carbs into a state of languor.

Suddenly, I taste the acidity of fear breaking through the syrupy taste. I look up to see Andres hesitating. "By the way, if you wanted to talk about tonight—"

I hold up a hand. "I'm good. I'd rather not. Not now."

He bobs his head at this. "Noted."

I'm exhausted and mentally drained. Yet, all I can think about at this moment is the way a bit of syrup shines on Andres's lip. How a beauty mark I never noticed before graces the small dip at the base of his throat. How his shirt drapes across the hard muscles of his chest.

And the way my throat cloys with warm, gooey honey every time he looks at me. My gaze flicks to him as I taste his desire.

When I stretch out of the chair, his eyes watch me, trace me, *scorch me.*

My mouth opens to say something, anything, but Andres gets up abruptly and makes his way to the living room. "You must be tired. I'll let you sleep."

My shoulders sink because even though the honeyed flavor of his desire pools inside my mouth, he's holding back, and I have to respect that. "G'night."

He settles on his back onto the couch cushions and stares up at the ceiling. "Good night, Delfi."

I drag myself to his room.

The smell of him bathes everything, washes over me. There's a worn dresser and mirror taking up most of the space, a framed picture of him on a mountaintop, and one of him in graduation robes smiling brilliantly with two beaming parents—Detective Douche acting human for once.

But no girlfriends I note, a little too relieved. Not that I have any right to be.

I pick up his jacket hanging over the back of an office chair, and I can't help it; I hold it up to my face. I glance up at the mirror, catching the longing in my reflection, and hastily drop the jacket to the floor.

Bed. I need to go to bed. I almost died tonight, and I'm not thinking clearly.

I flop onto the mattress on the floor, made up with crisp, wine-red sheets.

I shouldn't be here. I shouldn't have invaded his space and gotten him involved in any of this. Whether he's been investigating this on his own, I don't think he knows the full extent of what las Palomas can do, and even I don't know how exactly Teardrop and Silver Fox fit into all of this. The haunting image of my mom delivering the warning swirls around my head. No se metan donde salir no puedan.

Right now, I'm breaking my biggest rule: Get out if it feels right. Get out if he means anything at all to me.

Get out.

Get out.

I sit up, scramble for my bag, and head for the door. I'm about to fling it open when there's a knock.

My hand stills on the doorknob. I suck in a breath, silently counting to three before slowly opening it.

Andres stands right outside. His hair a fury as if he'd ran hands through it over and over again. In the space of seconds, something has changed, as if something caged inside him had just been released. The air crackles with a wild energy.

I will come undone if he keeps looking at me like that.

Andres comes closer, so close that his heat is mine, melding onto my skin.

"I'm not sure what I'm doing," he says.

"Ditto."

I reach out and yank him toward me by the shirt. Andres grabs my waist, consuming the last bit of space between us.

I pull him even closer until he's toppling into the room. Until we're falling

falling

falling.

His bed captures us, dips to cup our bodies. I wriggle his shirt up. He lifts his arms, letting me pull it over his head. Letting me do anything.

"I want to kiss you," I breathe.

He swallows, and nods.

I push him onto his back, tumbling onto him. I straddle his waist and he looks up, waiting. Vulnerable.

Without taking my eyes from his, I remove my shirt. Cold air cuts through my skin and burns to mist.

He sucks in a breath as he takes me in. All of me—slashed with darkness, striped by the light of the streetlamp outside. Like a blank page waiting to be written. His face lights with desire, and I trace his lips with my fingers. The curves of his jaw.

As I lower my mouth to his, I pause. I want him to make a choice, even if it's a little one.

And he does.

His lips are treacherously soft. The sweep of his tongue on mine singes like ice. I could live in this kiss. *This is just lust.* The words play over my mind like a mantra.

We grasp at each other, and he runs his hands up my arms until I wince when his fingers snag on my bandage.

"You're bleeding." He sits up, still holding me in his lap.

"It's nothing," I say, trying to meet his lips again, but he moves away, stretches to turn on a lamp.

I flinch away from the bright light, feeling as if I've been doused with cold water.

"When'd you get hurt?" He inspects my arm.

"It's not that bad." But then I notice that I have, in fact, blood running down my arm.

"Not bad? You're bleeding like crazy."

He gets up off the bed, and I groan. Every flushed part of my body going cool. I gather his comforter over my chest. He comes back with an even larger first aid kit than the one in his guest bathroom.

"I already put a Band-Aid on it," I say, practically pouting.

He sits cross-legged in front of me. "Well, it didn't work." Andres uses a wad of cotton to sweep up the blood off my arm, sending a wave of shivers over my skin. He winces when he peels off the useless bandage. "When did this happen?"

And just like that, the night's events crash over me. My knees go weak, and it's a good thing I'm already sitting on the bed.

"When we were in the water. I think one of the barnacles cut me."

He curses. "When I pressed you against the pier?"

I flinch as he cleans up the wound with an alcohol wipe. "Yes, Andres. When you shielded my body with yours like a damn Captain America."

He chuckles at this, looking up at me with a softness in those earthy eyes that kills me.

I tilt my head, going serious. "I never did say thank you."

He seals my cut with a sturdier bandage. "You don't need to." A half-smile forms on his lips. "Just doing my duty."

The moment's still charged and heated, but by something gentle and sweet. I savor it on my tongue like the most delicious fruit.

I can't help it. I reach forward and whisper a kiss onto his mouth. "Thank you."

He touches the ends of my hair. "You're welcome. I hope you know . . . what I said in the warehouse, about you being the toughest person I've ever met . . . It's true. Sometimes your strength scares me. It's fierce and overwhelming, but it's what I like most about you."

"I'm not always strong," I say. "At least I don't want to be."

His gaze remains fixed on my face. "I know. Sometimes, I don't either."

We both know we're treading on thin ice here. Any movement and everything will shatter completely with the cracks already placed there by our past.

Andres breaks free first. His hand drops from mine and I know it's for the best. It has to be.

"I'm going to take a shower," he says. "I'll see you in the morning."

Once he's gone, I wait before creeping outside to his living room. It's already daylight outside, and I hurry to gather my things, listening to make sure the shower is still running.

I hurry over to his dining table and write the only clue I can give him for now on a piece of loose paper: *Las Palomas (Cuba)*.

This way, it's not stealing, but an exchange of information. I need something in return. I know the picture is around here somewhere. I move around books, flip through more horrific crime texts. The water's still on, so I know he's—

"Looking for something?"

I scream. Like a drama thriller wife-found-her-husband's-lover-with-an-axe-in-her-bedroom scream. "Jesus Flipping Christ, Andres, are you trying to kill me?"

Then I notice what he's wearing. Or not wearing. One of his hands holds a flimsy looking towel around his waist, which does nothing to hide the exquisite cut of his body. The muscles on his lower abdomen form an arrowhead that practically demands I look in a certain direction. He's most assuredly trying to murder me right now.

He clears his throat. "Is this what you wanted?"

"Um, what?" For a second, I think he means something completely different, but then I see the photo in his hand. The one not clutching the towel.

I almost say no. Almost apologize, but isn't it better this way? Isn't it better for him to be disappointed in me yet again, to place me firmly in the *Nothing More* space? I can't trust myself when it comes to him. Because as much as I've lied to myself over and over again, I know deep down I like him. Like *really* like him. Too much to let him get hurt.

"What do you want me to say?" I force my body to go languid, a cat that's scratched but still wants to be petted.

"I would've given it to you if you'd asked." He smiles, but I can tell he's hurt. "Here, take it."

He keeps his distance but places the picture on the table. "But I want it back. Three days and you bring it back. I already took a picture of it with my phone, but if the face scanner can't pick it up, I need the original."

"Fine," I say. "Deal."

"Fine," he says, jaw working. "And your phone's alive again. I left it on the counter."

"Thanks," I say. Without making eye contact, I walk by him, grab my phone, pick up the picture, and slip out of his apartment.

Outside, I shoot a quick text to Lela asking her to meet me and clench my phone to my chest. Like a mantra, I repeat in my head that it's better this way. There could never be anything more between us.

Still, the bitter thought does nothing to ease the pain in my chest.

TWENTY-FIVE

Miami, November 20, 2016

LELA

I don't know what I was thinking getting involved with all this in the first place. Gilberto's warning rings in my head like a reoccurring nightmare. *I suggest you keep any future visions to yourself. For you and your family's sake.*

The conversation with Gilberto yesterday has replayed in my head about a million times. By now, he's definitely skipped town. I don't know how to tell Delfi that I've lost our primary lead, and that Gilberto didn't even take my warning seriously. At least we learned Silver Fox's real name, and though he didn't outright say it, he knew our mom. He knew Idaly and Emiliano before they were killed.

Ethan grabs hold of my hand, and we tread the pathways while I wait for Delfi to show after her urgent text from this morning. Every time we've taken this walk through the gardens of Cauley Square, I secretly hope the labyrinth of foliage and antique surprises will seal us in. That we'll be closed off from the world for a while longer. But it never does, and this place is no longer the safe haven it used to be.

We stop a good distance away from the small chapel where Delfi and I found our mom. I still have vivid flashes of her blank eyes as she delivered las Palomas' warning.

Ethan takes us over to a wrought-iron bench with vintage wagon wheels on each side and pats the space beside him. I rest my head on his shoulder, legs swung over his legs, and my arm looped through his.

He tucks me closer, kissing the top of my head. "Have you thought about what you're going to tell Delfi?"

I groan, burying my face in his shoulder. "I don't know. I don't even know if the trabajo to protect him would've worked. And what would I have done anyway? Rub spiritual grease on his forehead and chant?"

Ethan grimaces. "Yeah, that's weird."

"I felt like it was all BS. Like it was a fool's errand, and Gilberto knew it too."

Clearly Zuela doesn't know what she's doing either and Delfi keeps trusting this woman, eyes closed. If Zuela's right, and there is a Cuban secret society hunting down brujos, Gilberto, Teardrop, and whoever else is in trouble will need more than an oil tincture.

Now he's gone. I think about how Delfi would have handled the situation. I should've demanded answers about what he knows about my mom, about us. A part of me feels like he recognized me, but Gilberto was tight-lipped and paranoid with an expert poker face. Which I guess I can't blame him for, considering. It's clear by Gilberto's reaction though that our help isn't needed nor wanted, and he wasn't willing to help us in return.

"You did the best you could," Ethan says, twirling the frayed hems of my cutoff shorts.

I realize how exhausted he looks, and I wonder if he got any sleep last night. When he looks down at me again, his eyes are puffy, red in the corners.

I want to ask if anything's wrong. If he's still been isolating from his family. I flash to the memory of my sister's numb face when they called to tell her about Christian. All at once, the fear of the curse strikes at my chest like a bullet.

His thumb comes up to trace my lip, the wind rustling the trees as if the garden were a song. A warning.

"Ofelia Mila!" My sister's voice clashes against us. Pops the bubble of silence.

Ethan and I spring apart as Delfi runs up the cobblestoned path. Ethan jumps up from the bench, studying a nearby flower with the intensity of a botanist.

"There you are." Delfi's wearing an oversized shirt and sweats and looks exhausted. She shuffles forward and plops down on the bench, right on my feet, forcing me to make room.

Delfi does a double take toward Ethan who waves half-heartedly.

"Oh. What's up? I didn't know you were here too." She looks at me with a pair of raised brows. "Cozy spot, ain't it?"

I give her clothes a pointed look, ignoring her question. "Eventful night?"

She throws her head back and lets out a pained groan. "You wouldn't even believe."

"Same."

This makes Delfi sit up again. "Really? Spill. Did you scope out the place with the red crane?"

"Yeah, we found the place." I glance at Ethan. "And . . . I met Silver Fox. His name's actually Gilberto."

Delfi's eyes look ready to pop out of her head. "You confronted him without me?"

"Gilberto had already packed up and was about to leave, I didn't have a choice," I say defensively.

"You could've called me first!"

"I did! I was up all night staring at my phone waiting for a response from you until I got your call at 3 a.m. from a random number, acting all cryptic."

Ethan clears his throat. "I'll let you two catch up," he says, and there's a veil of sadness over his features that's unusual for him. Something beyond disappointment that coils my insides. "I'll call you?" He directs the question at me.

"Okay . . . sure. I'll wait for your call later then."

He waves, and in my heart, and only there where it's safe, do I tell him not to go, to stay so we can tell Delfi we're together. In my mind, I stride over to him and kiss his beautiful mouth until that pained look disappears. Until I'm sure everything will be all right. But the words stay locked in, finding no purchase in the thick heat of the garden.

Once he's gone, I can tell Delfi wants to say something about Ethan, but I quickly jump into the story of yesterday's bizarre encounter with Gilberto. I describe the memories I saw when Gilberto tried to stop me from entering his place—the dying Cuban dictator in his hospital bed and the robed figures surrounding him, and then how the vision just fizzled out somehow. I tell her how he reacted to the psychic protection juju Zuela made and his reaction when I mentioned the cops.

Delfi grabs my wrist. "What do you mean the visions fizzled out? He cut you off? Can he do that? Like a block?"

An errant wind snakes through the trees, agitating the ferns.

I shrug helplessly. I've been thinking about this, too, but for different reasons. If it's true, and he did block me, then maybe I could learn how to block myself too. I can stop walking around everywhere with my hands tucked close. Stop worrying that I'll pick up a random object that'll make me see things I don't want to know.

Maybe I could even block the curse.

"Let's hope it wasn't permanent." Delfi stands and digs into her pocket. "I was following my own lead last night at an abandoned boatyard. The boat Idaly was on the night she died was registered there. *This* was among all the ritual stuff we found at the boatyard."

"'We' as in you and your ex?"

"Never mind, just see if you can pick anything up." She holds out a photo impatiently. It's an old Polaroid, but I immediately pick out Idaly and Gilberto among the group.

"It's them," I say. I recognize all of them from either visions or dreams. The man at their center with skin like creamed coffee, and eyes that draw you in and hold you there—Teardrop. Someone who possibly shares our blood.

"Are you seeing anything?" she asks.

The picture in my hand is glossy smooth and flimsy thin, but I sense nothing else. No flashes, no memories. I shake my head. "Nothing."

Delfi sighs. "What did he do to you? You should've never gone to see him without me."

"I told you, I didn't have a choice. He wasn't going to stick around much longer." I gesture to her clothes. "Plus, you ditched me for some guy. I just wanted it over with so we can move on with our lives. I'm so sick of this. I went and I warned him, he didn't want our help, case closed."

Delfi stands up, hands curled into fists. "Are you serious? I went out last night for the same reason you did, to find information so we can stop a killer. Not to move on with my life, but to save somebody else's! To keep *us* safe. Andres almost died trying to help me. Don't act like I've been sitting on my ass making out with some guy."

"What do you mean you almost died?" I ask.

"It's fine," she says uncomfortably. "Teardrop showed up at the boatyard, and he had a gun."

"What?" I'm practically yelling. "And you were worried about *me*? So then he's not the victim."

"I'm not sure yet."

I throw my arms up. "Don't you get it? We don't know *anything*. We've been the ones putting ourselves and others in harm's way by asking questions. By digging. There's a reason Mami didn't want us knowing anyone else from her family in Cuba. Don't you think she would've kept in touch if she'd wanted to, if she'd thought it was safe? Besides, we don't know what we're doing yet. Tasting emotions and seeing visions isn't exactly the superpower you think it is."

"That's not all we can do! You just don't want to admit it to yourself. You don't want to learn. We can't just let whatever happened to Idaly happen to Gilberto, or to our possible relative. If you don't care—"

"I never said I don't care!" I hate when Delfi gets in my face like this.

"Then do something about it! Own up to the fact you're a badass bruja and have a community of other people like you, people like Zuela who can tap your potential, who could stand beside us when we offer them *real* help. Don't make that face—maybe if you stop being so thirsty for Ethan for one second, you'd see what you can *actually* do with the gifts you've been given."

My spine goes straight. "Oh that's rich coming from you! Where'd you sleep, Delf? Huh?"

"I haven't slept!"

I get up, stalking through the same garden Ethan and I'd traversed mere hours ago, only now it feels like the heat is too heavy, the shade growing thick with the sense of watchful eyes.

Delfi's right at my heels as we walk home. "Do you want to end up like me? Do you want that guilt hanging over *your* head?"

I take the steps to our apartment two at a time. "Oh my god, you always act like it's not my curse, too. Like I don't know what's at risk."

At the top of the stairs, Delfi yanks me back by my shirt, something she's done since we were kids to get my attention. "You don't know! I'm always shielding you from the most painful parts, but you don't see that because you're too busy thinking about yourself!"

I pull my shirt from her grip. "I've *never* put myself first in this family. I'm always watching over you, making sure you don't get hurt as you're running into things without thinking. So tell me, what don't I know, Delf? Enlighten me, please!"

Her face is a mask of fury. "The fire was Dad's fault!"

I stop. "What?"

Her voice shakes. "The fire at the Eighth Street house wasn't an accident. He *hated* us so much he wanted us to burn. Because of this stupid, *stupid* curse!"

I try to register what Delfi's saying. She might as well have pushed me down the stairs. "No—that's not true. Mom told us what happened, it was a candle—"

Delfi's face pales as if her words have caught up with her. She reaches for my hands, but I pull away again.

"I saw him do it, Lel," she says quietly. "He knew I saw him do it and he didn't even care. Because that's what the curse does to the ones we love—changes them until they don't even know who they are anymore."

Tears push at my eyes, stinging and hot. An unbearable pain spreading through my chest and I don't think I can breathe past it.

"Lela?"

I barge into the apartment in a daze, Delfi close behind, pleading for me to stop.

I stop when I see my mom hunched on the floor, facing us. All my thoughts clear bullet-fast.

She's crouched in front of a broken floorboard, hugging herself like a vise. I pause, wondering why the room is so dark, before realizing that our apartment is full of living shadows. The maldeados weave beneath the doorways, slither under our couch, and slick over our skin.

I flinch as the coolness of them sweep across my cheek. They surround my mom as if waiting for her word. But that's not possible. She can't see them.

"Mami, oh my god!" Delfi's first to react, rushing inside and kneeling in front of her. Mami's eyes are unfocused, checked out. "Lela, help me with her!"

I snap out of it, moving forward to help Mami up. I notice the rotten stench coming from the broken floor. I peer down and hidden under the floorboards are the scattered remnants of mason jars filled with a sticky substance gone dark. I see our princess dolls from when we were kids, covered in the honeyed substance and wrapped in twine. There are tiny maggots crawling over everything.

"Mami . . . what is this?" Delfi asks in a trembling voice.

Instead of answering, Mami topples forward and collapses.

TWENTY-SIX

Cuba, March 25, 1980

ANITA

Anita knew the initiation would test her devotion. Knew it would change everything. But she did not expect this.

"To purge the poison threatening our country, sacrifices will be made. Sacrifices are necessary for the greater good." Her mother addressed the initiates, but Anita knew the message was for her. Mamá Orti gestured toward the bruised and battered man—toward Elder Madroño who was once one of their own. Though no one would believe it by the way las Palomas looked at him now. "This man committed crimes against la revolución. He will rot in a jail cell but his alma can serve a greater purpose."

Anita was trapped, watching the horror unfold before her as the vasallos led Madroño to the center of the room and tied him roughly to a chair. She would go to hell for this. God would surely punish her. Anita was certain.

"Today, a maldeado will be made in your honor. To serve your will and to strengthen your position in la Orden de las Palomas." Mamá

Orti drew her eyes down in disgust at Elder Madroño. A man her mother must've known since she was a child. "And you. Anything you'd like to say?"

Madroño's eyes were too swollen for him to see but he faced Mamá Orti's general direction and spat on the concrete floor. "I am free of all of you. What more could I want?"

Mamá Orti leaned forward and grabbed his chin, sinking her sharp nails into his skin. "I hear Yalené and the children are still in Cuba. Should I pay them a visit and send them your best? Maybe your eldest would like your vacated position?"

The man sank impossibly lower, suddenly meek. "No. No, leave them be. They're of no use to you."

Mamá Orti rose again. "Yes, not a drop of power between them, you said. What a shame. Not every lineage is strong." Madroño and Mamá Orti shared a meaningful look. One that seemed to barter with buried secrets between them. Anita wondered if he'd paid something for his family's freedom. Finally, Mamá Orti turned away and flicked her fingers dismissively. She rejoined the others and a vasallo came forward to tie a grease-stained cloth over Madroño's mouth.

The Elders stood by the fire raging from the oil drum where a vasallo still heated the branding iron. Flames licked high into the perforated ceiling that allowed in black-speckled glimpses of sky. An Elder broke apart to stand before Anita and her friends.

Elder Amoros, Gilberto's father, gestured to the vasallo holding the metal rod high in the air to approach—no.

It was to mark them. They meant to claim them like cattle. A violent tremor worked its way up Anita's legs.

The Elder began with Idaly. Her scream was like a jolt of electricity against Anita's skin. The vasallos held Gilberto down next in case he flinched, though he remained stoic. He met her eyes and mouthed for her to *run*.

She couldn't go through with this. *This* was too much. To take a man's soul to gain power. To brand her friends so brutally. Was this what was expected of her for the rest of her life? To be the regime's blade? That was not who she was. That was not what her gift was meant for. She thought about praying to her orishas, but she was ashamed to call them to this place and invoke their wrath at the twisted use of her abilities.

She couldn't.

"Stop," Anita croaked, but again her voice was too low. Too muffled. The maldeados chittered in her ear. They were as trapped as she was.

The Elders picked up their chant. The swell of their pitch prickled her skin. They circled Madroño, hands upraised. His wild, red-strained gaze met hers as Anita was forced to hear the whimpers of her friends as their necks stung and bled.

The vasallo turned their dead eyes to her next, the iron rod hot in their grip as another held her in place.

Anita felt every bit of her go scorching hot with rage as if at any moment she'd raze this place to ash. Her mind went dark. The force of her magia del alma tearing at her throat. They wouldn't do this. Las Palomas could *not* do this. She would put a stop to it, regardless of the consequences.

Anita closed her eyes and called to the maldeados.

Listen, she told them, and the room went still.

The Elders turned to her and the approaching maldeados as if they could feel the command as well. *Aid me. Listen.* The spirits cried and spun around her, whipping her robe like a sail.

"Ana." Her mother's command was sharp but she ignored it. Even Madroño had gone still.

She could taste the bitterness of her fury. She could hear the rapid heartbeats of the Elders as each maldeado materialized and waited.

The Elders' fear was exquisite.

She savored the look on her mother's face. Anita sensed las Palomas combining their powers, using it to push against her own. She looked toward her friends, realized they had lent her their strength, reinforced her powers with theirs. She pushed back.

Stop them, she commanded the maldeados. And the corrupted spirits knew exactly who she meant. The maldeados clouded around the Elders, forcing them to their knees like pious worshippers. The vasallo dropped the branding iron, the metal going cold and useless. Anita ignored the Elders' cries of surprise and met Gilberto's wide-eyed stare, gesturing to the tied man. Gilberto rushed to release him.

Anita knew she'd crossed a line she could never take back. The combined power of her friends was too intoxicating. She knew with each passing second her control faltered, had only gone this far because of the Elders' surprise. But she couldn't stop now even if she wanted to. Her arms raised, her head tilted back, she drank it all in. For once in her life, she no longer felt weak. She felt invincible.

Gilberto's shout of pain drew her back. Anita opened her eyes. Her mother stood before him with a raised staff and a wrathful expression. In one quick movement, Mamá Orti shoved her palm to his chest and sent Gilberto crashing into a pillar. He slammed into the concrete and crumpled to the ground.

Anita screamed, her control vanishing as the maldeados sprung from her hold and disappeared back to shadows.

She felt the Elders' hold on the spirits fall right back into place, as swift as a guillotine, and the maldeados wound around her arms again, holding her still as Elder Amoros hauled the prisoner up.

Quicker than Anita could cry out, the Elders finished the trabajo that would sever Madroño's spirit from his body. The Elders each ripped a strip of fabric and threw the pieces into the oil drum, sending up a lash of fire.

It was too late.

Anita could already see Madroño's blank stare—empty of anything human. The slithering shape of a new maldeado whipped about the room and joined the roiling dark mass of the others.

Her skin pricked with lingering power as her mother approached.

When Anita lifted her eyes to Mamá Orti's face, she prepared herself for her mother's wrath. Instead, she saw the last thing she ever expected. In her mother's eyes, beyond the admonishment, was something she'd never seen before—a glowing pride.

TWENTY-SEVEN

Miami, November 21, 2016

DELFI

I dreamt of doves last night. Their white creamy bodies elongating and turning to smoke, molding to maldeados. Of hands, small, gloved hands that could belong to Doña Aura or someone else, twisting the maldeados into something ugly and wrong. I dreamt of a bright red moon and my hand reaching out for Lela before she could fall, but all I grasped was her necklace until it snapped.

To say I never want to sleep in a hospital room again is an understatement.

Mami makes a noise in her sleep and my heart twists in on itself. Fear and anger warring for attention. I'm scared I brought this on somehow. That maybe Teardrop had followed Mami home and confronted her. Maybe she *had* been hiding from her family in Cuba. But Teardrop had already been watching us for a while, so why strike now? Did I drive him to it? Once he did that trabajo thing on me at the boatyard, maybe he discovered I was the one there, snooping through things I shouldn't.

But according to the doctors, Mami's been sick for a while now. Another thing she's kept secret. She was dehydrated and anemic, and a sudden drop in blood pressure caused her to faint. Possibly due to stress or a sudden spike of adrenaline. I toy with the black stone of my azabache, gathering its protective warmth and immediately all the warring flavors in my mouth dull until I can relax.

It's impossible that she wasn't aware of the maldeados surrounding her last night. They weren't just present in the room, but seemed to be anticipating her command. What kind of power would it take to draw so many maldeados?

I watch her eyes move behind her lids in restless sleep, and I wonder how I can even trust who she is when everything she's told us has been a lie.

❖ ❖ ❖

By afternoon, we're waiting for the discharge papers. I hate how the entire hospital smells like antibacterial soap and tastes like a nausea-inducing syrup of all the most awful flavors—the acrid flavor of pain, muddied with grief, anger, and confusion. Mami's under strict instructions to rest this week, and I'll make sure she follows through.

"Delfi, siéntate." Mami picks at the Band-Aid on her hand, where they'd put in the IV. I stop pacing and sit on the chair beside her. Lela quietly stares out the hospital window, which only faces the AC units, but she's been like that all night. The tastes coming from her are rotten with misery, and I know I caused it. Her grief for our dad is one I'm all too familiar with, because he's been dead to me since that night too. I've just had more time to let him go.

I have only one parent and my questions for her boil beneath the surface, but I have to tread carefully or Mami will shut like a clamshell.

I watch her nibble on the sugar-free, carb-free, flavor-free cookie they brought her earlier and ask gently. "Mami, what's been going on?"

Lela turns and cuts me a glance. *Don't push it.*

Mami places the cookie down, grimacing. "Nada, I'm fine. You heard the doctor. Stress." Her expression softens as she pats my hand. "I'm a single mother, Delfi. Stress comes with the job, but I'll be okay. I have you two, and that's all I need."

"Yeah, but what about—"

"Ay, Delfi. I'm tried. We'll talk later, okay?"

My jaw clenches, feeling a mixture of sour hurt and betrayal. She goes back to watching a novella but I need to ask about the stuff we found, about the maldeados swirling around her. About the fact that she's a bruja. Lela clears her throat and I go back to pacing until the nurse comes in with the discharge papers and a ready wheelchair.

I'd gone back home this morning once they assured us Mami would be all right and cleaned up the mess of whatever she had been hiding beneath the floorboards. I'd had to fill the hole with boiling water and vinegar to get rid of the maggots first, and I probably stopped to gag a million times, but once I'd cleared those away, I saw the obra for what it was—some kind of ritual for protection. Not magic, not brujería, but a Santería ritual.

I mean, she's always been private about her Santería practice, and always felt it best we don't get involved, and we respected that because the practice is very personal to the individual. But the obra was clearly about me and Lela. It was the same dolls she'd taken from us when we were kids, their dresses sewn with different colored ribbons representing different orishas, like blue for Yemayá, white for Obbatalá, and even purple for Oyá—the deity of storms and death. The honey, the type of herbs and grains, the shaved offerings of sweet cakes, everything suggested a measure of protectiveness, but wrapping our dolls up in twine, that's control. I also found a bundle of hair that I suspect is mine and Lela's from when we were kids, wrapped in a pañuelo. I had cleaned what I could, then put what was salvageable in a bag and left it on her bed.

What's weird is how everything spoiled. I consider texting Zuela to ask what the hell could be going on, but this feels private. Even if I'm frustrated at Mami for keeping secrets from us, this is between our family.

I wait for the right moment to ask Mami more questions, but nurses and doctors keep showing up. And when I see the bruises on her arm from the IV, the dark circles under her eyes, I'm scared to push too far.

Maybe Lela's right. Maybe we have done all we can to help these strangers, related or not, and pushing it any further will only get someone I love hurt or killed. I swallow hard.

Downstairs, while they load Mami into the passenger seat, Lela comes around the car and we do one of those awkward maneuvers where we can't get around one another. We haven't had time to talk since rushing to the hospital. All that built-up fiery rage has gone cool like an ember. Still hot but not enough to burn.

I was so pissed, and I know I shouldn't have said the things I said, even though a part of me is relieved that my father's secret is no longer only mine to bear. I just didn't want to believe that we've done all we can do. I thought that if Lela could only realize how unique and full of magic she is, the good that she can do with it, she would want to join me in using our powers to help people, instead of throwing her future away on a relationship that can never work.

If only I could find the right words, the ones that are more honey than vinegar.

Lela hesitates, as if she reads all this in our single shared look. I can taste the fiery anger from her, the vinegary guilt sweetened by her love and sorrow. The same emotions pitting the inside of my stomach are raging through her and she surprises me by pulling me toward her in a hug and clenching me tight. As if this was just any other fight.

I catch Mami watching us from the car's side mirror and squeeze my sister back.

"I'm sorry it was your secret for so long," she whispers, and a frigid, forgotten part of me finally melts.

I wipe under my eyes. "I'm sorry for pushing you into something dangerous."

Lela shakes her head. "You just have such a big heart."

At this I make a face.

"You do. Even if most people have to climb a chain-link fence to get to it." She lowers her voice. "I wanted to help the others too, Delf. I really did. But we might be putting them in more danger by getting involved. Gilberto's leaving. They're both powerful brujos, stronger than we are. Maybe they both have somewhere safe to go. Maybe the visions will stop now because we played our part and now our focus should be on protecting our family." A stab of guilt pierces my gut. Lela glances inside the car at Mami. "We have to watch over her. She needs us now more than ever. Maybe there's a way we can earn some extra cash, help her with bills. And if you want to teach me about tarot reading or whatever else you do at Zuela's, I'll try, okay?"

I feel a lump build in my throat. It's a compromise, and I'm happy she's not done trying to develop her gifts. Lela's right, she should stay out of it, and Mami, too. But I'm not ready to give up yet. I don't think Gilberto realizes there are brujos right here, willing to help him stand up to las Palomas, and we're not his enemy, and I'm still not 100 percent sure my possible relative *is* the enemy. My job here isn't done.

But I don't say any of that. If Lela can compromise, so can I. For now.

"You're right, Lel. You're always right."

TWENTY-EIGHT

Miami, November 23, 2016

DELFI

Just because Lela decides that we're done chasing visions, doesn't mean the visions are done with us.

It seems ridiculous to play fortune teller with Mami still recovering, but it's been four days since Andres and I nearly died at the boatyard, and I'm done waiting around for something else to happen. For the next ball to drop.

New visions have been sinking their teeth into my dreams. Just last night I saw myself reaching for my sister again under a red moon, of a wall of flames between us. She doesn't tell me about her visions anymore, and I don't ask, but I know she's seeing something too. I can taste it in the bitter early morning air when she wakes up in a cold sweat.

There must be a reason that we're receiving the visions, and the intensity and frequency of them tells me we're on the cusp of something major. Something bad. After googling, I learned the blood moon isn't just a figment from a nightmare, but a real astrological phenomenon. And thanks to Sahara winds blowing from the East, a blood moon is supposed to appear tomorrow night. It's too much of a coincidence for me to ignore.

I'm tired of waiting around, of waiting for either las Palomas to send another warning or "Uncle" Teardrop to lurk around. If there is going to be a confrontation, I'm going to pick the place, and it'll be under my terms.

So I'm going to set a trap.

I barge into Zuela's store with a stack of event flyers in my arms advertising our tarot readings. I've already covered the socials, skipping Facebook, which is the only one Mami has access to, letting everyone else know where to be tonight.

Look for the enormous caravan parked outside, prime location courtesy of Ethan's stepmom. Whoever's looking for us can't miss us.

Zuela's ringing someone up, but she glances up at me and says, "Hola, mi niña!" in her loud-ass Cuban voice, making the skittish customer in front of her jump.

"Hey, Zuze! You got a sec?" I ask, placing the flyers by the entrance.

She hurries around the counter. "Dime, mi niña."

"I need your help," I lean in, lowering my voice. "Remember that trabajo you told me about that draws in someone's energy? You said we could use it to draw in a lover for a customer or draw in money."

"Yes . . ." she says, as if knowing where I'm going with this and not liking it.

I press on. "Well, what if I used it to draw in a brujo's energy?"

She takes a step back. "Delfi." The phone starts ringing, but she grabs hold of my arm, looking me dead in the eyes. "They're not strays, mi cielo. You cannot simply lure a brujo and expect them not to bite. Especially not the ones you are thinking of."

"But—"

"It's too dangerous, Delfi. We'll think of something else. Don't worry."

She releases my arm and rushes over to the blaring phone.

My nails dig into my palm. I know she's only trying to keep me safe, but playing it safe is no longer an option with las Palomas involved. "Can I go grab your spare tarots?" I call out.

She answers the phone while nodding, jabbing a thumb to the back of her store. My heart feels whittled to a splinter but there's no backing down now.

Once I'm back there, I step carefully around the giant porcelain San Lazaro statue and the platters of coconut husks and head to the psychic side where I know she keeps her book of trabajos. The ones that require a bit of alma magic. I'll just need to be quick about it.

I make my way to the wooden chest she has on the floor and open the false bottom. Her notebook's inside. I glance around, then skim through its pages until I find it. I'm able to read Zuela's scribbled words in Spanish. *Like attracts like. Power attracts power.* She lists out what's needed to draw another's energy, like a calling card. Maybe it's how she draws in customers. Her list of ingredients isn't too hard to find—in fact, she has plenty back here that I can pinch and the rest can be improvised. I take a picture of the page with my phone as her voice trickles from the front of the store, still occupied.

If I could call to Gilberto, then I'll have a chance to get the answers my sister wasn't able to get. I'll do whatever I need to get him to talk. I could bring him to Zuela and show him he doesn't have to run and hide for the rest of his life. I'm not the enemy here, and maybe if he trusts me, he'll be willing to help me figure out how to protect my family from las Palomas too. If he brings Teardrop, I'm not sure what I'll do—blood-related or not, he shot at me, but it was before he saw my face. I'm really banking on the fact that he wouldn't have hurt me had he known I was the one there snooping.

I pluck the herbs I need from Zuela's shelf and a red string, pocketing them, then hurry out the store like my ass is on fire.

"¿Ya te vas?" Zuela asks, surprised I'm already leaving.

I'm halfway out the door. "Gotta run. I'll see you soon though!" I know she'll forgive me. She's said it before: *Don't second-guess fate when it's handed you a gift, for she rarely gives out second chances.*

• • •

My hair still reeks of dye, but it's as black as it was always meant to be. Now there's no telling Lela and me apart, but I've kind of missed that.

I check my reflection once more, swiping away the lipstick at the edge of my mouth. Taking a sweep around the interior of the caravan, I make sure everything's in place. The candles are lit, the table's arranged with my tarots and a collection of purity stones. I turn down the volume on the flute music that someone must've swiped from a wax and facial spa. Probably Ethan.

Annoyance bubbles up at the thought of him.

Just because I'm sorry for the way I said it, doesn't mean I regret warning her. I mean, what the hell is she thinking? It explains so much. Why Ethan's been walking around looking like a sullen Nosferatu. I hope she ends it soon because if she doesn't . . .

Ya, I can't think about this now. I shouldn't fill the caravan with negative juju before the trabajo.

I light a match. Here goes nothing.

The herbs smell like lemongrass and something nutty. I spread the smoke throughout the caravan, taking extra care around the windows and door. I take the safety pin I'd left soaking in alcohol and prick my finger, letting the drops of blood fall to the ashtray I've filled with water. Had to improvise a bowl somehow. Once the water turns slightly pink, I douse the incense bundle and say, "Gilberto." Again and again for good measure because his name is the only one I know.

Nothing happens. Like at all. Did I do it right? I pick up the ashtray, peering closely at the floating flecks of ash. I blow out a frustrated breath. I should've known it wouldn't be that easy. If Zuela was here, what would she say? I tap my lip. *A trabajo is only as good as your intent. Use your magia del alma. Stop holding back.*

My alma magic. But whenever I've tried to use my abilities on my own, without her guidance, I've always screwed it up. Either it hasn't worked, or I've gone too far. I feel a stab of guilt over how I tried to control Andres with the maldeados.

But I know that's exactly what Zuela would tell me to do. And she's never led me wrong before. Even though I'm doing this behind her back.

I suck in air, holding the jittery water in my hands. My alma. My alma. I coax it out, and a rich vibrating hum starts low in my belly. It's there waiting patiently like a cat, curled warmly in the deepest parts of me. The words come from there, from this place I'm just getting to know, just learning to trust. The loudest part of me I've had to keep buried, I let her out to see the light.

I call to him again. *Gilberto.*

The ashtray cracks right down the middle. The water sloshes to the floor, then disappears into a cloud of vapor that spreads like a thick fog around the caravan. A crawling sensation starts at the back of my neck, spreads down my arms to my fingers. For a second, I can't see. The fog is too thick. I have a moment of panic before the fog disappears and I'm left with nothing but the cracked ashtray in my hands.

I take a look around but nothing else seems any different. Did it work?

My phone lights with a message from Andres. I haven't spoken to him since being in his apartment and coming home to find my mom surrounded by maldeados. I almost don't check the message now, afraid it'll throw me off my game, but curiosity gnaws at my chest.

Screw it. I open his message.

i need that picture, delfi.

Another one comes through.

tomorrow morning.

I sigh, a needle popping the hopeful bubble that shouldn't have been there in the first place. Lela's been keeping the picture close, hoping she'll eventually get some sort of read off of it, but she hasn't sensed anything yet.

Before I can respond, there's a tap on the caravan's door before it opens. I take my seat, crossing my arms over the table.

showtime. I text Lela.

A woman walks in. Mid-to-late forties. Expensive clothes and handbag. A common creature of the art scene in upscale Wynwood. Our first ever tarot client.

She stumbles back a bit when she notices me waiting, doing a double take. "Wait. You were in the art gallery a second ago." She squints. "Weren't you the one who read my palm?"

A smile sweeps across my face as I gesture for her to sit. Lela walks in behind her and takes her place at my side.

The woman looks startled as she takes in our identical movements, our hair, our features, our clothes. Simultaneously we ask, "What would you like to know?" We know customers eat this shit up.

She wrings her hands. "Oh, this is freaky."

My sister and I look at one another. It's not the first time I've heard that, but never has it felt so good. Might as well have fun while we wait.

TWENTY-NINE

Miami, November 23, 2016

LELA

I help the last customer off the caravan, guiding her gently by the arm, listening to her reminisce about her fourth husband. Delfi and I realized quickly into the tarot reading that she wasn't interested in her future, just wanted someone to listen to her stories of the past, but she was too sweet for it to bother us.

Her grandson comes running in from the art gallery to help her into the car, and she tells him to get her checkbook from the trunk.

"Gran, I'm not going to pay her with a check." He walks back toward me, digging out his wallet. "It's twenty, right?"

I nod and take the money from him, but he doesn't leave. The guy's closer to his midtwenties with the same long nose as his grandmother.

"If I didn't have to take her home, I'd ask if you wanted to go back into the gallery with me."

I feel my face flush and give a nervous laugh.

He's being polite, I guess, but getting hit on has always made me uncomfortable. "Sorry, I don't—"

"Hey!" Ethan comes jogging from his truck with a dark look that I've never seen on his face before. It sends a shiver of dread down my spine. "You need something?"

I don't recognize this Ethan. I'm not sure if he's planning on shoving the guy, but I step in between them just in case, gripping his jacket.

"Ethan, I'm fine." The moment I touch him, he stops dead in his tracks. He shakes his head, and the fury in his expression melts into unease.

The guy puts his hands out. "My bad, I was just leaving."

Ethan watches as he leaves, then turns to me. "I . . . I'm not sure what that was about but I'm sorry. I just haven't heard from you lately and I thought—"

"You thought what?" I say. "That you can't trust me?"

"No! I don't know, I thought he was bothering you—but really, I'm not sure why—" He grabs hold of my hand but I shake him off.

"We both know why."

He looks skyward as if warding off my words, but there's no hiding from this anymore. There never was, and after Delfi told me the truth about my dad—I can't risk it. I won't, not when it comes to Ethan. My heart calcifies to stone. It drops into my stomach, making every breath hurt.

"Can we please talk about this tomorrow?" He cups my face, his fingers cool as metal.

I look up at him searching. "Eth, we can't put this off forever." I know when something's wrong. I don't want it to be me, but I know it is. It's why I've been avoiding him. "I think we need space."

He backs away, and everything inside me tightens and throbs like salt meeting a wound.

"No, I can handle it," he promises, his beautiful face drawn. "I'm just a little tired."

"Then go home and rest," I try to appear as reassuring as I can. "We'll talk more later. I'll come over tomorrow, okay?"

He swallows hard, placing a feathered kiss on my forehead. On my cheek and on my lips, warm and sweet. When I return the kiss, an image pops into my mind of him crying in his room. It was the briefest reel of a memory, like an error on a film. Something I was never meant to see.

"I love you, Ofelia. I love you so much."

"I know. I love you, too."

And that, that's the problem.

THIRTY

Cuba, April 1, 1980

***

ANITA

The trees were acting strange today. Anita had never seen them so restless. She was on her way home from school, the only place she'd been allowed to go since the initiation a week ago—a freedom Mamá Orti had promised would be over once las Palomas regained strength to perform the taxing ritual and finish marking Anita as one of their own. None of her friends had been able to meet under las Palomas' renewed scrutiny.

She hated that the last time she'd seen Gilberto, he'd been in pain—crumpled against a wall, left to face whatever his father had in store for him because of Anita's impulsive actions. Anita tried to forget the image of Madroño's blank stare, a soul carved empty, but it was impossible to wipe from her memory.

As she walked, maldeados weaved like a cool river through her feet. The air shivered with growing unrest.

Go back, go back, they whispered. *Go back, brujita.* She knew her mother would be waiting for her at home, but Anita couldn't stop the snag of worry from creeping up her neck as she cut through the winding pathways of Parque Miramar. Her steps led her back to the city, through the cramped alleyways, where she could see a plume of smoke rising toward the sky in the distance. The entire city of Miramar was thick with the sense of something building.

Anita's heart raced as she could hear the pounding of feet surrounding her from other streets but couldn't tell which direction they were coming from. They came from everywhere. Anita didn't have time to scream before a stampede of people slammed into her. Crowds were pouring out now from their homes onto the streets, all heading in one direction.

It was chaos. She didn't know what to do, what was happening. People were coming in a furious wave, and she was a pebble against the current. Someone tumbled into her, and she lost her bag. She landed hard on the pavement. Feet crunched over her hands, but before she could cry out, someone slid their arms under hers and hauled her up.

Her brother whipped her around to face him. "Are you okay?" Rafa cupped her chin, inspecting her. "I was just on my way to find you. It's happened, Anita! They crashed the bus into the embassy and people are leaving!"

A wave of shock ran through her. It was here. Their chance was here. Rafael pulled on her arm, weaving them into the stream. But where was Gilberto? Where were her friends?

"The plan!" she cried over the clamor. "We're supposed to meet them at the plaza!"

Rafa paused. "We might not have time!" But she planted her feet in defiance.

He looked skyward for a moment before relenting. "Fine! But if they're not there, we leave." He tugged her past the clashing bodies, flying through the alleys of Miramar until they reached the plaza. They both searched the crowds. She could no sooner turn around then change the ocean's tides, but by god she wanted to. It was all happening too soon. If they waited any longer, el Comandante's soldiers would swarm in and they'd miss their chance to claim asylum, but she couldn't leave without them. Without *him*.

Just as she thought this, Gilberto's determined face appeared in the stream of people, Idaly and Emiliano following close behind. Gilberto broke through the crowd as if wading through a storm and crushed his body to hers.

"Ana, you shouldn't have waited. You should've gone ahead, what if—"

Anita shook her head. "It doesn't matter. You're here now. You're all here now."

Her brother pulled at them both. "Yes, and if we don't go soon, we'll all be stuck here."

He was right. If ever there was a chance to leave, it was now. And she was going to take it. She wanted to start over with her new family.

Together, they fell into the wild current of hope flooding the streets. A tide she prayed would lead them all to freedom.

THIRTY-ONE

Miami, November 23, 2016

DELFI

I pull away from the door. Even from inside the caravan, I could hear the distinct pitch of Ethan and Lela arguing outside, the soft hum of Lela's pain-filled voice. I know what it's like to get swept up in the promise of love, but I also know what it's like when it ends.

Lela shuffles back into the caravan, red-eyed and quiet. I know better than to say anything, so we pack up together in silence.

We hear the rattle of the caravan's door. My entire body tenses.

"We're closed for the night," Lela says, but no answer comes.

A man walks in. Teardrop.

Immediately the intense taste of tobacco coats my tongue. His eyes sweep across the interior of the caravan before moving from my sister to me. He has long hair that stops short of his chin and a hard, thin line of a mouth that hooks into some semblance of a greeting.

My heart hammers behind my ribs. His posture is calm, indicating he means no harm, but I recognize that spark of anger in his dark eyes. The same fire I've seen in my family's eyes. But this isn't some familial reunion, and I realize too late I've made a mistake.

"Like she said, we're closed," I say, hating the shake in my voice. When I cast the trabajo, I was expecting Gilberto. I didn't think it'd be *him*. I was hoping it wouldn't be him. I look nervously to see if he might have his gun.

Teardrop takes another step inside, and I swipe my phone from a shelf. Lela shoots me a frantic look.

He makes a placating gesture. "Wait." His accent is thick and sleek like maple syrup. "I only want to talk, and then I leave. Quick. I won't hurt you."

My mouth goes dry. For once, there's no assault of flavors, no inkling of intentions or emotions. It's like he's blocked me from using my power.

I hate it.

The only thing I can go by is the sincerity in his tone. I subtly open my recording app. If he does decide to make a move, I'll have it on audio, uploaded to my cloud in seconds, get it to Andres somehow.

The man makes a curious path around the caravan, picking up the smudge stick I'd used for the trabajo and taking a deep whiff. He pockets it and then lingers over certain things, taking his sweet time as if daring me to make a call.

"What do you want with us?" I demand.

"Strange, I came to ask you the same thing."

He drapes himself onto a chair, crossing one leg over the other, as comfortable as a lounging panther. Even if he is our relative, he could be the killer sent by las Palomas. He could be slowly hunting down all his old friends, including Gilberto and my mom because they left. He could be here because I found his secret boatyard for unsavory deeds.

"We weren't looking for *you*," I say.

"And yet you summoned me."

From his suit jacket, Teardrop produces my tarot cards. I look to the vintage cigar box I keep them in, wrapped in a slip of silk. The box is propped open, the silk spilling out like disemboweled guts.

He shuffles the cards in his hands, then flicks out three cards across his crossed leg. "Tu sabes, I used to do this as a kid, when I was about your age. Tricks for tourists, fortunes and truths for bil-lete. But I also did them because I found it to be a release."

One by one, he turns over the cards, and I gulp as I see them. "To let go of some of that built-up—how you say? Power? Gift?" he leans forward. "Curse?"

"You still haven't told us what you want," Lela says. "Why have you been following our family? Is it—is it because you're related to us?"

Surprise—then pain registers on his face. "If we are related, let the cards be my advice to you." He shows us the first card. The Devil. "There's something haunting the two of you. Something you can't get rid of." He picks up the Eight of Cups next. "This one is interest-ing. Let go of what drags you down. At least that's how some see it. For me, it's more of a warning card. A warning to walk away from things that don't concern you."

I suck in a breath. All he's done is give us a non-answer and now . . . a threat?

"You two have been busy, I see," he continues, picking up the final card. He makes a sound with his tongue as if it's the gravest of news. The Ten of Swords. It's a grisly illustration of ten endless swords impaling a supine figure. "Now, this card tells me your path ends in no good. No good at all. If you're not careful, maybe even death."

One by one, the candles we'd made sure to blow out bloom to life. Lela jumps beside me, trying to get as far from the taunting flames as possible.

I glare at him. "Are you finished? Or should we call the cops now?"

He gets up and places the cards on the table. "Simply a playful prediction. But before I go, answer me this—" Any amusement is cut clean from his face. "What exactly do you wish to accomplish by sending out a beacon of power for every brujo to show up here? Are you trying to get yourselves killed? What are you playing at?"

Shit. He means the trabajo I did to call Gilberto. I must've messed it up somehow.

A look of surprise crosses my sister's face, but she recovers quickly. "We don't know what you're talking about. But you could start by telling us what *you* know, and with none of that ambiguous crap. I've seen you. You know where we live, you know where our mother works, and you were there when Idaly died. So what are *you* playing at?"

Lela's ballsy demands surprise me, but she's right. If anyone needs to answer questions, it's him.

"And what were you doing at the boatyard?" I ask.

Teardrop looks between us incredulously. He pinches the bridge of his nose. "Igualitas."

He grumbles, calling us the same. But the same as who? As him? As our mom? He studies us for a few uncomfortably long seconds, and he gets that distant look I recognize, like the one when I get a rush of taste or Lela touches something with memory attached. An inward look.

He takes us in again. "I didn't understand before, but I do now. You haven't had the proper guidance. You need to keep away from things you don't understand." He pulls down his shirt's collar, revealing the puffy scar of a brand—a dove and a snake. "*This* means they're searching for *me*. If you two keep showing up where you're not meant to, who do you think they'll track next?"

"So they're after you?" I say. He's not the hunter. A part of me feels instantly relieved. "You can trust us. We can help you."

The pain in his expression is instant and raw. "There is no *we*. You're free of this. I mean it. Stay. Away."

He's afraid, I taste. But not just for himself.

From his pocket, he withdraws a small brass object and places it over my tarot cards.

A fancy Zippo lighter—the one I'd swiped from Zuela before going to the boatyard.

"This belongs to you." He looks directly at me.

A flash of pain pierces my shoulder, a sudden release as if whatever hook and line had been attached to me since that night at the boatyard is withdrawn. He did have something of mine. He *had* been tracking me.

The man disappears from the caravan, leaving us reeling as we stare at his vacant chair.

Lela walks over to the lighter, almost as if afraid to pick it up. She holds it for a moment before her eyes water, as her eyes stay focused and clear of any visions.

She rubs her palms over her face, gathering herself before turning to me. "Care to explain what he meant by a beacon of power?"

• • •

By the time Lela and I get home after locking up the caravan and taking the wrong bus twice to throw off anyone who might be following us, it's 2 a.m. and we have to sneak in to not wake Mami. Even though if she were awake, she'd probably be avoiding us, like she's been doing since they let her out of the hospital. She claims she's either too drowsy from the meds or that she has a headache anytime we try to ask her questions.

The house is quiet and cold. Lela and I don't speak as we both collapse onto our beds. I figured I'd pass out from exhaustion the moment my head hit the pillow, but the adrenaline is still coursing through my body like a riptide.

Lela's not faring any better, because I can hear her whimpering in her sleep. My sister's accusation still rings in my head after I called Zuela and she reamed me out, then explained exactly how I messed up the trabajo so badly.

"You stole a spell that signaled every brujo within a sixty-mile radius?" Lela yelled. *"Might as well walk around with a flashing billboard that reads 'Kill me next!' You promised you'd let this go!"*

I hadn't exactly promised, but it doesn't mean I didn't do something wrong. Guilt makes me toss and turn. Shielding my phone's light under my comforter, I open Zuela's text and reread it.

ay, delfi. i'm so disappointed. we're supposed to work together.

I shut my eyes, curling deeper into my sheets.

I hear the phone ring and I scramble to silence it but it's not mine. I whip the comforter off, and Lela's sleepily pawing for her phone on the nightstand. Our clock reads 6 a.m. I must have drifted off.

Lela looks at the screen, and her expression makes my stomach plummet.

"Who is it?" I ask.

"It's Ethan's stepmom." Lela scrambles to sit up, answers the phone, and puts it on speaker. Holly's voice is high and reedy, which is already unlike her. She starts with, "Now don't freak out." Which has the complete opposite effect. "But I need you to come back down to the gallery. There's been a fire."

THIRTY-TWO

Miami, November 24, 2016

LELA

I can't describe the insurmountable fear that shot through me as we raced back to the gallery. Even after Holly assured me that no one had been hurt in the fire, the panic didn't dissipate.

The fire in the caravan started soon after midnight, right after we left. The police investigators said the damage was minimal, likely an accident, but as I'm staring at the flurry of doves perched over the gallery's roof, their curious, long necks bent, I know this was another warning from las Palomas.

"Oh, honey. Don't worry," Holly says, coming up beside me. I put away my phone. I can't even count how many times I've called Ethan already, but it keeps going straight to voice mail.

"They don't get reception out at sea," Holly continues. "But I left them a message. Ethan's dad took him out to Boca Chita Key last night to cheer him up, and they're usually back by noon."

To cheer him up. Probably because of the fight we had. Because I've been distancing myself and maybe I made things worse, made the curse take hold faster.

A heavy weight settles over me, along with the morning air's cold bite. Holly has to leave, so we offer to stay with the officers until they finish examining the caravan. We say goodbye to Holly and tell her we might not make it to tonight's Thanksgiving dinner she invites us to every year since Mami is always working. We don't usually celebrate the colonist holiday, but we do go for the free food. And if I'm being honest, we go so we're not constantly reminded of how small our family actually is.

Finally, they tell us it's clear to go in. When I walk inside, I want to sink onto the floors and sob. The eye-watering smell of burnt fabric and wood hits me first, carried by the subtle scent of singed lemongrass. The entire back portion of the camper looks charred, sooty. All his hard work to make this perfect for us. For me—ruined in a flash.

The investigator follows us. "We believe that's the culprit right there," he says, pointing a pencil to what remains of a built-in shelf. There are the remnants of an exploded glass jar that used to hold our smudge sticks and a row of candles burnt down to the wick.

I shake my head. "I'm one hundred percent sure I blew out every candle last night."

His mouth purses in a doubtful expression. "Like I said, accidents happen."

Delfi turns on him. "This wasn't—" But I put a hand out to stop her.

The guy has already made up his mind, and delving into what we *think* happened will lead to an entirely different set of questions that we can't answer. Besides, I haven't forgotten what Gilberto said, *la policía in Miami can't be trusted*. Maybe it was Teardrop, maybe he didn't think his verbal warning was enough. Or maybe it was someone las Palomas sent, drawn to the caravan by that same damn trabajo Delfi did.

"At least it's not that bad," the investigator continues, and this time it's Delfi holding me back. "You're lucky someone called when they did. Any longer and the fire would've spread to the front of the cabin."

"Who called it in?" Delfi asks suspiciously.

The investigator looks up from his notes. "Oh, someone that was driving by." He lifts one of the pages. "Andres Navarro. Good kid. Mentioned he knew one of you."

My sister and I lock eyes. There's a weird expression on her face as she says, "Yeah, we know him."

"Well, that's it for us here. Tow truck is on its way."

"Tow truck?" I ask a smidgen too loudly. "But you said it was still operational."

The investigator snorts, scratching his neck with the end of his pen. "Oh, it is, but we can't just let you take it. It'll be checked into the police impound until the owner retrieves it."

Ethan. Ethan needs to claim it, but there's no telling when he and his dad will be back on land and get my messages. Another pinch in my throat.

I look at Delfi. I don't even bother asking how much the impound costs, because I know we can't afford it. Mami's car was repossessed one time and it took an entire two weeks' salary to get it back.

I see my sister's hand clench, then with a wink in my direction, Delfi squares her shoulders and steps closer to the investigator. I step back as the maldeados peel from the sooty darkness and weave their way over to him.

Delfi shakes loose her hair and lowers his clipboard with a finger so she can look him deep in the eyes. The investigator's nervous expression smooths as the maldeados begin to wind their way up his ankles.

"You know what I think?" Delfi starts, and already he's nodding. "You should let us take this little problem off your big, strong hands."

◆ ◆ ◆

As soon as we pull up to Andres's building in the caravan, Delfi takes off in the direction of his apartment. I go after her, even though what I actually want to do is run to the marina and wait for Ethan at the dock. Although I told him last night we needed space, I want to see him, make sure he's okay. Yet instead, here I am, following Delfi as always.

I catch up to her right as she starts banging on Andres's door. "I don't know what Andres was doing at the caravan last night, lurking around like a creeper, but I plan on finding out," she mutters.

Delfi bangs on his door again, and Andres finally answers.

He peers outside with a wary look. When he sees it's just Delfi, Andres hangs his head in relief. "Jesus."

"Nope, just me," she says.

"What time is it?" He looks at the watch on his wrist.

She flicks the picture up between two fingers. "I come bearing gifts."

He tries snatching the picture from her hand, but she moves away. It's then he notices me standing there. He releases an exhausted puff of air. "Great. As if one of you isn't enough."

Since Delfi doesn't get to the point, I do. "Our caravan mysteriously caught on fire last night. How did you just happen to be there in the middle of the night to report it?"

Delfi shoots me a look, but I shrug. Andres looks down the hall, his mouth pressed tight. He deliberates for a moment, before grabbing his keys and locking his door. I cast Delfi a dubious glance.

"I can't explain why I knew to go over there, but I can introduce you to someone who can," Andres says. "We can go now, but I can't fit both of you on my bike."

◆　◆　◆

The stark yellow and teal caravan with its lacy windows and big, fat white tires looks even more incongruous among the Corollas and Civics of Andres's parking complex. As if we stole it from the *Stardust* movie set. But as we walk up to it, we can smell the stink of ash.

"How are you driving that thing around?" Andres circles the front of the caravan as if it'll grow teeth and eat him. "I thought they would impound it."

"Never mind that." Delfi waves away the question. "You still haven't told us who we're supposed to meet and why."

"Look," he says. "I told you my grandma is a santera. I visited her last night, thinking she could tell me more about las Palomas. Thanks for the tip by the way—"

Delfi does a half-hearted salute.

"Anyway, she explained the whole Cuban cult thing, and told me some troubling things."

"Like what?" I ask. "Besides the obvious."

"Like, the fact that she knows they've been on a hunt for a few people. People with abilities like yours. She said she had this bad feeling about last night, said she felt something drawing her to someone, and then she mentioned you by name. We think someone was messing with some serious magic."

I glare at Delfi, and she looks away. She'd promised she would drop it, but I should've known better. And now, after Delfi's little stunt with the stolen trabajo, there really is no going back. It seems everyone with an ounce of magic, including anyone associated with las Palomas, is *definitely* aware we're here now.

Andres looks a little sheepish. "When I left her place, I got worried. I saw your tarot flyer on Instagram, so I just passed by to make sure everything was all right, and it's a good thing I did."

Delfi's expression is soft, almost gentle. I don't think I've seen her look at someone like that before.

"Did you happen to see anyone by the caravan last night?" I ask. "Any . . . doves?"

His brows scrunch. "No, nothing like that. I think you guys should meet my grandmother though. Maybe you'll have other questions that she can answer."

"Maybe she could help me with my block." I hadn't wanted to voice it before but it's impossible to ignore. At last night's tarot event, I was running on pure intuition because the truth is, I haven't had another full vision from an object since Gilberto's. And a part of me actually misses it.

Delfi grips my arm. "Why didn't you say how serious it was? We could go to Zuela for that. She could help." But then Delfi's face falls. "I mean once she cools off."

Andres cuts in. "Who's Zuela?"

"Doesn't matter," I say, opening the caravan door. "We need someone who can help us now. Neither of us can afford to be weak in any way. Not if we now have brujos coming after us. I don't want to be ambushed again."

"Wait, who ambushed you—"

I let Delfi fill Andres in on Teardrop's visit as my phone gives a sudden, violent chirp from my back pocket. My hands fumble for it, fingers clumsy as I swipe at the screen.

"Hello? Ofi?"

"Eth—" I choke out in relief.

"Oh my god. Are you all right? I just got everyone's messages."

"I'm okay," I say, though I'm not sure how true that is. "But—the caravan."

"That doesn't matter. I can fix it. As long as you're okay. I'm so, so sorry. I should've been there. I never should've left." There's a thump, as if he tripped, which is very much like him.

"It's okay," I say. "I'm just glad you're—I'm glad you called me."

"I didn't mean to scare you, I swear. I was just trying to clear my head. I just wanted to— I'm sorry."

My throat constricts. "Me too."

"Can I see you?"

"Don't you have to stay for Thanksgiving dinner?"

"I could come back later," he says. "They'll understand. This is more important right now."

"We'll be right there." After I hang up, I tell Delfi and Andres we need to make a stop before we go meet Andres's grandmother.

◆ ◆ ◆

When I finally see Ethan, when he's finally right in front of me, I feel like my lungs can fully expand.

After a quick introduction to Andres, Ethan hops in and takes over as driver, having more experience with the caravan. At a stoplight, he reaches across to grab hold of my hand.

"I've missed you," he whispers.

I make sure no one's watching, and they're not. Delfi and Andres are too caught up in some battle of wills to notice anything else.

I wrap my hand around his, buzzing and a little cold. The fading sunset plays with the golds in his hair. There's a bit of darkness rimming his eyes, but other than that, he looks fine. More than fine. He's as beautiful as ever. Especially when he looks at me with that searing warmth.

"I missed you too," I say.

His responding smile makes me have dangerous thoughts. Makes me believe that maybe everything will be okay. He lifts my hand to place a gentle kiss over my knuckles, and I hold on as tight as I can, for however long I'm able to.

Andres directs Ethan to his grandmother's modest yellow house at the end of a cul-de-sac. He tells Ethan to park under the mango tree since there's a lopsided Cadillac parked all messed up in the driveway.

Andres shakes his head. "Mimi's a menace when she drives."

Despite it being so early in the day, the sky is dark. The sun hides behind a gathering of gunmetal clouds. I don't care who sees, I hold Ethan's hand as we follow Andres down the path of stone steps to the front door, weaving past a lovely garden full of flowers and a collection of stone frogs. Something you'd expect from your grandma's house. Not that I would know.

Andres glances back at Delfi a few times as we reach the metal gate. I think he's nervous, and I get it. There's something deeply personal about meeting someone's grandma. A level of familiarity I don't think my sister has ever crossed before, even if this visit is borne out of necessity.

Before Andres can knock, the door swings open, and my eyes nearly fall out of my head.

It's her. Stormy gray hair braided down her back. Earth-rich skin, tight over sharp features. She doesn't smile when she opens the gate. She doesn't even seem surprised to see us, as if our appearance here was inevitable. It's the woman from the red tent.

Doña Aura.

THIRTY-THREE

Cuba, April 6, 1980

ANITA

When they'd first arrived at the Peruvian embassy along with the other asylum seekers, Anita had thanked the saints for the balcony they'd managed to claim. Although the five of them were squeezed onto the space with ten others, the balcony was high in the air, away from the shoving and feverish press of other bodies.

But they could barely move, and after the scorching heat of the second day, Anita's gratitude was gone. The Peruvian embassy grounds were full beyond capacity, the manicured lawns now a sea of people. Anita had listened to the soft, frightened murmur of conversation, the wailing of children from inside until the voices began to dull. What frightened her the most was the pallid complexion of Gilberto and her friends. Their marks were still red and angry, healing from the branding iron, and she worried they would get an infection. With Rafa's help, Anita had to keep holding her friends back from jumping down and fleeing back home.

They described the feeling as an urge to return, so strong it was making them sick. As if the mark worked like a beckoning trabajo to lure them back. Anita and her brother tried what they could to ease their friends' suffering, even calling to the maldeados, but the more they used their alma magic, the worse the sickness became.

As they fought off the magic, Idaly sobbed softly, face buried into Emiliano's chest. Gilberto had his head down between his knees and every so often Anita would rub large circles against his back to remind him he wasn't alone, but there was little comfort she could offer him while they waited to hear if they would be granted asylum by the Peruvian embassy.

When the others had drifted off into a restless sleep, Anita whispered to Rafa, "What do we do if they can't fight the urge to return? How do we keep them safe?"

Her brother looked over the sorry state of them. "The mark is still fresh. We knew it wouldn't be easy, but it will get better. We'll have to limit our alma practice and never trust others beyond our circle. It's the only way we'll all stay hidden."

Limit her magic. Although she had often rejected what she was, her power had always been a part of her. The grief wormed its way into her heart knowing she'd always have to hold that part of herself back. A hefty price for freedom.

Faint from hunger and fatigue, and the unrelenting heat, Anita's muddled mind kept drifting to her mother. Of visions of her showing up, taking them back. She knew she was hallucinating when she envisioned Mamá Orti cradling her in her lap as she must've done when Anita was a child. When her father was still alive. Anita dreamt of a different life, free from curses and blood. A life she had no need to escape.

Finally, on the third torturous day of being stuck inside the embassy, they received word that the Peruvian embassy would grant immunity to the asylum seekers, even at the risk of breaching their country's tenuous peace with Cuba. For now, Anita and her friends were safe. Even las Palomas couldn't risk meddling at this scale of political affairs. Anita's relief grew when Gilberto admitted that the mark's pull was beginning to subside, fading over time and distance. For the first time, it seemed possible that they might actually be able to escape.

All that remained was for el Comandante to approve the asylum seekers for emigration, and after nearly a week of what Anita truly thought would be the last days of her life, the comandante made the declaration. He'd had enough, making his revulsion clear. For those who wanted to leave, they were welcome to go. He no longer wanted the anti-revolutionaries to pollute his country. The traitors. The venom was spread to those who stayed loyal to him, as evident by the massive crowd gathered outside the embassy gates holding bats and broken bottles.

Anita and her friends were forced off the balcony by the Peruvian embassy soldiers and were given paperwork that declared them an "emigrating people" with diplomatic protection. But the hope that Anita felt was quickly replaced by fear when she was informed that they were to go back home and wait for further news from the Cuban government.

Rafa began arguing with a soldier in a beret, but their heated words seemed distant, as if she were underwater. She knew he was begging the embassy soldiers to let them stay until it was time to go, to keep them behind the gates, but it was no use. As the militants escorted them all outside, Anita was too weak to fight back. Her friends were too weak to fight back.

It was all wrong. They were forcing them back out onto the streets of Cuba where Anita knew they weren't safe. Where las Palomas would make sure they would never leave again. It all felt like one big joke. She couldn't go back home now. Her mother would never let her escape twice.

Please, she begged. But her words were too quiet, swallowed by the sounds of protesters outside.

"Traitors! Ingrates!" They jabbed signs at even the children with images of crudely drawn white-haired Americans surrounded by worms, implying that those fleeing were as unwanted as bugs. "Cuba for those who work! Out with the anti-socialists!"

These were her people, her fellow compatriots, who couldn't see what she saw. They had decided to ignore what had befallen their country since the revolución. It should infuriate her that they couldn't see that they too were controlled, they too were oppressed. But she knew it was not all black and white, and exhaustion was blanketing her. More likely, the crowd was coerced to share el Comandante's ire through propaganda and militant intimidation.

She'd always heard the dissent whispered, in her school, by the maids, in the pockets of conversation she'd catch walking through the city. But people were afraid of who might overhear and throw them in jail, or worse, disappear a family member. Like the boy from the infirmary who'd helped her and her friends get away. Anita had gone beyond their murmured whispers of rebelliousness and had risked everything to escape. But in the end, she was right back where she had started.

As soon as they passed through the embassy gates, Anita felt someone grab her roughly by the arm, and she screamed when she spotted the emblem of la Paloma Eterna on his armband, but she was too weak to shake them off. It was only then that Anita noticed her brother and the others had been shoved down to the ground by more militants. Las Palomas' soldiers had found them the second they left the safety of the embassy, just as she had predicted.

As the militants forced Anita into the back of a jeep, she saw Idaly being pulled away from Emiliano, heard Rafa and Gilberto screaming for her, but there was no fighting her way out.

As the jeep pulled away, Anita allowed her eyes to finally drift shut, because she already knew where they were taking her.

Back to the hacienda and the brutal heart that governed it.

THIRTY-FOUR

Miami, November 24, 2016

DELFI

Mimi, this is the girl I told you about, and her sister," Andres says. "We have questions we hope you might be able to answer.

I back away, almost falling into *Mimi's* prickly rosebush. I never would've been able to guess they were related. There's not much resemblance except for the deep barrel of their eyes that seem to capture too much.

Doña Aura keeps her face impassive, but I can taste the tart pop of surprise, along with the smoky burst of her power. She recognizes me too.

"The ones with the visions." She breathes in deep, and with a scrutinizing look at me and Lela she says, "¿Andresito, en que te has metido?"

What have we gotten *him* into? More like what has Andres gotten *us* into?

I point an accusing finger at her. "Are you working with las Palomas? Have you been the one sending all the warnings?"

I realize that the warnings only began after we ran into her at the festival. I picture her manipulating our mom like a ventriloquist, sending the flock of doves to the caravan.

I look at Andres, and I feel a deep stab of pain in my chest. "Were you in on it together? Were you just using me?" Lela grips my arm, pulling me back.

Andres holds up his hands. "What are you talking about? I brought you here so you could ask her questions, not so you could attack her. How do you know each other?" He looks back and forth between me and his grandmother.

I try to get a read off her but all I taste now is what's reflected in her expression. Utter confusion.

Doña Aura unlocks the metal gated door between us. "I think you have the wrong idea. I remember you from the botanica and then again at that festival, briefly, but I don't know about any warnings. And I would never work with las Palomas."

Andres's impatience escalates. "My grandmother would never harm anyone. All she ever does, all she *ever* done, is try to help others."

My sister looks uncomfortable, sharing a glance with Ethan, but says, "We thought Doña Aura may have had something to do with Idaly's death." Doña Aura startles at the name. "There was this trabajo thing Delfi did on Idaly's locket, and the wax melted when we got near your tent, which meant you were the last person who spoke Idaly's name before she died."

I chime in, "Plus, there's rumors that, ugh . . . that you do some pretty defensive magic or . . ." I trail off.

"That's bullshit—" Andres starts, but Doña Aura raises a hand.

"I don't blame you for being wary. Like I used to tell Andresito, more clever is the fox for his slyness than his teeth. But you have the wrong impression of me and my relationship to Idaly."

Lela and I share a look. She did know Idaly, and by Andres's lack of surprise he already knew this. His grandmother had been his source all along, not his dad. That's why he was so invested in this case.

Doña Aura steps aside. "Perhaps you would like to come in and form your own opinions?"

◆ ◆ ◆

No matter who it is, you can't go into an elderly Spanish household without accepting a coffee or a snack, so while Doña Aura prepares the espresso in the kitchen, Lela, Ethan, Andres, and I sit awkwardly facing each other on the two loveseats, with my sister at my side and Andres to my left. The worn-in recliner at the center is obviously reserved for the owner of the house.

My leg bounces up and down. "I don't think this was a good idea."

Lela places a hand over my knee. "Let's hear her out. Besides, I still need help with removing the block on my powers."

Andres leans forward, steepling his fingers together. "Is the block on your visions?"

To my surprise, Lela answers. "No, it's for, I guess, my specialty. Besides the other psychic stuff, I can see memories from touching certain objects. And I was getting even better at it, until I went to visit Gilberto."

Andres gives her an inquisitive look.

"He's the Black man from the photo," she explains. "We found out where he was staying, so I confronted him and when I touched his ring, I saw robed figures surrounding the Cuban president—las Palomas. But he cut me off from the vision, and since then, I haven't been able to get a read off anything else."

Andres's eyebrows hike up. "You knew where one of them was staying? Did he give you answers? Did he confirm who las Palomas sent after him?"

Lela shakes her head. "No, he gave me a bunch of non-answers. He didn't trust me."

I cross my arms. "Don't give us that look, *Andresito*. Up until a few minutes ago, I had no idea you knew who Idaly was all along."

"I didn't *know* Idaly," he says defensively. "My grandmother just told me about her when she saw her on the news." His expression turns slightly panicked. "Wait, let's rewind for a second. What about you? Do you have the same ability as your sister?"

"Wouldn't that be fun?"

"Delfi."

I taste a flicker of tangy disquiet.

"No, but I can taste emotions."

Now he goes still, and I lean closer because it's instinctual, and maybe because part of me wants to make Andres uncomfortable. "Like right now, you taste like—" My tongue runs over my teeth. "Green apple, and a hint of sweet, sweet cinnamon spice. I mean, I could only guess at the emotion, but I would say it's something like unease with a hint of . . . sensuality."

"Ew, okay. That's enough," Lela says. "I think he gets it. His grandma's literally in the other room."

I smile, but Andres does not. In fact, he looks like he's going to be sick.

"There's also that curse thing," Ethan provides oh so helpfully. Ethan backpedals when he catches my glare. "That ugh . . . you know—" I could seriously strangle him.

"We're cursed," I say with a grand flourish because there's no point hiding it now. "The Sánchez women, we can't let ourselves fall for someone without damning the recipient. Cute story, huh?" I stand, suddenly feeling claustrophobic. Just how long does it take to make espresso?

"Is that true?" Andres asks. His voice is soft. Too soft.

Again, I run my tongue along my teeth, this time to rid myself of the overwhelming taste of emotions choking the room.

"Yeah, it's whatever."

I don't like the tenderness in his expression. And there's something else there too. Paired with a sunny sweet flavor, another emotion swirls in his dark eyes, like a dawning understanding. Like hope.

I sit down again as Doña Aura comes into the room carrying a tray of little coffee cups and Andres jumps up to help. After handing them out, I take in the thick creamy layer of foam on top and the mouthwatering scent of Café Bustelo. Oh my god. I haven't had this in forever.

"This is so good," Ethan says, and we all echo the sentiment. But I'm having a hard time drinking more with Andres's Mimi staring me down.

She breaks the silence, her tone matter-of-fact and stern. "It was dangerous what you did. The trabajo to call to others. You were lucky it was only a small fire. It means las Palomas don't want to hurt you, but they may want something else."

I place my cup down. "Like what?"

She shakes her head. "I can't pretend to know how those people think. Which is what I would tell Idaly when she asked for my help. She wanted to cut ties with las Palomas, remove her mark and join my ilé—my spiritual community—and I was willing, but we are not equipped to protect anyone with that level of strength. Not while the Elders are still alive. Las Palomas aren't just magically powerful, they're politically powerful. I helped with what I could, marring her mark enough that it wouldn't pull her back to las Palomas, where she could attempt to live a normal life, and I would buy the items she needed for her religious practice. Like me, Idaly was a practitioner of Regla de Ocha-Ifá." Another name for Santería. I notice she doesn't mention her alma magic.

"That's why the police couldn't decipher Idaly's Paloma mark," Lela says. "She went to you to get it removed?"

Doña Aura unconsciously rubs a spot on her neck with a pained look. "There is no removing it, but we tried our best to impair it. She was visiting me often and I came to think of Idaly as a friend, until . . . well, I knew the moment she stopped showing up that my efforts hadn't been enough. I most likely *was* the last person to see her and speak her name, but I promise, it was said with affection."

Doña Aura looks squarely at me. "As far as my so-called defensive magic, I'm a palera with an open connection to my ancestral spirits, and I am not ashamed. I have my practices that deal in protection and, yes, my own defense, but not to attack, and never with ill intent."

We stare at each other a while longer, each of us assessing the other as we had done in the botanica. Whatever she sees in me makes her sit back and relax her shoulders. And all I can taste from her is the soft peach flavor of sincerity. Guilt wriggles itself into my skin at having thought so little of her.

Andres shows her the picture of Idaly and the group. "Mimi, could any of her friends have had something to do with her death? Did any of the others approach you to remove their mark?"

She takes the picture, putting on her reading glasses to peer at it closely. She taps a finger on the fair-haired boy wrapped around Idaly. "Idaly's husband was killed before I met them, but she spoke of him often. This is him, isn't it?" I nod, and her expression falls. "A shame. The others, I don't recognize, and I'm not sure whether they could be involved in her death. From what I understand, Idaly had fled Cuba with other members of her family a year ago, but she never spoke of them. I believe it was to keep them safe. Do I want to know where you got this, Andresito?"

Andres clears his throat. "Probably not." She gives him a disapproving look and he fidgets despite the fact that she's a quarter his size. It's actually kind of sweet.

Doña Aura doesn't have any of Zuela's warmth or extroverted flair, but there is something genuinely comforting and motherly about her. An openness I wish my actual mom would share.

Andres leans forward. "What about that symbol the cult uses on their members, could you tell us more about it?"

Her knuckles blanch as she places the photo over the coffee table.

"The dove with the snake," she tells him, nodding. "Every practitioner in this area knows las Palomas by this symbol. La Paloma Eterna. I've seen it since I was a young girl in Cuba, but until Idaly, I had no idea they marked their own. Las Palomas were infamous but secretive, though their political power has diminished in recent years because of Castro's decline. I knew Idaly needed protection from them, but it was not my business to know why."

"So it's true," Ethan says. "The dictator's got spiritual bodyguards. It'd explain how he's managed to survive like fifty assassination attempts."

"Six hundred and thirty-eight," Andres corrects. "According to a documentary I watched."

"You watch documentaries?" Lela asks.

"All the time."

Lela gives me an appreciative look, and I feel strangely proud that she sees he's smart and perceptive. Broody and hot is just a bonus.

"I still don't get why they would pick off their own members," Ethan says.

"Cults work a lot like gangs." Andres rubs his fingers over his chin. "You're either with them or against them."

"Worse than a cult," I say. "The people in the picture are brujos." I look at Lela. "Like you and me. As for what the other brujos can do, who knows? But we know they're powerful—" I stab a finger at

Teardrop in the center of the picture, at our potential "uncle." "He made sure we understood that last night, and the night at the boat-yard." I give Andres a quick glance, unsure of how much he's told his Mimi. "Anyway, from what we've seen, the people in this picture are familiar with alma magic."

I consider asking if Doña Aura's heard of our mother, but I hesi-tate to tie her name to any of this, to incriminate her in any way no matter what part Mami plays. With one look, I can tell Lela feels the same.

Doña Aura clasps her hands. "Do you know a lot about your gifts? Do you have a godparent guiding you?"

"I have Zuela," I say. "She's taught me almost everything I know."

Doña Aura tucks loose gray hairs behind her ear. "I see," she says, in the same careful tone Zuela uses when mentioning her, and I'm convinced there's a rivalry going on.

"I don't have a guide," Lela says, and something in me twists—as if I've left her to fend for herself all this time. "Do you think you could help me with a block? So I can sense if there's a memory linked to this photo?"

Doña Aura's mouth tugs at a smile. "Sí, I could help with that."

She gets up and tells us to follow her to the backyard, but when the boys stand up, I point back to the kitchen. I know Lela's already nervous enough as it is. "Why don't you guys wait here? Make your-selves useful and make us a sandwich."

Ethan starts to protest but I level him a look. "Please," I add, and Andres watches me in that new way of his—like now he understands something about me. Again, a sunny yellow taste spreads across my tongue, wraps around my heart, but it's still too new of a taste for me to decipher.

I grip my sister's hand, letting her know she's not alone in this. She never has been. "Ready, babe?"

THIRTY-FIVE

Miami, November 24, 2016

LELA

Doña Aura leads us to a small studio in her backyard near a noisy chicken coop and under a massive framboyan tree with its large bottle-shaped petals littered on the ground. "It is vitally important to release any spiritual interference from the body," she says as she unlocks the door. "Or it'll take root like a sickness. A gift like yours was never meant to be contained."

I understand what she means. At first I didn't notice it, but lately, it feels like I've been missing something, that I haven't fully been myself.

Delfi stands back when we walk into the divining shed, taking in the clutter of saints, shells, and staffs. Her head tilts in confusion. "Don't you keep it separate? Your alma magic from your religious practice?"

Doña Aura pauses, her braided silvery hair catching the light. She watches Delfi carefully. "I don't believe they are separate from one another. The gifts of my family lineage and my spiritual practice makes me who I am. There is no dividing that. It dictates everything I do, all my intentions. But that is my choice. Others work through their own cultural teachings, but for me this feels right. You'll have to decide on your own what gives you peace."

I sit on one of the mismatched dining chairs in the corner as Delfi stays huddled beside the woman, asking whispered questions as they go over the items they'll need. Doña Aura lists all her steps out loud so we can follow along and I hear the word *despojo* a time or two so I know they're gearing up for a cleansing.

Delfi watches Doña Aura intently as the woman consults the Obí coconut shells, says a few prayers in another language, and gathers items off her wall-mounted shelves. I don't think Delfi has ever seen this side of our mother's practices, and I have to admit it feels nice not to be the only one in the dark.

After a bit, Delfi directs me to the center of the room's concrete floor, straightening my shoulders so I'm facing her. My mirror.

"It's going to be fine," she says, her voice low. "But I'm going to need your help, Hermanita. Only you can sense where the threads of your magic disconnect. Don't be afraid and look carefully."

"I don't know what that means. What should I be searching for? Is it like a vision?"

She waves away the questions, only tightening the knot in my stomach. "This isn't time for logic, Lela. Use your intuition. You. Are. Magic. Embrace it, *feel* it, and stop pushing it away."

"It's important to do as she says," Doña Aura warns. "We can only do so much on our part, but it is you who has to reach within yourself and mend the disruption. Or you risk making the block worse and losing a part of your gift for good."

I feel her words like a choke hold.

"But that's not going to happen," Delfi says reassuringly. "I have never, ever doubted what you can do when you set your mind to it."

My sister forms a chalk circle around me. From where I stand, Doña Aura makes a bundle of long-stemmed herbs and wraps them together in ribbon.

"Ready?" they both ask, though it's not really a question.

I nod, even though I'm most definitely not ready. Where are the instructions? Do I just stand here? Delfi said I should be searching for the disconnect, but searching where? And what if I make it worse? What if I lose it—my magic?

How often have I wished for my abilities to go away? But now when faced with the actual possibility, my whole being recoils.

Doña Aura begins a prayer that reverberates through my bones, then nods encouragingly at Delfi, who joins in. The vibration increases until it's gotten hold of my ribs, cinching the bones tight against me.

My sister lights a cigar for Doña Aura, and the woman puffs and puffs on it until all I can see is gray. Until the world is nothing but smoke and song and flashes of quivering light.

I grow dizzy as my sister appears behind me with a rattler. She shakes it over my head, near my shoulder, in a circular motion around my back, down my legs. All the while repeating the prayer, the words bounding in my chest.

Then she disappears in the smoke that consumes the small space, making my eyes sting. Doña Aura appears holding the bundle of vibrant green herbs, hitting it along my skin.

The chanting gets louder, the distinct static sound of maldeados joining in a chorus. My heart begins to pound faster and faster until I'm sure at any second it will burst free from my body. I want to scream, but beyond the rainforest of sound, the prayer, I don't think anyone could hear me.

I'm afraid.

This isn't my world. I never wanted to disobey my mom. Never meant to dabble in magic. I should have listened to her.

Slips of oily shadows materialize near my feet and tangle around my ankles.

I'm afraid.

I'm afraid.

The slithering shapes coil around me gently, caressing me like a mother, brushing up through my hair, tenderly sweeping against my cheek. They whisper calming things, calling to a part of myself that's weighed down by fear and denial.

My magic. They call to my magic. And, finally, with an intoxicating rush of power, I release it.

I'm no longer in the room filled with fog and ceramic saints. I'm in a space where everything is alive. Where everything has value and memories are tied to the very fabric of its latticed cells. Now I see those threads like a network of silver, a web of thoughts I can follow.

I find the block placed on me easily. It's right there on my sternum, a straining golden knot over my center, plain and visible. The knot itself is simple, put there by someone else, but tightened by my own fearful heart.

I unravel it, tugging and pulling until the magic flows through me once again.

Distantly I hear my name, but I'm too preoccupied to answer. The flow of what Gilberto tried to keep hidden blazes in my mind—what I would've seen had I delved into the vision from his ring before he cut me off. The images, voices, emotions all boil over, swirl into the well of my gift.

I see an image of him surrounded in smoke. A giant, red moon above him. His face in terror.

"This is the second time you've made her pass out like this. Are you trying to kill her?" Ethan's voice echoes through my thoughts, rouses me from the trance. He must've heard a noise and come running. The cold floor presses against my back.

"Shut up. She's waking up. Lela? Lela, it's okay. It's over."

I know, I think I say out loud, but I must not have, because she repeats it twice more.

"Is she all right?" Andres now, but farther away, as if giving them space.

"I'm fine," I say, and I realize my eyes are still closed. I work to pry my lids open.

Doña Aura hands me a cup of water and I sit up to gulp it down. Except it's not water. I sputter as the acidic liquid burns down my throat.

The old woman gives Delfi a serene shrug. "I thought she could use something more fortifying."

Delfi blinks. "Did it work?"

I can barely nod, I'm still trembling so hard. "I saw what he's been blocking from me. And something else—I think something's going to happen to Gilberto during the red moon."

Ethan pulls out his phone, typing into it quickly then reading. "Um, says here there's a supermoon—" He speeds through the rest of the article and reads aloud, "Coupled with a dust storm blowing in from the Sahara, this supermoon will provide a unique experience for sky watchers, as it'll shine a brilliant bloodred." He looks up, face panicked. "And it's happening tonight."

Something's off in Delfi's expression, but she presses on. "But we don't know *where* Gilberto is going to be. You think you can see what's tied to the photo now, Lel?"

"I've got this."

At least I think so. The buzzing sense of power under my skin isn't as unsettling now. We're starting to understand each other. The more I've pushed it away, the more volatile and overwhelming it'd become and maybe I just need to trust it more.

I'd been trying to cut a part of myself out, and I sort of wish I hadn't spent so much time being afraid. Being resistant. I'd let what others had called me, had thought of me, get in the way of how I saw myself.

Without the barrier I've taken so many pains to construct throughout the years, the magic washes through me, settling in its rightful place. I'm a powerful bruja—I can tell by the strength of the magic as it settles comfortably into my skin.

When my sister places the picture in my hands, I'm wrenched away.

This time I don't fight it. This time I dive into the memory.

A gust of breeze comes in from the north, cool and briny as an oyster. Only the Malecón and rocks keep the choppy sea from reaching the lit city.

She leans back against a post, holding a camera to her eye. "Go on, smile, Rafa. You look as if you're sucking in your stomach."

"I am, now hurry."

There's a laugh, a rough, raspy one.

Idaly squirms under Emiliano's heavy arm but pulls him closer, as if she could combine them into one. Her smile is frozen in place. Between them and Gilberto, Rafa poses in the middle, foreboding as ever with a clever glint in his dark eyes. Gilberto beside him stares straight into the lens as if looking right into the photographer's soul. It makes her throat go dry and her stomach knot.

The camera shifts to eternalize the four of them, capturing the whole of the Malecón and the glittering ocean. She thinks perhaps it's the most beautiful sight she's ever witnessed.

Click. And the camera's brought down.

I can see the photographer now. The striking young girl skips to stand with the group, the camera bouncing by her hip.

Gilberto moves close so no one else can listen. "Will you keep it by your bedside, Ana, and think of me?"

When the girl's neck heats, the flare of her eyes become unmistakable, unique in their fire.

I recognize them instantly, each one marked for death. Maybe even Ana.

As my gaze adjusts back to Doña Aura's divining room, I look at my sister.

"What did you see?" she asks.

I sway in place, connecting the face from the vision to the one I know so well. The face I've known all my life.

"Mom. I saw Mom."

THIRTY-SIX

Cuba, April 20, 1980

___

ANITA

A morning fog coming in from the open window clung to the inside of Anita's room as she stared at the ceiling. There were military jeeps parked outside, as they had been for the past two weeks. She was told they were there for protection to keep them safe from the chaos and riots breaking out over the cities, but she knew they were there to keep her locked in the hacienda forever. But how would she leave anyway? She'd already *tried*, and it was no use. They'd caught her and brought her right back. All their plans for freedom had just been a fairy tale.

Anita heard someone shouting outside. At first, she thought it was just another protester, but then her breath caught as she recognized the voice. With effort, she got out of bed and approached the open window. The haze was beginning to subside and dark anger was sweltering in its place.

She looked down to see her brother at the doorway of the hacienda, one of las Palomas' soldiers poking a rifle at his chest. Looking at the state Rafa was in, she was reminded of what they'd been through at the embassy. His skin was boiled from the sun, face sunken in from the days of hunger.

"What business brings you here?" the militant barked.

"Let him through," her mother's voice boomed from inside the courtyard. "He's my son."

Anita hurried out of her room as Rafael was escorted inside like a criminal. As if they were preparing him for the firing squad. She went to the exterior hallway overlooking the courtyard and watched them from the balustrade, careful to stay out of sight.

Anita spotted Mamá Orti by her garden box. She held a sharp blade, snipping off the ends of a vine. "You've come right on time."

"I'm here for Anita." Rafa crossed his arms, and she knew it was to keep himself steady. As brave as her brother was, their mother made them both feel like small children. "I know about the initiation," he said.

"Did you want to be invited?" her mother responded with another quick snip.

"How could you do that to her? How could you make Ana do something that goes against her nature?"

"Please," she scoffs. "How could I what? Show her how to live up to her potential? How to come into her own power? Our gifts are inherent to who we are. It is you who wishes to go against our nature."

"No, this is *your* world, not hers. You had no business initiating her into that cult!"

Anita's hands gripped the metal railing.

Mamá Orti wiped the blade against her dress. "You know," she began. "I always told your father that we spoiled you. Gave you everything you could ever want. The best tutors in Cuba, food, comforts . . ." She lifted an arm heavy with beaded bracelets, and the sound rang out like a storm. "You think it's so easy to dismiss your duties now to your family, to your country? Do you think everything I invested in the two of you was for *nothing*?"

"We didn't ask for any of this."

"Oh!" She moved toward him. "As if we receive what we ask for in this world. You need to grow up, niño." Her features turned vicious. "Do not think I don't know about your little infirmaries in the city. It is a disgrace. These gifts do not come without a price. Your sister is learning. She will adapt. As will you."

"We don't want anything to do with this. Especially with you!"

Even from the second floor, Anita could see her mother flinch at his words. She was surprised to see actual pain lanced through her mother's features.

"Fine. I've let your delusions go on for too long. Whether you want it or not, you are a de Armas, and you have a sacred duty to el Comandante. To your country."

Mamá Orti made a signal and two militants emerged, encircling Rafael. He shouted for Anita and tried to run past them and up the stairs, but they clamped onto his arms, kicked in the back of his knees.

"You can't do this!" he yelled. "I have our safe passage papers now! I *will* leave this godforsaken place, and I will take her with me!"

Mamá Orti simply smirked and gestured to his pockets. One of the soldiers withdrew the papers tucked inside, stamped like a train ticket.

"You've wasted your time in that embassy. Went hungry and suffered for nothing because of your own stubbornness," Mamá Orti said.

Rafa seemed to think something over and he went slack in the soldiers' arms. "I'll take her place in las Palomas. You can mark me, just let her leave."

Thankfully her mother shook her head at this, not even considering it.

Mamá Orti took in a fortifying breath. "I know this is difficult, Hijo, but one day you'll understand. This will always be your home, you and your sister's destiny. It is what I have worked for all these years. Now, take him away and remind him of who he's meant to be."

No. This was not her destiny. Rafa's fear shook something loose inside her. Anita knew what awaited him if they took him to el Comandante. Torture or death, Anita had enough blood on her hands. She would not let her brother suffer that fate.

"Stop!"

From the top of the stairs, she swayed, appearing no more than a ghost. "Let him go!"

Her voice was hoarse, the first words she'd said in days. Still, her rage was enough to draw the maldeado spirits to her side.

Anita walked slowly down the steps, murmuring her words of intent. She was done hiding.

"Go back to bed, Ana," her mother commanded. "This doesn't concern you."

Anita stared down at the two armed men. She couldn't stand the sight of them. A surge of vicious intent welled inside her.

She wanted them to feel pain. She needed them to fear her as she had once feared them.

"Anita," her mother shouted, but she wasn't listening.

The courtyard turned gray with fog as if a storm were brewing within the hacienda's walls. The militants and her mother watched her, Mamá Orti's eyes narrowed as if assessing how far Anita could go. Even her brother, weak in their arms, had fear in his expression. Not for himself, but for her.

The wind whipped at the framboyan tree, dead leaves scattering like rain. The static of ghostly voices surrounded them, the maldeados winding up the militants' legs and torsos, encircling their throats.

Anita whispered a command and stared at the two soldiers as their sneers disappeared, as their complexions began to redden. They released her brother, clawing at their necks as the air rushed from their lungs.

She commanded the maldeados to squeeze tighter. *Let them fear me.*

Their eyes rolled back. Above them, dark clouds gathered.

"Have you had enough?" Mamá Orti asked, bored, as if Anita were only throwing a tantrum.

She hadn't. She ordered the maldeados to squeeze again and the two men slumped to the floor, asleep or dead, she wasn't sure. Her mother was powerful, but she was alone. No other Elders were here to lend her strength.

Rafa shouted a warning. "¡Cuidado!"

Another militant stood at the threshold, pointing a pistol at her. Anita felt her hold on the maldeados waver. She glanced at her mother's stoic face.

Would she really allow him to kill me? She wondered. *Could I mean that little to her?*

But before she could find out, the militant slumped to the ground in a shower of dirt. Behind him stood Gilberto, holding a broken flowerpot.

His gaze found hers and she felt her heart swell. "May I come in?" Her smile was small but alive.

Rafa rushed up to her, sensing she was moments from collapsing. Days of barely eating, days of that heat, and lonely gloom of the resulting weeks caught up with her.

Rafael wrapped her in his arms. "You can stop now, Hermanita. I'm here. I've got you."

But they weren't finished yet. Anita used the last bit of strength to push against her mother's magic as Mamá Orti tried regaining control of the maldeados.

Rafa was pulling her through the courtyard toward the door where Gilberto was waiting. Anita tried to speak, but all she could manage was to release the tears trapped inside her. He smelled like her father. He looked like him too, skinny and sunbaked, except for the beauty mark under his eye—that came from their mother.

Gilberto stepped forward. "Idaly and Emiliano are in the car already. People are leaving by the thousands! There are countless boats waiting to take us to la Florida. We have to go now. The riots are turning deadly."

Anita wouldn't be able to hold their mother off much longer. Rafa scooped down to grab one of the fallen militants' keys and the safe passage papers they'd taken. "We'll take their jeep. No one will mess with a military vehicle. Vámonos!"

Now that they were actually leaving, she was filled with grief. Despite everything, she loved this island. She loved its cities, its land, and vibrant people. But there was so much suffering here too. So much danger and forced silence. Too much blood that would eventually stain her hands forever.

"Basta!" Mamá Orti picked up her knife. Anita braced herself. But instead of advancing, her mother used it to draw blood from her finger, then painted a symbol over her palm. Anita couldn't hold them anymore—the shadowy spirits slithered toward her mother in a flood of darkness.

"You would abandon your mother as if I were nothing?" she spat at her children. "After all I've given to you? How could you both be so *ungrateful*?"

"Ungrateful?" Anita's words were low but sharp. "My whole life has been dedicated to making *you* proud, and yet you never were.

You talk about giving, but I've given you all that I am and still it was never enough." Anita walked up to her mother. "I'm done trying to get you to love me. I won't stay here and let you do to me what you did to Papi."

She stared straight into her mother's depthless eyes. This time, she refused to back down.

"Ya, let's go . . ." Rafael tugged her back, urging her toward the door. He'd broken his connection to their mother long ago. It was Anita who clung by a thread for so long.

"Your father was a drunk!" Mamá Orti slashed the knife against the tree, cutting through her father's initials. "A useless womanizer."

"Because of you! Because you don't know how to love, you never have. You poisoned him," Anita said. She knew she was being unfair but she couldn't stop the words from coming out. "Just like you tried to poison me by forcing me to join las Palomas!" She backed away, grabbing hold of Gilberto's hand for strength.

Mamá Orti's nose flared. For the first time in Anita's life, she saw her mother's eyes fill with tears. But then the hurt quickly morphed into wrath.

"You keep thinking with your heart, Ana, not with your head. When are you going to learn, niña, that love is a sickness?"

"How would you know?" Anita spat. "You've never loved anything besides your power. You've always put your faith in the wrong people."

The room was thick with electricity, the maldeados with two different sheens turning on one another as Anita and her mother's powers warred for space.

"It seems I have." Her mother stepped back. "Go ahead then, leave. But know this, Hija—" She gathered herself up, yet her voice was breaking. "I curse you. I curse you to live by your own words and choices. If my love is poison, then yours and your children's will also be. Because your blood is mine and there is no changing that."

With that, Mamá Orti spat on the ground, a hiss of smoke rising from the tile. The moment her mother completed the curse, she looked up at Anita—a deep, unfathomable grief knowing there was no one left who'd mourn her.

As Gilberto ushered Anita to the waiting jeep, she felt something ancient take root, sinking deep into her heart.

THIRTY-SEVEN

Miami, November 24, 2016

LELA

Ana. That was my mother's name before she changed it to María Sánchez so my father wouldn't find her. There's no mistaking who I saw. Not only did they all know my mother. But they loved her.

My heart feels as if it'll slip from my chest. To have it confirmed— to know she was directly involved with las Palomas, a part of their group, makes me realize I don't know her at all.

We were right, even though we really didn't want to be.

We had Ethan give Andres a ride to his place, opting to go home alone. Delfi and I needed to speak to our mother on our own. Our EZ Ride driver eases onto the paved path leading toward Cauley Square, framed by giant trees with tendrils that remind me of hair.

Mom used to tell us a story about trees like these. The reason they grow twisted toward the sky is because of Doña Magdalena, the mortal who fell for a sun god and was buried underneath these trees, the branches reaching for her lost love in the sky. When Delfi and I were little, she often told us stories about a sad old witch who lived alone in a castle waiting for her lost children, or about a magic sea that could transport you wherever you wished.

As she spoke, I'd be enraptured by the fire in our mother's eyes. Latch on to her every word, especially when she'd pause for effect. Through the stories, I'd glimpsed pieces of her past that she never spoke about. Cuba and the home she left behind became fairy tales. Any family we might've had—grandparents, cousins, aunts, uncles— became characters.

But if we ever pressed about her past, for the truth at the heart of her stories, she'd tell us her family died long ago. She came to the United States alone, fleeing a turbulent government, and had nothing or no one tying her down. Her life in Cuba no longer existed.

I came here to start over. Eso es todo—that's it, nothing worth remembering, she'd said.

Honestly, I'm not even sure if all these years of hiding were because of my dad, or if instead we were just running from Mami's past. From the cult she got involved in.

Delfi gently smacks my thigh. "Look."

Craning my neck, I spot a moving truck right outside our building.

Delfi's already got her door handle in a death grip. "Why is there a moving truck here?"

But we already know why. Before the car's put into park, my sister and I are already out the door.

I'm running for the stairs. Delfi's right behind me as we jump the steps two at a time. We have to weave around stuffed garbage bags and old decorations I'd forgotten we had.

"Mami?" I call, rounding the entrance to the apartment. I stop cold.

Delfi pushes past me. "What the hell is going on? Why's all our shit in boxes?" She stalks across the bare floor, ripping open the nearest un-taped box to pull out one of her jackets that says CALM YOUR BITS.

We find our mother in the kitchen, clutching the house phone to her chest, staring off into space. All the confusion and anger rush out of my body.

"Mami?" I go up to her, gingerly taking the phone from her hands, and she lets me, her face still empty.

I place the phone to my ear and hear a woman's voice, "Aló? Aló?"

I respond to the woman in Spanish. "Yes, hi. Who's speaking?"

"Ay, sorry. Tell her I'm sorry for the bad news. I only thought she should know. Someone should."

"Know what?"

But my mom finally snaps awake and snatches the phone from me, slamming it in its mount. I look at the caller ID, and it's a foreign number.

"Who was that?" Delfi asks.

Mami ignores her and hurries into her room, coming out with old dresses and scarves spilling from her arms. She drops the clothes by the door, already piled high with our stuff. Her eyes are puffy and red, raking over the room as if assessing what else she can carry.

"Please talk to us," I say.

Mami finally stops to look at me. "We're leaving. Ahora mismo."

"Like hell we are," Delfi says, grabbing on to her box of things.

"Cuidadito como me hablas," Mami admonishes because we never talk back to her this way. "I want everything in the truck tonight. Between the three of us, we can do it."

"Why do we have to be out of here tonight?" Delfi demands.

"Because there's no time!" Mami cries.

We're interrupted by the sound of flapping wings. We turn toward the open door to see a dove land on the pathway. Then another. And another.

Mami flinches, then makes the sign of the cross over her chest before running to slam the door. In that moment, she confirms that she knows all about las Palomas, and that's why we're leaving.

"Recojan sus cosas," she orders.

Delfi barks a laugh. "I'm not going to pick up my stuff. I'm not going anywhere. You can't do this to us again. We're adults now."

"You are still my children, and I am your mother." Her voice is low yet firm. "You do as I say. And I am telling you we have to go." Another glance toward the door, where to my horror, I think I can hear the sound of more flapping wings, more doves arriving.

"Mami," I say, "Delfi's right. We know you're just trying to do what's best for us, but we need you to answer our questions."

She makes an exasperated sound. "Not you too, Ofelia." She stalks into the kitchen.

I'm left here with my mouth open. Not me? *Not me too?*

Why, because I'm supposed to follow her, eyes closed, all the time? Because I'm not supposed to have an opinion? Delfi can get away with throwing a fit, but not me. No, I can't question why she's always told us magic was bad, that I should never open that door, that I should stifle who I am, when she was apparently a powerful bruja in her teens. Well, I'm tired of being left in the dark—she's kept us there long enough.

I stride into the kitchen after her. I'm too pissed to cry. I'm too pissed to be her good little Ofelia. Delfi scrambles after me, and I think for once how nice it is to be the one followed instead of the one always trying to catch up.

I slap down the photo on the kitchen counter in front of our mother. "Could this be why you want to leave? Your cult friends found you?"

Mami's face goes red. She slams down a glass cup wrapped in newspaper that miraculously doesn't shatter. She opens her mouth, but then she takes in the photograph.

My mother goes still. Her gaze zeros in on the picture, and it's as if the room is depleted of air. She breathes it all in through one great rush.

I flinch at the wounded keen my mother makes. I almost take the picture back, hide it in my pocket, where it'll keep from hurting her.

She lifts the photo to her face with shaking hands. And still, it's not enough. She stares at the figures in the picture as if she weren't here with us but instead there with them. In her past.

"Where—where did you find this?"

"We've been having visions of them, Mami—your . . . friends," I say, steeling my nerves. "Visions and warnings."

"Visions," our mother murmurs. She traces each face as her eyes fill with tears.

I nod. "*We knew* we had to look for them. I didn't want to at first, but then we realized they were being murdered. We couldn't save them, but we wanted to save the ones who are left."

"The ones who are left?" she asks, emotion throttling her voice. "Who was murdered?"

A silence falls over the three of us. Finally, Delfi points at the two figures whose faces are crystallized in my mind forever—Idaly and Emiliano.

A tear breaks free and tumbles down Mami's cheek. "No." She looks at us, dazed. "How long ago?"

"A few weeks ago," Delfi says. "Idaly and Emiliano died here in Miami. We saw them being killed in the vision, by a brujo commanding maldeados." Mami covers her mouth. "We've been trying to warn Gilberto but he doesn't trust us, and this other man with the birthmark—"

Mami looks down at the picture again, tears building in her eyes.

I need to know. "Is he . . . is he our family?"

Sorrow lines my mother's face.

"Yes." Her voice is wafer-thin. "Rafael is my brother. Your uncle."

◆ ◆ ◆

The notion of family beyond our little circle still hits me like a physical blow to the chest. We'd actually met our uncle at the caravan. Our suspicions were right.

Mami sways on her feet before pushing past us into the living room. The flutter of bird wings outside our home is unbearable. We've explained most of what's happened over the past few days, and she's not exactly taking it well. But we still need her to fill in the blanks.

"Mami, I know this is hard," I say. "We know you've kept a lot of secrets from us, and it's hard to come clean now, but we know about the cult. La Orden de las Palomas? We'll understand if you got involved somehow back in Cuba. Everyone makes mistakes."

Mami stops, and her anger glazes over my skin like a living fire.

"*Mistakes?*" Her face twists. "You two have no idea what you've involved yourselves in. These people are not just some *cult*." She spits the word. "They are part of one of the most powerful aquelarres in the world. Entienden what it means to stand in the way of these people?"

She's not listening. She keeps grabbing bags, trying to make her way out the door. But Delfi stands in her way.

"And how can we understand anything if you've kept *everything* from us?" Delfi matches our mother's stance, a crackle of shadows slithering near her feet. I notice the way Mami's gaze flickers over them. As if she's perfected the ability to pretend the maldeados aren't there.

She hoists the bags higher. "Move," she commands in a tone that would usually have us both backing down, which almost works since the maldeados snap to attention around her. They seem caught between Delfi and Mami's wills.

"No," Delfi stands firm. "Not until you've explained."

Mami implores me with a look, but I shake my head. "We deserve the truth."

She keeps her chin high, but I see the tremble. "Everything I've done—*everything* I've sacrificed was for you to live free of all this."

"But we've never been free of it." Doves begin tapping against the windows as if proving my point. "Our abilities can't be prayed away, and you've even made yourself sick by holding back your magic. Haven't you?"

She looks away.

Delfi wraps her arms around herself. "You've left us to figure things out on our own, Mami, to deny one of the biggest parts of ourselves. I am sick and tired of holding everything in because we can't tell each other the truth about who we are! You can't dictate our lives anymore."

Our mother gives an incredulous laugh, dropping everything to the floor. "You—born and raised here, with all the freedoms this country has to offer—say that *I* have dictated your life? You have no idea what it's like to live under someone's control." Her voice breaks. "When your whole life you're taught to stay quiet, be obedient, don't ask questions. *A de Armas knows their place.* Follow their rules even when it means going against everything you are! Follow even when it means taking the souls of others!" Mami covers her mouth as if she can take back the words.

Delfi moves toward her, but Mami waves her off. Our mother sinks down to her knees, our things scattered around her. Each sobbing shudder she emits kills a piece of me.

She's right. I didn't know. I didn't know my mom lived with this much pain. Even after what happened with our father and all the times we moved, she always put on a brave face for us. Always made us feel like everything would be okay, but inside she was hurting as much as we were. If not more because she's been completely alone with her secrets.

When I look over at Delfi, all the fury has leached from her too. We drop down beside her, gathering our mom between us like a pearl within a sand-beaten shell.

"I don't want to keep pushing you, Mami," I say. "But there are people in danger. Specifically, tonight during the red moon. We need your help, but most of all, we need the truth."

I bring out the picture again, wrinkled but intact.

My mother releases a rattling breath at the sight. She doesn't need to say it. Looking at Teardrop, at Rafa, there's no mistaking the similarities between him and my mother. The penetrating dark eyes and crooked smile, the low brows and cut jawline—placed side by side, the features would match any of ours.

"Tell us about them," I say. "Tell us about our family."

Delfi moves her finger over to Gilberto. "Was he—"

"He was a friend," our mother says, wiping her cheeks and regaining some of her steady control. "We were all friends, all children of the Elders. We—we thought we could have something different than what our parents had in las Palomas." Her tone darkens. "But what could we do? Las Palomas are not something you bring down. Its reach is global. Its power infinite. If Rafael and Gilberto are being hunted now, it's because they tried to leave las Palomas, to have the same freedom I've been allowed all this time. The freedom they sacrificed for. I've been shrouding us from las Palomas all these years, but something's happened recently. My protection obras have weakened. Nothing I do seems to be working,"

Delfi and I share an uneasy look. We have a feeling we know why her efforts haven't worked. It's because we've been digging where we shouldn't.

"If las Palomas realize you are of Mamá Orti's lineage, they will hunt you down and force you to continue her"—Mami's mouth twists in disgust—"her *legacy*. I can't let that happen. I won't."

And with that, Mami mumbles a set of indecipherable words I feel in the pit of my stomach. Chittering, the maldeados ooze with a glossy sheen beneath the doors and through the cracks of the windows. They silence the birds outside.

THIRTY-EIGHT

Miami, November 24, 2016

DELFI

H old up," I say. "What does that even mean? Who's Mamá Orti? And what legacy are you talking about?"

Mami tries to get up, but I grab her hand. The tenderness I tasted a moment ago hardens with the tang of impatience. I realize it's the first time I've picked up emotions from her this strongly, as if I've finally found a way around the magical barrier she's kept firmly in place. Now it's like she's let some of her guard down, like she can finally be herself.

Mami snatches her hand away, pausing. "She's the most powerful and dangerous of the Elders. Or she was." A deep inhale. "She is also your abuela, and that phone call was from her nurse."

"*What?*" Lela's face pales and I know mine mirrors hers.

A living grandmother. I can't believe it. And the most powerful bruja on top of that?

"Wait." I straighten. "What did the nurse say? Is she okay?"

Mom's chin trembles. "No. She's dying. She has been for a while."

"God," Lela whispers. There's a sharp taste of anger coming from her and it melds with my own.

"How could you keep us from her?" I ask. "How could you cut us off from our grandmother?"

Mami looks defensive. "Because if your grandmother knew where we were, she would betray us to las Palomas. She would not show us mercy."

I pick up on the effervescent taste of uncertainty. "But she must've kept track of you somehow, to have your number after all these years. Wouldn't they have come for us by now?"

"I don't know," Mami says. "I never understood my mother, but she's never been forgiving. Even Mamá Orti's gift ranged more in the ability to exact justice or . . . prolong curses."

The word *curses* hovers in the air. Does that mean what I think it does? Was she the one who cursed us? My mother reads the question in my eyes and gives a tight nod in response.

Any fantasy of a loving grandmother is squashed in a heartbeat.

"I loved my father," Mami says, catching me off guard. "He was everything to me, but he was also a shell of a man who filled himself with drink and a festering regret until the last of his days. I can't defend my mother. But the grief he caused her became her fuel, a fire she channeled into her destiny as an Elder. Any bit of softness was pummeled out of her until it became steel. That's the mother I knew—unrelenting steel. I can't imagine what Rafa had to deal with on his own."

"All the more reason to have his back now." I jump to my feet, pulling Mami up from her knees and straightening her blouse. It's what she would do for Lela and me on the first days of school, before a recital, or whenever she wanted to instill bravery in us. "Like Lela said, tonight specifically it's important we do something. We've had visions of him and Gilberto being captured by las Palomas during a red moon, and that's happening tonight."

"I can't." Mami tries backing away, knocking into the entry table.

"He's your brother," Lela reasons, but Mami's retreating again. I can see it in her expression. Can taste it in the tartness of fear.

But Lela isn't taking no for an answer. She swipes the picture from the table and reaches for our mother's hand. I think at first it's to comfort her, but then my mother's gaze goes unfocused. My mouth fills with the scent of salt and airy cold.

It's the taste of a memory. I realize this is the first time Lela's done this—invite someone into her power so confidently. I reach out, grabbing hold of their hands, and catching the tail end of the vision.

The girl dangles her legs off the sandy seawall, laughing when Gilberto nearly loses his footing on the rocky shore below. He gives her a playful scowl before joining Emiliano and Idaly by the water.

She keeps a quiet vigil over the vast ocean, stirring only when her brother swings his leg over the muro to sit beside her.

"Everything all right?"

She tilts her head, watching the horizon. "What kind of life do you think we'd have over there?"

The boy looks out over the ocean thoughtfully. He grabs hold of her hand and smiles. "One of choices, Ana. One of possibilities."

I'm thrown out of the vision as our mother snatches her hand back, the picture dropping to the floor.

She touches her fingers to her wet cheeks. "How did you—how could you have that memory?"

"The memories are tied to this day in the picture. It's part of what I can do. I'm an ojo," Lela says in a wavering voice that gains strength with each word. "I'm only starting to figure it out, but this is what we meant. We have these gifts, and there's no more tamping it down. It's in our blood. The visions, the captured memories. I'm starting to think that's only the beginning. I want to see what we can do when we don't let fear get in the way."

Mami takes a deep breath. "¿Y tú?"

When I see Mami's expression, not fearful but curious, maybe even proud, I feel this unbearable pressure lift from my shoulders. As if I'd been carrying around a secret for far too long and it's finally being exposed to the light.

"I can taste emotions," I say, "*And* I can do this."

I grin as the maldeados fill the room like a blanket of night sky, eyes glittering like stars.

"Ay, Delfi." My mother covers her mouth, glancing around the room. "You control so many maldeados at once."

Hearing Mami's concern, I let the power seep from me, ask the shadows to leave. The room lightens but the shadows stay in the corners, thickening. The maldeados aren't quite ready to go yet.

"No, not control. They just—" I spread my arms. "They like following me around. They've helped me before, sent me messages. They're not so bad."

"They like your power," my mother tells me. "It gives them substance. The maldeados are the remnants of restless spirits, shadows of—"

"Yeah," I say. "I know. I've been learning."

I reach out and take my mom's hand, and Lela takes the other.

"If you want to leave, I understand," Lela says. "I won't hold it against you, Mami. Neither of us will. We love you *so much*, but we're staying here. We have to help Rafa and Gilberto, and we can't keep running our entire lives."

"We're de Armas," I add. "We're going to make Las Palomas realize they're screwing with the wrong family."

Lela squeezes her hand and shoots me a look. "We don't have to bring down the aquelarre . . . yet. Let's start with saving Gilberto and Rafa and standing our ground."

"Zuela said there are powerful communities all over the world that las Palomas respect," I add. "We can band together and make our own. You said we have Mamá Orti's blood and her power in our veins. Once we show them what we're made of, las Palomas have to take us seriously. They'll leave us alone. And we won't have to hide anymore. We can face them."

The maldeados begin to creep forward as my excitement grows. Their shadows pulse with the same energy racing through me.

"Zuela, eh?" My mother asks. "You've been talking to that woman in the botanica?"

I give a sheepish nod.

The taste of her regret takes me by surprise. "It should've been me," she says.

"You did your best, Mami." Lela says. "There's no guidebook for this."

But I stay quiet, because I agree, it should've been her. Mami should've been the one guiding us.

"Okay." Mami squares her shoulders and wipes her eyes. "I have a way of drawing my brother's attention. But for this to work, we'll need to go somewhere he has a strong connection to. At least somewhere he's been before."

"All we have is the address where Gilberto was staying," Lela says. "But I don't think he's there anymore, and I'm not sure if Rafael ever visited."

Mami's mouth hardens, not liking the idea of Lela having risked herself like that. Which is why I'm hesitant to suggest the place where I risked *my* life, when my uncle almost shot me because he thought I was sent by las Palomas.

Lela seems to pick up my train of thought because we both make up our minds and say, "The boatyard," in unison.

Mami raises a brow but decides not to question why. "I'll need certain supplies." She checks her watch. "And my botanica's already closed."

This is where I come in, though I'm not sure how Zuela will react, considering the last time I saw her I'd lied to her face. I force a big smile. "I know just where to go. How would you like to officially meet another badass bruja from the block?"

THIRTY-NINE

Miami, November 24, 2016

─────

LELA

On the way to the botanica, Delfi calls Andres. She puts the phone on speaker so I can hear, too. He has about enough time to say "hello" before she's filling him in on our plans. She asks—well, maybe *demands*—that he check Gilberto's apartment first just in case he stuck around.

"We'll reconvene here at the botanica," she goes on. "Ethan knows where Gilberto lives, so he can take you. I'll text you his—"

"I got it," Andres cuts in. "Your sister already texted Ethan. He's here at my apartment."

I give her a wide-eyed look.

"Oh?" She nestles closer to the phone. "You two hanging out now?"

He pauses. "Just discussing things."

Delfi tries muffling the phone by pressing it against her chest. "They're totally talking about us."

I shrug. "So what? They're hanging out. I think it's cute."

She brings the phone back up, and Andres says, "It's not cute."

In the background, Ethan chimes in. "I mean, it's kinda cute. You did make me bomb-ass pancakes."

I smile. The sound of him relaxed and happy coats my heart in honey.

"I was hungry . . ." Andres protests.

Delfi pinches the bridge of her nose. "All right, all right, enough. Can I count on you for this?" The smile on her face disappears, and her voice lowers in a rare flash of vulnerability. "I can't—I can't have anyone else's death on my conscience."

"I won't let that happen." There's an intimacy in Andres's words that I know are meant solely for my sister. I lean away from the conversation.

We make it to the plaza and already I can see the giant moon peeking out from the clouds with a fiery orange tinge. The red moon from our visions.

Delfi stops me from gnawing on my thumbnail, reminding me to calm down. We watch as Mami hesitates before turning left toward the botanica instead of right for the bakery. It's instinct, but it's also self-preservation.

On this side of the plaza, everything's mostly closed save for the liquor store and Zuela's neon LA BOTANICA MAGICA sign. As we walk up to her shop, Zuela pushes open the door, sending the bells jangling, and peers outside with a grim expression, tangerine lipstick stamped over the tight set of her mouth. She wraps a bony hand around Delfi's wrist and yanks her in, leaving Mami and me to hurry after them.

As soon as we're in the botanica, Mami clenches her cardigan to her chest. Her face pales. So many items clamor for my attention, radiating with vibrant energy. Since Doña Aura's despojo, everything's been heightened again, but I find myself less resistant to the pull. Maybe even a bit curious about which objects will set off a vision.

We wait while Zuela hugs my sister, then gives her an earful about respecting privacy. Over Mami's shoulder, the dying wisps of smoke from a snuffed cigar draw my attention to the cash register. I glimpse a stack of red-marked notices—most of them with Final Notice stamped on the front. I guess the botanica business isn't booming.

"There is much turmoil in the air," Zuela says, lighting a candle for la Caridad del Cobre, Cuba's patron saint, and placing it on a pedestal.

"There are rumors el Comandante is dying," she explains.

"There are always rumors," Mami sighs.

Zuela stops what she's doing. "Yes, but this time, it's true."

"If he dies, would that mean no more Palomas of Order?" Delfi asks.

"Orden de las Palomas," I correct.

"A la contraria," Zuela says. "Las Palomas will need to grow stronger than before. They'll need to secure the political position and set themselves up as the protector of the next president."

"El Comandante's brother." Our mother rubs at her cross necklace.

Zuela finally takes notice of Mami with an edge of sharp curiosity. "That's right. If anything, this means the Elders are even more desperate to secure their successors and tie up any loose ends." At our questioning expressions, she elaborates. "With el Comandante gone, the Elders' almas are mostly depleted—their magic was tied to him long ago, sustaining his life. It's time now for a new generation to reign." She watches my mom as if she expects a reaction to this. And she gets one. As much as Mami tries to hide it, her jaw stiffens to a knife's edge.

"Is that why she's dying too?" I ask.

Our grandmother. Mamá Orti—the strongest member of las Palomas—gave everything to this one man, and now death has come to claim them both anyway. I look at Delfi and catch her disappointment. Despite everything we know about her, it hurts that we'll never even get the chance to meet.

Mami shakes her head. "No, she's been sick for a long time." She gives us a pointed look, meaning, *Don't say anything else in front of this woman.*

"It's all right, Mami." Delfi releases a heavy breath. "I've already told Zuze everything. She's been the one guiding us and keeping us safe."

I think "guiding" slightly oversells it, but regardless, a shadow of hurt falls across my mother's features.

Zuela approaches my mother, a glint of awe in her eyes. "Then it's true, you are related to an Elder. Considering your daughters' gifts, it must be a mighty bloodline. Could it be Ortencia de Armas, perhaps?"

"I don't speak about my family to strangers." My mother brings herself to her full height, which wouldn't be much to behold if not for the crackle of power I feel around her. I can't believe she was able to hide it for this long. No wonder she was making herself sick.

Instead of being offended, Zuela nods. "I understand, you've been hiding your roots for so long, it's not easy to speak of them now." She rounds the checkout counter to pluck a felt bag off one of her shelves. "Now, my Delfi mentioned something along the lines of a beckoning trabajo. Seems I've misplaced one of my own."

The use of *my Delfi* was obviously not lost on our mother. For a few heart-rending moments, I imagine the entire wall of candles sputtering with flame, but the tension is gone just as quick.

"Yes," Mami says firmly. "I need dried yerba mala and un hilo sagrado—" *consecrated thread.*

Zuela places the items on the counter. "Oh, and something sharp. Will this do?" She brings out a serious-looking needle.

Mami flinches, then nods.

She brings out her purse, but Zuela places a hand over hers. Zuela's eyes flare as their skin meets. That same look Delfi gets when she tastes emotions. I'm sure it's the same expression I wear when an object's past sucks me in. The room grows dark, the edges of my vision catching sight of the maldeados as they creep forward.

Mami pulls her hand back, and the entire room clears once again.

"It's on the house," Zuela says with a hitch of breathlessness, respect gleaming in her eyes. "Anything for a de Armas."

Delfi leans across the glass counter. "Enough dramatics, Zuze, you're scaring them." Zuela winks at her. To Mami, Delfi asks, "How does it work?"

Mami briskly begins arranging the items for the trabajo. It's disorienting to see her here, the place she forbade us from even looking at, seeming so out of place yet also in her element.

"Es sencillo," Mami says. We watch as she plucks one of her own hairs and twists it around the silvery sacred thread, the gestures familiar to her. "I would do this as a child when I hadn't seen my brother for a long time." She frowns to herself, breaking apart the dried flower, rubbing the powdery residue on the center of her palm as if she were applying perfume. "Rafa couldn't stand it. He says the sensation felt like a hundred ants crawling beneath the skin of his hand. Una picazón"—*an itch*—"until he'd resolve himself to visit me." Mami places the pouch with the needle into the side pocket of her purse, beginning to wind the thread over and over around her hand.

"But I'll need to finish the trabajo in the boatyard. It only works if I do it in a place he's been to before, a place he has a connection to. It would work when I was younger because I'd call him home." She gives us a careful glance, still coming to terms with the fact that we're also a part of this world now and that she can talk to us openly about magic.

I remind myself to close my mouth before I catch flies.

Delfi lays out our plans for Zuela, explaining that we're going to lure my uncle and Gilberto to the boatyard and convince them to stand with us against the Elders. Zuela assures us that she'll reach out to her coven and that the local practitioners will also stand with us. With las Palomas in their weakened state, and no Guardias to succeed them, we can form our own circle. If the only thing these people respect is power, then we plan on showing it to them once we convince Gilberto and our uncle to join us.

Mami and I get ready to head to the boatyard while Zuela and Delfi stay behind to gather up supplies and set up defensive charms to keep us free of psychic attack. Hopefully more potent than the protection trabajo she did on our necklaces. I don't like the idea of being apart, but Zuela needed help. She'd asked us both to stay, but there's no way I'm leaving Mami on her own, and Delfi seemed weirdly adamant about us splitting up. I wonder if she'd had the same vision I'd had, and if like me, she'd kept it hidden, hoping it was just a dream. A wall of flame between us, our necklaces breaking apart, all under the red moon. Maybe she figures if we're apart, it can't happen.

When the boys show up with confirmation that Gilberto's hotel room is vacant, Mami, Ethan, and I set off for the boatyard while Delfi stays behind with Zuela and Andres.

As we drive over, dread rises in my stomach as I watch my mom stare restlessly out the window to the red moon, still winding her hand over and over with the sacred thread. We've been down this road before, trabajos to call to others doesn't always work as planned. You don't always know who'll show up.

FORTY

Miami, November 24, 2016

DELFI

I hoist Zuela's heavy-ass bag into her car parked behind the botanica. The trunk's already filled to the brim as Andres walks up with the last thing we'll need—a caged pigeon—and places it gingerly in the back seat. It's meant to send a white flag of sorts to las Palomas and draw their attention, and not for sacrifice, which I'd originally assumed. Apparently, Zuela's bringing out the big guns.

I watch the crimson moon drag across the sky and worry again if I made the right choice by letting my family go on without me. There was a bad energy in the boatyard and I don't like the idea of them being there alone, but we can't convince las Palomas we're a force to be reckoned with without the right tools and weapons. Still, the dream of my sister falling, of me being unable to reach her, replays in my head. The longer we're apart tonight, the less likely the vision is bound to come true.

From the pile of objects in the trunk, I grab a small ceremonial blade and tuck it in my pocket. Andres gives me a look.

"What?" I say. "It's not stealing. I'm just borrowing it until this is over."

"Whatever you say." He crosses his arms and leans against the car, but he's smirking. Which is halfway to a smile. The first miracle of the night. "You think we're ready for tonight?"

I like that he says "we." I shrug. "As ready as we'll ever be."

My gaze lingers on the dimple forming on his cheek. The way he doesn't shy away from any of this, as if I've never been too much for him. I take out a blessed silver coin from the trunk. "Here, for protection," I say. "Your muscles can only get you so far in life."

A drip of caramelized sugar slips down my throat as he takes it and does some casual coin flick before pocketing it. "Thanks."

Andres's calm presence is soothing my nerves. I look up at the red supermoon, taking in the orangey tinge cast on our tan skin, the crisp air of the chilly night, and the sounds of buzzing insects like the giant, disgusting palmetto bug flying right at my face—

I shriek, practically scrambling over him. "Oh my god, oh my god. Did you see that? It was clearly targeting me!"

Andres's laughter builds slowly. "Every time I think: Does nothing scare this girl?" His shoulders shake. "It's gone now, don't worry."

I push off him. "It's not funny. Those things carry diseases!"

"Thank god you managed to escape. Sure you don't need your protection coin back?"

"Look at that, he jokes." I poke at his chest, ears burning. He stills my hand. Holds my fingers over the wild thrum of his heart.

He leans in. "You're cute when you're angry."

My breaths get shorter. "I get angry a lot."

He grins down at me. "Exactly." In the space of this moment, something shifts between us. When he looks at me like this, there are no lies, no tricks, only the unbearable truth that I like him too much, and he knows it.

Andres bends down to kiss me, tender and soft. Vulnerable, like a confession.

"Delfi . . ." He runs his thumb along my cheekbone. "You know you make everything incredibly difficult."

I nod slightly. "I know."

He kisses me again, and I hold on for as long as I can.

"I probably shouldn't be doing this again." A kiss down my neck.

My heart hammers behind my ribs. "Probably not," I say. I know I should stop, but then he crushes his mouth to mine again, and I forget to breathe.

"It's like you've put me under this *spell*," Andres murmurs. "I can't stop thinking about you—"

At the mention of a spell, I go cold.

I'm struck by the fear that maybe I've somehow bewitched him, cast some sort of magic I didn't even realize I was doing. Maybe his attraction to me is just another one of my compulsions. And maybe my attraction to him is the *what if* and the *what could be*, and none of it is real. Spells and curses. My love life, everyone.

I break away. "Then you should listen to your gut."

He grimaces. "I knew that was the wrong choice of words the moment I said them. I—I didn't mean to offend you. I shouldn't have said—"

"You didn't. Offend me that is," I say smoothly, trying to rub away the taste of him from my lips. "Anyway, our focus should be on getting to the boatyard right now. I should check on Zuela."

He runs a hand through his cropped hair, his gaze still heavy with need. "Is it—it's this love curse thing, right? That's why you keep pushing me away?"

"No one said anything about love. Besides, you're the one saying you should stay away."

He follows. "Because I can never get a read on you! I don't understand what you want."

I stop. "What *I* want? I deal with enough from my family, Andres,
and I don't have space for anything else. I just want to have something *fun*, that's just for me. No strings attached." I roll my shoulders,
stressing how *free* I am.

"I don't believe that."

· I lift a brow. "You think I'm trying to make this into something
more? I know what this is . . ." I gesture between us. "*Lust,* and neither of us are going to be satisfied until it's out of our systems."

The darkness only masks some of his hurt. "That's not what this
is. At least that's not only what this is."

"I don't know what you want me to say then."

He strides closer. "What I want is for you to admit this is more
than—"

Before he can finish, maldeados lash out from the dark and coil
around us both.

"Delfi, what's going on?" he yells as we struggle against the shadowy spirits.

"I don't know!" I cry out.

With a hiss, the maldeados tighten around me until all I can see
is pitch black.

FORTY-ONE

Cuba, April 20, 1980

ANITA

Emiliano drove the five of them in their stolen jeep north, up the hilly streets, toward the Port of Mariel. They were going to La Playa Mosquito, a beach that'd been closed off and designated for processing political exiles. From the back seat, Anita watched as Idaly clutched her lover's hand until her knuckles turned white.

There was no time to waste, not only because people were leaving Cuba in droves but because they knew las Palomas weren't going to let an entire generation of initiates go so easily.

They rode in tense silence. Anita sat between her brother and Gilberto, trying to wring her mother's parting words from her mind.

After a while, Gilberto leaned close and intertwined his fingers with hers. "Are you here?" he whispered, trying to catch her gaze. "Or are you very far away?"

She sighed, leaning her head against his shoulder. "I'm not sure where I am."

"Here," he replied, bringing their hands up to his chest. "You are here with me."

A smile barely touched Anita's lips but her heart warmed all the same.

"We're going to get through this," he whispered. "I promise I won't leave your side." He squeezed her hand as if reassuring himself as well. "Your mother didn't mean it, you know? Don't lend power to her words. Don't allow it to take root inside you."

"You don't know her," Anita said. "She meant every word."

Rafa cleared his throat, but before he could say anything, Emiliano spoke up from the driver's seat.

"I can see the coast. We should leave the jeep behind. We don't want to rouse any more attention."

They got out a good distance from the port, hiding the jeep to rot or be looted, and quickly made their way to the port's entrance—a narrow stretch of beach covered in military tents and rickety wood docks spearing a bay where there were already hundreds of boats, waiting to be filled with asylum seekers. Now that el Comandante had announced that all who wished to leave Cuba could do so, the crowd was massive, and it was only going to get worse.

It was complete and utter chaos. Supporters of el Comandante— and those too afraid not to be—stood behind metal barricades, mocking the long lines of refugees waiting to be granted access to the beach to board the boats. This mass public shaming was one of the many ways el Comandante enforced order. Years ago, in the beginning of the revolución, another intimidation tactic was televised shootings of those who remained loyal to the previous president.

Anita knew a lot of the people screaming at them and throwing rocks were pressured and threatened by el Comandante's soldiers to do so. A way to demonstrate to the Cuban people, *See, this is what happens when you don't agree, when you go against your government. Your own people cannot stand you.* Knowing much of it was a political ploy didn't lessen the hurt that Anita felt, the shame deep down that she was turning her back on her people while they stayed and suffered.

Like her mother, el Comandante would not give in without leaving his mark.

"Let's be thankful we can blend in." Rafael led them all to the other side, behind a group of women holding their Bibles. They were Jehovah's Witnesses, likely leaving for religious freedom. There were also men and women dressed all in white, proudly wearing their eleke beads, santeros leaving for the same reason.

Despite the cacophony of desperate voices, Anita could hear only the sound of her heart. Feel the unrelenting heat of the sun and see dark clouds forming, the wave of angry faces from the protesters jabbing signs toward all of them—there was no way they'd all cross that giant sea and live. None of them even knew what was on the other side but stories and fables.

They were almost to the front of their line, underneath one of the pitched tents. As she scanned the families huddled together, she caught the eye of a young girl glaring back at her. She looked familiar, but Anita couldn't place her despite the unique green of the girl's eyes. An older boy grabbed the girl's arm and pulled her away as the lines began to move forward and Anita lost sight of them.

"Papeles!" a militant with pitch-black sunglasses called to them. "Have your documents ready!"

A fight broke out at the end of the line, jostling them forward. A protester had run past the barricades and grabbed a woman by her hair and the man beside her drove his fist back, striking someone in the crowd.

"Afuera la escoria!" "Traidores!"

It hurt to be called a traitor, even more to be considered human waste. The militants stared ahead, did nothing to stop the heckling mob. The soldiers were supposed to be there to maintain order and process safe passage visas, but Anita suspected they were mostly there to intimidate and obstruct. Most guarded the port's entrance, but at least a few dozen, barking orders, roamed the crowd of people that were slowly mounting the boats.

Once it was their turn, Rafa handed the militant their crumpled paperwork. They all held their breath as the man looked the papers over, his expression hidden beneath the dark shades. He looked from Rafa, then down to the stamped papers from the embassy. "You two traveling alone?"

Rafa drew himself up. "No, this is my family." He gestured toward Emiliano, Gilberto, and Idaly. Next to her, Gilberto squeezed her hand.

Idaly spoke up. "We're seeking religious freedom. We wish to practice our faith in peace."

"Where's your identification?" the militant inquired.

They handed their identifications over to the man one by one. The militant snatched them, making his annoyance clear. He scanned their names, looked up at their faces, and after a long pause, told them to wait.

Idaly gave Anita a terrified look, and Rafa and Emiliano shifted nervously.

Anita's heart thundered as they watched him walk over to the pitched tent to speak to the other militants. Occasionally, he would look up and stare at their group.

Anita felt the slight tremble in Gilberto's fingers and this time, she squeezed his hand.

The people in line behind them grew restless as the militant continued discussing their papers with the other soldiers.

"¿Qué está pasando?" *What's going on?* Someone called out.

Anita's heart sank as the militants stopped talking and stood up now, looking straight at their group. Slowly, they picked up their rifles.

"Rafa . . ." Anita warned.

"Don't worry," he replied, but he was interrupted by the sound of the protesters approaching. Some of them were now barging into the lines of people waiting to be processed. The militants had clearly stopped enforcing the barricades.

The first militant who'd taken Rafa's papers now came up to them, flanked by other soldiers. They began backing away, but the crowd pressed from all around. A militant appeared behind Emiliano, yanking him back by the collar.

"No! Let him go!" Idaly cried, but another held on to her flailing arms.

The protesters were getting louder, the commotion fueling their anger.

"¡Tú! Ven conmigo!" the first militant said to her brother.

Rafael looked at Anita, so many unsaid things exchanged in the blink of an eye. Anita felt the breath robbed from her lungs. He exchanged a meaningful look with Gilberto, an understanding in the space of a moment. Then the militant grabbed hold of her brother.

Anita screamed as Rafael swung at the guard, hitting him in the jaw, only to fall back when two more guards piled on top of him. In an instant, he was surrounded.

As Anita shouted for Rafa, Gilberto clamped on to her arm, dragging her back and away into the mass of people. Anita realized Rafa was creating a distraction, allowing Gilberto and Ana to get lost in the crowd.

"I'm sorry, Ana. We have to go," Gilberto whispered as he pulled her away.

"No, we can't leave Rafa and the others!" she shouted, trying to break free of his grip.

"Ana, it's too late. If we don't go now, we'll all be trapped. This was Rafa's choice."

"No!" she yelled again, but soon she was caught in the tidal wave of people and had to run or be crushed under them. From what little she could see above the heads, her brother was still creating a distraction. He was an animal set loose, a lion slashing away at any who came near him.

Then a horde of people rushed forward, taking advantage of the confusion to run toward the boats, fueled by the fear that there wouldn't be enough ships for everyone, that el Comandante would change his mind. Even some of the protesters seemed to be trying to escape. But they all pushed her farther away from her brother.

"I can't leave him," Anita said desperately.

"He'll join us as soon as he can. They all will."

Together, they rode the current of people seeking freedom toward the docks. Anita saw flashes of sweat-stroked faces, desperation blurring the features that would typically determine ages or gender.

A man pushed past her, hitting her shoulder hard, and Anita slammed to the ground before scrambling up.

"Ana!" Gilberto touched his hand to her skin, and it came away bloody. "It's okay. We're almost there. I'll mend it on the boat."

Anita nodded. She had to believe her brother and friends would come. She had to have faith.

They squeezed onto the docks, where dozens of shrimp boats sagged under the weight of countless people. Anita saw women holding children in pañales, boys hanging off the sides of the boat as if they'd fall over at any moment. The heat and the crush of people threatened to kill them all before they'd even left the harbor.

"Gilberto, they're here." She spotted a group of militants plowing through, getting closer. Anita knew their time had run out.

"No, look, this boat is leaving." A deckhand was making quick work of the ropes as the boat prepared to leave the harbor, already overflowing with refugees.

"¡Una más!" Gilberto shouted to the ship hand. "¡Una más!"

The deckhand shook his head until Gilberto rushed forward and grabbed him by the shirt collar. "Please, just one more. A woman." The deckhand hesitated, then nodded, gesturing for him to hurry as Gilberto released him.

Anita whipped around to face him. "No, there's two of us."

"I know," he responded, smiling sadly.

"No. No, I will not leave you. I will jump into the ocean before I leave here without any of you."

Gilberto was resolute. His hair was in disarray, his dark skin slick and drawn, yet he was the most beautiful man she'd ever seen. He ran a thumb over her cheekbone, and amid all the cries and hysteria, he reached down and kissed her. A kiss that sank into her skin down to her heart like an anchor.

"I will love you always, Ana. Always," he said. And before she could believe him, he pushed her.

She fell back into the arms of the deckhand, who tossed her to the desperate hands of her fellow countrymen. The crowd swallowed her up into the ship, ignoring her screams, which were too indistinguishable from the million other sounds of anguish and desperation. A woman shushed her as if she were a child, thinking perhaps that her tears stemmed from relief.

The boat pulled away. She felt the rock of the waves beneath her, and the vertigo of leaving land—her homeland. It was a feeling she would never forget until her dying day. She scrambled over dozens of people to reach the boat's stern so she could see the dock.

She searched frantically for Gilberto in the crowd but couldn't find him. Couldn't see his face or her brother's or Idaly's or Emiliano's. They were all gone. They'd made all these plans, thought up all these dreams together. Of all of them, she was the least worthy of escaping. She'd always been the one too afraid to dream. Yet here she was, the only one to sail away.

As a storm brewed on the horizon, Anita grew cold like a stone. The harbor shrank from view, growing smaller and smaller until it disappeared entirely. Until everything she'd known was gone for good.

FORTY-TWO

Miami, November 24, 2016

———

LELA

I see the disappointment on our mother's face, reliving a loss she experienced decades ago. She's giving up hope. We've been at the boatyard for too long. The red moon's already dipping toward the horizon, and there's still no word from Delfi and the others, no sign of our uncle. Ethan gives me a bleak look when he tries calling Andres instead. No answer. I try not to panic as my mind flashes to the vision of Delfi, wreathed in flames.

We're too late to stop las Palomas, and we're not strong enough. Even with Zuela and her friends, even with all of our combined gifts, how could we ever have stood a chance against a cult that powerful? I can't even break a love curse.

"I'm sorry, Mami," I say, but she waves me away, her expression lined with sorrow.

"If I could have an ounce of your bravery," Mami says quietly. "You have done more than most would've tried. There's no failure in that."

But I do feel like I failed. I want to punch something. I want to scream. Why can't this one thing go our way? Why can't anything be easy? We develop our powers and still can't do a single positive thing with them. We found out we have family . . . and now we can never meet them.

"Maybe we should call it off," I say. "Head back to the botanica."

"Wait." Mami grabs my wrist, stilling me. The two of us sense it. A slight change in the air like an approaching storm. A sharp wind whistles through the trees, the cicadas voicing their displeasure.

"What is it?" Ethan asks, but we shush him.

I feel a crackle of electricity on my skin. Power.

We watch the edge of the clearing to a dark grove of trees, the three of us holding a collective breath.

I'm focusing so hard, I almost don't hear my mother's gasp, almost miss the moment when the two men step into view.

Gilberto and Rafael come out from the trees like two spirits of the night. Even from this distance, I can see their expressions are dark and foreboding. When our eyes meet, Gilberto's gaze briefly sparks in recognition, but then he focuses on my mother with a longing that makes my heart hurt.

The man from the caravan, *our uncle*, stops mid-stride, scratching at his palm. As they walk up to us, I can see they're slightly out of breath, as if they raced here.

Mami covers her mouth with her hands. "Rafa . . ."

All around us, the maldeados swarm from the forest. Watching. Waiting. As if called to witness this reunion.

Our uncle gathers Mami in his arms, squeezing hard enough to hurt. It's only for a moment before his thoughts seem to catch up and he pulls away. He speaks to her in Spanish. "No. *No.* You never should've called to me. Do you have any idea what you've brought on yourself?"

More than anger, there's a terror he's struggling with.

I want to defend her, but this isn't my fight. This moment belongs to them.

"You don't have to remind me," Mami says, her expression pained. The maldeados begin to circle them. "I know very well what I've done by calling you here. I understand the risks. I always have. But my girls . . ." His attention flashes to me with the same intensity he had in the caravan. What I had mistook as aggravation back then was concern.

"My girls reminded me that I am not an island," Mami continues. "That I have family, friends"—a feathered glance at Gilberto—"and an unfinished responsibility to put an end to this. We will not run anymore, and neither should you."

His features twist. "Why do you think I didn't reach out to you before, eh? You think I sacrificed all that so I could put you right back into danger?"

"Yet you came looking for me. You came to my home, to my job. Don't pretend you didn't have a hand in involving my daughters. Besides, what makes you think I wanted your *sacrifice*? Once again, Rafa, you're deciding for me. You've never asked me what I wanted." Her voice fractures. There's a sudden gust of wind as the maldeados swarm forward in an agitated mist. "I would've stayed with you in Cuba. I would've faced anything by your side. You stole my choice. You both did."

She turns to Gilberto, whose face shudders with shame.

"You broke all your promises."

"Then you would never have had this life," Rafael says, gesturing to me and the space where Delfi should have been. "I wanted to give you a chance to live, even if that meant I took away a *choice*."

My mother's tears break free. "That's not how this works. Each of us should have the freedom to determine what's worth fighting for. I've decided it's time to stop hiding, to stop running, because

I have been, Rafa. I've been running my whole life, sheltering my girls until they couldn't confide in me." She gives me a tearful smile and takes my hand. "I *beg* of you to stand by my side and stop running too."

Gilberto steps forward. "She has a point, compadre. There's nowhere we could go that they'd stop looking for us and we still have the mark. If we stay here, and if we can band together, las Palomas will have to accept we have formed our own circle, and that we are under someone else's protection."

"We know someone who can help weaken your marks," I say, thinking of Doña Aura. "If you stay, we can help you."

Our uncle paces, ignoring this. "You want *their* protection?" he asks Gilberto. "Are they not the same girls you said would get us killed, if not themselves first?"

Indignation rises in my chest.

My uncle addresses me, switching to English. "You and your sister have been running around, flaunting your power without any consideration of the dangers you're attracting. I imagine tu hermana is out there right now doing something she shouldn't be."

"Don't talk to her like that!" Mami snaps. "It's not their fault. I wasn't—I didn't explain this to them. I wanted to protect them from this life." Her expression is conflicted. "I—I made that choice for them." With that, the tension in her body drains—with the realization of their parallel mistakes.

Ethan looks wary. I don't blame him. Our family drama has invited a forest crowded with agitated shadows beating like a living heart.

The fight seems to leave my uncle, too. I watch in silence as our uncle approaches Mami again. He calmly reaches into his pocket and withdraws a switchblade. A sound escapes me but before I can even react, he grabs Mami's hand and delicately slices away the tight thread binding her palm. The maldeados settle and there's a final gust before the forest is quiet. He tucks the blade away and rubs her swollen fingers with his.

"I'm sorry," he says. "Yes, I went looking for you. I wanted to make sure you made a life for yourself. I couldn't help it."

She looks up at him with a vulnerability I've never witnessed. "I would've done the same." The two of them embrace again, their anger breaking as they cling to each other. As if the years of being alone have finally caught up.

The sight is a jab at a bitter wound. How different our lives would've been had Mami been honest with us. Had we been honest with each other. Every truth laid bare. Every bad decision recognized. I finally get to see Mami for who she is, and I should just feel happy, but I also feel a sense of loss for all the years we wasted. For everything we hid from each other, every lie we told.

When I look at Mami and her brother together, my family reunited, I know that my tears aren't solely for them.

◆ ◆ ◆

Once our mom and uncle break apart, Mami beckons for me to draw closer. I expect her to have a similar reunion with Gilberto—the whole romantic, swept-off-her-feet moment with the man I imagine is her first love. But she avoids eye contact with him, despite his attempts to catch her attention, only murmuring her regrets over Idaly and Emiliano.

"They were being desperate," Rafa, my uncle, says harshly but not without grief. "We begged them not to speak to that federal agent. We got here a year ago, but we already knew how things worked here. Las Palomas have most of the police in their pocket. Especially here in Miami. Emiliano insisted the agent who'd approached them was different. The agent promised them protection in exchange for information on las Palomas but it was all mentiras. Emiliano and Idaly decided to trust them instead of us, but las Palomas found them."

"So you all remained in las Palomas? Even you, Rafa?" Mami asks.

He wipes a palm down his face. "We didn't have a choice, Anita. You know that."

The look of guilt on Mami's face makes him put an arm around her.

"We're just glad you've . . . you've done well," Gilberto says, but Mami still won't look at him. "Come on, Ana—are you going to stay angry with me forever?"

She ignores him, clearly still upset over whatever happened in their past. "How'd you escape, Rafa?"

"Fleeing Cuba was the easy part. Las Palomas are no longer as powerful as they once were. Staying hidden has proved more difficult," my uncle continues, indicating the empty spaces next to him. Spaces that should've been occupied by their friends. The grief in his eyes is haunting. "After we lost contact with Idaly, we also lost our connection to the bruja who was meant to help us weaken our marks."

Rafael takes a look around the condemned boatyard. "Why on earth did you choose this place to meet?"

"Delfi—my sister—says she saw you here and you had a confrontation," I say.

"What kind of confrontation?" Mami asks suspiciously.

My uncle grimaces, and I rush on, deciding now is not the time. "It's fine. Delfi found a picture of all of you in the building, as part of a ritual. We figured this was your hiding place."

Gilberto shakes his head. "It's not, but I know which photo you mean. They've been using it to track us."

I glance around as the woods take on an eerier quality.

"It was taken from our home after las Palomas ransacked the hacienda," Rafael says.

"Why would they ransack Mamá Orti's home?" Mami asks, baffled.

Rafael explains. "After you left, las Palomas wanted to track you down. They tried to pressure Mamá Orti to help them, but she refused and became withdrawn, and eventually she lost favor."

Mami takes a moment to soak this in. "I never knew that."

"I came here to the boatyard the other night because I knew las Palomas had someone stalking us with a connection to this place. A dangerous sifón with the ability to absorb powers, a powerful bruja who is gaining a reputation among las Palomas. I figured if I could get rid of the sifón, we could cover our tracks and leave, but then I saw your sister and I realized how deep you two had fallen into this. I knew I couldn't leave then. Not when a target had already been placed on your backs."

"And you knew who we were this whole time?"

Rafael's mouth tilts in a solemn smile. "I did, and I wanted to reach out to the two of you more than you could imagine, but I couldn't tell you who I was. I could only warn you to stay away." I nod shakily at this and feel Ethan's warm hand settle comfortingly on my back.

"Where is your sister now?" Gilberto asks.

"She's with her mentor. This woman named Zuela. She has a local community here that's willing to stand with us. She knows about las Palomas, and she understands what we're up against—"

Their faces have grown pale. Gilberto cuts in. "Did you tell her you called us here?"

"What?" I look at my uncle and Gilberto in confusion. "Of course we did. You don't have to freak out, she's bringing the backup to make sure las Palomas takes us seriously. They're coming here tonight to help."

"What have you done?" Rafael asks, searching the clearing and surrounding forest. The tension in his voice makes us all go on high alert. "We need to leave *now*."

"¿Rafa, qué pasa?" our mother asks. I notice with surprise that the maldeados have all cleared away, as if they too have sensed something is wrong.

"He's right," Gilberto says. "What was this bruja's name?"

"Zuela. I don't know her last name."

Our uncle curses. "Madroño. The sifón."

I feel as if the ground has opened up from under my feet.

"Madroño?" Mami makes a visible effort to remember. "Why do I know that name?"

"He was an Elder," Gilberto says gravely. "He was the one from our initiation."

"The Elder that was turned into a maldeado," Mami says in horror.

I feel a truth that's been struggling to latch on finally take hold.

"You never put a block on my abilities, did you?" I ask Gilberto. He shakes his head, his concern intensified.

"Listen," Rafael urges. "Whatever Zuela's told you, she's not who she says she is. Has she given you anything? Or tampered with something you carry with you all the time?"

I feel my necklace go hot—the blessed azabache, and nod.

"Damn it! I knew I'd seen her colors threaded around you both."

"Delfi's with her now," Mami says, panicked. "Is she in danger?"

"I'm going back to the botanica," I say. Ethan's already grabbing his car keys, and Mami and I begin rushing to the car. "Delfi trusts her completely. She won't see it coming."

But before we can get very far, before I can rip the necklace off, we hear the sound of many footsteps coming from the warehouse.

Zuela is the first to step into view. I sense the electric touch of malice.

She's bedecked in her many bracelets and charms, wearing a pulp-red suit, as if she's now fully ready to play the part of a wicked witch. She pushes my sister into the clearing. Delfi is tied up, a bruise blossoming over her cheek.

"No need to leave, amores," Zuela purrs. "We're all together now."

FORTY-THREE

Miami, November 24, 2016

DELFI

Lela cries out as Zuela's men push me and Andres forward, our hands tightly bound, my mouth gagged. The betrayal feels like a thousand glass shards ripping me open from the inside.

Three of Zuela's hulking men and the old brujas I'd met in the botanica surround my family, Ethan, and Gilberto. Zuela flicks her hand and the maldeados rush forward, cinching them in an oily grip.

Zuela cuts a cold glance at my uncle. "I haven't borne the name Madroño in a long time. As you'll recall, my father was *also* a traitor to las Palomas."

That look. I've never seen it on her. Even now, the tastes she exudes are foreign, nothing like what I've grown used to picking up over the months we've spent together. Revenge in the taste of spoiled fruit, desperation in the flavors of rancid wine. Tobacco nearly overwhelming everything else. They all rush into my mouth now. All this time, she's kept them hidden. She's way more powerful than she'd ever let on.

"How could you do this?" Lela cries. "How could you betray her like that?"

Zuela glances back at me. The studied picture of motherly concern. "Ay, mi niña. We have been through so much, you and I. You have no idea how much I owe to you and your sister—"

I want to bite through the cloth around my mouth, then rip her throat out.

"And for the love I have for you, my Delfi, I will not neglect the promise I made to be your guide through this. To teach you to embrace your gifts instead of stifling them." She looks at my mother then, and it's clear the disgust in her tone is meant for her.

With a scream, Mami breaks free from the maldeados, makes as if to charge at her, but she's wrenched back by one of Zuela's men, forced back into the circle as the maldeados wind around her body again.

I glance from our struggling mother to Zuela. My muffled words change from curses to pleas. *Please, please, please. Leave my family alone.*

"I'm sorry, Delfi." Zuela's expression melts into pity. "I have waited to return to my island for a very long time, mi niña. My rightful place is with las Palomas. I know in time you will learn to understand. It is your rightful place too."

"Zuela, please," Mami cries out. "I don't know how I didn't recognize you before. I am so sorry for my part in your father's suffering. For your family's suffering. I tried to stop it. I thought of you and your brother—"

Zuela's expression hardens to ice. "My brother is *dead*. He drowned during the Mariel when we were forced to leave everything behind because of my father's disregard for *our* needs. He was foolish and selfish, and las Palomas denied my wish to stay because he told them I was useless, that I had no power, in a pathetic attempt to deny me my legacy. A lie your mother was more than willing to accept if it meant keeping you, Ana, as her top prize for the comandante." She laughs without mirth, the taste of betrayal and hatred so bitter on my tongue. "Now those wretched husks need me. Their comandante is dying, and they would do anything to bring back their power. When they learn that I've brought them the heir to the de Armas lineage, that the de Armas power won't die with Ortencia, I'll be welcomed back with open arms, as their equal—no, as their only hope. Then they'll know what it's like to be useless."

Mami spits out, "I'll never go back with you."

"Why would I bring a traitor like you? Someone who has weakened her own magic for years?" Zuela says harshly. "No, I'll be bringing them Delfi and Ofelia, brujas who will soon be at their prime. You, I think I'll turn into a maldeado, just like I'll turn the rest of the old Elders."

Zuela lifts her hands to the sky in summons of her power. The other brujas in her coven join her, speaking low and urgent as a thick, suffocating mist gathers around the clearing, making it hard to see.

Panic beats inside me like a trapped bird.

My uncle and Gilberto are still held back by the oily slick bodies of the maldeados. It's the last glimpse I see of them before they're engulfed by the fog.

"Take the twins. Leave the rest," Zuela orders her men, she tosses one of them a set of keys and the man opens one of the boatyard's doors. She has the keys to the boatyard because it was *her* hideout. Not our uncle's.

The women of her coven chant louder. Words in Spanish that mean fire, chaos, death.

"No!" Mami screams, Zuela's maldeados dragging her toward the water. I try kicking the man holding me, but he yanks my arms behind my back until I'm sure my shoulders will dislocate. Another man drags Lela over.

Our mother manages to break free again, gaining control of the maldeados around her, a wave of power I can feel across my skin.

She's almost to us when Zuela steps in her way, clucking her tongue.

Zuela touches a sharp red nail to the center of my mom's forehead. "Time to dream, little dove."

"What are you doing?" Lela screams. "Leave her alone!" But it's too late.

Mom's eyes roll back, turning completely white as she collapses. White eyes like in our vision. Like Idaly before she was lured to her death.

Anytime I'd seen Zuela put others in a trance, she would blindfold her customers. She made me blindfold my sister in the botanica before transporting her spirit to Gilberto's. Zuela said it was to keep anything from coming back from the liminal place she sends people to, but now I know it was another lie. It was so I wouldn't see their eyes and recognize her handiwork from the visions.

My sister cries out as Mami convulses on the ground, struggling against Zuela's magic, as I feel my own alma magic held down like a chained, angered animal. Like I'm not in control of it. Like it's been blocked.

Zuela leans closer to us. "There's no need to panic. I am not a monster. My plans have nothing to do with your boys or your mother. They will survive the night. I promise." She gives me a smile that I want to rip off her face.

"How do I know you won't kill them once we leave?" Lela asks.

Zuela presses a hand to her chest. "Trust me. I give you my word."

My scowl is vicious. Like I'll ever make that mistake again.

"If you think we're going to go quietly. That I'm just going to let you—"

"Enough," Zuela snaps, as if Lela were being a petulant child. "I think it's time you join your mother. It'll be my gift to the two of you."

Zuela's cold fingers press onto our foreheads, and Lela and I crumble into sleep.

FORTY-FOUR

Tierra de Sombras

ANITA

It has been a long time since Anita has dreamt of the woods outside the hacienda.

Her neck prickles with unease. She has the vague sense she's forgetting something. A muted fight somewhere deep within her bones. But each time Anita tries grasping it, the feeling flutters away.

As she's done many times before, she ambles through the densest part of the forest, with its towering thick-rooted trees and spiked palms on either side of the path. She's always loved the fine beauty of these woods, whose branches only let the tiniest seep of sea air through, like a tune played only for her.

That fretful feeling tries to capture her again—*Hurry. Hurry.*

But then Anita sees him, and she stops thinking about anything else. He waits at the base of a tree, as if he'd been there all this time.

"Papi?"

His weathered face looks up at her, translucent. "You see, Anita? How the roots twist toward the sky like tangled hair? It's the story of Doña Magdalena."

She chokes on the sob building in her throat. She remembers this story. Remembers the way he'd gently pull on a strand of her hair, back when it used to curl. He's an echo, she realizes. The imprint of a spirit trapped in a moment in time. Trapped in this place, in the land of shadows.

She sits down beside him. His glinting eyes meet hers and his smile spreads like the breaking of a daylit sky. She repeats the words she'd once said as a child.

"Tell me about him, Papi. About the sun god."

Her father tugs free a cigarette from his shirt pocket in a gesture that makes her heart ache. He always smoked when he told stories.

"Ah, he was a jealous fool who didn't recognize the love of a woman when he had it right in his immortal hands."

She recalls the tragic ending. "A sad story."

Her father releases a torrent of coughs. The sound fills Anita with sadness, a worry for something that's already come to pass.

Her father puffs on his cigarette, and Anita listens because only her father could ever tell it so well. "Everyone knows the sun must set and night must have its sky. And so Doña Magdalena would kiss the sun god's golden brow every evening as he lay down to sleep in the west." Her father described the grand love affair between Magdalena and the sun god. How their love bloomed so hot it threatened to burn the world. How it ended because the sun god was tricked and made to believe his Magdalena was untrue.

"The sun god realized his mistake too late. When la Doña died, his morning tears spilled across Magdalena's grave and from it grew the thickest roots the world had ever known. Roots as thick and red as Doña Magdalena's hair. Right in this very spot."

Anita remembers how she would respond as a child.

"Then I never want to be in love." The words sting because life had made sure she never could.

The roots seem to sway around her.

A grave. That's what this place was according to her father's fanciful story. A place where a grand love once entered, stayed, and died. It was also the place where she would spend many afternoons walking with her father . . . Until she started growing up. Until she became too close to what he wanted to escape from. Then this place became the path she would take to reach the outskirts of the city, to find her father drunk on the streets. Half dead and half wishing it.

Like Doña Magdalena, love had burned him until he was nothing.

"Why, Papi? Why did you give up on us? Why didn't you fight for us?"

He looks at her, but his expression is somber. She's not sure if he can even hear her. He grows too faint to see, and she knows it's time to say goodbye.

"Your journey has only begun, bonita. Only begun."

She knows he's right. Her journey is nowhere near finished.

Gathering her strength, Anita stands and makes her way to the hacienda. Most people experience only one grand love in their lifetime. She has had two. Two beautiful daughters, and they needed her more than ever.

She hurries toward the hacienda, exactly as she remembered but with the undeniable signs of neglect.

Hurry, hurry, brujita.

She squints as a sharp glare of light comes from the lofted upstairs corridor. Her old maldeados have come out to see her. They form a path up the stair's wrought-iron rail, down the hall, leading to her mother's bedchamber.

Anita follows the shadows, dreading what she'll find at the end of this path, but understanding what she must do before it is too late.

FORTY-FIVE

Tierra de Sombras

LELA

The last thing I remember is Zuela's finger pressing against my forehead, and Delfi reaching for me. I wake to the mournful gaze of a porcelain Virgen María looming above.

I scramble back, knocking into an array of clay bowls filled with something sticky. There's a sense that I'm forgetting something, an urgent whisper that I'm not supposed to be here, but I can't make it out.

I look for Delfi, Mami, or Ethan but I'm alone. I can't see much in this dark room except for what the moonlight illuminates through the window. But I see enough. It looks like an altar—staffs and porcelain, saints and candles, all covered in a film of dust. I'm in some kind of shed, one that clearly hasn't been used for some time.

I find my way to the door, my hands skimming rough surfaces that I'd rather not look too closely at. I have the distinct impression I'm being watched. I realize the room is filled with maldeados, the spirits swirling around my feet, eyes glittering in the dark. Waiting.

As if sensing my erratic breathing, the shadows shift, curl around my leg like a docile cat. I hear it then. Or sense it. They want to show me something. They don't mean harm.

When my shoulders slowly relax, the maldeados funnel around the center of the room, shimmering against the moon, until a cloudy image forms. The ghost of a memory. A remnant of time replaying on a loop.

I see the translucent figure of a young girl crouched in the middle, her head bowed over a candle. The light illuminates her cross necklace, her straight nose, and firm mouth.

"Mom?" I say, and the girl looks up—her eyes studying the dark with fear. I realize I'm looking at my mother as a young girl. But she looks past me, and I feel a cold wind sweep through my body as another figure passes through me, another echo from the past. I see an older woman in a long dress, wrapped in dozens of beads. Her features are severe, calculating, protective. She stands over my mother with a blade. I gasp as she slices into her own palm and paints a bloody cross onto my mother's forehead.

My grandmother, I realize—this imposing figure is my grandmother. Mamá Orti.

Mamá Orti looks down at my mother. "You're distracted, Ana. Whoever's captured your interest, it needs to end."

"But I'm not—"

"Fidelidad, fuerza, y poder," Mamá Orti booms out—*fidelity, strength, and power*. "That is what moves this world. I am hard on you for a reason. Strength cannot sharpen without force. Power is only revealed when weaknesses are tested. Do not let yourself be led by those who seek an easier path, because it is only easier to get lost that way. Do you understand, niña?"

My mother stares down at her hands and I ache for her. For the love she lacked as a child and for all the love she never withheld from us. "Sí, Mamá."

"Good. Now go." Mamá Orti gestures for her to leave, and my mother scrambles to get away.

I watch the translucent image of Mamá Orti kneel where my mother was a second ago, grab the candle, and blow it out. She goes dark, but her words—her prayer—lingers in the air like a ghost. *Do not leave me, my child. Do not leave.*

I know I have to find a way out of here, have to wake up from this land of memories, step out from the shadows. I leave the shack and find myself outside in a vast field surrounded by rolling hills and neglected crops. The night is loud, with hundreds of insects and the agitated rustle of wind. But what captures my attention is the enormous Spanish-style hacienda looming over me.

Home, the night whispers. *Home.*

FORTY-SIX

Between the Veil

DELFI

I find myself staring up at a palm-leaf ceiling fan. Launching myself off the bed, I stare around a room I've never seen before in my life.

I feel like I'm in a dream, or a vision, but I don't remember going to sleep. My heartbeat is jackhammering, like when I get trapped in an elevator with too many people. The feeling that I'm stuck here against my will.

I thrust open the shuttered window to reveal the night, and a wide expanse of hilly land I doubt is part of Florida. Where the hell am I? I tear around the room looking for something to orient myself, but the room is small and devoid of personal effects. Even the bed is stripped.

I sense the stirring then. The maldeados gather in the room, pouring in from the window and coming in from the corridor to swirl around a mirror on the vanity. When I look into the mirror, instead of my wild-eyed reflection, I see my mother. But a past version of her, the Ana de Armas who was in the photograph. She's young, so young but already carrying that heavy burden in her expression I know so well.

She's reading a letter, pressing it to her chest with a dreamy smile. It's obvious she's in love. An expression I've caught on Lela, and on myself that's always followed by fear of what's to come. Another figure moves in the reflection. A woman with the unmistakable de Armas features. My grandmother.

By the door, Mamá Orti silently watches my mother read her letter. Her dark eyes flicker with so many emotions, including a tender expression that I just know would taste of heartbreak.

My mother looks up, catches sight of her mother. She hastily folds the letter, tucking it into the vanity's drawer. Her gaze blazes with worry as she waits for her mother to say something, to uncover whatever secret she'd been keeping. But Mamá Orti doesn't say a word.

The maldeados disperse, taking the memory with them.

This was my mother's room. Her house.

I make my way to the hall and down into the courtyard of the hacienda. In the center, there's a large tree where I find Lela waiting.

FORTY-SEVEN

Tierra de Sombras

MAMÁ ORTI

Ortencia de Armas knows what she must look like—a frail, withered old woman destined to die alone. Since her children left, she had prepared for death, welcomed it.

What she had not braced for was seeing her child again. She had stopped searching for her long ago.

Ana is no longer a child, but Ortencia would recognize her daughter anywhere. She is the spitting image of her father, but Ortencia finds that she no longer resents it. Only the memory of that resentment washes her in shame.

Ana inches her way closer to the bedside. There's a shimmer to her that makes Ortencia realize she's visiting from the land of shadows—here but also elsewhere. Her daughter's gaze lingers over her gray hair and the bones of her chest, visible through the thin fabric of her nightgown. As she's always been able to do, Ortencia reads the swirl of emotions on her daughter's face—hate, rage, affection . . . loss. She imagines it is this loss that makes Ana sink down at the edge of her bed.

"I do not know if I'm really here." Her daughter keeps her chin from quavering as she's always done. What Ortencia had once seen as weakness she now recognizes as her daughter's unwavering ability to withstand. There's a strength in her that Ortencia has always lacked. A strength to love and forgive. If there is something to gain from these many years on Earth, it is the ability to recognize one's own mistakes. It's why she had not said anything when she learned of Rafael and the others' plan to leave last year. She was too old to fight, and old enough to realize how much time she had wasted on what didn't matter.

But there is something else hovering over Ana now, the imprint of another bruja—one intending to harm—that makes the old fire return to Ortencia's bones. She reaches out and grasps Ana's arm with what little force she has left, solidifying her in the real plane of existence. "Wake up. You must wake up."

Ana's face strains. "I'm trying. I'm trying, but I can't."

"You're still too afraid," Ortencia says, and Ana snatches her hand back. An old pain lances through Ortencia's chest. Always her fault. Always . . . the wrong thing to say. The pain turns into a physical one as her lungs constrict, and she releases a wheezing cough. Ana's expression softens unbearably. Her touch returns to wipe the unbidden tears from Ortencia's eyes. Ana tries tilting a cup of water into Ortencia's mouth, but she can no longer drink. Ortencia knows this is the end, and it feels freeing.

"We are not alone," Ortencia manages to gasp. "They are here, too."

Ana straightens. "What do you mean?" Ortencia nods toward the door, where two young ladies stand. Though she can barely see anymore, she knows they are beautiful. Her granddaughters, whom she'd only ever met through her most wishful of dreams.

The three of them collide in whimpers and hugs in what a true family should look like. The sight brings Ortencia a deep comfort. Although Ortencia knows she is not deserving of it, she is thankful for it just the same.

Ana leads her daughters cautiously toward Ortencia with a fearfulness that cuts deep. As if Ortencia could do more damage than she's already caused.

"Mamá, these are my daughters. Ofelia and Delfi. Niñas, this is your abuela—the grand Mamá Orti."

She would laugh if she were able. There is nothing grand about her. Now her granddaughters, on the other hand, are marvelous. To her surprise, they each grab hold of her hands and hold tight. They swim in her vision, the pressure of their fingers like a balm to her dark heart. Her lips crack as she smiles up at them, hoping beyond anything that this is what they'll remember once she's gone.

"I . . ." When Ortencia strains to speak, Ana hushes her. But Ortencia is determined to say what she's wanted to for years. "I'm sorry. I know I don't deserve your forgiveness, but I am sorry."

Ana takes in a shuddering breath. She places a hand on Ortencia's arm, holding back her tears. "Maybe not. But I'll give it anyway."

Ortencia closes her eyes, pained and relieved and ready. "Here— you must press here . . ." She raises a shaky finger to the beeping machine beside her, to the switch that'll fix everything.

They raise panicked eyes to hers.

"What are you saying?" Ana cries, her face draining of color.

"Please," Ortencia croaks. "It . . . would be a mercy. Let me do this for you, for my granddaughters. I'm dying anyway."

Ana's face falls. She knows what she must do. She knows it is the only way. The only way to break a curse is to kill the bruja who cast it.

"Mom?" Ofelia's lovely voice trembles with the question. The girls have gentle hearts like their mother. It is a blessing.

"Mamá, I can't," Ana says.

"You must." She tightens her grasp around her granddaughter's hands, and not with her voice that is failing and weak, but with what remains of her power, she tells them all how much they mean to her. How it would free her soul to know her death righted a wrong.

To her right, Delfi's steely gaze tells her she heard. She knows. The three of them come together. They hold on to their mother as Ana touches a kiss onto Ortencia's head and finally turns off the machine. They help her tug off the breathing tube and tuck the sheets around her body to keep her comfortable. Ortencia's breath hums in pained relief, and it doesn't take long for her eyes to close as if falling into restful sleep.

But there is one last thing Ortencia must do. Her true legacy. The potency of whatever power holds her family here is reaching its height, building like a crescendo. Reality creeps in around the edges and Ortencia knows she doesn't have long before her family leaves this place, to the other side where a fight awaits.

With the last bit of her strength, every bit of alma Mamá Orti had ever radiated drains from her body and washes into her daughter like a cool stream. A gift in place of a curse. It's all she can do, and after all these years, Ortencia is at peace.

The hacienda dissolves around them.

FORTY-EIGHT

Miami, November 25, 2016

ANITA

Smoky air fills Anita's mouth. She takes in the midnight sky with a clarity she's never felt before. Despite the sadness soaking her heart, a powerful thrum courses through her skin, and with it, a dangerous anger.

That witch took her children. She knows the girls must've also woken from between the veil, although god knows where they are now.

She groans, lifting her cheek off the grass and staring up at the blaze coming from the warehouse. Panic beats at her chest. The girls! She struggles to get up, but her hands are bound by a plastic tie. Her clothes drenched as if she'd been thrown into the bay.

Beyond the terrible sound of a crackling fire and the consuming smoke coming from the boatyard, Anita hears Ethan and that boy Andres yelling back and forth to one another.

Even with bound hands, she scrambles toward them, slipping once on a smear of algae near the boating ramp, desperation making her clumsy.

"Are they in there?" she screams. "Are my babies in there?"

"Ms. Sánchez!" Ethan spots her, rushing forward. "No. No, they're not in the warehouse. I'm so glad you're awake. Zuela took them! She took Ofi and Delfi! I don't know where they went!"

Anita gives a sharp nod, her head still spinning. She has to work hard to control the vortex of power coalescing inside her. It seems her mother's death has opened something within her that had been welded shut through the many years of pushing away her gifts.

Ethan's own wrists are marked red, but they're free of any restraints. She holds up her hands. "Take this off me."

"Oh! I—I don't know how, but Andres does. Come—"

They flinch as a loud burst comes from the burning boatyard. The crackle of singed metal as part of the roof comes crashing down.

They find Andres struggling to hold on to a gushing fire hose unreeled from a large metal box labeled EMERGENCY.

"Hey!" Ethan runs up and switches places with him, taking over the hose and gesturing toward Anita. Andres hurries to her, not wasting time as he grabs hold of her wrists, loops one end of the zip-tie back into where it secures, and applies pressure. After a try or two, the plastic gives and slides right off.

Anita rubs her wrists. "What's going on?"

"They're in there," the boy says urgently. "Your brother and Gilberto are in the warehouse. I saw two of Zuela's men take them inside before those jerks threw us in the water and left. We've got to try putting the fire out ourselves."

She looks over at the burning building, panic needling its way into her, making her feel as if she were being ripped in half. Her girls aren't here. Her brother and Gilberto are in danger and she knows help won't come in time for them.

With the sudden appearance of spearing headlights, they fall back as a car comes careening down the dirt road and into the clearing. The car stops just short of hitting the concrete border rimming the water.

A figure launches out of the old Cadillac and runs toward them with surprising agility considering the woman's age.

"How can I help?" The woman with the gray curtain of hair directs the question at Anita. She gestures to Andres. "This is my grandson. I'm Aura, and I know what you are. I can lend whatever bit of strength I can. I'm here to help."

The woman is like her. Anita nods.

"I need to go in before the entire roof collapses," Andres says, taking off his jacket and bringing it up to cover his mouth.

Ethan's face strains with exertion as he aims the hose. "You won't make it. There's still too much smoke blocking the entry."

Anita runs up to the yawning wall of smoke, blocking their way through the boatyard's door. "Wait. We can temper the flames, but I need a moment."

The woman's clever dark eyes meet hers in understanding.

A drizzle has started above them, one which Anita could use in her favor. She collapses to the ground, burrowing her fingers into the damp earth. Aura mimics the movements. The reverberating words of prayer start deep in the pit of Anita's stomach, working their way up her throat. She starts by invoking Oyá. Aura recognizes what she's doing and repeats the words, the motions. As Gilberto had taught her long ago, if their magia del alma is part of the natural world, the most powerful connection to their spirit, it is then aché— the universal energy that gives life to all, manifested in the orishas. Anita had not forgotten the lessons, and it was in this moment with her magia del alma that she felt the most connection to her guardians. She needed them now more than ever.

The roots of her magic spread, carried deep into the soil where they erupt from the surface as bugs and worms wriggle away. But there's something else deep inside her, at her core. Her mother's strength. Her mother's gift.

Aura's voice rings loud and clear, lending strength to the obra. She spills nine coins onto the dirt as ebó. As one of Oyá's preferred offerings.

The boys watch in awe as the clouds above them grow swollen and dark. The sky seems to split down the middle. The first drops land on her cheek, gentle, before the downpour truly begins. The rain pelts their skin, ferocious in its intent. Finally, the water douses the flames enough that they can see inside, the smoke parting like a sea for them to enter.

The boys don't wait to ask if it's safe. They rush in while she and Aura hold the brewing storm above them in place, willing it to slow down Zuela's escape.

"Careful!" she shouts, trying hard not to lose her concentration. Trying hard not to let the panic of her missing girls consume her.

The night thunders around them. The rain continuing its torrent. In the distance comes the wail of approaching sirens. But they won't be here fast enough. The boys have been in the warehouse for too long. Maybe they can't find Rafa or Gilberto. Maybe they're too late. The storm spins out around her, taking on a furious life of its own.

Just as Anita's readying to run inside as well, the boys burst through the smoke, dragging her brother and Gilberto out to safety. Anita and Aura rush forward to help.

Both men are unconscious, but their chests rise and fall. They're alive.

"Go find your girls!" Aura says urgently. "I'll stay here with Andres and watch over them. Go."

"I'm coming with you," Ethan says.

All Anita can manage is a nod of gratitude. Snatching up a shard of broken glass, she runs to the water. In her mind, she conjures the images of her girls as babies, making her intent clear, strengthening the threads that binds her life to theirs. Threads she cannot let be severed by a bruja's greedy hands. She thinks of the first moment they were put into her arms after a harrowing delivery. She could always tell them apart. Always knew which cry belonged to who. Which laugh.

Anita presses the glass shard into her palm, hard. Ethan flinches but stays still. He's already learned that magic has a price.

Through her memories, she recalls watching them grow. How they learned to say their first words. She remembers their heartbreak over their father over and over again. And the boys she had to turn away, along with the ones that stayed. She can feel Ethan's anxious presence beside her now, but this magic is a slow build. A mother's request to the stars and moon. And perhaps a message to her own mother.

Help me find my children. Lead me to them and give me the strength to set things right.

She watches as the drops of her blood fall, and the water laps it up. Tastes it before the rush of knowledge washes through her. The bay grows restless as if the ocean were hungry for more.

"I know where they are now," Anita says. "But we'll need a boat."

FORTY-NINE

Miami, November 25, 2016

DELFI

I have a hard time clearing away the fogginess of Zuela's magic, but I know I have to snap the hell out of it.

An engine rumbles to life beneath us. Lela's waking up beside me. We're crammed into a boat's damp cabin that smells like stale cigarettes and fish. There's a porthole where I can see the lit marina and the plume of smoke behind it already growing small in the distance.

Zuela pokes her head in to check on us, then begins to stride away when she sees we're awake.

"If you hurt them, I swear I'll kill you!" I yell after her. "I will never—*ever* forgive you!"

She ducks back in and blinks as if I've hurt *her*. "Delfi—after I gave you the opportunity to meet your grandmother? See the family that was taken from you? It's too late for your mother, but your grand-mother's position is still yours to take. Everything you wanted—power, family, community. The chance to make a difference, to make your mark. It's yours. *It's ours.* We are the next Palomas. We can remake it in our own vision, don't you see?"

Lela's arm presses into mine. All my wants and desires twisted into something sour. None of this is what I wanted. Not like this.

God, how could I have been so oblivious to her manipulations? How did I not see it sooner?

Zuela gets closer, leaning over me, whispering as if this were a secret between us. As if she were merely sharing something *special* with me, as she's done so many times before.

"I know this is difficult to understand, cariño. It's painful for me too, and will forever change who we are. But I promise you will be stronger because of it—" She caresses my cheek, her eyes softening.

"Don't touch me!" I shake off her hand. Zuela's orange-red lips harden.

"Understand this, niña—those two men are traitors to our country. I swear I didn't know they were your family in the beginning, but it doesn't change what they did—they abandoned their comandante, their country, when they were needed most. After they'd been given all the luxuries of the world. Everything I was denied growing up because my father was a selfish idiot." Her words lash with old bitterness. "I had no idea why you two had the connection to these traitors, but when you came to me with your vision of Idaly, you have to realize I couldn't waste this opportunity to have my life back."

"So you killed them?" I cry.

"You were there," Lela says slowly, realizing. "Both times. With Emiliano and on the boat with Idaly. *You* orchestrated their deaths."

Zuela scoffs. "Keep painting me as the villain pa' que tú veas. I am the messenger, and they were the message that needed dispatching. You think they've never killed anyone? You think they were in la Orden for this long and never once had to do what they were commanded to do? Do you think your mother is innocent too?"

"She would never," Lela growls. But my mother's words come ringing back in my ear: *You have no idea what it's like to live under someone's control . . . Follow their rules even when it means going against everything you are! Follow even when it means taking the souls of others!*

But Zuela wasn't trying to escape this kind of life. She was trying to use us as her ticket back in.

"Now, keep quiet and hold tight. There's a storm coming." With that, Zuela turns on her heel, closing the accordion door shut and sealing us inside. My sister and I knock against each other as the boat rocks. Zuela wasn't lying about one thing—the crack of thunder and choppiness of the waves catch up to us quickly.

I can tell the moment we've left the bay because the boat picks up speed, the landings after each crest larger and rougher.

"This crazy-ass witch is taking us to Cuba!" Lela says, trying to balance on her knees so she can look out the porthole. As if she can see the island from here. "But there's no way she'll make it past the Coast Guard."

"Unless they were paid off," I say.

"Then what are we going to do, Delf? We can't just give up."

I readjust myself, a sharpness digging into my back pocket. Hope flares inside me as I remember the ceremonial knife I jacked from Zuela's trunk.

I flip onto my stomach, turning my back to Lela.

"Um, what are you doing?" she asks.

"Back pocket," I say. "There's something there that might cut the zip ties."

She awkwardly maneuvers until she can pull out the small, bejeweled knife.

"Where'd you even get this?" She doesn't wait for an answer, fumbling around until she can reach my bound hands. "Let me know if I'm cutting you."

We freeze as the boat slows down and we hear someone running across the deck. I can feel every reverberating footstep. Someone else joins them at the front of the boat, and as I peer out the Plexiglas hatch, I see one of Zuela's men, a linebacker-huge guy come into view. He's scanning the horizon, expression tense. And I worry this dull, ceremonial knife won't be enough to save us.

"¿Qué está pasando?" Zuela asks from above deck. "Who is that?"

We sit up, both of us craning to look out the porthole window. The storm rages on, but the full moon illuminates the speedboat heading straight for us, getting closer and closer by the second.

"Hurry," I whisper to Lela. "Keep cutting my ties!"

The steps pound back toward the helm as the motors roar louder, but it's no match for the quickness of the other boat.

As Lela is sawing away, I notice something dark crawl over the side of the speedboat, then another thing, followed by an avalanche of inky shadows that seem to be flowing across the surface of the water to us like a giant oil spill. I have to repeatedly blink to make sure I'm seeing this right.

"It's Mom," I say excitedly. "It has to be."

Lela cranes her neck to look, still working on my ties. "That's Ethan's boat!"

A surge of affection punches me right in the throat. "Shit. I love that kid."

"Me too," she says, but much softer.

Now the speedboat's caught up, and through the veil of rain, I spot Ethan at the wheel keeping pace and my mom beside him, black hair loose and wild like a war banner. The lightning illuminates her, the sky erupting with electric veins.

She looks like a queen. A deity come down from the heavens to exact her punishment.

She pushes her arms out toward us, the boat sputtering to a stop as the engines release a loud whine.

"Did it!" Lela jumps just as the door crashes open, and Zuela bursts inside in a fury. The knife goes spinning under a cabinet. Zuela yanks us both up by our arms, and I quickly shove my hands back so she can't see that my ties have been cut.

"Your mother thinks she can intimidate me with this light show!" Zuela pushes us to the deck, her hair coming loose from its bindings. Her expression strains as she focuses on my mom, attempting some sort of magic. She screams in frustration when it doesn't seem to work.

I crouch to keep from toppling overboard, trying to hold on to Lela. My mind is unable to make sense of what I'm seeing.

Our two boats circle each other, caught at the beginning of a whirlpool. The wind and sharp drizzle pelt me from every direction. The two guys at the helm of our boat struggle against the maldeados clogging the engines. Their hands seem to sink into darkness and stay there. Another maldeado takes hold of the wheel, locking it into place. I know it's all my mother's doing. Even from this distance, I can see the power radiating from her and feel the immenseness of her alma navigating this storm.

"No," Zuela murmurs. "She's been dormant for so long. She can't block me—"

I lend Mami every bit of strength I can muster.

Mami's fierce gaze meets mine and Lela's and she sags with relief as the storm loses some of its fury.

"Give me my daughters, Madroño!" she yells. "Or I swear the only coven you'll join is the one waiting for you in hell!"

Damn, Mom. My mouth curves as Zuela's grip on us tightens. She puts on a brave face, but her fear is like touching the tip of my tongue to a 9V battery.

Zuela locks on to my sister with a calculating look I don't like at all.

"How about an even trade?" she calls back.

My eyes narrow in confusion, but then she shoves Lela forward, hands still bound, into the choppy seas.

"No!" My mother and I scream. I reach for my sister, but only grab the thin chain of her azabache necklace as she plummets overboard. The chain snaps in my hands, and the protective stone goes clattering across the boat deck. My vision, at last come to horrible life.

Lightning tears through the sky and the storm only worsens as Mami grows frantic. Ethan doesn't hesitate; he dives into the angry sea after Lela while Mami scrambles to take the wheel.

I rush to the railing to see Lela's head disappear beneath the waves and also try to jump in after her, but Zuela yanks me back. A sting pricks my neck as Zuela pulls me to her, a knife held to my throat.

"Time to choose, Anita! Save the one or lose them both!"

"Please," I beg. "*Please*, Zuela, let me help find her."

"Quiet," she says, high and reedy, the knife pressing deeper. "Your sister will be fine."

A cry of relief explodes from me as Ethan and Lela break the surface of the water. The waves threaten to take them under again, but Mami tosses Ethan a lifesaver. There's too much going on for Mami to maintain her careful command of the maldeados, so as Mami hauls Ethan and Lela back toward their boat, our motors roar back to life. The maldeados skitter away from the wheel and one of Zuela's men takes control again.

I feel it in Zuela's confident grip, see it in the frantic expression on my mother's face—I'm not going to be joining my family.

The spirits slip away as Zuela regains command of them, except for a few that linger. One maldeado slips up into my sleeve like a lost pup. Like a friend.

The hot press of tears clogs my throat as Mami helps haul Ethan and Lela up onto the speedboat. My sister's coughing and vomiting gallons of seawater, but she's alive. They're safe. They're all safe. With every rock of the boat, Zuela's knife tightens.

My eyes meet Mami's glassy ones as she tries to figure out what to do next. I try to convey to her that it's okay. I'll be all right.

"Take me instead!" Mami pleads, and Zuela scoffs.

"It's too late for that now! They won't take a traitor like you," she shouts. "¡Ahora, sáquennos de aquí!" she commands.

My nails dig into my palms as the boat gives a lurch forward, and my mom screams in anguish for us to wait. To stop. To give back her baby.

My chest rises and falls. The sight of her pain is too much. I catch my sister's urgent gaze, even across all this space, and everything seems to go quiet. I feel a current of electricity over my skin, Lela's voice filling my head louder than thunder. *Let me in.*

And I do.

The vision comes through like a bolt, desperate and loving. Lela shows me a vision—a dream she's kept locked away. She shows me what I have to do next.

I reach for my azabache and pull, ripping it off my neck. A sifón, my sister says, telling me all I need to know. Zuela's been tampering with my power since we met, but she's done bleeding me of my own magic.

I call forth a swell of something dark and lovely rushing up through my feet. A sweet current, electric, like strength.

The maldeado hidden in my sleeve now peeks out from my collar, perching close to my ear—and its whispers feel familial, ancestral. *Delfi. Muéstrale el poder de una bruja de Armas.*

And I will. I'll show her the power of a de Armas witch.

I let my eyes fall shut, allow my body to surrender to that intoxicating rush of magic. I pull it from the sea, from the blood moon and stars. And from the powerful women of my family.

It's a reminder of what I am and who I come from.

In my mind, an imposing woman appears wrapped in silk and scarves. Her face like mine and my mother's. My grandmother. Powerful and strong, how she must've looked in the prime of her life. She whispers a word from a language I never learned. But I understand the meanings of heat and life and fire. In my mind, I hear the echo of Lela and my mother's prayer over and over again, offering me their strength.

"What are you doing?" Zuela asks as my body goes limp. She tries to pull me upright. "Stand up. Stop this!"

One of Zuela's men rushes forward to grab hold of me too, but it's too late. I've gathered the strength of my family.

I stiffen in their arms, then splay my hands on the boat's edge. The magic erupts from inside me. An inferno burning across my skin. The fiery heat builds until it catches, until flames spread across the deck, making their way to the motors.

"You stupid girl! You've damned us all!" Zuela screams in rage, still brandishing her knife. The two remaining men grab life jackets and dive overboard to safety.

In the distance, a helicopter approaches, cutting through the storm. Ethan's boat is too far for me to swim to, the waves pushing us farther and farther apart.

"No, no!" Zuela cries, releasing me and hurrying toward the helm. She tears through the compartments, searching for a way to tame the flames, but whatever she finds, it won't be enough. The only way this boat will be extinguished is when it's underwater.

"It's over, Zuela," I say. "We need to jump now! The boat's going to explode!"

She shakes her head, expression fraught.

"Just go," she says, body curving over the wheel. The knife clatters to the floor. "There's nothing left for me back there."

The fire inches closer to the motors. The roar of a rescue chopper hovers overhead, and already I can spot a rescue swimmer being dropped dozens of feet above me.

"Come on," I say, perched on the edge of the boat, the fumes overpowering the air. "This can't be worth your life. You have a choice, Zuela."

Zuela's eyes reflect the fire as she gives me one last look. One full of affection and now stained with grief. "This is my choice, cariño. The only one I've ever been given."

"Zuela, wait—"

Everything flashes in a searing white light. The blast throws me back, delivering me into the sea's waiting arms.

FIFTY

Miami, November 25, 2016

LELA

My sister is surrounded in flames, just like in my vision. I watch as the boat explodes, screaming as her body plunges into the water. I feel like I'm shattering into a million fragments. Like I'll never be whole again.

• • •

The Coast Guard chopper is calling for us to stay back. Ethan's trying to keep control of the boat, while my mom restrains me by the waist. Because I want to jump back in. I need to find Delfi. I need my sister to be okay.

• • •

I'm trembling all over, the rain pelting my face. The chopper shines a beam of light over the ocean where a Coast Guard diver disappeared under the waves, searching. We all hold a collective breath. Mami sobs with me, her terror keeping the storm strong.

◆ ◆ ◆

But then two heads break the surface, and a rescue basket is lowered to bring them both up.

◆ ◆ ◆

I hear a strangled cry, and even though it sounds miles away, I realize it's mine.

FIFTY-ONE

Miami, November 25, 2016

LELA

Getting to the hospital had taken entirely too long despite Ethan gunning it. Luckily, Andres called to tell us Delfi's airlift had gotten there quickly. She was hurt but awake, lucid. My uncle and Doña Aura had been with him in the waiting room. Gilberto was also being treated. But they were all safe.

It felt like a part of me had been turned off, disintegrating, and I wouldn't be whole again until I saw her. My other half—I couldn't imagine life without my sister. I wouldn't survive it.

The streets had been chaos as we neared the hospital. There was a residue of hazy smoke from the fireworks being set off, the remnants of a colorful explosion in the sky. We'd heard a cacophony of shouts barreling into the night coming from all directions. The banging of pots and pans. The revving of engines at full throttle. We even heard people singing on our drive here, waving the Cuban flag, which told us it had nothing to do with Thanksgiving.

After leaving the unsettling quiet of the marina, it was like entering a parallel universe where nothing made sense.

As Ethan maneuvered the car through traffic, my mom had held me tight, pressing my head close to her chest as if she'd rather have me back in the safety of her womb. Ethan had turned on the radio trying to figure out what was happening. He flipped past a country song, a sports station, until he finally left it on a Spanish channel with the host talking a mile a minute.

We'd all zoned in on the host's rambling, the words taking on a life of their own. Completely altering a reality we felt was certain. A stationary truth.

Cuba's revolutionary leader, el Comandante, the dictator . . . dead.

Dead.

The man was ninety years old. It's not like it should've come as a huge shock, but it did. He was a fixture, the boogeyman, an icon of Cuban identity steeped in oppression and revolution.

My mom had taken a deep, shuddering breath, grief lining her expression. Not the reaction I'd expected, considering all the times she'd scowled at the mere mention of the man's name, but then I'd realized it served as a reminder of her mother's death.

They were both gone now. Their fates intertwined in death as they were in life.

Now in the hospital room as Delfi sleeps, and Mami prays quietly by my sister's bedside, I read the captions on the silent TV. All news outlets are covering the story. A reporter's interviewing a Cuban woman who calls the Comandante un asesino, a murderer. She sobs as she recounts the story of when she left her family and Cuba behind. Another man is shown and he's singing a very different tune. Saying he's disgusted with the revelers, claiming the Comandante made plenty of mistakes but was a fighter of US imperialism to the very end.

The distant chant of "Cuba Libre" can still be heard outside.

He's dead. He's truly gone. After everything I'd heard all my life, all I'd learned of Cuba's bloody history, I don't know how to feel about it. There's a distance between Cuba and me that no amount of stories or pictures could ever bridge. I never went through what my mom or thousands of others did.

Even if I can't celebrate, I won't judge those who needed to.

I come away from the window. Delfi groans in her sleep, a deep, pained sound I've only ever heard her make when she's sick. Mami reaches forward and grips her hand, kissing the back of it.

My sister's first reaction when she saw me was to smile. Pointing to her bandaged face, she said, "Now they can tell us apart."

And I'd been the one to break down in sobs. Even now, my throat tightens, the space behind my eyes building pressure. I haven't been able to sit down. When I do, I want it to be beside Delfi, at home, and arguing about which show to watch.

I walk over to Ethan, as restless as I am. He slides a hand across my shoulder.

"You hungry? Want me to get you something from the cafeteria? Maybe a cookie?"

I blink up at him. "Do you know I love you?"

"I know." He gives my mouth a peck. "Cookies and coffee coming up. I'll be right back."

I squeeze his hand in thanks, watching him head toward the elevators, where he passes by Andres and the detective that I remind myself is his father.

His father holds Andres by the shoulder, and they're locked into an intense discussion that I'm worried might turn into a fight, but after a moment, the detective brings Andres into his embrace and holds him tight.

Andres comes over when he spots me. "Hey. Is she doing any better?"

I nod. "The doctor said the pain medication would make her sleepy, so it was expected. And Delfi did request that he give her the good shit."

He laughs. "That sounds like her."

"So what'd you end up telling him?" I nod toward his dad. "You know, about Zuela?"

He sighs. "What could I tell him? She didn't exactly leave any evidence behind. Not that it matters. Emiliano and Idaly will just become two more unsolved cases in a sea of hundreds."

My smile is small, sympathetic. "But *we* know. They'll always be remembered."

"Yeah." He leans against the wall. "My dad's just glad we're all safe. He wasn't exactly thrilled to learn I'd gotten so involved in this."

I look up at him, reading his face. "And why did you?"

Andres stares into the hospital room where Delfi sleeps, covered in bandages. For the first time, I notice his hands fidgeting with a large silver coin—the kind I'd seen in Zuela's shop for protection. "I'm not sure. For Delfi, if I'm being honest. There was . . . a pull. My grandmother helped raise me, taught me how to soak messages in honey and lay a glass of water under my bed for bad spirits. She taught me to pay attention to these feelings. I felt that connection to her and couldn't resist."

I follow his gaze into the room. "Magic has a way of doing that—sucking you in. I'm glad you didn't resist."

He gives me a half-smile. "Me too." We watch as his father interrogates my uncle Rafael, who, like another hardheaded relative, had refused treatment and is now putting some kind of ointment he stole on his arm. "And I'm guessing having a dad detective might've played into the interest too."

"Maybe," he admits. "But after this, I'm finding a nice, boring desk job."

I laugh, tilting my head toward my sister. "Yeah, good luck with that. From the looks of it, you just have a thing for danger."

As I go off to grab the coffees and the bag of goodies from Ethan before he spills it all over himself, I hear Andres mutter, "I guess I do."

FIFTY-TWO

Miami, Months Later

DELFI

I'm sitting in our caravan, setting up for our next tarot client, when I find the cowrie shells in La Botanica Magica's signature velvet pouch. I don't know why I keep them. I'm still not at a place where I can use them in my practice, but they're all I have left of the botanica and my time spent there. And they're a reminder of Zuela. Every time I try to figure out how I feel about her, the mix of emotions I taste is just too much, and it gets stuck in my throat until I can't speak.

It's complicated seems to be my go-to for everything lately.

How do I feel about Zuela's death? *It's complicated.*

When strangers ask how I got the still-healing burns across the side of my face and neck, I tell them *it's complicated.*

Mami says the Sánchez Curse is broken and that we can heal and move on. Well, that's complicated, too.

I can't erase Christian or my dad from my past. And who's to say love isn't a curse on its own? I loved Zuela, and *she* was willing to

murder my whole family. So yeah—complicated. But my new thera-
pist says it's okay for things to be complicated, and I've just got to
believe that.

I lean over to turn on the electric candles, and for a second, I
think I see a weaving maldeado out of the corner of my eye, but it's
just my own shadow. It's impossible anyway. With Gilberto's guidance and Mami's help, we'd set the maldeados free so they could
ascend spiritually or return to their family's ilé as protectors, as
eggun. A part of me misses them, but I know they've found peace.

I tuck away the cowrie shells, adjust my body-hugging corset, and
finish prepping the rest of the caravan for the influx of guests. Today
I'm dressed for our first gig since "the incident," hosted right in our
backyard—Cauley Square's very own annual Renaissance Festival in
the forest. Lela's late, and she better hurry, because I have a perfor-
mance slot tonight. It feels good to be dancing again.

I open the curtains, allowing the sun's rays to spill into the caravan, and my heart lurches as I see Andres hovering outside, as if
debating whether to come in or not.

"Coming inside?" I call out the window. He blushes and heads to
the door.

We've been taking it slow since I got back from the hospital. We've
been texting and there's the occasional call, but I haven't been ready
to see him yet. We have so much history, so much hurt between us
and I worry that forgiveness feels like too much to ask from him. But
today, something made me send him the invite to the event, hoping
that he'd show.

I try to keep my breathing even as he steps into the caravan.

"Wow," he says, cheeks reddening further, as he takes in my getup.

I strike a pose, accentuating my already accentuated assets. "Am
I everything you imagined a fifteenth-century psychic wench to be?"

His mouth curves, the tension easing. "My expectations have
been exceeded." I gulp. "It's really good to see you, Delfi."

"It's good to see you too." I rub my arm and gesture to the medieval utility belt slung around his jeans. "And in costume."

He taps the belt. "Yeah, well, your sister and Ethan kind of cornered me before I got here. Said I was ruining the Ren Faire vibe."

I smile until I notice he's looking at the trail of scars across my collarbones.

I force a laugh. "I'm sure I look pretty different from the last time you saw me."

He perches on the edge of the table, holding me with his dark gaze. "I'm glad to see that you're healing."

"And that my eyebrows are back." I laugh, but again, it's hollow. "But yeah, I got lucky. There's not much permanent damage." Not visible at least.

He chews the inside of his cheek as if working out a particularly troubling problem. "Well, I'm here if you . . . whatever you want, I'm here."

"I know," I say, because even though it doesn't make sense on so many levels, I know he's still willing to show up every time. I move closer to him slowly, waiting for a flinch, waiting for a sign that he doesn't want me near him, but it never comes.

He turns his hands to me, palm up, and I slip my hands into his. His arms wrap around my waist, his head on my chest as I hug him tight. I know he can feel the wild thrum of my heart by his cheek. I know he can hear the part where I say *I'm sorry* over and over again.

When he pulls back and cradles my face in his hands, his eyes shine the color of freshly tilled earth. And when he kisses me, the taste is spring sweet, the promise of a new beginning.

FIFTY-THREE

Miami

LELA

Holding tight to my dress skirts, I wriggle myself onto the metal bleachers I'm positive didn't exist in medieval Europe. Then again, neither did the peg-leg pirates nor the butterfly fairies I spot in every row in front of me. It's authentic-ish for the event, which is good enough for me. Though I'd never admit that in Dr. Guzman's presence—the department chair of the anthropology division, author of over forty published research findings from all over the world, first Latina to graduate from her college in '88. I mean, I can go on and on and risk another full-on nerdy panic attack, except at least now she wouldn't be here to witness it and call me *cute*.

It was already hard enough to impress her when I took her last two labs. I need to show her I'm the perfect candidate for her full-ride scholarship program to Brazil next summer, focusing on Candomblé, another diaspora religion syncretized with West African traditions. I'm thinking of shifting my focus to religious studies, considering my family are practically walking, talking encyclopedias and at last, we can talk about our heritage.

There is a world of opportunities for me here and anywhere else. And I'm not alone when I need to face any hurdles. I'm confident, and most of all, I'm content.

The jousters ready themselves on either side of the field, their horses pawing at the ground, ready to charge. My family joins me in the bleachers, Ethan sliding a cup of fresh-pressed lemonade into my hands and a cool kiss onto my cheek that leaves the lingering scent of lemons.

My mother sits on my other side, and I slide a look at her, wondering about her reaction to the casual PDA, but she's caught up in conversation with my uncle and Gilberto.

Tío Rafael insists on Gilberto sitting beside my mother, and winks at me as if it was his ploy all along to get the two together. Except Mami would never admit that she and Gilberto are a couple despite their nightly cafecito dates on our porch and the way they danced at a wedding we crashed last month.

Honestly, judging by the way they make any excuse to brush against each other or have yet to spend a day apart, I wouldn't be surprised if the next wedding we crash is theirs. I swoon just thinking about it. Of course, Delfi will insist on being the maid of honor.

My sister appears with Andres in the row behind us as if sensing the thought. Andres and Ethan greet each other like two little kids as if they didn't just hang out for the whole day while Delfi and I did our tarot thing.

Delfi squeezes my shoulder and gives Ethan a little hair ruffle. "God, you guys aren't going to become one of those annoying social media couples that combine their name like Bennifer, are you?"

I raise a brow. "God, you're not going to be one of those annoying sisters que se mete en todo. Wait, never mind. Too late." She already sticks her nose into everything.

Andres tries to smother a laugh. The joke is lost on my poor Anglo Ethan.

Delfi stretches her arm, pulling us into a hug. "That's right. Get ready for the ultimate third wheel." She shoots Andres a careful smile, which he returns, and I know the last thing we need to worry about is her being a third wheel. With our group, we have enough wheels to move the caravan.

She leans over to bother our uncle, but they're so evenly matched in quippy banter they only end up tiring each other out. Finally, Delfi has found her match, and I love seeing the fiery spark reignited in her. I know she's needed it. We cheer on the remainder of the match in true Cuban fashion—which is to say too loudly and with dramatic flair. When our jouster wins, Mami whoops, jumping up and hugging me tight. She pulls Delfi into the embrace, squeezing us until I'm sure the moment has become something else entirely. Until it feels like home pressed into their arms.

Once we sit, Ethan leans in, biting into a honey cake that leaves his lips glossy. The sun slants between the clouds to bring out all the colors of his eyes, like a rare treasure I've unearthed.

"I'm guessing the red jouster's brutal defeat is not why you're smiling?"

I shake my head. "I'm just really, really happy."

He grins, kissing me once with his honeyed mouth. "Good, that was the plan all along."

ACKNOWLEDGMENTS

If any part of this story stuck with you like a hitchhiker ghost, I hope it only conjures some semblance of happiness.

Like all stories, this one took me on a journey. I thought why not write about my experience as a Cuban-American, but wouldn't it also be important to include my father's path as an exile? Then again, it needs magic, murder, and mayhem. I tried to stuff so much lived and imagined experience into this story, and it will forever carry a piece of me. I couldn't imagine a better way to debut.

I have an entire village to thank for this book coming to life. To my agent, Danielle Burby, thank you for reading this story in a day and for skyrocketing my career dreams to the stars. Proud to be a Mad Woman, knowing I have your endless support and unwavering enthusiasm.

My eternal gratitude to my editor, Tiffany Liao, who took her magic chisel to the massive boulder of words, vibes, and plots I presented her. Whose encouragement, thoroughness, genius insight, and incredible patience made this story into what it is today. I'm only the Color-Coded Queen because you made me so, and I take my new title with the upmost honor.

TJ Ohler, your notes and check-ins were incredibly valuable. Thank you for your support and for reading this book a bazillion times. Huge thanks to the entire Zando Team: Molly Stern, Sarah

Schneider, Andrew Rein, Allegra Green, Nathalie Ramirez, Anna Hall, Amelia Olsen, Chloe Texier-Rose, and Sara Hayet. The production team for making sure the manuscript was in tip-top shape: Neuwirth & Associates, Janice Lee, Mikayla Butchart, and Rachel Kowal. Couldn't be more grateful for the talented trio behind my stunning cover: designer Aurora Parlagreco, art director Lindsey Andrews, and artist Liliana Rasmussen. Thank you for bringing my girls to stunning life! I'm a lucky one to have had such a gifted bunch launching my story.

This book would've taken way longer to finish, and gone in a completely nonsensical direction, if it weren't for the gentle guiding hand of my Las Musas mentor, Nina Moreno, who happens to write some of the swooniest, most emotional stories I've ever had the privilege of reading. So thankful for the Las Musas Mentorship program for connecting so many authors together and making dreams come true.

Incredibly thankful to some of my early readers like Katherine Toran, Julie Vohland, Briana DiCicco, and Sabrina Rodriguez for their insight. My alpha readers, Tara Lundmark and Kelly Barina, I can't express how valuable your support has been all these years. Not only did you push me to be a better writer, but your stories have always struck inspiration in me as well. Karalyn Spencer, you're a star and I'm forever grateful for your friendship. Sher Lee, what would I have done this debut year without you? Lucky to be your friend. Stephen Gallifrey, thank you for being the sweetest. My Do the Words Group: Isabelle, Misty, Shelly, Hetal, and especially its founder, Erica, thank you, couldn't have found a cozier, more motivating Slack group. The entire 2023 debuts group, so proud to be going out into the book world with such talent. Finally, my Miami Girls Writing Group and overall amazing humans, Yeneisy Pineiro and Alexandra Someillan, I love y'all. I'm so proud of you both. Bring those gorgeous words into the world; I believe in you.

Any inaccuracies or unintentional misrepresentations are solely my error, and mine alone. But I would be remiss to not specifically thank Dr. Solimar Otero for her wealth of knowledge on all things Santería, Palo Mayombe, and Cuban Espiritismo. For the thoughtful insights and deep dive she did more than once to lend richness and authenticity to *A Tall Dark Trouble*. Dr. Otero's book, *Archives of Conjure*, especially, was invaluable in its wisdom during research.

My friends and familia, los quiero tanto! To my mom, for not only birthing me, but for encouraging my writing passion every single step of the way and being the kindest human. My dad, for his endless stories of growing up in another country, with another set of rules and customs. Thank you both for letting me forge my own way and always thinking the best of me. I love you.

My sister, I admire you so much. You're brave, you're authentic, you're beautiful. I hope you always know how much I need you in my life. My brothers, you guys are cool too. No, but seriously, I adore all of you.

My kids for always keeping me humble. For keeping things interesting and fun, thank you. I love you more than words, and that's saying a lot.

My husband, Leonardo, you've always pushed me to be the best version of myself. Couldn't have imagined, nor written into existence, a better life partner. You're my truest and best love story.

ABOUT THE AUTHOR

Fueled by the magic of espresso, Miami-born **Vanessa Montalban** channels her wanderlust for far-off worlds into writing speculative fiction for teens. She's a first-gen graduate from the University of Central Florida, where she received her bachelor's in creative writing with summa cum laude honors.